I KNOW A PLACE

REST STOP AND OTHER DARK DETOURS

PRAISE FOR NAT CASSIDY

"[A] platter of phobias… Luckily, for every scare, there is a sense of resilience and a laugh in the face of fear to get you there."
—***Fangoria Magazine***, on *Rest Stop*

"Nat Cassidy is quickly becoming one of those names in horror—along with Tananarive Due, Keith Rosson, and Silvia Moreno-Garcia—that inhabit the 'go to' section of my brain when it comes to picking up new books. They always delight, intrigue and horrify. Guaranteed to deliver."
—**Patton Oswalt**

"Somewhere between *SAW* and Sartre, there's a detour. Nat Cassidy's *Rest Stop* is that roadside attraction, a funny, beautiful, and scary novella that leavens its introspection with blood-spatter and a dusting of spider legs. It's great!"
—**Adam Cesare**, author of *Clown in a Cornfield* and *Influencer*

"Nat Cassidy is a master of creeping fear, of urban unease, of uncanny dread and outright horror."
—**Ramsey Campbell**, horror legend, on *Nestlings*

"[Cassidy has cemented] his status as one of horror's all-time greats."
—**Rachel Harrison**, *NYTimes* bestselling author of *Play Nice* and *Cackle*, on *When the Wolf Comes Home*

"A blood-soaked freakout that does for gas stations what *Jaws* did for beaches."
—***Kirkus Reviews***, on *Rest Stop*

"Poignant and nasty as hell, Nat Cassidy's Rest Stop is a thoughtful and sharply written chamber drama that veers off the rails into a profoundly devastating cosmic splatter spectacle."

—**Eric LaRocca**, author of *Things Have Gotten Worse Since We Last Spoke*

"One part Stephen King's *Desperation* and one part *Green Room*, this is like a perfectly satisfying gas station hot dog—greasy, made of surprisingly complex components, and viscerally rewarding."

—***Publishers Weekly***, on *Rest Stop*

I KNOW A PLACE

REST STOP AND OTHER DARK DETOURS

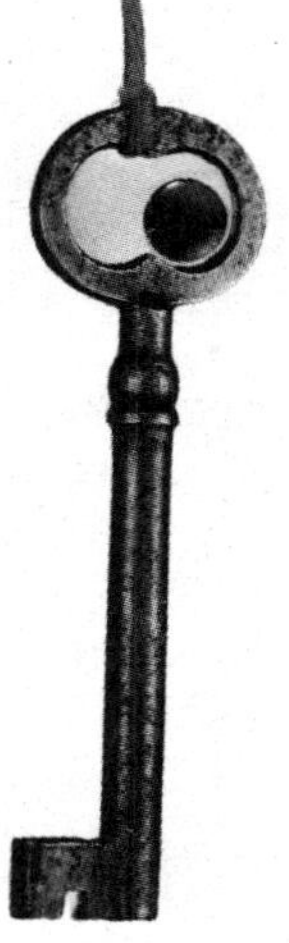

NAT CASSIDY

Content Warnings can be found at the back of this book.

A SHORTWAVE BOOK

SHORTWAVE PUBLISHING
Publisher's full catalog available at:
shortwavepublishing.com

SIMON & SCHUSTER
Worldwide sales and distribution:
simonandschuster.biz

Publisher's Note: No generative Large Language Models or Artifical Intelligence were used during any part of the production of this book.

FIRST SHORTWAVE EDITION — MAY 2026

COVER AND INTERIOR DESIGN
BY ALAN LASTUFKA

10 9 8 7 6 5 4 3 2

ISBN 979-8-89732-016-5 (Paperback)
ISBN 979-8-89732-017-2 (eBook)

Short stories are keys and this book is for the locksmiths.

For Richard Matheson, Kelly Link, Ray Bradbury, Carmen Maria Machado, Robert Bloch, John Langan, Charles Beaumont, Nathan Ballingrud, Stephen King, Brian Evenson, Peter Straub, Hailey Piper, Mariana Enriquez, Clive Barker, Eric LaRocca, Joe Hill, Stephen Graham Jones, Ramsey Campbell, Paul Tremblay, Clay McLeod Chapman, Rachel Harrison, Tananarive Due, T.E.D. Klein, R.L. Stine, Nadia Bulkin, Junji Ito, Paula D. Ashe, Joyce Carol Oates, Manly Wade Wellman, Anton Chekhov, Lisa Tuttle, Michael Wehunt, Angela Carter, Laird Barron, RJ Joseph, Karl Edward Wagner, Philip Fracassi, Michael Shea, Tyler Jones, Denis Johnson, Alvin Schwartz, Thomas Ligotti, John Hornor Jacobs, Anthony Boucher, Joe Lansdale, Ananda Lima, Jon Padgett, Robert Westall, Jeremy Robert Johnson, Raymond van Over, Daphne Du Maurier, Amy Hempel, and Harlan Ellison. Just to name a few.

It's also for you, if you'll come with me.
Let's open some doors together. . .

I KNOW A PLACE

REST STOP AND OTHER DARK DETOURS

THE DETOURS

INTRODUCTION
STEPHEN KING

These stories are fucking great. They rule.

Basically that's all the introduction *I Know a Place* needs. But, sad to say, that won't do. It's not an introduction, it's a blurb. It would look perfect on the cover, only then it would say *These stories are f*cking great.* Because bookstores are—theoretically, at least—places for the whole family, and *These stories are fucking great* might cause impressionable children to become degenerate serial killers.

That might sound ridiculous, but it's not as off-track as you might think, because most writers of terror and the supernatural started as impressionable children. Nat Cassidy didn't grow up to become a degenerate serial killer, but I'm guessing that he loved tales of horror and the supernatural as a kid. As did many of the stars in the genre, such as Ray Bradbury, Robert Bloch, and Richard Matheson. As did I.

In his excellent biography of Jerry Lee Lewis, Rick Bragg gives a perfect anecdote concerning the artist, not as a young man, but as a child. Jerry Lee and his parents walked up the road in their town of Faraday, Louisiana, to see their relatives, the more well-off Swaggarts. (Jimmy Swaggart, who would become a hellfire evangelist, was Jerry Lee's cousin.) The Swaggarts had a piano. Jerry Lee told Bragg, "I didn't know what it was, I just knew I had to get at it."

My guess is that Nat Cassidy felt the same way when he read his first scary story. Given his age (he was born in 1981), it might even have been—*horrors!*—one of mine. For sure *something* he read made him get at it.

To turn the key to wonderland.

The result, a few miles down the road we all travel, our talent carried on our backs or in snakeskin traveling bags, is this book. It's full of stories that are fucking great. They rule. I'll write a little bit more ("Play your harmonica, son," as Lightnin' Hopkins liked to say), but that's really all it comes down to.

Fucking great stories.

They rule.

Case closed.

I've heard Nat Cassidy on Neil McRobert's podcast, which is called *Talking Scared*. He's a well-spoken, thoughtful critic with that rarity in well-spoken, thoughtful critics: an actual sense of humor. I picked up his third novel (fourth, if you count *Steal the Stars*, the novelization of a podcast), *When the Wolf Comes Home*, thinking I probably wouldn't like it, because in my experience, well-spoken and thoughtful critics often make boring-as-shit storytellers. They have a tendency to think too much about what they are doing instead of just whaling away.

INTRODUCTION

To my surprise and delight, *When the Wolf Comes Home* was terrific, full of scares and good old-fashioned gory fun. The final-girl main character, Jess, is totally relatable, and there's a scene involving Halloween display that blew my mind. It was a fine and scary novel.

Mr. Cassidy wrote me an email, mentioning how one of my idols, John D. MacDonald, wrote an introduction to my first book of short stories, *Night Shift*. Nat didn't come out and say "Why don't you do me a solid and pay it forward," but the implication was clear. Based on *When the Wolf Comes Home,* I agreed. Although as I have said, all the introduction needed to say was they're fucking great, they rule. If they hadn't been, I would have found an excuse. Possibly an inoperable brain tumor.

Don't expect me to summarize any of these tales, which Cassidy calls "dark detours." Horror stories, suspense stories, tales of the *outre,* are fragile. They have a tendency to shatter under analysis, partly because the best of them have a sting in the tale but mostly because it's like explaining a joke. When you do that, it's no longer funny. (I think I just mixed a bunch of metaphors. Go on and sue me.)

All such stories (maybe all fiction) are detours, I think—they diverge from the main-traveled roads. They all start with a *What if.* In "Rest Stop," the longest story—and in my estimation, the most terrifying—starts with an Everyman named Abe who stops at the kind of convenience store we all know, the kind that sells gas outside, Slim Jims, Twizzlers, and discount cigarettes inside. Nat Cassidy asks *What if* there was a lunatic right out of a slasher movie lurking in that store. *What if* he killed everyone except for the unsuspecting Abe, who only stops because he's having a snack attack. Oh, and *What if* there was a snake and spider house just down the road, one of those shirttail roadside attractions like the World's Biggest Ball of String (Kansas) or the World's Biggest Frying Pan (Iowa). *What if* the two things worked together to create hell for Abe and a compulsive page-turning thrill ride for the reader?

What if a guitarist eking out a living in cover bands found a way to travel back in time. *What if* he kept John Lennon from meeting Paul McCartney in 1957? And *What if* this guitarist actually *BECAME* a superstar calling himself. . . wait for it. . . the Beatle?

What if a little kid who loves Christmas was visited by a foul-mouthed elf from Santa's workshop? And *What if* this elf, Twinklebottom by name, told the kid he could save Christmas by being naughty instead of nice? This one's a story that would have been perfectly at home in a *Tales from the Crypt* mag from 1953, with art by Graham "Ghastly" Ingles or "Jolly" Jack Davis. Sicko that I am, I could easily visualize a Christmas tree looped with a garland of intestines, eyeballs for bulbs, and a dripping heart on top.

As a young writer, I mourned the passing of the horror comics and so-called "shudder pulps" like *Weird Tales*, feeling those were markets I could have sold to. It's possible that Nat Cassidy missed the passing of skin mags like *Adam* and *Cavalier* for the same reason. They published genre fiction between various thought-provoking pictorials of topless nuns and nurses who remembered their caps but somehow forgot the rest of their clothes.

The shudder pulps are long gone. So are the horror comics. The skin mags have been replaced by Pornhub. None of the stories collected in *I Know a Place* appear to have been previously published in magazines. Some were published as chapbooks, others in anthologies ("Nice," the story about the weirdo elf, was originally published in a book of winter-themed stories). Many are seeing publication in this book for the first time, and one ("A Fruiting Body") has a previous (and current) life as a performance piece.

Yet one thing is constant both in Cassidy's stories and my *Night Shift* stories, many of which were published in the aforementioned skin mags: they have lead-ins so potent that you just about *have* to read on. The first line of my story, "Night Surf," is this: "After the guy was dead and the smell of his burning flesh was off the air, we all went back down to the beach." The first line of "Trucks" is, "The guy's name was Snodgrass and I could see him getting ready to do something crazy."

The first line of Nat Cassidy's "Rest Stop," which is destined to become a classic, is "All is either darkness or chaos." In "Run for Your Life," the narrator (and future Beatle) begins by saying, "This is not a confession". . . although it is. Of course it is. A page later, when the story *really* begins, he informs us that he started playing with the Beatles when he was ten. . . in 1998. What a perfect lead-in to a time travel story. Am I right or am I right?

The most important thing about these stories isn't the punchy first lines or the sharp characterizations. There is humor, twinkling stars in a mostly black firmament, and there are moments of writing so sharp you could shave with them. (In "Lunar Eclipse," he writes. "Innocence is simply experience that hasn't made up its mind yet.")

The most important thing about these stories is their sheer readability. If it was an album, it would be like CCR's *Cosmo's Factory* or AC/DC's *Highway to Hell* (at least for me; your mileage may differ): not a bad track on either side. Nothing in *I Know a*

Place goes clunk. It's as good a book of fiction as you'd want. So enough of the bullshit.

These stories are fucking great. They rule.

So read them.

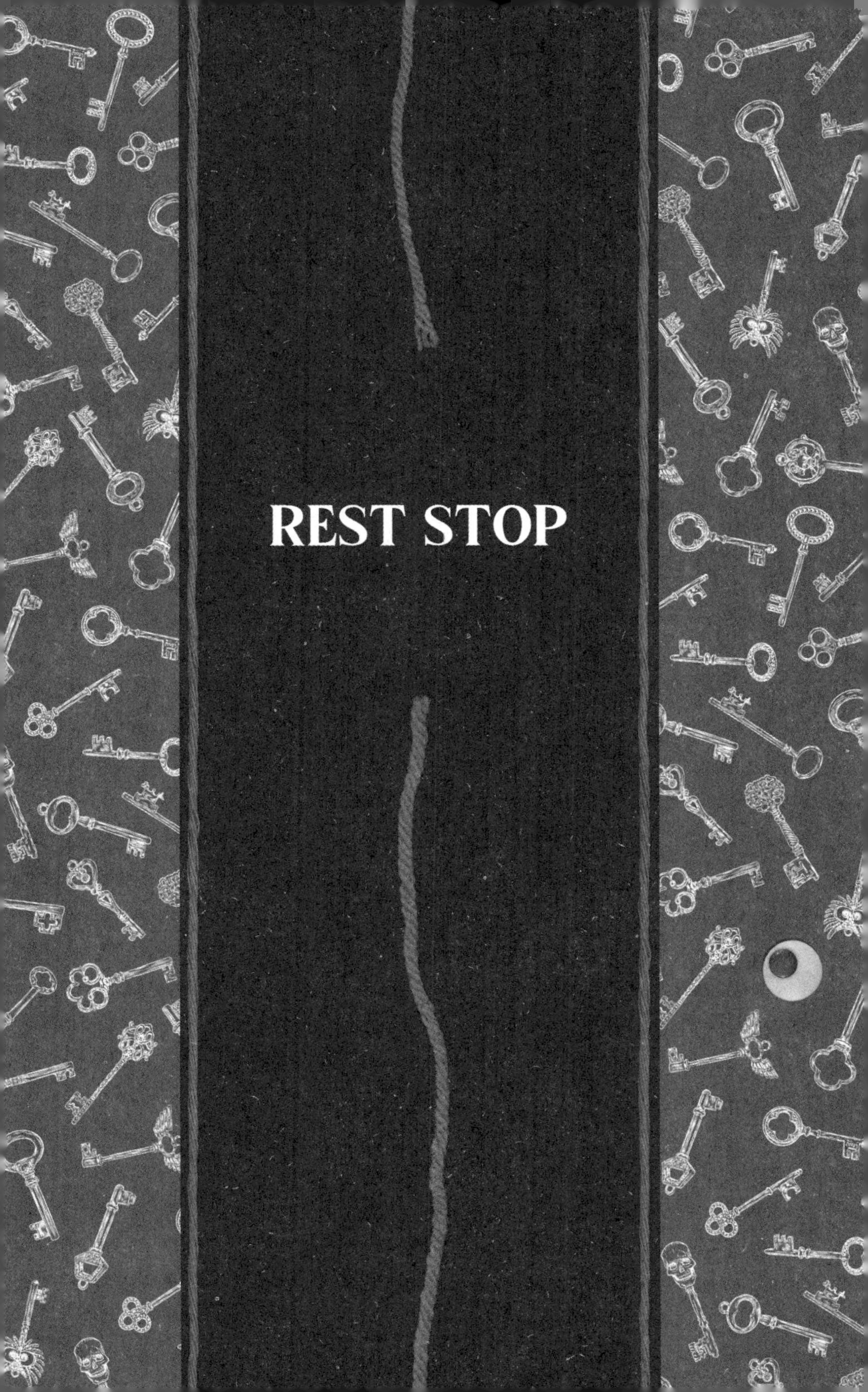

REST STOP

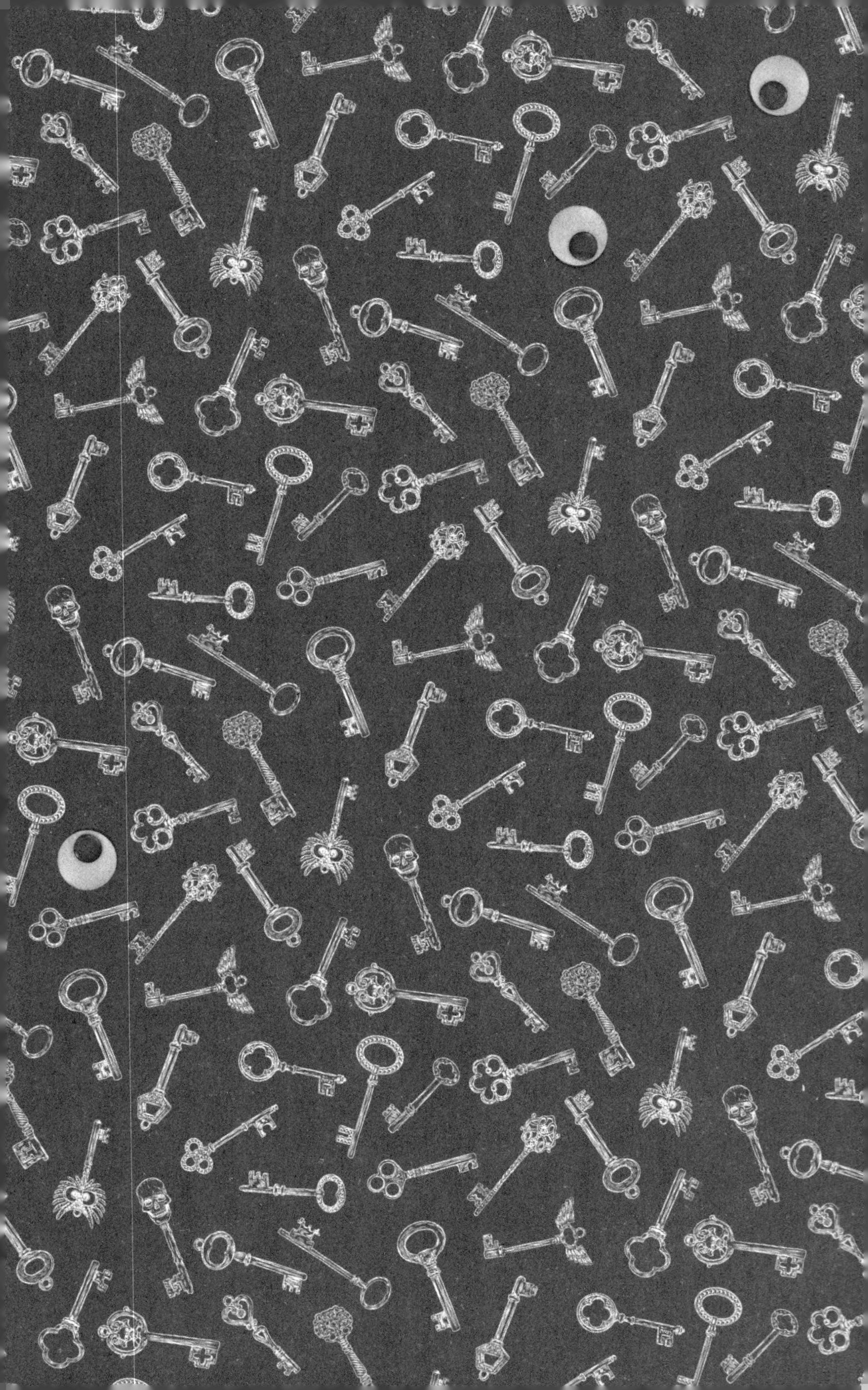

THE BIG BANG; LET THERE BE YACHT ROCK; BROKEN HEARTS; MOTHERFUCKING SNOBALLS

All is either darkness or chaos.

The deep space obscurity of midnight or the careless incoherence of lights and colors speeding past, expanding, tumbling, destined only to wink out in the rearview. Barely any form, let alone any meaning.

Until—

Splat!

A bug the size of an adult human thumb collides with his windshield, presenting its insides in a wet bouquet across the glass.

"Sweet Jesus!" Abe exclaims.

"What?" His older brother's worried voice, coming from the phone plugged into the dashboard. "What happened?"

"Nothing. Just a huge fucking dragonfly or something. Christ. Thing was big enough to have a social security number."

"Well, it's summer," his brother says, always helpful.

"Yeah. Thanks."

Abe engages the wipers. The remnants of the bug smear across the windshield in stubborn, arcing streaks. He tries adding a little windshield fluid. The bug refuses to be forgotten.

For the briefest of moments, Abe feels a touch of something like dread at the base of his spine, though he has no idea why.

"Look," he tells his brother, "can I get back to concentrating on driving? Or do you need to tell me another thirty times how I should've left earlier?"

"Hey, you're the one who decided to still be on the road at," a pause while his brother looks at a clock somewhere, "one forty-five a.m."

"I'm also the one who explained I have a gig in a few days and had to cram in a rehearsal before I get stuck at somebody's hospital bedside for the foreseeable future."

"It wasn't Bobbe's idea to have a stroke before your big gig, Abe."

"It's not a 'big gig,' okay, it's just a 'gig.' But thanks for the condescension."

"You're welcome."

"And if anyone would purposefully time a stroke to fuck with my life, it's Bobbe."

His brother declines to respond. He's exhausted too; Abe can hear it.

"I'm hanging up now," Abe says at last. "The road is starting to look like the end of *2001*, so I gotta focus."

"Please be safe. We don't need you to die too."

"Bobbe would be furious about being upstaged. If she *does* die, which I still don't think is possible."

"The doctors said—"

"I know."

"And mom really wants you here before that—"

"I *know*. Can I please hang up now?"

"Lemme know when you're like an hour away. You sure you're okay to drive? You have me worried now."

"Yes. I'm only at risk of purposefully driving myself off a cliff."

"Abe."

"I'm fine!"

"Fine. Just, one last thing—"

"What? Jesus!"

"*That*. Can you cool it with the Jesuses and the Christs? You know how much she hates that. I don't know if she can hear anything right now, but. . ."

Abe snorts. "Hey. Maybe I can make her mad enough to snap out of her coma."

"Ha. She might wake up to yell at you for being a bad Jew."

"She'll hop out of bed just to write me out of the will, like she did to Uncle Mike for being rude to her at that dinner once."

"And his kids too. Don't forget she wrote his kids out. Just 'cause he asked her to stop being racist to the waiter."

"Hey, what if she wakes up and the stroke has made her an actually pleasant person?"

"That'd be a miracle."

"I might start believing in God then."

The brothers fall into brief, guilt-tinged giggles, thinking of their own emotional infarctions with their not-so-beloved grandmother: Bobbe Meydl, their mother's mother, the only grandparent they've ever known.

Then they remember they're grownups, not little kids sharing a bedroom. They repeat their goodbyes and disconnect, leaving Abe alone in silence.

It was a long enough call that the playlist Abe had been blasting doesn't automatically come back on, so for the moment, all he has is the sound of his wheels barreling over the mostly empty highway to underscore his thoughts.

So many thoughts.

He considers turning on the radio, or maybe listening to a podcast. He doesn't do that, though—because it's August, deep in the cursed year of 2016, and all anyone can talk about now is the upcoming election. The blonde, bloviating businessman versus the blonde, cackling e-mail lady. Abe takes a little comfort that E-mail Lady's all but guaranteed to win, but still. What a shit-show. As if this year hasn't been traumatic enough. Bowie dead. Prince dead. George Martin dead. Alan Rickman dead. Chyna dead. Abe fuckin' Vigoda dead.

And, of course, Abe's own troubles. His *tsuris*, as Bobbe would call them, no doubt in her sneering, mocking way.

"Splat," he whispers, almost like an invocation. It's hard not to stare at the base reduction left on the glass.

He pulls up the playlist he'd been listening to earlier. Stabs 'Play' with a vengeance.

The next song begins. The Doobie Brothers. "What a Fool Believes."

During the day, Abe, who is the bassist/vocalist for a death-metal-math-rock duo called Darwin's Foëtus, hates—despises—*loathes*—shit like the Doobie Brothers. But alone in his car? Barreling down the open throat of midnight on a barely peopled highway in the middle of the country for a trip he desperately does not want to be taking? There's only one proper response any mortal being can have to the smooth vocal stylings of Mr. Michael McDonald.

"FUCK YESSSSS!" Abe punches the steering wheel in celebration and starts scream-singing along. As with all Michael McDonald songs, he only really knows the vowel sounds, but that doesn't matter.

What matters is he's looking past the bug guts to the dark road beyond.

xxx

He'd lied to his brother. There'd been no last-minute rehearsal. The main reason Abe hadn't left the house until the last possible moment was because he frankly just didn't want to go. So he'd puttered around his apartment, finding things to take his attention. A sock drawer that needed to be culled of socks with holes in them. A refrigerator that needed emptying. A beloved Ibanez BTB745 that needed new strings. He would've kept finding important tasks like that forever if his brother hadn't called to ask how the trip was going.

In fact, Abe's bandmate Ty had *begged* Abe to rehearse, but Abe was ducking Ty's phone calls and texts for weeks now. The only time they'd spoken since setting the gig up had been when Abe let Ty know he had to go out of town yesterday.

That had freaked Ty out. He started whining, pleading—just a quick rehearsal, please, just to make sure we're on top of our shit.

Abe assured him he'd be back in time for the show, and then

left him on read. Was, in fact, enjoying making Ty twist in the wind a little.

Ty is always annoying before a show, even under normal circumstances. He likes to pretend each and every performance is that scene in the movie where the record exec sneaks into the back of the club and is so blown away by the talent onstage that a major label contract is offered on the spot. Abe doesn't think record execs are even a thing anymore.

But Abe knows why Ty is so concerned about this particular gig.

Ty might say it's because of their *previous* gig at Club Congress. That disaster. He'd say it's because they need to prove themselves—to the venue and to each other, that their band is worth saving.

But Abe knows what's really on Ty's mind.

The Doobie Brothers are fading out now. He stops his scream-singing, says her name to his empty car with a mourner's sigh.

"Jenna."

Two soft syllables that slice like razor wire.

Oh, Jenna.

Beautiful, quixotic, intelligent-eyed Jenna.

Smart, funny, passionate Jenna. Awesome fashion-sensed Jenna. Who always cheers loudly for their songs even when no one else is in the crowd, and who's never afraid to call you on your bullshit when your lyrics are clichéd or problematic.

Darwin's Foëtus's next gig is going to be Jenna and Ty's first "official" gig as a couple. *That's* what Ty really cares about. Impressing his new girlfriend. Making her proud. Making her want to be scooped up in his arms afterwards, so they can sneak away somewhere to celebrate and probably—

"Fuck," Abe exhales, horrified to feel an actual tear leaking out of his eye. He wipes it away, embarrassed and furious. Christ, he has it bad for this girl.

Don't call me a 'girl,' he imagines Jenna saying. *I'm thirty-one years old. Also, watch it with the C-word, remember?*

The next song on his yacht rock playlist begins. "Summer Breeze," Seals and Croft. Abe turns the music up to try to drown out his thoughts.

Two a.m. on the dot now; precisely the number of cars that are sharing the highway with him.

Out of the deep-sea darkness, a billboard floats past. Wavy, kitschy letters proclaiming:

TRUMBULL FARMS
SNAKE AND SPIDER HOUSE
Visit . . . If You Dare
NEXT EXIT

Flanking the lettering are a few photos of—surprise, surprise—snakes and spiders. Truth in advertising. Always nice to see.

That'd be a cool spot to visit during the day. Maybe on the drive back. Kill a little more time before showing up and relieving Ty's anxieties. Plus, it'd be nice to visit some of nature's more pleasant creatures after being around his grandmother.

Thinking of creepy crawlies, his gaze is drawn to the guts on the windshield again.

Oh, Jenna. I'm the bug. You're the windshield.

He wants to roll his eyes at the sentiment, but refrains. The movement might cause more tears to spill out.

What about Bobbe? What's she in this metaphor?

"The darkness," he mutters, and gives a wet chuckle.

Even stupid, golden retriever-brained Ty knows how Abe feels about his grandmother. One rehearsal, Ty had been reminiscing about his own perfect and cherished Nana, who baked cookies and still sent birthday cards with a ten-dollar bill tucked inside to her precious grandson.

Abe had scoffed. "That's wild. My grandmother's one of the worst people I've ever met."

"Your *grandmother*?" As if grandmothers were some trusted brand. "Seriously?"

"Seriously." Abe started fiddling around on his bass. Minor key riffs and runs. "For just a taste: she tells me I'm a failure *every* time I see her. Those are her exact words. 'Abraham, are you still wasting your life?' That's how she says hello."

"Damn." Ty followed along on guitar.

"And let's see. . . She chased my mom with a hammer once for dating a Black guy in the '70s. My mom ran away and lived in a park for a few weeks after that."

"Fuck!"

"Oh, and she's the *worst* whenever she meets any other immigrants. She'll start quizzing them on where they're from, and then start telling them how *she* had it worse as a child. That they should be glad they're not *her*—which I'm sure they are. I've seen her spit at people. I've seen her flip them off to their face. She's rude. She's mean. And the only reason she's not constantly being beaten with sticks is because she's this tiny old lady."

"She sucks."

"She *really* sucks."

"Why is she like that?"

Abe shrugged. "The war? She grew up in this tiny village in Poland that got sandwiched between the Nazis and the Commies and—"

"Oh, man, did she get sent to a *camp*?" Ty whispered it, the way he did whenever he spoke of something serious. Like he expected to get in trouble. Beautiful, dumb Ty.

"Nah," Abe replied. "Some extended family did, but she got to stay with some family friends. I guess things didn't actually get bad for her until right *after* the war. I dunno. Trauma's trauma, but I think some people are still just born assholes."

Suddenly—*splat*—he finds himself wondering: what would *Jenna* be like as a grandmother?

Their whole impossible future flashes by in an instant. They have kids, grow old, watch their kids have kids. Jenna becomes one of those cool grandmas with tattoos and a record collection. She curses and makes naughty jokes and sips whiskey (but never too much). She has long, silver-blue hair—or maybe a wicked bob—and every time she looks at Abe she smiles a warm smile that says, *look how far we've come*. That says she's never once regretted her decision to fall in love with a man who, sure, doesn't look like your everyday romantic hero, but who has a heart of gold and fingers of—

"ABE!" He shouts at himself. "FUCKING STOP IT!" He whips his head back and forth.

This is all way too depressing. Not even summer breezes blowing through jasmine can keep the midnight blues away. He's also getting hungry. And thirsty. More than that, he wants sugar. Lots and lots of sugar.

He should get gas, too—and maybe wipe off the bug guts from his windshield before the idea of driving off a cliff really *does* become tantalizing.

As soon as he has that thought, a radiant green and white sign with the image of a gas pump emerges from the darkness.

"And the Lord said let there be a gas station, and it was so. Hallelujah and amen."

Mouth watering at the thought of Icees and beef jerky and, holy shit, some Hostess motherfucking SnoBalls, Abe glides smoothly onto the exit ramp.

PARIAHS; BIGGEST PARTS; UNPLEASANT FRIENDS

The parking lot isn't empty. Two other cars sit next to each other near the entrance to the gas station's convenience store. There's also a powder blue VW Westfalia that's as far away from those two cars as it can get while still being parked up at the front. It looks like some pariah animal at the local watering hole, not welcome to hang with the other gazelles or hippos.

Abe pulls into his own spot, then sits for a moment.

The song on his playlist has changed to "Biggest Part of Me," by Ambrosia.

Another legitimately good song Daytime Abe would never admit to liking, full of complex changes and interesting harmonies. It actually might make for a delightful (and safely ironic) cover. He can imagine singing it onstage, looking out into the crowd, making direct, unequivocal eye contact with Jenna. She'd probably laugh. Not a mocking laugh but a delighted one. A laugh that would settle into a warm, appreciative smile. It'd probably make her happy. It might make her blush.

It might even make her *think*.

He angrily turns off the engine, killing the song.

Snacks first, then gas and windshield cleaning. Let that bug have a few moments longer to be memorialized in this cruel, stupid universe.

He's reaching to unplug his phone from the dash when a text comes in. His brother, who apparently doesn't sleep. The message reads:

All still good? Updated ETA?

"Ugh! Leave me alone! Fuck *everybody*!" Abe snarls, flipping off the screen.

He quickly gets out, leaving his phone in the car.

xxx

As he sulkily trudges his way to the front door of the convenience store, he passes by the blue van. He's already started to anthropomorphize it—poor loner van, probably too awesome for the other cars to appreciate. *I feel you, Lonely Westfalia.*

A band he once knew called the Benson Ashe used to tour around in a green Westfalia, and that had always seemed like a fun time, so Abe gives this one an appraising look.

All its windows are curtained from the inside. Totally private. Probably means they do a lot of drugs in there. Rock on, Lonely Westfalia; live your truth.

Then he notices the license plate. A vanity plate. It takes him a moment to understand what it means, but as soon as he does a shudder ripples through him. Suddenly, not being able to see inside the van seems like a very bad thing.

"Jesus," he whispers.

We're not friends anymore, Lonely Westfalia.

He hurries over to the store, now desperate to get inside. This parking lot has gotten too dark and it feels like that van, with its impenetrable windows, is swelling in size, blotting out what little light there is.

When he reaches the front door, he turns back around, as if to double check what he just read.

The front license plate is the same.

CR8 H8

Create Hate.

APPLE PIE; SILENT SCREAM; A QUICK BATHROOM DETOUR BEFORE HITTING THE ROAD

Safe inside the store—so bright, so blissfully cool after even just a few moments of the muggy summer air—and he feels better. Sometimes capitalism knows how to hold you just right.

Abe starts wandering up and down the aisles, idly scanning snacks, keeping his head down so as to not make eye contact with whatever psycho owns that van outside. Soon enough, he's lost in his snack options and his thoughts.

Maybe it's because she's dying, but Abe's been thinking of his grandmother a lot lately. Thinking *as* his grandmother. Her accented, sneery voice will randomly buzzsaw into his brain, offering all sorts of unwelcome, unhelpful commentary. As he starts grabbing brightly colored treats off of the well-stocked shelves, here she comes again.

No wonder this country is so fat and lazy. Look at all the poison they stuff into their faces. Disgusting.

Abe shakes his head, not just at the sentiment (*fuck you, Grannie, this food is dope*), but at the implication. Because whenever she said something disparaging about "this country," it carried the implication that *Abe* was among the fat and lazy too. That, in fact, Abe was an avatar of horrid Americanness. *That's me. Abraham Yehuda Neer, right up there with baseball and apple pie.*

He supposes he *gets* it. To an extent. Meydl always looked at Abe and, to a lesser extent, his brother, as not just creatures from another planet but as betrayers of their true faith and culture. After everything she and her family went through, it makes sense she'd be a little sensitive about stuff like that. But it's called assimilation, Grandma. It doesn't have to be a *bad* thing. Hell, their ancestors might've done well to do a little bit more of that over the millennia—maybe then they wouldn't have been such a frequent target.

And it's not like Abe doesn't want to be Jewish. There's a lot he digs about the religion, the history. Contrary to what he joked to his brother earlier, he's not necessarily against the idea of the existence of God, either—or at least a God-like *Energy* out there. It's the arbitrary rituals he doesn't care about. Being Jewish is cool and all, but who in their right mind ever volunteers for extra homework? Who doesn't love the occasional pork chop or cheeseburger?

Sometimes he wonders if maybe Bobbe's unpleasantness isn't actually more generational than religious. He has another friend, a metal bassist named Win, who's half-Korean and has a similar relationship with his grandmother. Win's *halmoni* lived through her own horrors during the war, courtesy of the Japanese, and Win thought the things she witnessed were a big reason why she'd never been, let's say, interested in social niceties. "I mean, that entire generation's gotta be *so* messed up, right?" Win said over post-show beers once. "That's the thing about a world war. Everyone gets bit, no matter where they're from."

Abe supposes that might be true. On the other hand, hadn't he met plenty of nice old people with faint numbers tattooed on their forearms when he was a kid? People who radiated a love of life? Why should Bobbe's travails give her license to be such a shit all the time? Why should anybody's? We're all in this mess together. We're all just bugs against the windshield of time, right?

Looking for an amen, he finally glances up at the other customers in the store and his thoughts cut off abruptly as if somebody screamed in his ear.

No one screamed.

Quite the opposite. Except for the crinkle of the bag of Corn Nuts in his hand, this place is silent as a tomb.

Because there *are* no other customers.

The store is completely empty. Abe's been so wrapped up in his thoughts, it hadn't registered until just this moment.

"The hell?" he mutters.

The Icee machines whir. The refrigerators hum. And yet. . . not a soul around to operate or browse through any of it. Not even someone at the counter.

Weird. Especially considering the three cars in the lot. Where could everyone be?

"Uhhh. . ." He gives a stupid, disbelieving laugh.

He goes to the front door. Looks out into the night. The cars are still there. That van—

(*create hate*)

—is practically leering at him.

For the first time in his life, he actively wills the voice of his grandmother to come back into his head. Keep him company. Chide him for being silly.

She's totally silent too. Of course she is. When has she ever chosen to be helpful?

He turns back to face the store. Scan it from this angle. Still no signs of anybody. Next to him, the newspaper stands blare headlines and photos about, what else, the election. Both candidates, frozen in mid-roar. Here in this gas station, even *they're* rendered mute.

"Okayyyyy. . ." He tries to shake off the unease, get back to his supply-gathering. Any second now, a clerk will emerge from the backroom and make things feel normal again.

As he reaches the beverage section, something catches his attention. Something on the floor.

He bends down to get a better look.

It's a small, plastic googly eye. The kind a kid might glue onto a craft project and then shake so the pupil rolls around.

Huh.

Much like the smeared guts of the insect against his windshield, for some reason this little plastic circle fills him with a heavy, unspeakable dread.

I think I wanna get the fuck outta here.

"Yeah," he mutters. "Good idea."

Except, he really should pee. He has hours and hours left of his drive and, if this stop is spooking him so badly, maybe he should avoid stopping at any other middle-of-nowhere gas stations before the sun comes up. Don't look a gift toilet in the mouth now.

Fine. Peeing will be his final attempt at buying time. If he comes out of the bathroom and the place is still empty, he'll grab his snacks, leave a ten-dollar bill on the counter, and make tracks. And if he just so happens to grab more than ten dollars' worth? Well, you shoulda been better at your job, Check Out Guy.

He crosses over to what's clearly the bathroom: a plain white door on the opposite wall, in between a beverage case and a display of shirts and hats and a couple ice scrapers.

There's a sheet of printer paper taped to the door:

No Key.
If It's Locked, It's OCCUPADO

Under which someone had handwritten:

THAT MEANS
"SOMEONE'S POOPING"
IN FRENCH

Great. Buncha comedians run this joint.

He puts his hand on the knob, then stops. What if everyone's hiding in there right now? What if he walks in on an orgy-in-progress, three cars' worth of naked weirdos, holding their breaths and their naughty bits, waiting for Abe to leave so they can resume their midnight game of Fill 'er Up? What if the Create Hate guy is their fuck maestro and this is how he goes about cr8ing?

What if they ask him to join?

Best excuse I'd have yet to keep Bobbe waiting, I guess.

He turns the knob and pushes the door open.

A completely empty and unremarkable bathroom stands before him. Just a single toilet; not even a stall to hide behind. Not occupado. No one pooping in French.

Abe sighs, maybe in relief, maybe in disappointment, and steps inside.

THE POINT OF THE JOKE

The dread recedes a little but doesn't disappear. The sound of his peeing feels too loud, too exposed, so he starts humming the first yacht rock song that pops in his head while he finishes up.

At least his body feels a little relief.

Peeing is the best. Whoever invented peeing was a stand-up guy, hyuck hyuck.

When he's done, he steps to the sink to rinse off his hands. Studies his face in the mirror. An all-too-familiar thought:

This is not the face of the guy who Gets the Girl.

Gets her to laugh, maybe. Gets her a thoughtful present for her birthday, maybe. But outside a Woody Allen or Adam Sandler movie, where the point of the joke is that the nebbish somehow has sex appeal, no one's throwing themselves at someone like Abe's feet. With his wavy, thick hair that covers his head fully but doesn't *do* anything interesting. With his skin, still faintly marked from a merciless bout of teenage acne. With his somehow simultaneously pudgy and scrawny frame. With his prominent, oh-so-semitic nose, which one particularly nasty bully in middle school had dubbed his "Jew Beak." *That* had prompted Abe's first—and, up until a few weeks ago, his only—fight.

Hell, Abe barely even looks the part as a *musician*. He'll never forget that one gig where the club owner asked him, "So, you're the band's manager, right?" That's when Abe had decided to grow his hair out, no matter how awkward it looked.

Despondency over his severely dented heart replaces his dread for the moment. He stares at his stupid, shmuck face in the spotty, streaky glass of the gas station bathroom. Examines every angle.

It's time to admit it. Jenna and Ty make sense. Jenna can have her pick of literally any human she wants, and Ty is a big, handsome, Übermensch rockstar with a jaw that doesn't quit and a good boy sweetness. Abe can play the bassline of a death metal song in 9/8 time while screaming lyrics on top of it, and he's pretty good at *Super Smash Brothers*, but he doesn't have much else to recommend himself. Besides, what was that old Groucho Marx quote? "I wouldn't want to belong to any club that had me as a member?" Something like that.

Just like that, he decides he's just going to be happy for Jenna and Ty. Hey, if Ty and Jenna make it work, at least Jenna will be around more. She'll come to more rehearsals, more gigs, more afterparties. She can tell more of her corny jokes in her dry, wicked monotone. She can show Abe more panels of her sci-fi graphic novel-in-progress. They can get into more arguments about movies and books. Just friends, but still: friends.

That's right, Bobbe Meydl says. *Be happy for them. She's not one of us anyway, Abraham. Stick to your own kind.*

"Yeah," he grumbles. "What I really want is someone who'll turn into you in a few decades, Bobbe. That's some hot shit."

Okay, so maybe he's a little bitter. Know what the best cure for bitterness is, though?

"I'm gonna get me an Icee *and* some SnoBalls *and* some goddamn motherfuckin' Fruit Stripe gum if they have it," he tells his reflection. Mirror Abe gives a resolute nod.

He dries his hands on his pants and is planning the exact combo of flavors he's going to dump into a single Icee cup when he bounces off the door and stumbles backwards into the room.

"The fuck?"

He tries the door again.

It won't open.

The handle goes down, popping out the handle lock he'd depressed when he'd entered the bathroom, but when he pushes on the door, it sticks fast in its frame.

Is he not pushing the handle down far enough? He puts his shoulder into it.

Still no luck.

Has he somehow. . . locked himself inside? He's done a lot of clumsy, stupid shit in his life, but this would be pretty impressive. How would it even be possible? The only lock he can see is on the handle and he'd heard it diseng—

There are four holes a few inches above the handle. The faint outline of a box around them. A smaller, equally faint outline across the seam of the door. Like a deadbolt had once been there, and. . .

. . . and what? Moved? To the other side of the door?

"The fuck," he says again. Quieter, but no less baffled.

He presses on the door. It *does* feel like something at approximately that height on the other side was holding the door shut. Perhaps he'd been too busy reading the dumb jokes on that stupid sign to notice there'd been a deadbolt on the outside of the door?

Maybe. But the thing about deadbolts is they don't engage automatically. Someone's gotta slide them in place. And that deadbolt obviously had to have been pulled back when he'd opened the door in the first place. Which means. . .

A sick, churning feeling in his guts. His heart begins to pound.

"Hello?" He shouts into the door. "*Hello?*" Then, stupidly: "Someone's in here!"

He continues to shake the handle. Surely, this has gotta be a mistake. Someone cleaning up for the night didn't think to check if the room was occupado first. Or maybe a little kid wandered over and slid the lock shut while his mom was grabbing some late-night snacks? Maybe that's where that weird fucking googly eye came from?

Doesn't seem likely. Then again, neither does a bathroom door with a deadbolt on the wrong side.

Finally, he stops. Catches his breath. Tries not to let panic surge too high inside his chest.

Pressing an ear to the metal, he listens carefully for any noise on the other side.

The empty gas station convenience store—which he now knows *can't* be empty—offers nothing in return.

FEARLESS; WRITING ON THE WALL; NOISES IN THE CEILING

A few more pounds on the door. A few more shouts.

"*Helloooo*? Is anyone out there? This friggin' door is locked or something! This isn't funny!"

He presses all over the door, as if there might be some sort of secret panel. Nothing.

Finally, with a great roll of his eyes, he leans his forehead against the metal surface, weakly whacking the door with the bottom of his fist.

"Come onnnnnnnn."

When his energy peters out, he peels himself away and begins pacing the room, taking stock of what's in here with him.

A toilet.

A thin plastic brush and a plunger with a moderately thick wooden dowel.

A sink. A soap dispenser. A mirror (Mirror Abe gives a sympathetic head shake: you believe this shit?).

There's also a vent in the ceiling towards the center of the room. The vent hangs down a little from its aperture. Maybe he can grab onto that and pull his way out through the ceiling? He files that thought away as a Worst-Case Scenario sort of idea.

Other than that, there's not much of note beyond a few random phrases scribbled onto the wall, mostly clustered by the toilet paper holder. Prime real estate for bored squatters. "Be fearless — fart as loud as your anus allows" and "THINGS I HATE: 1. GRAFFITI 2. LISTS 3. IRONY" and "Trump 2016 MAGA," under which someone else had scrawled "I just shit out a better president."

There's also one sentence written on the wall opposite the mirror. Abe reads it carefully, in case it's somehow a clue.

SALLY SPARROW DUCK NOW

"Awesome," he sighs. No idea what that means, but he's pretty sure there are no indications anyone else has suffered his particular problem in this room before.

Time to get drastic, then. Time to kick the fucker down.

He stands in front of the door, sizing it up like a boxer trying to intimidate his opponent. Abe hasn't been to the gym in a minute and leg flexibility isn't one of his key selling points as a bassist. There's also nothing to really hold onto for balance, so he's just going to have to try to hammer kick this bitch from a freestanding position.

"Piece of cake," he huffs, already out of breath at the thought of it. Maybe he'll get one less sugary treat once he gets out of this mess.

"Fuck that. When I get outta here, I'm eating every Twinkie

in the place." He swings his leg up and out, hitting the door with all his might.

It shakes in its frame but, overall, seems pretty unimpressed with his efforts.

He kicks again.

He kicks a third time, as hard as he can—so hard he almost loses his balance and goes careening backwards, just barely managing to stay upright and not Crocodile Mile his way into the piss pool on the floor.

The door remains unmoved. Either Abe is weaker than he likes to imagine, or the deadbolt on the other side of the door is screwed in mercilessly tight.

Okay. Kicking isn't going to work. Neither, he learns a few moments later, is ramming his shoulder against the door. All he gets is an ache along that side of his body, and some hot, private embarrassment for his troubles. That deadbolt must be pretty heavy-duty.

Now what? Just wait for rescue? Chalk this up to bad luck and/or being careful what you wish for when he wished for an excuse to be late to his destination?

A noise. Barely audible. A low *rumblethunk* in the ceiling.

His mouth goes dry.

"Hello?" He clears his throat. "*Hello?*"

Another thump. The air conditioning coming on?

Yeah, that must be it. Just the air conditioning.

Definitely not the sound of someone crawling through the ceiling towards him.

Definitely not the soft titter of someone giggling.

Abe has a couple seconds where he's able to convince himself he's just being paranoid.

Then the biggest spider he's ever seen falls, as if pushed, out of the vent and drops to the floor.

BORIS

A prank.

Some plastic gag toy. Has to be.

No way are there real spiders *that* big. The size of his actual hand.

The fake spider lays where it fell. Immobile. Inanimate. Which makes sense because the only other times Abe has seen a spider like this are for Halloween decorations, and thankfully, Halloween decorations aren't—

The spider scrambles towards the wall. Very fucking alive. Very fucking real.

Abe goes rigid. He'd piss his pants if he hadn't already gone.

"Is. . . somebody up there?" Abe asks the ceiling in a high, tremulous voice. Gentle. Almost absurdly soft. Not wanting to agitate his new companion. He listens hard for any movement above. The ceiling is low, maybe eight feet? Seven and a half? Abe could scrape it with his fingertips if he jumps, and the thought of someone crouched so close to the top of his head, quiet, listening, lurking, is beyond unsettling.

Regardless, there's no response.

Back to the spider. It's given up trying to crawl up the wall. Now it's tucking itself into the corner, hopefully as scared as Abe is. Even from this distance, he can't help but marvel how hairy and angular the thing is. Like a spider cobbled together with discarded rat parts.

"Uhhhh, so where'd *you* come from?" Abe asks, putting on his best chill, go-along-to-get-along demeanor. He doesn't know if spiders appreciate such things. "You, uh. . . from around here?"

A sign flashes in Abe's memory. Trumbull Farms.

"An escaped convict, maybe?"

The spider only glares at him. Abe can feel the multiple eyes sizing him up, breaking him down.

"You're a tarantula, right? You look scary but you're pretty docile? You've just got a bad reputation? I can dig that."

If Abe ever had occasion to visit Trumbull Farms, he would have seen this particular specimen on display—not a tarantula, but a Sydney funnel-web spider. The signage would've informed him that the Sydney funnel-web spider isn't deadly. Not usually, at least. But it *is* "a favorite here at the Farm, because, as you see, they're not shy! In fact, they're quite aggressive. And those fangs can bite down hard enough to break a mouse's skull!"

Now Abe raises his voice, again trying to reach the (maybe? possibly?) person in the ceiling. He feels like a supplicant, begging some remote, inimical deity.

"Hey, this is really funny. Super funny bit. I dig it." He listens for a moment. "Is this being filmed?" Another long pause.

"Maybe I can help you out? I did theater in high school? And I did improv for a couple semesters in college? I could. . . y'know, help you with bits and. . . stuff?"

The presence in the ceiling—if there is one—stays silent.

Meanwhile, the spider raises two of its front legs. It makes Abe think of a magician preparing onlookers for a feat of wizardry. He doesn't like it one bit.

"Look, little guy," Abe gulps. "I don't want to hurt you. And I'm like four hundred times your size, so I probably *could* hurt you. So, just stay over there, okay? We're just gonna be super chill roommates until someone comes and lets us out. Cool?"

The spider's other legs ripple; each one briefly lifting off the ground, testing its readiness.

"I'm just gonna go. . . over here." Abe backs towards the opposite wall, pressing himself into the most diametric corner possible. "Super chill roomies. No stress. All good. Do you know The Who? John Entwhistle? One of the greatest bassists of all time? He's got a song called 'Boris the Spider.' Fucking dope song, it's—although, he. . . he kills the spider with a book at the end, never mind, you don't need to hear it, it's not very good. But the name's cool, right? Boris?"

The spider puts its legs down. It seems mollified.

"Yeah. Boris. We're cool, Boris. Best buds, me and Boris."

Meanwhile, Abe looks around for something to murder Boris with. Just in case.

Nothing reveals itself. Neither the toilet bowl brush nor plunger look serious enough to deliver a killing blow. He could maybe trap Boris under the upturned trash can. But probably he'll just have to resort to a good ole fashioned stomping—and for some reason stepping on something so big, so *complex,* as Boris the giant spider makes him wanna barf. He'll feel the exoskeleton break. He'll feel joints dislodge. He might have to do it multiple times.

Fuuuuck.

His grandmother pipes up. *Pathetic. Your goyishe friend with the chin would never be so afraid to kill a little spider. . .*

Before he can assure his imagined grandmother that he's not, in fact, afraid, Boris makes the first move.

"Whoa, whoa, what are we doing?" Abe tries to back further into his corner.

Boris has taken a few tentative steps forward, sticking close to the base of the wall. Now, a few more steps. And a few more. In no real hurry, which somehow makes it even worse, like watching the tide roll in while you're buried up to your neck on the beach. Abe decides maybe the toilet bowl brush or the plunger don't seem so useless after all. He circles around the room opposite Boris, a slow-motion pursuit.

Of course, both the brush and the plunger are tucked behind the toilet, so when he finally reaches his destination, Abe has to turn his back on Boris to pick his weapon. He opts for the plunger, which then gets tangled up with the brush. He has to jimmy it out of its place for a precious second or two.

When he turns back around, Boris is gone.

The wall that Boris had been skimming against is empty. All the walls of the small square room, in fact.

"Fuck. Where'd you go, Boris? Fuck! Where'd you g—"

The huge spider is already at his feet. Rearing back. Lifting its massive fangs, which Abe can see with horrible clarity.

Boris means business.

"NOPE!" Abe tries to do several things at once. He tries to swat Boris with the plunger. He tries to kick Boris with his shoe. He tries to run away.

What he manages to do is flick the top of Boris with the plastic end of the weapon in his hand and also take a half step to the side with his right foot. His foot meets the puddle on the floor and then, in apocalyptic slow motion, Abe loses his balance and falls onto the tile.

The graze with the plunger knocked Boris back a few inches and stunned the spider momentarily. But now Abe is laid out before him and Boris isn't going to miss the opportunity.

The spider rears up again. It's grown somehow—at least the size of a small dog and its fangs are long, black daggers jutting from two thick extensions that look like a child's drawing of bodybuilder biceps.

Those fangs come straight for Abe's face.

Then, somehow, the next thing Abe knows: Boris is flattened against the floor and the heel of his left hand is radiating with ice-white numbness.

Abe scrambles away, at first just relieved Boris doesn't pursue. He starts to put together what happened. He'd swung his free fist down onto Boris's back before Boris could strike. He'd done it out of pure panic, so hard and frantic that some of Boris's guts had shot out of his spinnerets.

Even though the thought of touching that hairy carapace still fills him with panic-barbed nausea, Abe reaches forward, picks up the still-twitching spider, and hurls it with all his might against the wall. As his hand grips Boris's body, Abe thinks, *this doesn't feel right, my hand doesn't feel right,* but his thirst for vengeance is stronger. Boris the Spider, the would-be face-biter, now lays upside down, legs curled, against the wall, fully shrunken to the size of an impressive—but *real*—spider.

Abe staggers to his feet, breathing hard. The kind of breathing that brings with it low, gravelly vocalizations. Eventually he gathers enough grunts to form a sentence.

"Fuck you, Boris! Never liked that song anyway."

He stares at the spider for about five full minutes.

His hand won't stop throbbing. His pinky and ring finger aren't curling the way they should. But at least the crisis is over.

Hoping some cold water will numb the pain a little, he heads over to the sink, and that's when he remembers where Boris came from.

"You fucking enjoying this, asshole?" He calls over his shoulder to the ceiling, running his hand under the tap. The water helps—but only a little. "Having fun? You *dick*? Super hilarious prank! I think I've got piss all over me. And I have a gig in a few days and I might've just broken my fucking h—"

Movement catches his eye in the mirror. His words cut off.

He spins around, hoping that what he thinks he saw in the glass isn't what's actually coming out of the ceiling vent.

It is.

Oh God, it is.

And it's in this moment Abe realizes—perhaps belatedly—that none of this is a prank.

It's in this moment he realizes how fucked he truly is.

He begins to scream.

Louder than he's ever screamed in his soon-to-be-ended life.

NAMELESS; WHAT A FOOL BELIEVES

There are thirty-two different species of rattlesnake that can be found in the United States. The smallest species, the aptly named pygmy rattlesnake, averages around twelve to fourteen inches, boasts vibrant dorsal splotches, and is very rarely fatal to humans. Chances are, though, when someone imagines a rattlesnake, it's the classic Western diamondback. Grayish brown scales the color of dirt, white lines outlining darker, hexagonal patches along its back, golden eyes in a permanent glare, venom easily capable of killing an adult human if left untreated. This breed tends to range from three feet to six feet in length and weighs about two to four pounds.

However, there's a breed of diamondback that can be found in the southeastern part of the country, and they're often a foot longer and several pounds heavier than their Western cousins. In fact, the largest rattlesnake ever recorded in the United States was an Eastern diamondback: over eight feet long and close to fifteen pounds of coiled, scaly muscle.

What begins to emerge, head first, from the bathroom ceiling vent isn't *that* large. But it *is* an Eastern diamondback, and not a small one. It's the sort of specimen a Snake and Spider House might display with special prominence, for children and adults alike to gasp at in fear.

Abe is gasping. His initial screams have turned into ghosts of themselves.

He's also weeping. A helpless, awed kind of weeping. Shaking his head. Moaning, "No, no, no, no."

The snake ignores Abe's refusals. It continues slowly and intractably outward. Not cautious, more like. . . skeptical. Maybe even annoyed.

Its tongue flicks out.

Scanning.

Probing.

Already, it's the size of Abe's hand and forearm, and there's no sense that the end of its body is anywhere near. Somewhere in the ceiling, its rattle whirs, ghosts of cicadas on a summer day.

In a few minutes, gravity will take over. Then, Abe understands, the snake will not be trapped in the room with him. He will be trapped in the room with it.

He picks up the plunger from where it fell during his spill to the floor and backs away as far as he can go. His left hand throbs harder and harder. His eyes never leave the snake, but he can feel the locked bathroom door in his peripheral vision, taunting him, pressing down on him like the compactor of a garbage truck.

His legs want to give out, but he wants as little of himself near the ground as possible.

When the snake finally drops down onto the wet tile floor, it makes a thunderous noise.

Like a heavy stone falling into a shallow puddle. Like a war drum played in the rain.

xxx

The snake swirls into an enormous coil where it landed, close to the toilet. No cute name for it, like Boris. It's too massive, too elemental for names. It stares back at Abe. Flickers its tongue at him.

"Oh God," Abe wheezes through a pinhole throat. He tries to appeal to the person in the ceiling once more. "Are you still up there? Please let me out? Please stop this? Please! Please, God, please!"

Oh, Bobbe says with a luxuriant sigh, *now you believe in God. Now you pray.*

He's barely even aware of the voice in his head. He's as close to actual disassociation as he's ever been.

Why is this happening?

What did he do to deserve this?

How can he hope to survive?

He doesn't know.

He doesn't know *anything.*

The crushed and curled body of Boris lies near his feet. So small now. Trivial, even.

Will he look the same way when he dies? After his blood congeals in his veins? Will he land face first into that piss puddle and taste piss as his lungs suck in their final breaths? Will he be eaten, or will he be left to rot, perhaps alongside the serpent that kills him? Do rattlesnakes eat their victims?

He doesn't know *fucking anything!*

Another voice pipes up in his head.

You don't have to be afraid of a stupid snake, man. You're a monster slayer! You defeated Boris the Spider with your bare hands! Even Frodo couldn't do that shit.

Usually Abe hates—or at least barely puts up with—Ty's Boy Scout enthusiasm. Now he's desperate for it. Even if he doesn't believe a word of it. There's no defeating what cannot be named.

The snake holds its rattle up and shakes it, agitated. The sound moves through Abe like an electric shock. The bathroom's too small; Abe can't back up any further and he's still too close for the snake's comfort.

"Go into the corner, you fuck," he growls. "You've got more room behind you."

The snake doesn't listen. Its head rises up a few inches and bobs back and forth. *Flicka-flick-flick*, its black tongue, a visual stutter.

It's going to strike.

He's seen random internet videos of how fast they launch themselves forward. Like horizontal lightning. He's also seen what rattlesnake venom does. It turns your blood into Thanksgiving cranberry sauce. The canned kind that slides onto the plate in a quivering lump.

It's going to hurt. A lot. He wants to cry. He wants to put the plunger down, sit, and sob about the unfairness of it all. All he'd wanted to do was take a leak and now—

Unfairness is the law of the world. Bobbe's voice again. *I tried to teach you that and you refused to listen. When I was a little gir—*

"Oh my God, SHUT UP!" Abe shouts—and without intending to, he stomps his foot in petulant rage.

The snake actually flinches a little. Shrinks back into itself. As surprised as Bobbe Medyl might be to hear Abe yell like this.

There you go, Monster Slayer, Ty says. *Scare that fucking snake!*

"SHUT UP, SHUT UP, SHUT *UP*," Abe shouts again. Aware that he might ultimately be making the snake more upset, but for this brief moment he doesn't care.

He starts stamping his feet and, without even thinking, he begins to huff out a death metal version of "What a Fool Believes."

"He came from some! Where! Ba-gg-ina! Long! A! Guh!" he shouts in a glottal growl that's half Michael McDonald, half Satan Himself.

The snake has no idea what to do with this.

Abe realizes that the toilet seat is up and an insane plan flashes in his mind: get the snake wrapped around the plunger and somehow get it into the bowl. Close the lid, sit on it if he has to, but get it in the bowl and out of his sight.

It's impossible. It's impractical. But it's also:

"WHAT A FOOL BELIEEEEVES!" he bellows. "HE SEES! THE WAH MAH HAH NAH POWER!"

He has to act fast, while the snake is confused. Jab it with the plunger like a snake handler.

Don't think, bro! Ty again. *Just do it!*

And he's about to. He really is.

Then he hears something at his feet. A *shhh* whisperrasping across the tile. He can't help but look down. Just for a microsecond.

Something has been slipped into the room from under the door.

A note.

Someone outside has passed him a note. What the absolute, everloving f—

He turns back just in time to see the rattlesnake launching itself towards him.

SNAKEBITE; LONDON CALLING

It doesn't hurt like he thought it would. He supposes it's shock. His nerves need a moment to collect themselves before reporting on the agonizing end that's in store for his body. The clotting suffocation.

Then he realizes what actually happened.

The snake's aim was just a tiny bit off—or maybe Abe also happened to move the plunger as his body turned. Instead of Abe's flesh, the snake latched its fangs into the black plastic of the plunger.

Even a quarter of an inch in the other direction and its venom would be pulsing through Abe's chest right now.

Sheer, dumb luck.

That's all it was.

The plunger was in his dominant hand—the one not swelling up like a balloon animal right now—but when the snake's not-inconsiderable weight was added, the plunger fell out of his grip and clattered to the floor. Now the snake is writhing and twisting and Abe realizes its teeth are stuck in the thick plastic. It can't detach itself yet. He has to act fast.

Despite his nerves' shrieking protestations, Abe wraps both hands around the wooden dowel, avoiding the thrashing rattle like it's a scorpion's tail. With all his goddamn might, like Paul Simonon bringing his bass down onto the stage floor of the Palladium on the cover of *London Calling*, he starts slamming the snake against the wall. It doesn't do much damage; the softness of the plunger must be buffeting the blows. Abe can sense the snake's fangs beginning to wriggle free from the plastic, so he reverts back to plan A. He dashes towards the toilet.

Just as the snake's fangs finally escape the plunger, Abe manages to drape the snake over the rim of the bowl, with the snake's head dipping into the water. Before the fucker can squirm out, Abe slams the seats down onto the snake's upper back and then sits as hard as he can. The solid resistance of the reptile underneath is horrifying—a metal pipe wrapped in muscle. But after a few bounces up and down, really putting his weight into it, he feels something inside the snake break. Its rattle whips, spasms, twitches. . . and finally stills.

NOTES; THE BEST SONG YOU EVER HEARD; HANNUKAH PRESENT; THE PROCLAIMERS

Abe sits there for a long time.

Panting.

Sweating.

Tingling all over. Carbonated by adrenaline.

A long time.

Years, maybe.

What finally gets him to move is remembering the note on the floor. He stands up, amazed at how suddenly sore and tired his body is, and waddles his way to the door.

Before he picks the note up, he checks back with the snake. Definitely still dead. But unlike Boris, the snake seems to have grown in death. Abe can't believe how much of it trails out from the closed toilet lid. Like a giant necktie. Its defeat feels impossible. He should absolutely be dead now.

He gives a weak shout through the door, "Why are you doing this?" His voice sounds so small for such a mighty gladiator. "Hello? Will you just talk to me?" Then, absurdly, he tries: "I'm not mad. I promise."

Worth a shot. Might even be true. But like all his other attempts, it goes unanswered.

xxx

It turns out to not be a note. At least, not in the way Abe expected. The white piece of paper slid under the door had been folded in half to act as a simple envelope. When he picks it up, what looks like confetti rains down from inside.

No, not confetti. After he retrieves the bits that fell—grateful none of them fluttered over to the piss puddle—he sees they're five pieces of candy wrappers, each cut to show one letter, like a ransom note that had forgotten its glue.

Before he can indulge himself in thinking maybe this is all just some random garbage that happened to blow under the door, his brain puts together the word the letters are spelling. He even recognizes the source of each letter.

The Y is from a Hershey Bar.

The O is from an Almond Joy.

The U is from a bag of Sour Patch Kids.

The R is from a Snickers.

And the E is from a 3 Musketeers.

Abe suddenly feels very cold.

"I'm what?" he asks. "I'm *what*?" He pulls on the door. Pounds it with his good hand. Kicks it. He screams: "I'm WHAT?!"

But he knows the answer.

Doomed.

Fucked.

A goner.

Dead.

The suddenness with which he whips around almost makes him fall. He's *positive* the snake is moving.

It's not. It's still draped over the rim of the toilet bowl. Still totally immobile.

But there's that vent in the ceiling. Anything could come out of there next. And Abe is so tired. He's been lucky—amazingly lucky—twice. No way he'll be lucky again a third time.

And his hand hurts so badly.

He's doomed. Fucked. A goner. Dead.

A memory tugs at the back of his brain. Some anecdote or lesson he'd heard about death. About already being dead.

He can't chase it down, though—instead, he gets distracted by another soft rasping noise across the floor.

A new note has been slid under the door.

"Fuck you!" Abe screams. "Why are you doing this to me?" No answer. "I'm not gonna play your fucking games, asshole! LET ME FUCKING OUTTA HERE!" His voice cracks. He sounds like he's going to cry. *Joke's on you*, he thinks, *I'm not going to cry*, and then feels the warmth of tears spilling down his cheeks again.

It only takes him a few moments to arrange the letters from this second note into a word. Longer than the first, but he's almost disappointed it's over so quickly. For those blissful seconds, his brain is occupied with something other than blank terror.

The G is from a bag of gummy bears;

The O from a Mr. Goodbar;

The N from a Crunch bar;
Another N from a bag of Corn Nuts;
And the A from a bag of Lays.
You're Gonna

"Die," he whispers. "The next one is going to say 'Die.'"

He has to wait a while to find out, sitting there, staring at the gap at the bottom of the door—but of course, he's already lost any real sense of time. It could be dawn, it could be the next evening, it could be fifteen minutes since he first discovered he was locked in. Darwin's Foëtus has a bit they love trotting out at gigs, called "Schrödinger's Pop Hit." Abe and Ty talk about it in between every song, telling the crowd that it's their most popular song and that they'll get to it soon since they know it's what everyone is really there to hear. Then they'll finish their set and if anyone asked afterwards about why they didn't play that one song, they'll say, "But wasn't it the best song you ever heard?" Not quite nailing what Schrödinger was all about (and Ty could attest to this, given he actually majored in quantum physics), but it's all in good fun. After all, as long as the song remained unplayed it could exist as both the best song and not.

Now, I've been Schrödinger-ized, Abe thinks. *I'm living and dead. Just waiting for someone to open this box and find me in my true state.*

He tries to chuckle at the thought. Fails.

He also tries chasing down that earlier memory. Something about death being foregone, about brokenness being inevitable. It continues to elude him, but he thinks it has something to do with glass?

Doesn't matter. It won't help him. Nothing will.

Soon enough, one more white sheet of paper slips under the

door, folded in half, pregnant with cutout letters.

Abe feels he doesn't even need to review the letters inside. There will be three squares and they'll spell out D-I-E.

Curiosity gets the better of him, though, and he peeks.

There are only two letters.

The B is from the sticky, cloying wrapper of a Honey Bun.

And the E is from a bag of Cheetos. The tiniest bit of residual orange dust still clings to the plastic.

"Huh?" he whispers. *You're gonna be. . . ?*

Gonna be what? Gonne *be* dead? Bad enough being tortured by a gleeful psychopath; does the grammar need to be tortured too? Or, worse: is his captor working towards quoting that damned Proclaimers song?

More time passes. Abe stands there, no longer able to think of anything other than what could be going on out there, what word could be next.

A strange, tangy, meaty smell seems to be emanating from under the door now. And did he just hear a faint, wet sloshing coming from the depths of the store? And giggling?

Eventually, another note appears.

This time Abe leaps for it, like it's a Hannukah present.

Before he opens it up, he notices a distressing detail. The white paper is smudged with dark red. Just a tiny bit, in the corner of one side of the ad hoc envelope.

Nope. I'm gonna be. . . ignoring that detail.

Four squares inside.

The letters are easily arranged, though not easily explained.

G, from a Good & Plenty box.

L, from a Jack Link's beef jerky.

A, from a bag of Smartfood Popcorn.

D, from a bag of Snyder's pretzels.

He hears a squeaking noise and assumes it comes from his own throat.

"Glad?" he whispers to himself. Baffled. "What am I going to be glad ab—?"

Then another noise—one that makes Abe bolt upright and spin around. A soft, brief, high pitched squeal coming from the airducts.

It could just be the air conditioning. Or it could be some gibbering horror, squeezing its way through the dark hole in the ceiling to join Abe in one more fight to the death.

You're gonna be glad you only met Boris and the snake so far.

Abe backs all the way up against the wall, heart hammering, mind spinning with all the nightmarish possibilities.

Somehow, what happens next is worse than anything he could've imagined.

The lights cut out.

Abe is plunged into complete darkness.

THE HAIRLIP MAN

Now the room is full of noises: a wail, a sob, a moan, a cry. All Abe.

Not the dark, please, don't leave me in the dark where I can't even see what's about to come out of the ceiling next, no, no, no—

He shuts up once he realizes someone is also standing in the room with him.

There, in the corner. On the opposite side of this tiny, dark room.

Abe can't see anything, but he can definitely feel the unmistakable presence of another human body.

He can also hear breathing—not his, someone else's. He holds his own panicky, keening breaths just to be sure, and—yes. Someone else is breathing in here. No doubt about it. *Oh God.*

A fear he hasn't felt so keenly since childhood stabs into him.

The Hairlip Man.

The Hairlip Man is in here with him.

The Hairlip Man is going to watch as whatever drops next

out of the vent finally fills Abe with enough poison to coagulate his blood and kill him. The Hairlip Man will smile his secret, charming smile while Abe dies in the dark.

For all her complaining and kvetching and reveling in the misery that was her life, Bobbe Meydl never went into too much detail about the incidents that had traumatized her as a child. She liked to keep it vague and mysterious: "If you knew the things that had happened to me when I was a little girl in Poland. . ."

But there was one detail she'd shared with Abe.

He'd been seven years old. For reasons he can't remember, Bobbe was staying with them for a few days, sleeping in his room while he slept in a pillow fort out in the living room. He'd been so excited about this new arrangement—he loved forts, and he loved the living room because that's where the television was.

The only problem was, he was coming off of a series of weeks where he'd been having terrible nightmares. Midnight shriekfests that sent him running to his mom's room for comfort.

It had been long enough since he'd had one of these night terrors that he'd kind of forgotten about them, in the way only children can do. Something about sleeping in a new location must have brought them surging back.

Instead of running to his mom's, though, he ran to his own room. Weeping, terrified, desperate for the familiar. Bobbe Meydl was sitting up on his bed, blinking sleep from her eyes.

"You have nothing to be afraid of," she'd said, stroking hair after he'd breathlessly reported what had happened. Lest he think she was trying to comfort him, she followed up with: "You don't know what being afraid really is."

Abe had been defiant, though. "I do! I know all about monsters!" Suddenly it was imperative to him that he convince her. He began rattling off all the scary movies he'd seen (or, more accurately, heard about at school). Freddy and Jason and Chucky and, and, and.

She listened, face pulled in its usual perma-scowl, eyes glittering with smugness. When he finished, she smoothed his hair one last time. He'll never forget the tingle that sped through his body when she did so—that desperate appreciation of her physical attention.

"This is how I know you're a child, boychik," she said. "Your monsters are ridiculous. They are circus clowns. When evil comes, Abraham, it does not wear a mask. It looks as plain as day. I was a little girl when I learned that. The Hairlip Man. . ."

She trailed off. He demanded she tell him what the phrase meant.

She stared at him, then said, "I don't know if he was a Russian or a German. I only know he was so handsome. Except for that one tiny detail, which made his face human. I memorized that face as I watched him do what he did to my mother. As he loomed over me. As he chased me into the woods."

The Hairlip Man.

Abe felt his eyes going wide. Felt a different kind of chill spreading through his body. He didn't even know what a hairlip was—let alone that it was really spelled *harelip*—but it conjured surreal, horrible beauty.

Perhaps she would've told him more, if his mom hadn't come in then, yelling at his grandmother to stop, to not tell little Abe "that story."

Bobbe Meydl had received her daughter's outrage with a

grin—a devilishly delighted one, Abe thought later. She liked scaring her grandson. "I had to live through it—he can't bear to hear it from the safety of his pillows?"

He never thought to ask for more details later on. She'd told him enough. The Hairlip Man was firmly planted in his brain from then on. For the next several years—up until high school, really—whenever Abe had another shriekfest in the dark, it was because the Hairlip Man had come for him at last, the fine hairs that made up his lips rippling like underwater kelp.

Now he knows: the Hairlip Man has found him again.

glad glad i'm going to be glad i should be glad because i'm not going to die alone he's going to be here with me in the dark and

"Shut up."

Abe hears the voice next to his ear, as real as the pain in his hand, the aches in his muscles.

"Shut *up*."

The voice is sharp, like a slap to the face. He physically twitches when he hears it. Then it became deliberate, without sympathy, like hands squeezing a throat shut.

"Don't let him win. *Think*."

He heeds this strange, new voice and shuts up. Takes a steadying breath—which is still very much unsteady. Tries to think.

What are his options? If he lets himself stand here, panic churning in his chest like a hot tub gone haywire, imagining what might be pouring out of the ceiling vent, he's gonna literally lose his mind. He might wind up bashing his brains out on the wall or floor like one of those desperate orcas he heard about, purposefully ramming their snouts into their tank to escape their amusement park prisons.

But what to do about the person in here with him, watching him? Can he really hope to fight a human blind when fighting just a spider in full light took so much out of him? He's an out-of-shape bassist—what will he do when this stranger is suddenly next to him, grabbing him, *touching* him—

"No one's in here and you know it," that other, sharper voice insists, and then he realizes—it's *himself* who's speaking. Bobbe's no-love attitude, but out of his throat. "You've been staring at every inch of this bathroom for at least a couple hours now—how would anyone have gotten in without you noticing?"

That's true. He doesn't *believe* it, but he can't argue with it.

Regardless, there's still the matter of other critters dropping from the vent to join him. That's a *very* plausible threat.

First thing to do, then: make his eyes adjust as much as possible. He squeezes them shut, counts to five, and when he opens them again, he's able to see a little bit more than before.

Better. As far as he can tell nothing is skittering towards him yet. The light coming from under the door helps a little bit too, and—

Looking down at that crack of light, he notices something white and rectangular on the floor.

Another note.

At first, the usual dread surges through him at the thought of what new word in this torturous puzzle waits for him to decipher. Then, a more confounding thought:

Why would the person tormenting him slip him a note and *then* cut the power so he can't read it? Abe was obviously being held by a psychopath, but that? That just doesn't make *sense*.

He thinks back to what happened the moments before the

lights cut out.

"Wait. . ."

He slaps his hands against the wall behind him until he feels the telltale ridges and shapes of a light switch.

He flicks the switch in the opposite direction.

The fluorescents blink back on. A sickly yellow, blue stuttering that makes his eyes water a little.

"Son of a bitch," he says in a shocked gasp. "Goddammit."

The laughter comes first. Great gales of it. Laughter until his abs hurt.

Then come the sobs. They burble out of him in hitching, gulping waves. He tries to quiet them down as quickly as they arise, but somehow that makes them even stronger. He's at their mercy until they finally ebb a few minutes later.

"Son of a bitch," he says again, wiping the tears and snot with his forearm.

Ever mindful of the vent in the ceiling, he walks over to the sink and splashes some water on his face.

He makes brief eye contact with his tear-puffed face in the mirror and then immediately looks away. He's feeling relief. He's feeling embarrassment. He's feeling anger—fury, even—at how vulnerable he is in this fucking room. But underneath all these things, he's feeling something which scares him and disturbs him and keeps him from being able to look at himself.

Gratitude.

A warped kind of gratitude.

Being trapped in the dark caused a new level of fear to spike through his body. When the lights came back on, when he realized it had just been a mistake and that his captor was trying to kill him and/or drive him insane, *but at least wasn't leaving him alone in the dark*, Abe felt grateful for that bit of kindness.

"Jesus fucking Chruuuuh," he mutters. He wants to puke.

There's a toilet right there, bro, he imagines Ty saying, and if there wasn't the dead body of a large rattlesnake draped inside, he might take the opportunity.

Aren't rattlesnakes still dangerous after they're dead?

Abe vaguely recalls more random shit from the internet. Texas farmers sent to the hospital because of bite reflexes from dead snakes or something. Doesn't matter. The toilet is off limits for the sheer gag factor alone. If he has to puke *over* that horrible snake body he might never stop.

No puking. Just thinking. Puke later. Survive to puke another day.

That new note on the floor beckons him.

He goes over to pick it up, but stops when he reaches the light switch by the door. He gives the room one last suspicious look.

"I really thought someone was in here with me," he mumbles.

Bobbe answers—in her own voice this time.

Fear will do that. Fear makes you stupid.

But it wasn't just fear or him being stupid. It was the *breathing*. He would have sworn he'd heard breathing.

Partially as an experiment and partially to just confirm what had happened, Abe reaches over and turns out the lights again.

Perfect darkness.

Perfect silence.

No breathing noises this time.

Had Abe imagined the breathing before? In the same way his eyes had imagined the shape of a (*Hairlip*) man in the corner?

Or maybe . . . had his captor been on the other side of this door, listening? Breathing heavily?

Whoever is trapping me in here is very *interested in what I do.*

How can I use that against him?

Abe turns the lights back on.

Then he bends down to pick up the note, curious to see what he's supposed to be so glad about.

ELEVEN

HEARTS HEARTS HEARTS HEARTS HEARTS

No ransom note letters this time.

No familiar snack food labels turned into diverting jumbles.

Just four simple words, followed by an array of crudely simple hearts, handwritten in what Abe really, *really* hopes is reddish brown ink.

You're Gonna Be Glad You Stayed In There

Abe runs the sentence over in his head again and again. He thinks he understands what it's implying, but he just can't let himself believe it. There has to be some other, deeper meaning.

You're Gonna Be Glad You Stayed In There. . .

That implies he's going to be let out. It might even imply. . .

"No," he whispers. "Don't fucking mean that."

Thinking of how he'd simply had to turn the lights back on to escape the darkness, he puts a trembling hand on the doorknob.

You're Gonna Be Glad You Stayed In There. . .

"Please, fucking, *no.*"

He turns the knob and gives the door the faintest of pushes.

You're Gonna Be Glad You Stayed In There. . .

The door gives way. Just a crack for now, but he can tell there's no resistance.

God help me.

The deadbolt outside has been disengaged.

The door is unlocked.

How long had it been unlocked?

How long has he been able to escape?

Before he pushes the door open all the way, though, another question comes to him. The million dollar one.

(*you're gonna be glad you stayed*)

Should he?

He steps outside.

xxx

As with the giant spider, Abe's first thought is this must be a prank.

The entire convenience store—so shiny, so immaculate when he'd first come in—is slathered in red. Not an inch untouched.

Someone must have screwed in a couple of those novelty boudoir bulbs or something. Or maybe heat lamps? Is that why I'm sweating so hard?

Two things prevent his brain from buying into such nonsense.

All the clumps of darker, blacker, wetter red.

And the stench, which hits him like a physical wall. That thick, meaty smell, dialed up to a million.

The convenience store has been bathed, drenched, literally painted in blood.

Organs are dumped haphazardly across the floor and on shelves.

Other, larger masses reveal themselves to be human bodies—at least three of them, nude and slumped in undignified positions.

Abe's throat closes as his gorge rises. He wants to cry, vomit, eject any and everything from his body onto the floor, and hey, why not: insides are apparently meant for the outside in this hellish abattoir.

His brain keeps processing details of the scene. Like what looks like a set of lungs draped over the coffee machines. Or a semi-deflated heart resting below the nozzle of one of the Icee dispensers. Or the arcing streaks that tell him the blood must have been literally mopped onto the floor and slathered across the walls and beverage cases. He even remembers those faint sloshing sounds from earlier. Which means, somewhere, there's probably a mop bucket full of—

Stop looking. Just move. Get out of here.

Yes. Good idea. As far as he can tell, no one else is currently here with him. His path to the front door looks unimpeded. In fact, he can even see his car. Just on the other side of the glass front of the building.

He moves as quickly, quietly, carefully as he can. His shoes stick and squelch, leaving thick prints in the red underneath.

His eyes fall on the nearest body, posed face down and ass up against one of the beverage refrigerators. Several long objects protrude like tail feathers from its rear. The ice scrapers, plunged in deep.

Are these bodies real? Do they belong to the owners of the other cars outside? Or employees of the store? No way to know.

He stares a moment too long, waiting to see if there's any movement. Any survivors—or, worse, anyone *pretending* to be dead, like in that one *Saw* movie. . .

Another detail. One he really wishes he wasn't beginning to see. The body he's looking at isn't red because it was painted with blood like the floors. That's the corrugation of muscle.

Much of this person's skin has been removed.

Abe almost retches again.

Okay, really *time to go.*

He's about to break into a run when, on the other side of the store, the door to the backroom opens and someone comes through, dragging a heavy bulk that can only be another corpse.

Abe freezes.

The corpse-dragger drops the newest body to the blood-slick floor, gives their own lower back a stretch, and turns around.

Hard to say for sure, but based on size and shape, Abe assumes the figure is male. Dressed in all black. Form fitting black pants. A long sleeve black shirt.

His head is covered in holes.

Fathomless, black holes, honeycombed in row upon row across what should be the stranger's face.

Abe's stomach plummets.

"Oh!" the hole-faced stranger exclaims, voice bright and cheery. "I was wondering when you'd come out! Didja see all this?"

He gestures to the room. When he moves, the holes on his face waggle slightly, and Abe quickly understands they're not holes. They're huge, dilated pupils.

Googly eyes. Affixed to some sort of mask.

That mask has a strange glow around the edges, but Abe doesn't get a chance to observe further. Laughing like a loon, the eyeball-man suddenly breaks into a full sprint, bolting right for Abe.

Abe feels his mind yank apart in two directions—run for the door! run for safety!—and his body takes over. He turns for the closest option, the most familiar.

He barely makes it back to the bathroom in time. He slams the door shut behind him and engages the handle lock, just as his whooping, guffawing pursuer collides with the metal on the other side. The door rattles in its frame, but the handle lock holds.

More thuds. More maniacal laughter.

"I saw you! I SAWWWWW YOU! Hooo! Hooo!"

A small shape skitters in from under the door.

Abe flinches and kicks it into a corner.

Another googly eye. Staring up at the ceiling.

The laughter continues.

Abe can only back further into the bathroom, joining the dead spider, the dead snake, and sob in response.

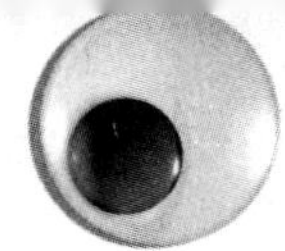

RESCUE AT LAST; ANOTHER ESCAPE ROUTE

Sometime later—hours, maybe—Abe hears sounds which, at first, he assumes are more mask-muffled hoots of laughter.

Then Abe sees red and blue lights under the crack in the door.

Not laughter. Sirens.

Rescue.

He hears indistinguishable shouts. The comforting melody of authority. The percussive rattle of gunfire. The silence that follows.

"I'm coming out!" Abe shouts. "Don't shoot!"

He opens the bathroom door and sees the eyeball-man sprawled on the bloody ground. Body riddled with bullet holes, like a mocking replica of his mask.

Officers stand over the psychopath, guns still smoking. Other officers flood into the store.

One notices Abe. "Put your hands up!" the officer shouts, but Abe is already complying, grateful tears running down his face.

The cops see that Abe's no threat and usher him out of the

store into the blissfully muggy night. They wrap arms around his shoulders and the feeling of comfort is exquisite.

Not as exquisite as the sight that greets him outside, though.

He has to blink several times before he can really process it. The strobing lights from all the vehicles make it hard to see. But once his eyes adjust, there can be no doubt.

Jenna is here. Waiting for him. Her own face, tear-streaked, as well.

"I was so worried," she says, and runs to him, wrapping her arms around him in a desperate hug.

"What—?" All Abe can do is stammer. "How—?"

She gives a wet laugh, wiping at her eyes before placing her hands on his cheeks as if she can't believe he's really real. "They traced your phone. Because you were using your map, they were able to reverse the satellite feed and find out where you were."

"That's" (*impossible*) "amazing," he says.

"You're amazing," she says, and kisses him. Her lips are firm but soft and sweetly flavored with tobacco. Heavenly. He breathes her in. If he could just smell her upper lip forever, every moment up to this point would have been worth it.

"But wait," he asks, pulling away, hating himself for breaking the moment. "How did they even know to start looking for me? And why are you here with them?"

Jenna's eyes search his. Her heart-stopping eyes, framed so perfectly by lashes as alluring as sea anemones.

"Oh, baby," she sighs, and pulls him close to whisper in his ear. "Because you're daydreaming."

"What?" He blinks.

He's back in the bathroom.

Sitting on the floor opposite the door.

The body of the spider, the snake, the puddle of piss, the glaring fluorescent light.

"You're daydreaming," she says again. Only, the voice isn't coming from his head. . . is it? His ears are ringing—a constant, high shriek from the stress of everything—so he can't tell for sure. But, just like when he was trapped in darkness, he's almost positive he's hearing a voice from outside his skull.

It's not coming from his own throat this time, though. This time, it sounds like it's coming from. . .

The mirror?

"You're daydreaming, stupid."

He can't see the mirror from where he's sitting, but the direction of the voice is unmistakable. So's the tenor of the speaker. It's not Jenna; it's his grandmother.

He sighs.

"Eat shit, Bobbe," he mutters back. Actually out loud. Who cares? Let him sound crazy. This might be the last conversation he ever has.

"*You're* the one eating shit," she says. "You're pathetic. Running away. You could've made it to that front door. You *chose* to be trapped."

"No, I didn't."

"Yes, you did."

"He could've followed me outside! He could've gotten me before I even got to the front door!"

"You're telling yourself that."

"Can you maybe try having empathy for once in your miserable life? Why are you always such a judgmental. . ." He holds back. Calling his grandmother a bitch seems like a heresy that can't be undone, even if it's all just in his head.

"See?" He can hear her smug grin. "Weak."

"I can't just run at him. I need a weapon or something."

"Your mind is a weapon."

"Great. Lemme just scoop that out and throw it at him like a fucking water balloon."

"Excuses, excuses, always with the excuses. 'I can't do this; I can't do that.' You've been trapped in that *shtusim* well before you found this bathroom."

Abe squeezes his eyes shut. "Shutthefuckup, shutthefuckup, shutthefuckUP!"

Then, suddenly, an idea. That dim anecdote about broken glass. He still can't remember the specifics of it, but. . .

His eyes pop open and he leaps to his feet, pulling off his overshirt and wrapping it around his not-broken fist.

His grandmother is still in the mirror, castigating him, mocking him, decrying him—him and his entire worthless generation. Great. Let her. Just makes it all the easier to—

Crack!

A single punch to the glass leaves a spiderweb in the center. It actually feels exquisite to hit something.

Crack, crack, crack!

A few more blows and several shards loosen and fall to the ground.

He picks up the largest with his wrapped hand.

"I've got a weapon now," he says.

Shut his grandma up too.

Or is she simply daring him to put his money where his mouth, his wrapped fist, might be?

He looks at the door.

Do it. Do it now. He won't be expecting it, and you've got a weapon.

"Yeah," he whispers. "I do."

But the memory of that awful, hooting laughter, the grisly decorations. . . Now that a physical confrontation is guaranteed, Abe finds himself staring at that solitary googly eye on the floor.

When evil comes, Abraham, it won't be wearing a mask. . .

Well, this time it definitely fucking *is.* And look how many other people are dead already. Eyeball Guy's clearly got psycho-strength. What if he also has a gun? That'd drop Abe well before he can get into shard-wielding range. It's good he's found something in this bathroom he can use to defend himself, but it's not like he's suddenly invincible.

Strategy. Think. Is there a way to avoid running into the guy? A way to avoid—(*those awful eyes*)—being seen? Or, at the very least, get the drop on him?

Abe tears his gaze away from the plastic eye on the floor, looks around his all-too-familiar prison. His sights land on the ceiling vent.

He'd heard someone crawling around up there, before Boris and the snake were dropped down. Which means someone was able to get up there. Which means. . .

He looks at the rest of the ceiling panels. Reachable, if he stands on something.

Something like the toilet.

Maybe there's another escape route that's been available to him this whole time.

THIRTEEN

SPECIMEN; INVINCIBILITY STAR; MURDERER

"Dude." Ty's voice, coming from one of the mirror shards on the floor. "How is this a better plan than just running out and fighting the guy?"

Abe ignores him, focusing instead on balancing on the toilet.

"Careful of that snake! Remember—"

"I know," Abe grunts in reply. "Posthumous bite reflex."

"Good name for a song, right? I read online that those fuckers can still bite hours after death, and they're still chock full of poison."

"It's venom," Abe mutters back. "And you only know that because *I* know that, because you're just a fucking voice in my head."

"Ouch, dude."

Both toilet lids are closed on top of the snake's body, but it barely compacts under Abe's weight. He rocks unsteadily on tiptoes, having wild thoughts of princesses and peas.

He could just pull the snake out and throw it in a corner, but he doesn't want to look at the fanged mouth of that thing ever again. It's okay. He can balance.

He takes a breath before pushing up one of the popcorn panels above him. His entire body feels clenched in a preemptive wince, too aware there could be any number of other spiders and snakes waiting up here—legless horrors and horrors with too many legs. That said, nothing else has made an appearance through the vent since the rattlesnake, so he's reasonably confident nothing is waiting for him.

He's half correct. In the darkness above, nothing crawls out to surprise him, but he *can* make out two brown boxes around the panels nearest the vent. On the nearest box, he makes out some words stamped on the side—"*Trumbull Farms*" and "*specimen transport*"—and shivers a little in recognition. Boris' and the snake's rides, he presumes. Hopefully at least empty now.

Abe tries to scan the rest of the shadowy landscape. If this is going to be a viable option, he'll need to find a way out of the convenience store that's ideally not the same way his tormentor used.

However, that means he needs to lift himself higher to see further into the ceiling space. Which also means inserting more of his face into the dark realm of the New Trumbull Farms.

A quick prayer to any deity within prayershot.

He plants his elbows into the joints of the ceiling panel and lifts.

The effort of holding himself up like this is agonizing. The uneven toilet lids rock under his tiptoes. He won't be able to balance like this for long. He clumsily rotates himself around to get a better sense of the landscape.

Another box is staring him right in the face. It had been behind his head this whole time.

Several spiders and a thick, centipede-looking monstrosity crawl along its side. Not empty at all. And barely two inches from his nose.

"Fuck!" He hisses. Flails. Tries to shove the box away. His legs kick impotently, toes searching for purchase. In the shuffling, he accidentally puts too much weight on the nearest ceiling panel and it gives way. Down it—and he—goes.

He plummets to the hard tile floor, narrowly missing cracking his back on the toilet.

The pain is symphonic, but tempered by the realization that he'd succeeded in tilting that surprise box towards the now-busted ceiling panel and it's currently raining insects onto him. Spiders. Centipedes. God knows what else. He can hear their horrid bodies plinking against the floor, into the piss puddle. He can feel hundreds of legs scrambling against his skin, settling into his hair.

It's too much.

He bolts to his feet, swatting and stomping, not giving any creature a chance to bite him first. A merciless killing machine.

He hears himself scream-singing again, beyond hysterical this time—is he reciting Doobie Brothers lyrics? Billy Joel? Cannibal Corpse? He doesn't even know. It's just words and howling.

He used to hate killing bugs. Not just because they grossed him out, but because he always felt guilty killing anything that had an instinct to save its own life. Even cockroaches. He always assumed this was a side effect of Jewish guilt. An entire religion obsessed with constantly escaping near-extinction—how could you approach killing another living thing cavalierly?

Now, those thoughts are galaxies away from his mind. All he

can think is kill, kill, kill. Leave nothing uneradicated.

Sometime later, the scream-singing comes to an end. He stands victorious, gasping for breath, surrounded by the bodies of his demolished foes. Nothing stirs in the room besides him. And, granted, he might not feel it even if he were, but he doesn't think he's bitten anywhere.

A miracle. And something even better: right now, he feels fucking invincible.

He feels like Mario after touching a star. He feels like he just got off the stage after a particularly cathartic and well-received scream-fest, not a single wrong note played.

Now! Go, now!!

His panting breaths come out like growls.

Not wasting a second, even to think about what he's doing, he tightens his grip on the mirror shard and yanks opens the bathroom door.

The guy in the eyeballs-mask isn't in sight. Abe strides purposefully and speedily towards the front door. Shoves it open. He feels like he can see in all directions right now, and like even the goddamn ocean would part for him.

The night air is the most beautiful feeling he's ever felt. He could almost cry. But not yet—crying will be reserved for later. He can feel his invincibility starting to waver, his legs starting to shake.

He heads straight for his car, then almost jumps when he notices: the van's gone. Its empty spot in the parking lot is as surreal and uncanny as an expert magic trick.

Did the guy up and leave? One final mindfuck?

No matter. Abe pats his pockets and for a moment thinks he doesn't have his keys, but then they're in his hand and he's fumbling with the unlock button on the key fob. Everything is working out exactly as it needs to. Almost done with this nightmare.

He's just about to open the driver's side door when a hand touches his shoulder.

"Help—" a soft voice whispers.

Abe's manic invincibility surges back. Still not even sure any of this is really happening, he spins around with (*snake-like*) speed and starts mercilessly pumping his shard of glass into the unwelcome stranger's guts.

ASSAILANT; AN UNLUCKY KID; NO SURVIVORS; SELF-DEFENSE

"stop. . . stop please. . ."

It's the weakness of the voice, not the resistance of flesh against fist, nor the hot blood gushing over his hand, that clues Abe in that this is real, not another daydream.

He would never daydream someone making such desperate pleas.

He stops stabbing. Takes a step backwards, along the side of his car, to get a better look at his assailant.

Assailant. That's rich. You're the one who just ventilated his torso.

He's looking at a young man. A kid, really—probably only a year or two out of high school.

Thin. All elbows and Adam's apple. A faint spray of acne. A mop of unruly hair. Huge, innocent eyes. Even huger now, in their shock.

The kid is hunched over, holding his stomach where Abe just

introduced a new series of speed holes, but Abe is able to see the kid is wearing baggy jeans and a huge, red and white polo shirt that bears the gas station's logo on the upper-left of the chest.

A loose black backpack was slung over the kid's right shoulder; now it droops off of his elbow.

"Sorry," the kid wheezes. His voice is high and reedy. Barely pubescent. "I'm—"

He collapses against the car.

Almost instinctively, Abe steps forward to catch the kid before he hits the ground. He's babbling apologies, too.

"No," the kid manages in a high, quavery voice. "My fault. I shouldn't have snuck up on you, I was just. . . stuck in the storeroom so long, I was so glad to see some—ohhh, God." He loses his ability to speak in a wave of wooziness. His eyes roll up, revealing the whites. Abe thinks he might even pass out, but the kid manages to stay conscious with obvious effort.

"Fuck," Abe says. "You're hurt bad. Um. Fuck!"

The clerk's midsection is slick with blood. He's so heavy. Almost dead weight already.

"Did you see him?" The clerk asks. "The. . . eyeballs?"

"Yeah."

"Any. . . other survivors?"

"No."

The clerk gives a wheezy laugh. "Then I woulda done the same thing." He hisses in pain clutches at his stomach wounds. "I'm so stupid. . . Didn't want to make too much noise, so I didn't yell first. I'm really sorry."

"Stop apologizing! I'm the one who's—I've gotta help you. We gotta get you to a hospital."

"Feeling. . . dizzy. . ."

He's probably losing too much blood. He might not even make it to a hospital. Shit. Fucking shit.

Leave him, his grandmother hisses in his head. *You're so close.*

"We've gotta stop the bleeding." Abe's eyes fall back on the convenience store. "There are bandages and stuff in there." Abe doesn't move, though. Not yet. Because. . . well, what if this is a trap?

The clerk looks at him, bent over his wounds. His eyes are so big and brimming with tears. It's as if he reads Abe's mind.

"You don't know me, man. Just go. Get help. Save yourself. *Please.*" He looks at least three shades whiter already. Like he's literally draining in front of Abe. Ashen circles above his cheekbones. His acne-haunted face slick with sweat.

Abe looks at his car. Looks at the man—the kid!—he might have just murdered. Looks at where the CR8H8 van *used* to be.

Don't you DARE, Abraham.

The clerk echoes his grandmother's sentiments.

"Don't." Voice cracking like a goddamn thirteen-year-old. He clutches Abe's arm with one bloody hand. "Please. Get out of here while you can."

The kid's hand feels so small against Abe's arm. So light. So desperate for Abe to be selfish. To be like his goddamn, awful grandmother. But what's the point of surviving if he sacrifices his damned humanity to do it?

"Hey," Abe says, breaking free of the kid's grip without difficulty and holding up his glass shard. "I can defend myself." He gives the kid a pained grin. "Or didn't you notice?"

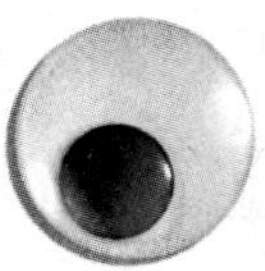

HUMANITY; BULKWARK; UNEXPECTED CONTACT

Stupid, he thinks. *Stupid. Stupid. Stupid. Stupid.*

It should only take, like, ninety seconds tops to sneak in, grab bandages, and sneak back out. But time has begun to pull itself out like taffy.

Every squeak of his shoes against the blood-slick floor becomes a nine-part symphony.

Every heartbeat becomes an extended drum solo.

Every breath, an open invitation for the door to the employee area to swing back open again and reveal the masked psychopath.

Where are the bandages? Why are there so many food products? Who needs this many goddamn snacks?

He can feel dozens upon dozens of eyes on him. In fact, peripherally, he notices one or two more of those damned googly eyes on the floor, where they must've fallen off of their mask or something.

His own eyes are busy darting to the backroom door, to the

bodies on display. He's waiting for something to move, to give him another cheap horror movie jump scare and come bolting straight for him.

The killer must be preoccupied skinning another victim or violating a corpse with automotive accessories, though. Or maybe he really did take his murder van and flee the scene.

All is silent and still.

Unbearably silent and still.

And the open door to the bathroom gapes like an audience member shocked and delighted to see Abe has returned.

At last Abe finds what he's looking for—why would health supplies be kept in the same aisle as antifreeze?!—and he fills his arms up and hurries back out into the night air, back tingling with the cold fire insistence that someone or something is behind him.

When he finds himself outside again, there comes that surprising feeling of invincibility once more. A giddiness. He's *alive*, goddammit.

Alive and with his humanity intact.

XXX

The van is gone, he keeps repeating in his head—a bulwark against panic.

The van is gone. The van is gone. The van is gone. The van is gone.

After ninety seconds in the convenience store, he gives himself two minutes to get the clerk bandaged up so he'll survive the trip to a hospital. This is an unconscionably risky thing to be doing—the sort of thing he's screamed at a thousand horror movie protagonists for doing on a thousand screens—but he can't stop himself. The clerk is acting like he's gonna bleed out otherwise.

"Keep a lookout for me," Abe tells him, while ripping open the bandages.

The young clerk gives a weak, but genuine laugh. "Just don't. . . tell me to 'keep my eyes peeled.'"

"Ugh. That fucking mask, right?"

The kid grimaces—maybe with pain or maybe with loathing. "I don't know if I'll ever unsee it."

Abe moves as quickly as he can. He's done all he can to mitigate the risk of staying here for these additional few moments. He's sitting in the driver's seat; the clerk is in the passenger seat. The keys are in the ignition. The engine is on and the convenience store is in full view. They're ready to peel out at the first twitch of danger—or the first sound of that horrible van returning.

Getting the kid into the car had been no easy task. He's not a large young man, but he was so weak it took both of their best efforts to get him seated. In fact, Abe's a little dismayed at how sapped his own energies have become. His adrenaline is ebbing.

Now, the clerk is leaning back to give Abe easier access to the gashes across his midsection. While the kid talks, Abe cleans and bandages up his wounds.

It had been a slow night, the clerk explains. "I was working in the backroom on stock stuff, which I hate, so I had my earphones in. Took me a while before I realized someone was shouting in the store. I came out to see what was going on—some. . . *guy* had come in. Wearing that mask. All those eyeballs. And he was yelling. There were two other customers and two employees, and he was yelling at all of them, almost like, like a preacher. He was saying he'd come to show them his 'creation.' He wanted to 'create' for them, whatever that means."

Abe swallows. He hears his throat click. "Hate," he says. "He wants to create hate."

The clerk looks at him with his wide, wet eyes that seem to say, that makes perfect sense.

"What happened next?" Abe asks.

"Well, that's when I noticed he had this knife. The biggest knife in the world. And he was blocking the front door, so no one could get past him. He slashed one of the customers. Then he threw the knife at another customer." He gestures to the spot between his eyebrows. "It just. . . sunk in. Never seen anything like it outside of a movie before. Trevor, one of the other clerks, tried to wrestle him down to the ground. He was too fast. Too strong. He started choking Trevor. And that *wasn't* like anything I'd seen in a movie before. Choking in a movie is slow and quiet. This was, like. . ." His voice fills with tears. "I thought his fingers were going to sink right through Trevor's neck. I. . . I wanted to do something, but I was so scared. I was frozen."

The kid looks off to the side, ashamed.

Abe wants to tell him he knows how he feels; instead, he lets the clerk continue, rapt.

"Then all those eyes pointed right at me. He let go of Trevor and he just *rushed* at me. Full speed. Laughing, this high, awful laugh. He shoved me. Never been shoved so hard. I don't know if it was against a wall or the floor, but I slammed my head. Blacked out. When I woke up, I was in the backroom and everything was super quiet. There was a Post-it Note on me. Right here on my chest. It said, '*Enjoy!*' With a buncha hearts. I came out and saw. . . everything he'd done." He fights back a wave of nausea.

Abe has finished applying bandages. The wounds actually didn't look so bad once all the blood was wiped away. The kid pulls his shirt down, wincing, and smooths it out. "Thank you. Think you just saved my life."

"Yeah, well. We're not outta the woods yet."

They both look at the store. The blood inside glistens like cherry shellac.

"Why is it so quiet now?" the clerk asks. "Where do you think he went?"

Abe shrugs. "Maybe he. . . did what he wanted to do? Created what he wanted to create?" Abe realizes they're whispering. As if they're trying not to summon the monster back.

"You think he left us alive on purpose?"

Abe considers that. "What's the point of creation with no one there to witness it?"

The sight is almost hypnotic in its grisliness. Still lit up like an oasis in the dark.

Then his eyes focus on the bug guts, still smeared across the windshield. Splat. He snaps out of his reverie. They can't have been sitting here for longer than three or four minutes, but that's too long by half.

"Doesn't matter," he says. "We're outta here. And we're—What?"

"Your phone," the clerk says, pointing.

Abe had been so busy tending to the kid's wounds, his story, that he'd forgotten about his phone. His goddamn, piece of shit phone, plugged into the dash in its stupid little cradle.

It's ringing.

Someone is calling him *right now.*

The name on the caller ID makes Abe actually gasp.

"Who is it?" the clerk asks. He still seems weak, but his energy is returning. He's not as pale.

"One sec. Just. . . keep your eyes peeled."

Abe fumbles with the phone. He should be speeding away, calling the cops, but. . . this will only take a second. No internal voice tells him he's being stupid this time. Every character in his brain understands he needs to answer this call.

To confirm this is happening. To hear her voice.

"Jenna?" he asks, barely able to speak her name.

"Abe!" Jenna shouts on the other end. "Holy fuck, are you okay? We've been losing our minds over here!"

When he hears his name out of her mouth, he immediately breaks down in sobs.

But even through those sobs, he can hear her—really, truly, *actually her*.

She's rambling about how his brother has been wondering where he is, and so he called Ty and then Ty called her—everyone is worried. Abe has been MIA for hours and hours. Ty and Abe's brother decided maybe Abe got cold feet and was ghosting them, but Jenna—"you know how I'm a chronic insomniac"—volunteered to keep calling and see if she could get an answer.

"I dunno," she continues, "I just had a bad feeling. Like, something in the air. Like, you needed help."

She cares about him. She's attuned to him. How insane, after all he's gone through, that this is what his mind latches onto.

Still. No time.

"I—I—I can't talk right now, Jenna," he finally manages. "I'm at a gas station. I don't know where. By, um—" A name he'll never forget comes to him. "—Trumbull Farms' Snake and Spider House. If you look that place up, you'll know where I am, just a couple miles away."

"Trumbull Farms?"

"Yeah. Someone tried to kill me. All night." He has to stifle a laugh at the insanity of that accurate statement.

"What?! Abe, are you—?!"

"I'm still in danger, so I gotta go. I gotta call the cops. Maybe you call them too? I gotta get distance. But. . . But it's gonna be okay, Jenna. I think I can believe that now. It's really good to hear your voice."

"Wait, but—"

Somehow, the hardest thing he's done yet tonight is hang up on her. But he does it.

Before he puts the car in reverse, he wipes at his eyes. Takes a deep breath.

"Wow. You really love her."

The clerk's voice comes from a million miles away. Abe actually almost forgot he wasn't alone in the car.

"Love? I. . . I don't know about that."

The clerk is leaning back in his seat, almost at a diagonal against the window. Looks oddly luxuriant, but his breaths are coming shallowly and his voice is thin.

"Love is so hard," the clerk says. Wheezes.

Abe says, "Let's get outta here. Once we're on the road, I'll call the cops, and—"

"Wait. Before you start driving. Can you do me a huge favor?"

Something about the guy's demeanor has completely changed, and it's ringing all of Abe's alarm bells. But he doesn't know why.

Nothing overtly threatening is happening. If anything, the guy seems almost. . . too relaxed.

"I've got asthma," the clerk says, chest rising in short little bursts. "It gets real bad sometimes. I can feel an attack coming on. Can you help me out?"

Abe feels a coldness creeping over his shoulders. Something is wrong. Something is very wrong. "What do you need?"

"Can you get my inhaler out of my backpack?"

The guy's backpack is sitting in the footwell. An unassuming black JanSport. Loose and floppy and seemingly empty.

"It's the only thing in there. You can't miss it."

"We really gotta go," Abe says. "We've wasted too much time already—"

"Please?" The clerk wheezes. *That's not an asthmatic wheeze, is it. . .?* "I could die if I don't have it. I'd do it but it hurts too much to bend. Because of the stab wounds. And if you're driving, then you can't get it either and—"

"Fine." If Abe had time to take that call from Jenna, he has time to do this. Fifteen seconds at most. Five, even.

But those alarm bells. . .

Abe reaches over and grabs the backpack. Unzips the top and sticks his hand in for the inhaler. There's a charging cord for a laptop but no—

White hot agony stabs into his hand and flares up his arm. He yelps, in surprise and pain. Wrenches his hand out of the bag.

No no no no.

Dangling from teeth sunk into the pinky-side of his palm is a thin snake. Alternating bands of black, yellow, and red. A black head.

And the clerk lets out another sigh.

And Abe realizes the quality of those shallow breaths.

Not asthmatic.

The clerk gives a satisfied, post-orgasmic moan. "Oh, *thank you.*"

OLD FRIENDS; FOREVER

Abe stares at the snake with clinical shock as it wriggles in mid-air, attached to his palm.

Then he looks back at the clerk.

The clerk is grinning the biggest grin Abe has ever seen. A grin that somehow adds decades to the clerk's boyish face—centuries—because only something truly ancient could feel a joy like this.

Abe's other hand is broken, of course. But now everything seems to be going numb, so he somehow manages to open the car door with his broken hand and throw himself backward onto the asphalt.

The snake finally lets go and slithers off into the night. Abe tries to do the same, backing away from the car, crawling across asphalt and concrete towards the safety of the convenience store.

Already, he's feeling sluggish.

Moving through molasses.

Nerves on fire.

Agonizing bursts sparking through him.

Concrete slabs drying around his limbs.

He's never moved so slow. Even the blood in his veins, turning into a hardened sludge.

The passenger side opens and the clerk slides out of the car.

"So," he says casually, like he just facilitated an introduction at a cocktail party, "that was a Sonoran coral snake. According to the sign on its case, it's super venomous, but not *always* fatal. It's pretty good at not overdoing it with its dosage when it bites as a warning. We'll see if she really meant business, I guess."

He sticks a hand into another compartment of his now-snake-less backpack and pulls out a slightly curved shield with an elastic strap. His mask.

Googly eyes are still stuck all over it, but fewer than before. All this action must be making the eyes come loose, fall off. It's apparent how homemade the thing is.

There's something unusual about the surface of the mask too—something Abe might try to get a better look at to understand, but at the moment he's a little too preoccupied to care.

He reaches the front door to the store, somehow manages to pull himself up and inside, closes the door behind him. He looks for the locks on the door, sees one on the ground, tries to engage it but it's too complicated for his hands—one, broken, the other starting to inflate around its puncture marks. Plus, bending like this is making him feel even woozier.

The clerk saunters up to the door—too close, too late. He raps politely on the glass, his erratic smattering of eyes waggling.

Only one place to go.

One place Abe knows he can hide.

He gives up on locking the front door and stumbles across the snack displays until he reaches the bathroom.

This lock is much easier to engage. An old friend. He engages it as he hears the clerk skip his way through the convenience store, laughing.

Abe begins to laugh too.

No, cry.

No, laugh. Barely any energy to commit to either.

He slides down to the cold floor of the bathroom, joining the array of dead insects he'd left behind, and his eyes lose their focus. He stares towards the crack under the door, but really he's looking into the nowhere of nothingness.

"You're *such* a nice guy!" The clerk shouts from the other side of the metal. "It's seriously impressive! Like, you *really* try! Wow!"

Abe doesn't move.

"Honestly, though, it's good you didn't get on the road with me. Things were gonna get messy!"

Abe doesn't respond.

After a long, *long* silence, the clerk calls out again: "Just made it so your car won't start, FYI. We're stuck here together now. Maybe forever, I don't know."

Abe gives him nothing.

The room has been spinning ever so slightly, but whether it's the venom clogging his blood vessels or the stress of maybe losing his mind, he can't say. Doesn't matter. He kind of enjoys it. It's almost like being rocked to sleep.

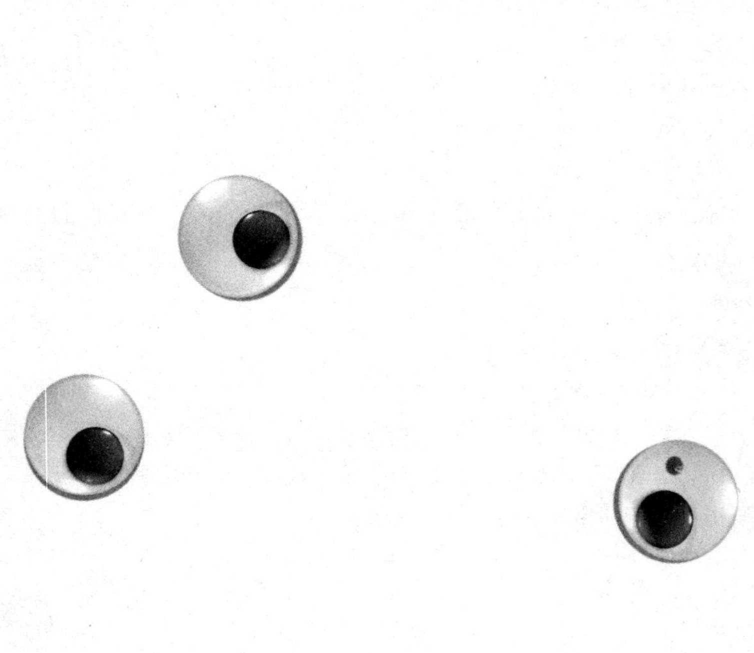

SEVENTEEN

RECEIVING LINE; FINAL GOODBYES; DEATH BEDS

"You were such a needy baby," his grandmother says from the broken glass on the wall and on the floor. "Oh, how you cried. I told your mother not to soothe you so often. It would only make you weak. I wasn't wrong."

He nods a little, perhaps in agreement, perhaps as a concert-goer enjoying one of the hits.

"Sometimes I would look at you and wonder, is this it? Is this what we fled destruction for? I didn't like thinking this, believe it or not. You think me such a monster, but I don't *enjoy* this disappointment. It tastes horrible, Abraham. I simply wanted my grandchildren to remember where they came from. I wanted them to plant roots that couldn't be torn from the soil like mine were. Like my parents' were. My cousins'. Everyone we lost in the fire. I wanted my grandchildren to continue our traditions, because evil tried to take them from us, and what do we do in the face of evil? We do not say, 'Oh maybe you have a point, I'll keep it down, I'll put my faith and traditions away.' We spit in evil's eye and say, back to Hell with you, I come from a long line of survivors! That's what it really is, boychik. I simply wanted you to survive. Every part of you."

"Welp," Abe mutters. "Sorry, Bobbe. Looks like that's not happening." His lips feel thick and dry. "Kein ayin hara, peh, peh, peh."

"*Quiet*," she snaps. "You didn't let me finish."

Wow. Can a mental projection get offended? He guesses so. Or maybe—he chuckles at this thought—maybe this conversation is *actually* happening. Maybe he and Bobbe, each on their respective death beds, are in some shared, semi-conscious space?

Aw, good for us. Finally having something in common.

"I want to say. . . I was wrong about you," his grandmother says. He can hear the effort it takes to admit that. "You are a bad Jew. You never went to shul, you never honored Shabbos. But, Abraham, you are a *true* Jew. You have tried to endure."

"Didn't do a very good job of it, though, Bobbe."

"No, pupik," she agrees, kindly. "But that's not your fault. You know what I think? I think maybe the age you were born into, all these years of fat and comfort, this time between the great wars and whatever's coming next—and something *is* coming, you can feel it, can't you?—maybe this time has all just been some sort of. . . accident. An anomaly. Or a cruel joke. Or—"

"A rest stop," he mutters with a rueful laugh.

"*Yes*," she says around an appreciative smile. Then: "Are you familiar with the Buddha, Abraham?"

That question *really* takes him by surprise. He can't help but laugh. Like many other secular Jews he knows, he actually *has* dabbled a tiny bit in Buddhism. Something about that religion—its wisdom, its approach—always seemed particularly appealing to him. But to hear the word "Buddha" in his grandmother's voice? To hear her talk approvingly of any other culture? This either really *is* a conversation between two individuals, or his dying brain is throwing all sorts of ingredients at the wall while it struggles to stay online.

"I know, I know, I'm just an ignorant girl from a tiny village in Poland. You think I know nothing. But I have studied, too, Abraham. I have tried to make sense of this world. And a story sticks with me. A Buddhist teacher, with his students gathered around him—almost like a minyan, nu?—and he drinks out of a glass and says, 'I love this glass. It is so beautiful. It carries the water to my lips and keeps me alive. It catches the light. But if, one day, I accidentally drop it and it shatters, my heart breaks with it. I am so sad. So I must remember: being broken is the glass's truest nature. It will be broken far longer than it is whole. It is *meant* to be broken. It is *already* broken. How can I be sad then, for this brief illusion of wholeness?' Do you see what I'm saying, Abraham?"

Broken glass. That lesson he was searching for.

A strange feeling fills him. The opposite of snake venom.

"Thanks, Bobbe." He remembers the phrase she always ended conversations with, those rare occasions he spoke with her (was forced to speak with her) on the phone. "Zei gezunt and kim gezunt."

"You know what your problem is?"

His grandmother is gone. Now it's Ty's voice, coming from the mirror shards.

Oh great, is this a receiving line now?

"We don't have those in Jewish funerals," Abe mumbles.

Ty repeats: "You know what your problem is?"

Abe rolls his head on his neck, closes his eyes.

"I don't have any problems now. I'm ready to die."

"You know what your problem is?"

Maybe the fact that I've got a best friend who doesn't listen to me?

But no. This time it's not an imaginary conversation he's having. This time it's a memory. Ty *actually* said these words to him.

Okay, then. Bring on the memory.

One final moment before we turn off the lights and close up shop. No need for the whole worthless story to flash by. Make it a good one. Make it. . . *characteristic*.

Abraham Neer, this was your life.

LIFE

"Abraham Neer, tonight, you're gonna be a fuck machine. You're gonna be the T-1000 of jizz. They will turn your conquests into a billion-dollar film franchise. And you'll be awarded the Nobel goddamn Prize for your dong's breakthrough discoveries in perpetual motion."

With that, Ty handed Abe an overflowing fistful of condoms, each one a glaring neon. Abe recognized them from a previous club they'd played; offered for free in a fishbowl by the front door.

Abe looked at the collage of rubber in his palm. "Uh, what the fuck?"

The two of them were standing in the grimy bathroom of Club Congress. In thirty minutes, they were due to open a bill that had three other acts on it, but there was a decent crowd outside—mostly thanks to a nightly trivia event that had just finished up—and more than a few not unattractive women among it.

Not as many women as the over-generous amount of condoms

Ty just shoved into his possession, though.

"'What the FUCK' is exactly right, my man! You're radiating pure sex tonight. You're shooting off pheromones like, like a skunk. But *good.* A *sex skunk.*"

Abe stared at his friend through narrowed eyes.

"Ty. What are you doing? This is gross."

"Not as gross as all the. . . y'know. . . all the sweet, sloppy poon you're about to get. Man. Ugh." That was too much, even for Ty. He grimaced at himself, the confident wingman disappearing. Ty, the concerned Scout Master, took over—a far more comfortable role. "Sorry. Look, dude. I'm just saying you need to get out there, okay? Get in the game. I never see you chatting with girls after shows. I mean," he dropped his voice to a conspiratorial low, "when was the last time you even—?"

"Jesus Christ."

"Whoa! The *Bible* days?"

Abe felt his face burning. He gave Ty a light, but not altogether unserious, shove.

"Would you stop? I'm not a casual hookup kinda guy, you know that."

"You're not an any-kind-of-hookup guy, I'm starting to think."

"Shut up. There's someone I've been kinda thinking about working my nerve up to ask out. It's fine. Don't worry about it."

Abe tried to hand the wad of condoms back and Ty said:

"Okay, but. . . what if that person isn't single anymore?"

Abe's stomach dropped. "What? What does that mean?"

"There's something I gotta talk to you about, man. It's. . . I've been wanting to tell you this for a couple weeks now and I don't know how. It's. . . a little awkward."

Just like that, Abe knew what Ty was about to say. The way a patient knows what a grim-faced doctor is about to report. Or a spouse, waking up in the middle of the night to find highway patrol at the door. He felt himself disassociate while Ty stumbled through a probably rehearsed speech about how he and Jenna had begun "hanging out" and were "maybe going to try being official about it." A parade of soft, equivocating language. A real vibe shift from the vulgar braggadocio a few minutes ago.

After an eternity, Ty finished. He looked at Abe for a response.

"Well." Abe swallowed a hot stone coated in dried shit. "That's all super. Happy for you."

He suddenly felt like this bathroom was too small for a single occupant, let alone two. He tried to leave, and Ty stopped him with a hand on his upper arm.

"Can we talk about this?"

"Talk about what? She's a person, not a PlayStation controller. She likes you. That's awesome. You're dumb and handsome, she's smart and beautiful, it's great. Good for the gene pool. Here. Use them in good health."

He tried to hand the condoms back to Ty again—harder this time, practically punching Ty with them.

Again, Ty deflected the effort.

"We can't play a show with you pissed at me," he said.

"I'm not pissed at you."

"You're totally pissed at me."

And the thing was, Abe had never been more furious in his life. But it was a fury tinged with sadness. And it was a sadness tinged with fear. His heart was breaking at the prospect of losing this girl he'd developed overwhelming feelings for. But he also loved his friend and knew this was the sort of thing friendships ended over. He didn't want either to happen. But he also wasn't ready to swallow this indignity, nor embrace his future as a bystander to their relationship. Parts of him he never really thought about were suddenly flaring to life, reminding him of all the other indignities he'd swallowed in his life.

Suddenly, Ty's eyes lit up. "Do you want to hit me?"

"No, I don't want to hit you."

"Because you can. I'll allow it."

That made Abe laugh, a short, sharp snort. "What's the point of hitting someone if they allow it?"

"So you *do* want to hit me!"

"No! I want to get out of here and forget this fucking conversation."

This all seemed to be happening beyond him. Like he was watching a movie. He just wanted to be out of this bathroom, be among the crowds of people not there for him, drown his sorrow in a whiskey-ginger (*her favorite drink too; she got you into drinking them*), scream out his feelings onstage.

A cruel, condescending smile smeared across Ty's face.

"You know what your problem is?" he asked.

Abe's jaw clenched. "What? What's my problem?"

"You want things so badly, but. . . I think *one* of the things you want is to never have to fight for the things you want, and that makes it impossible to, y'know, have those things! It's not even a vicious circle, man. It's a *stupid* circle."

Abe's temples throbbed. "You saying *you* want to fight?"

"I mean, I'd *rather* not, but sometimes fighting's what you gotta do. Sometimes it's even kinda fun."

"Well, you're definitely making me want to fucking punch something! But I also don't want to hurt my hand before we go on, so! Fuck!"

The bathroom door pushed open. Some hapless schmuck, looking to piss. Abe and Ty shouted at him in unison to give them some space and he fled, eyes wide.

When they were alone again, Ty asked:

"So what do we do?"

"I don't want *these*, that's for fucking sure." Another attempt to be rid of the stupid goddamn condoms. Another rejection.

"Nope. Sorry. Not gonna let you. You might hate me, Abe, but I'm still your friend, and I'm looking out for your best interests. You're going to use those whether you like it or not."

"I'm not going to use them, Tyler. People don't like me like that."

"You're totally gonna use them! I'm gonna help!"

"I'M NOT GOING TO USE THEM."

"Abe!" Ty yelled. "Do you know I waited so long to actually ask Jenna out because I kept waiting to see if you'd do it first? Even *she* thought you were going to! And you never fucking did!"

Abe knew Ty was trying to goad him into attacking. That's not why Abe ultimately did. It wasn't anything Ty said—not even that last horrible, painful admission that would make Abe's heart hurt for the rest of its beats.

It was Ty's faint, smug grin. It made Abe think of someone else. Someone antagonistic and condescending who loved reminding him he was a failure. That he always feared the wrong monsters.

"Fine." Abe dumped the condoms onto the sink counter, began ripping their wrappers open. "You want me to use them? I'll fucking use them."

Ty looked on, curious.

Abe held the first condom under the faucet, filled it with water, and tied off the top. Then he did it again to a second.

He held two heavy water balloons in his hands and glared at Ty over a sneering smile.

"You wouldn't," Ty said. Suddenly nervous.

"Yeah, you're probably right," Abe agreed. Then threw the first balloon.

It exploded on impact against Ty's chest.

Ty yelped.

Abe threw the second one at Ty's shoulder.

"Look how fucking cheap these things are, asshole! Condoms shouldn't break like that!"

Ty didn't hear him; he was too busy mourning over his soaked outfit, too busy grabbing another condom and filling it up under the other sink. "You fucking *dick*!"

He was, of course, far more athletic than Abe, and his aim was unsurprisingly truer. He hit Abe square in the mouth with his balloon.

The fight immediately paused—a moment common in every boyfight; breath-holding combatants waiting to see how serious a potential injury might be, if the action needed to be halted or if things were about to get really nuts.

Then Abe growled, "I'm gonna fucking *murder* you," and the battle was on.

They got through almost half the condoms, turning the bathroom into a legitimately dangerous water hazard, before a bartender came in to see what the ruckus was.

Abe and Ty were summarily kicked out of Club Congress, their position on that night's bill revoked. They were told they'd never play there again.

Typical Ty, though: he managed to beg and plead with the club's booking manager for a second chance. He was just too charming and sincere to say no to. Another gig for Darwin's Foëtus was put on the club's calendar—but it was made clear, any shenanigans this time and they were gone for good.

Confirming that new gig was the last time Abe and Ty had spoken, until yesterday afternoon, when Abe informed Ty about his grandmother's stroke. In between, Ty had sent plenty of texts: pleas for rehearsal, for seeing a movie, for just grabbing a beer and hanging out. Abe ignored all of them. He was sure Ty would rather be hanging out with Jenna anyway.

Sometimes, though, he did wonder if Ty was right. Maybe Abe just needed to move on, play the field a little, stop putting so much emotional stock in someone who was now unavailable. Someone who was even more desirable now *because* of that unavailability. And someone whose unavailability was, in part, due to his own cowardice.

Maybe Abe should go to a bar, go to a concert, try to have a fling or two. He even stuck one of those damn neon condoms in his wallet, just to have it, just to look at it and remember that moving on *was* an option. The world didn't *have* to be so cruel. His heart might have been broken, but. . . well, it was like some Buddhist monk had said. Being broken wasn't cruelty, it was simply the state of things. At least he wasn't dead, right? Right. And while there's life, there's—

Abe's eyes open.

NINETEEN

AFTERLIFE; ABE'S LAST CHANCE

He's not dead.

Somehow he isn't dead—at *all.*

In fact, he's actually feeling a tiny bit stronger. Still shaky and numb and a bit lightheaded, but sitting, resting, breathing, meditating, has helped.

Slowly, wobbly, he gets to his feet. Pulls out his wallet with thick, clumsy hands. That dumb, neon condom is still there. Glowing yellow, like an item in a video game.

He flexes the fingers of his bitten hand. They're swollen and stiff, but his thumb and forefinger are still relatively usable. Same with those fingers on his other, fractured hand. Two pincers, like a crab. Should be just enough to get the job done.

He bites open the wrapper, pulls out the thin prophylactic. Fills it with a little bit of water from the sink so it sags. Then he pumps some hand soap into it and resumes filling it with water.

Soon it's bulbous with soapy water. Enough to blind someone

with a well-aimed shot in the face.

That lone googly eye on the bathroom tile catches his attention and he realizes he'll have to convince the guy to remove his mask. To hit him in his *real* eyes.

Can he even make a shot like that? Damaged as he is?

Abe leans his head against the bathroom door. This time he actually prays—*Baruch atah Adonai, Eloheinu melech ha'olam. . .*

That's all he remembers in Hebrew. The rest has to come in English—but, hey, God should speak that, too, right?

Please help me get out of here.

Please, Adonai. Guide my hand. Help me survive.

Please. I don't want to break just yet.

He opens the bathroom door, the lock disengaging with a turn of the handle. For a moment, he worries the clerk might've locked him inside once more, but there's no resistance. The killer has been waiting for this final showdown. No need to prolong it anymore.

That said, once again the store appears empty.

Abe takes a step out of the bathroom, scanning for movement. Trying to summon every bit of action movie bravado he's ever seen or felt.

In this awful, straining silence, he gets the chance to really notice, dotted across the floor, the scores of random googly eyes that have been shed throughout the night. Like glitter after a party. Like rodent droppings. They all stare up at the ceiling. A final audience, at once avid and disinterested. Peripheral witnesses.

"If we're going to do this," Abe announces, "let's do this."

"Okay," a voice answers from the other side of the store. Muffled behind plastic. "Gimme a sec. I want you to tell me if something looks cool."

Abe tries to calm his galloping heart. Readjusts his hold on the soap grenade. He needs the bastard's eyes out in the open.

"Hey. How about no more masks, huh? Just you and me? Face to face?"

The clerk giggles.

"Come on," Abe pleads. "I've already seen you. You don't have to hide your face from me. *Please?*"

A long, considering pause.

"My face."

"It's only fair, right? Let me. . . appreciate the creator."

"Hm. Wellllllll, how about this?"

The clerk rises from where he was crouched behind a shelf.

He's not wearing a mask.

In fact, there's *nothing* above his neck.

He doesn't have a face at all.

Abe is so stunned by what he's seeing—by what he's *not* seeing—that the balloon squirms out of his grip and falls to the ground. It breaks open against the floor, spilling its contents uselessly, worthlessly across the tile.

Splat.

BROKEN; STAND-OFF; CHOREOGRAPHY; AN ANSWER AT LAST

Abe looks at the broken balloon at his feet. His grandmother might've commented on how inevitable this was.

She's silent, though. The whole world is silent.

Abe looks back up. Numb.

"Everything okay over there?" the clerk asks. "Did you drop something?" He cocks his neck, a pantomime of sympathy.

It's by that gesture that Abe understands what so startled him. The clerk *is* wearing a mask, after all—the same mask he's been wearing this whole time. But all of the eyes have finally been peeled off. What remains is a perfectly smooth, plastic-and-chrome mirror mask. Its flat surface reflects the store back at Abe and for that first moment, it had looked like there was no head at all.

The guy wouldn't have had any idea of Abe's plans, but it was still enough to make stupid, clumsy, shmendricky Abe drop his last, best hope. Dooming him.

"Doesn't matter," Abe says weakly.

"My face," the clerk says, "is *everything* now. Even your face! Do you see? Did it look cool?"

"Sure. Cool."

"Awesome. Okay!" The clerk holds up a knife. The biggest knife in the world. He waggles it, tantalizingly. "Still wanna 'do this?'"

Abe thinks about jumping back into the bathroom one more time. Locking the door. Coming up with some other plan. Maybe using the plastic scrub brush or one of the smaller shards of mirror glass.

He shakes his head at the idea. He's so tired. He won't forestall the inevitable anymore. He just wants to make it outside, at the very least. Be gutted in the fresh air.

He takes a small step away from the bathroom door.

The clerk responds with a hooting laugh and takes a big step toward Abe.

Abe might not have his balloon, but there's still plenty to throw. He picks up the nearest object off a shelf and launches it at the madman. Just a granola bar. It bounces harmlessly off the clerk's face. But it hit. His aim was true. So he grabs the next thing. And the next. And the next.

Chips. Pop tarts. Candy bars. Protein bars. He keeps a shelf in between them and throws everything he can. He only half-registers that he's emitting a hooting-laugh, too, the shadow twin of his pursuer's. A desperate, furious sound.

Gum. Bags of peppermint mints. Bags of circus peanuts. Bags of actual peanuts. All of them, hitting exactly where he's aiming.

Then, the door is behind him. It's *right there*.

Instead of throwing more snacks, he throws himself at the

door. His hands actually close on the handle—

—but before he can get the door open, arms wrap around his midsection and hurl him backwards.

"No!" Abe shrieks, and receives a hooting cackle in response.

He was so close!

Could've been a knife in his back, he supposes. The same knife the clerk is waving in an uh-uh-uh motion right now. You're not leaving that easily, the gesture says.

A stand-off, then.

Abe tries to feint for the door, but the clerk matches his every move. Then the knife whips forward and slices Abe across the arm.

Abe seethes in pain, feels blood seep down his arm.

Worse, he's close enough that now he can see himself reflected back in that awful, chrome mask. He looks so small. So distorted. So helpless.

"No!" he shouts again, pleading.

"No!" the clerk mimics. "No! NononoNO!"

Abe looks around for other options. Run to the backroom? Run back around the store and try again for the front? Pretty much his only options, but—

While he's thinking, the clerk springs forward with the knife and cuts another deep wound in Abe's other arm before darting backwards. Abe snaps out of his thoughts; he's getting too groggy, too sloppy.

As if that realization was all the clerk was waiting for, the clerk springs forward again and this time Abe manages to avoid the slice by jumping backwards. His reflection shrinks in the mirror mask.

"There you go," the clerk says, approvingly. He lunges forward again—and Abe jumps backwards again.

And again. And again. Both of them moving in sync like expert line dancers. . . until Abe's feet forget the choreography. During his next dodge backwards, he tangles clumsily with himself and the next thing he knows, he's staring up at the ceiling, his back throbbing against the tile floor.

The clerk is on him in a flash. Sitting on his chest, trapping his arms.

"Oops!" The clerk laughs triumphantly, pityingly. Abe squirms underneath. Trapped.

The clerk is heavy. *Too* heavy. He must be putting his full weight on Abe's chest, but there's no way someone his size can be *so horribly* heavy.

"Why?" Abe manages, trying to breathe. "Why are you doing this?"

The clerk lets out another guffaw. "Why?! Haven't you figured this out yet?"

"No," Abe wheezes. "Figure out what? Please?"

"Don't you know what's happening? Don't you know who I am?"

"No! I don't know anything!"

The clerk bends his head towards Abe's. Stoops with impressive, maybe impossible, flexibility.

"Buddy," the clerk says. Calm. Rationally. "You've been calling my name all night." His breath, huffing delightedly against the inside of his mask. "Ask me."

"Who. . . are you?"

"I'm *God*," the clerk says. His voice fills the world.

Abe stares back at his own terrified face and realizes the man isn't kidding.

TWENTY-ONE

GOD VERSUS ABRAHAM; THE RED SEA; NILS LOFGREN; COMPANY

So heavy. So unbearably heavy.

"What?" Abe asks dumbly.

The clerk gives another hardy laugh. "*You're* my creation. All of this is my creation. But I get *soooo* bored sometimes, so I come down to visit. To keep from going crazy."

"You *are* crazy."

"Ha! Yeah, well."

"You're not God, you're, you're—"

"*Everything.* Look at me."

The mask presses against Abe's nose. And maybe it's because it's so hard to breathe, or maybe it's the lingering effects of the snake venom, but Abe looks into his own terrified, bewildered eyes, sees the swirling prism of the reflective surface, and begins to understand. Yes. Yes, this may very well be so, his attacker may indeed be telling the truth. This man. This stranger. This crushing weight on his chest, dense as a dying star. This *is* God. *The* God. The one countless generations of terrified humans once worshipped. The one countless more generations try to pretend they *aren't* worshipping now.

The God of lightning in the desert. The God of twisted shadows on cave walls. The God of wrath. Of persecution. Of corruption. The God that demands proper nouns and capitalization. The God whose first commandment isn't kindness or empathy, but THOU SHALT HAVE NO OTHER GOD BEFORE ME. The God of sick jokes. The God of babies born without heads. The God of turtles born having to race to the sea with their first lungful of air. The God of ancient land disputes that turn into genocidal rugby matches. The God of the great cosmic punchline that is mortality foreknown. Of suns destined to implode. Of nerve endings that refuse to stop reporting pain. Of fathers who die of bowel cancer. Of hearts that won't stop breaking. Of promising futures and the unbearably slow deflation from pinprick disappointments.

"I can do whatever I want," the clerk—God—is crowing. "You're my creation! And I just wanna drink you up!"

Abe stares at his own face, braces himself for God to bring His knife down into Abe's fragile, mortal chest. Splinter his ribs, pop his lungs and heart, spray his chin with hot blood.

God doesn't do that, though. Instead, He starts casting around for something new. Something fun. He lands on an item displayed on one of the racks nearest them. "Ooo!" He reaches out and grabs it. A glint of light flashes before Abe's eyes. Something metal.

"Drink! You! Up!" God exclaims again, waggling the metal object in front of Abe. It takes a moment to focus on what it is: a souvenir bottle opener. The kind with a round mouth that encircles a bottle cap . . . and a sharp under-tooth that pops the cap off.

God sets the bottle opener on Abe's face and gets to work.

"Pop top!" God proclaims in delight. "Chug-a-lug!"

Abe feels the chill of the metal, then a digging. A scraping.

The sharp under-tooth bites into Abe's nose, his septum, his upper lip. The pain is exquisite. Symphonic. Multipart. Polyrhythmic.

The shredding of layer upon layer of skin. The cold, bitter metal, and hot, bitter blood. The uncompromising squeeze of the round bottle opener around the bulb of his nose. The frantic furrowing as God works the metal over and around and into his skin, like an overzealous dentist with horrible depth perception. The sounds of teeth and flesh being scraped.

The under-tooth chews into Abe's septum, up and down, up and down, back and forth, until, with a luxuriant rip, the septum separates from the cleft of Abe's upper lip. The flesh at the bottom of Abe's nose puckers backwards like a shirt bunched up against a chair, like blankets kicked to the foot of a bed, revealing a deepening hole, a third nostril in his philtrum where the bottle opener continues to dig.

Abe's mouth floods with blood.

My nose, he thinks dimly. *I always thought it got in the way.*

He's going to peel my face off.

God's going to peel my face off and I'm going to drown in my own red sea.

Nothing I can do about it. It's Moses who parts the sea. It's Jacob who wrestles and wins. All I can do is—

An unexpected image flashes in his memory. Nils Lofgren, executing somersaults while shredding lead lines during an E-Street

Band concert. Years ago, Abe had watched video of those moves and, ever since, had been desperate to try something similar onstage. He'd never played venues big enough to try, and was always afraid of getting tangled in cords, but none of that is an issue here.

—all I can do is roll with it.

God is leaning forward in His exertion. The weight is off of Abe's arms and chest a little. Abe scooches his feet and legs further up and, with a final burst of strength, pushes up. He somersaults backwards, taking God with him, flipping and scattering them both across the floor.

Abe staggers to his feet, the front of his face a copper-flavored waterfall. All the blood he can't swallow drools down his chin. Distantly, he feels the loose flesh under his nose trying to settle back into place.

Meanwhile, splayed out in front of him, God's mask has slipped off His face a little. He appears confused about what just happened. . . then His mouth brightens with a delighted smile. He rises, in no hurry. Adjusts His mirror mask so it's back in place.

Abe's move got him out from being trapped, but their relation to the door hasn't changed—God still stands between Abe and freedom.

Abe looks around for an escape route. Realizes, once again, his options haven't changed. Fine. Let him die amongst the bugs.

In a limping, clumsy run, Abe doubles back to the bathroom, his wet gasps of exertion barely audible under God's appreciative laughter and the tacky squelch of their shoes against the drying blood on the floor.

God follows, close behind, swiping the knife, easily closing the distance. Managing to get a few more knicks and slices in before Abe reaches the bathroom doorway.

Abe sees the puddle of soapy water a split second before his body takes control and leaps over the spill. His jump takes him face-first into the bathroom wall, but he stops himself with his forearms and turns around just in time to see God slip and literally fly up into the air before crashing down onto His back.

The crack of God's head against the floor makes Abe's teeth hurt.

God groans and twitches like an upturned turtle. As painful as the fall appears to have been, though, He won't be incapacitated for long. Already He's trying to get up on His elbows.

Abe doesn't think he can step over and sprint to the door fast enough, so he hustles to the bathroom and, straddling the draped body of the rattlesnake, lifts up the lid of the toilet tank.

It's heavier than he's expecting. Hard to hold, especially given his injured hands. But he brings it back over to the clerk and holds it high.

One of God's hands wraps around Abe's ankle. Abe reacts without thinking and, instead of bringing the lid down on God's head, he drops it on the arm holding onto his leg. The hand lets go and Abe is able to stumble backwards, losing his balance and landing on his butt back in the bathroom.

Looks like he broke God's wrist, though. The fingers of the affected hand are twitching and pointing in uncomfortable looking directions. God seethes in pain, in the effort of sitting up, spittle audibly spraying against the inside of the mask.

"Oh wow," God keeps saying in a monotone. "Oh wow. Oh wowwwww. Wow, wow, wow."

The porcelain lid has broken into shards. God picks one of

them up with His good hand and starts crawling on His knees and elbows towards Abe. The shard is jagged and brutal looking. A raptor claw.

"Wow. Wowee wow, wow. Wowowowowowowow."

Abe sees his own twisted fury and surprise as the mask approaches. The lower half of his face, mangled and ruined, drenched in a beard of blood and gore.

God advances on all fours. An animal on the hunt. One merciless, porcelain claw tapping on the ground. He's obviously hurt and dazed, His breath is ragged. But He's also not stopping.

Abe retreats in a reverse crabwalk, over insect carcasses, further into the bathroom until the cold, hard wall stops him.

He can't move backwards any further, only to the side.

God gets closer. Closer.

"Wait," Abe says in a breathy whisper. He has to spit blood out of his mouth to not accidentally aspirate on it. "Wait, please."

That changes God's droning wows to waits: "Wait, wait, wait, wait. Waitwaitwaitwaitwait."

Abe is in the corner now. Nowhere to go.

"Just one second," Abe gasps. "I just have to tell you something. It's important."

His own desperate expression, reflected back at him.

"What is it, little one?" God asks.

Abe swallows. It takes great effort. He has no idea what's going to come out of his mouth next. Only that he must fascinate his assailant.

"I love you," he blurts.

The clerk's head tilts. "What?"

"I *love* you," Abe says again. Staring at himself. "I'm so grateful for all you've done. All you've given me. Thank you for. . . for music, for sunsets, for laughter, for sex, for, for, for Icees and beef jerky and satisfying pees. Thank you for life! Thank you for so much life! I love you!"

God takes this in. Sits back on His haunches.

"You. . . I—? No you don't."

"With all my heart. With all my mind. With all my strength. I absolutely fucking *love* you." Puts all the sincerity he can into those three words.

God's shoulders twitch. Then He begins to laugh. Great, belly laughs. He pushes the reflective mask off of His young/ancient face to reveal delighted tears streaming down His cheeks. He keeps trying to speak and each time, another gale of laughter overtakes Him.

"That's—! That's the stupi—!"

Abe knew he might get a reaction, but the extent of this reaction is a surprise.

No matter. He takes his opportunity. Quicker than he would've thought possible, he reaches for the one thing in grabbing distance: the midsection of the dead rattlesnake. He yanks the snake from out under the toilet lids and whips it forward.

He misses God's face. It lands somewhere even better.

The head of the snake collides with God's neck. And even though it should be impossible, even though it defies every odd, the snake's posthumous bite reflex proves true.

Its teeth latch onto the Creator of the universe's throat.

Right into His carotid and jugular. Right next to His ridiculously-named Adam's apple.

God's eyes go wide with almost comical surprise.

Abe's own eyes do the same.

Dayenu, he thinks, and lets go of the snake.

God stumbles backwards, trying to laugh, trying to whoop, trying to pry the snake from His neck, trying to get to His feet. He finally manages to pull the dead snake off, but then He slips again in the soap puddle and flails backwards, making a real farcical performance of crashing into the nearest display of snacks.

In His flailing, one of the thin hangers holding snacks gets jammed into one of His eyes. It goes in deep. He begins to seize, blood transubstantiating into jellied cranberry sauce. He knocks snacks everywhere. Makes horrible choking noises. Spasming. Foaming. Twitching. His bowels let go. Piss darkens His pants.

It's an agonizing scene.

Abe takes no pleasure in it.

He simply watches from where he's slumped against the bathroom wall, enjoying the cool solidity of the tile and the quiet that eventually comes.

XXX

He sits that way for a long time.

Eventually, the outside world lights up with blues and reds. Is it real this time? He thinks so. But what's the difference? He's still enjoying the wall, its calmness, its simplicity. So much elegance in a wall. What a blessing to simply hold up a ceiling. What a creation.

His eyes never leave the clerk's face. The guy wasn't God after all, was he? Just some normal, damaged human being? And this was nothing more than an unfortunate encounter in an isolated gas station convenience store in the middle of the night?

Abe just keeps staring at that young, innocent face. Those eyes—one glazed and half-lidded in death, the other skewered and leaking. What stars imploded within those eyes? What universes were wiped out?

The first cop who finds Abe actually screams. Not just because Abe looks like pure hell, but because he's sitting there, practically carpeted in bugs.

A whole array has found him, trailing down from the vent and from a missing panel in the ceiling. Another box's cargo. Spiders. Centipedes. Taking their time to investigate what's happening below.

Abe doesn't show them any mind.

In fact, he feels blessed by their gentle company.

A MAN IN GOD'S IMAGE
A GOD IN MAN'S IMAGE

They found the van around the corner from the crime scene. Parked on the shoulder of the road. The clerk (who, of course, wasn't actually a clerk, just someone wearing clothes stolen from one of the dead employees) had moved it, presumably to aid in his fucking with Abe. Saving it for some big reveal. Perhaps if Abe had got on the road more expediently—if Jenna hadn't called—the clerk was going to point the van out before dumping the snake in his lap or something. No way to know. Things played out the way they'd played out.

It takes almost a year and a half of bureaucratic wrangling before Abe is able to buy the van from the police department.

He imagines they might be confused as to why he'd want it. Or maybe they're not. He doesn't really care. They take his cash easily enough.

Besides. Forensics cleaned it out thoroughly. There are no clues inside for him to find. It's just a van now.

He doesn't need any clues. He's not interested in learning more. He just . . . wants it.

First thing he does is give it a new license plate. Some random letters and numbers. No message. Something like a cramp inside his heart eases up a little when he does that.

Funny how the driver's seat feels like cold tile, though.

In fact, he *always* feels cold tile on his back.

And sometimes his vision seems just ever-so-slightly framed by tile walls.

Like he's looking at the world through a bathroom doorway.

xxx

Jenna and Ty are still going strong—they really *do* make sense as a couple, and Abe actually enjoys the dynamic of the three of them, whenever they're together.

It's not jealousy that keeps him from hanging out with them more often. It's a stranger reason than that; one he finds hard to articulate.

He doesn't always recognize them anymore.

He'll be having a good enough time, but suddenly he'll wonder, *Who are these people?*

Who am I around them?

What are we doing here?

What are we all becoming?

What have we become?

Then he'll think:

We're all just biding our time before we break, aren't we?

This is just the rest stop.

He's happy they're happy. He's happy happiness exists. Even if it's only for now.

But usually, he's much more comfortable alone, sitting against the cool tile, wherever he happens to be.

He doesn't know how much longer Darwin's Foëtus will stay together. He knows Ty wants to play out more—in part because he thinks it's good for Abe's healing process, and in part because the band has never sounded better.

The few gigs they've played have been marvelous. Abe's playing is impeccable. Even when he misses a note, it sounds incredible. And his singing has improved. All that screaming seems to have made his voice richer, deeper. The emotion he puts into the lyrics often leaves audience members in tears.

Abe never met his grandfather—Bobbe Meydl's husband, who died well before Abe was born—but his mom told him he was a cantor. He had the most beautiful singing voice, she'd say. He put all his pain and hurt into it.

In the middle of songs, Abe's able to forget everything. But he's not sure it's worth it. The way everything comes flooding back afterwards, it's like being bitten by some venomous creature—he knows it won't kill him, but he has to feel his blood congeal all over again.

xxx

The most effective way he's found to clear his mind is driving around in his van. When he's behind the wheel, all that matters is what's in front of him. And, of course, the cool tile against his back.

Sometimes it's just aimless driving.

Sometimes he makes the long trip out to visit Bobbe.

She's in a nursing facility now. Still holding on, two years later. Making the tiniest bit of improvement too. A wiggled finger. A blink.

He overhears one of her doctors say, *Honestly, I think she's too stubborn to die.*

Abe thinks, *Thank God for that. Baruch Hashem.*

He thinks, *L'dor, v'dor.* Generation to generation. Doorway to doorway.

He thinks, *Tikkun olam.* Of repairing the world.

He doesn't speak when he visits. He doesn't hold her hand. He doesn't feel that kind of sentimentality about her. He just sits by her side. Maybe that'll change one day—he feels like they have a lot to talk about. He wonders if she can relate to the strange thoughts and fantasies he's had lately. He suspects she can.

In the meantime, he's content to share space with her.

The bathroom walls feel very tight around him when he's there in the hospital, though.

He's not sure if that's a good or a bad thing.

xxx

He bears a lot of physical scars from his night at the gas station. Most extreme, of course, was from the damage incurred by the bottle opener. But with a few stitches and a little bit of time, mostly all that remains are a few thin lines bisecting his philtrum and upper lip.

In a way, it almost looks like the surgical remnants of a harelip.

He stares at it in the mirror a lot. It actually looks great. Dignified. Mysterious.

It does make him think strange thoughts, though.

I'm the Hairlip Man now.

He often wonders. . . could I ever be like my grandmother's boogeyman? Do I have that kind of evil—that kind of *h8*—in me?

He wonders, did that man *also* think of himself as God? Is that what it takes to be so cruel?

Abe remembers his own twisted, bloody image, reflected back at himself.

What kind of God would I be?

What kind of universe would I create?

Often when Abe goes driving, he starts before dawn. He likes to be in the van to watch the sun come up, then drive slowly around in the soft, pale light, when the backroads are empty, and he can take his time.

He encounters a lot of joggers on these drives.

Eager early birds, getting their exercises in before another day of blissful productivity.

He's fascinated by them. Stares at them from behind the wheel of his great big van.

Sometimes he's filled with such a rage it almost takes his breath away. They have it so *easy.* They're so fucking ignorant of what life can be like. Of how quickly things break.

He's started to have incredibly vivid fantasies. The kind that are so real they make him wonder if he really just *did it.*

Running them down.

Hearing surprised yelps and the chicken-bone snaps of their skeletons under his weight. Feeling the tires jump and twitch over their bodies.

Crunch.

Splat.

Sometimes he wonders if he should try it. Just once.

It would be so easy to nudge the steering wheel a little to the side, press a little harder on the gas.

He can imagine how easily the van would sail over their bodies, grind them into the asphalt of the shoulder.

He can imagine how the springs would compensate. How he would rock and bounce in his tile-wall seat behind the wheel.

Maybe, if he did it enough times, it would be enough to finally rock him out of place.

Maybe he'd be shaken free from his bathroom.

Some mornings, he thinks he could run down four or five people before the authorities even notice.

Is this the feeling of being broken? He wonders. *Or is it the process of breaking?*

Is this how it feels to refuse to break?

Or is every moment simply its own act of creation? Its own god, too holy for a name?

He doesn't know.

He always keeps the wheels on the road and pointed forward, though.

Steady as can be.

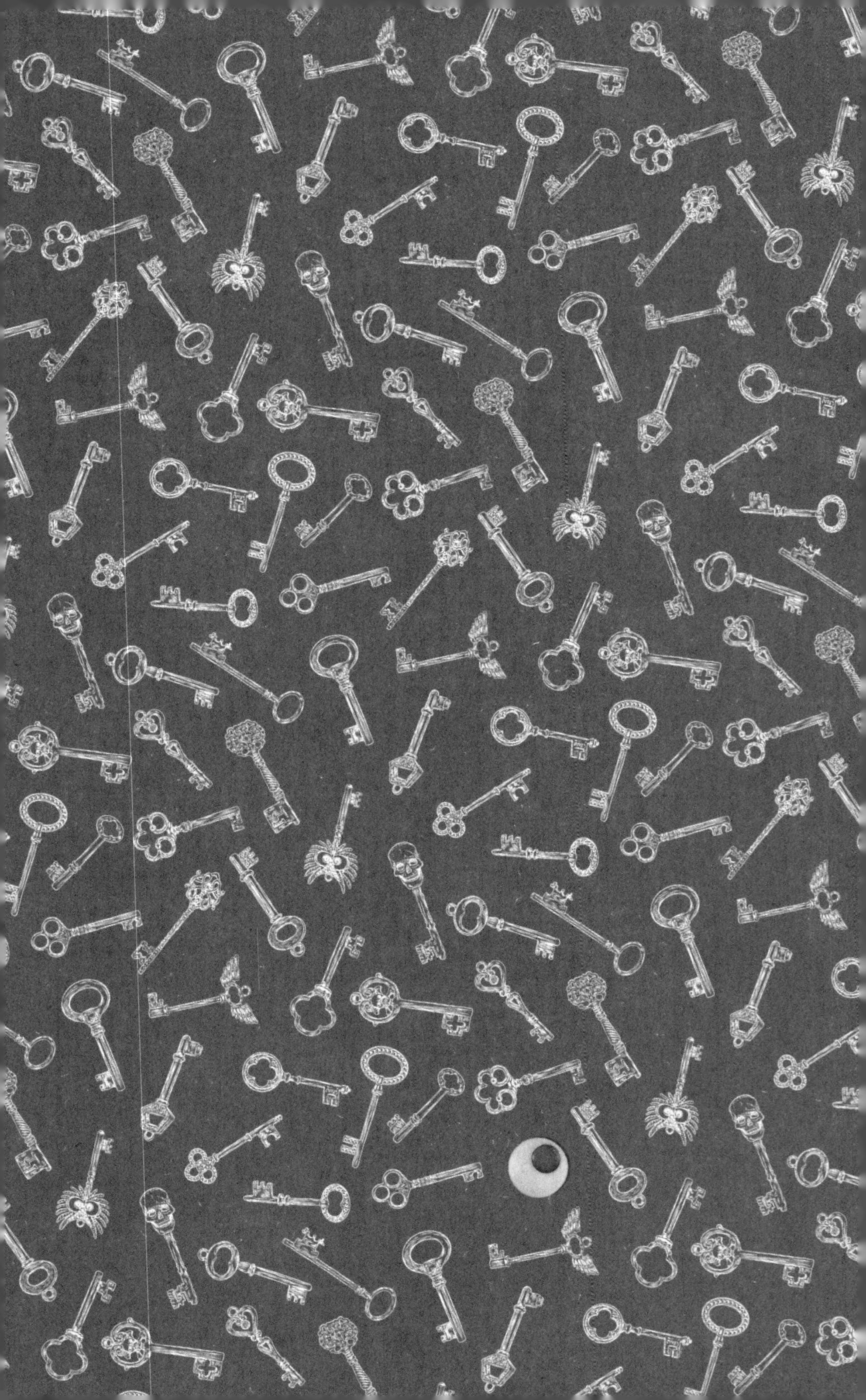

MEET-CUTE #1

THE UNLUCKIEST GIRL

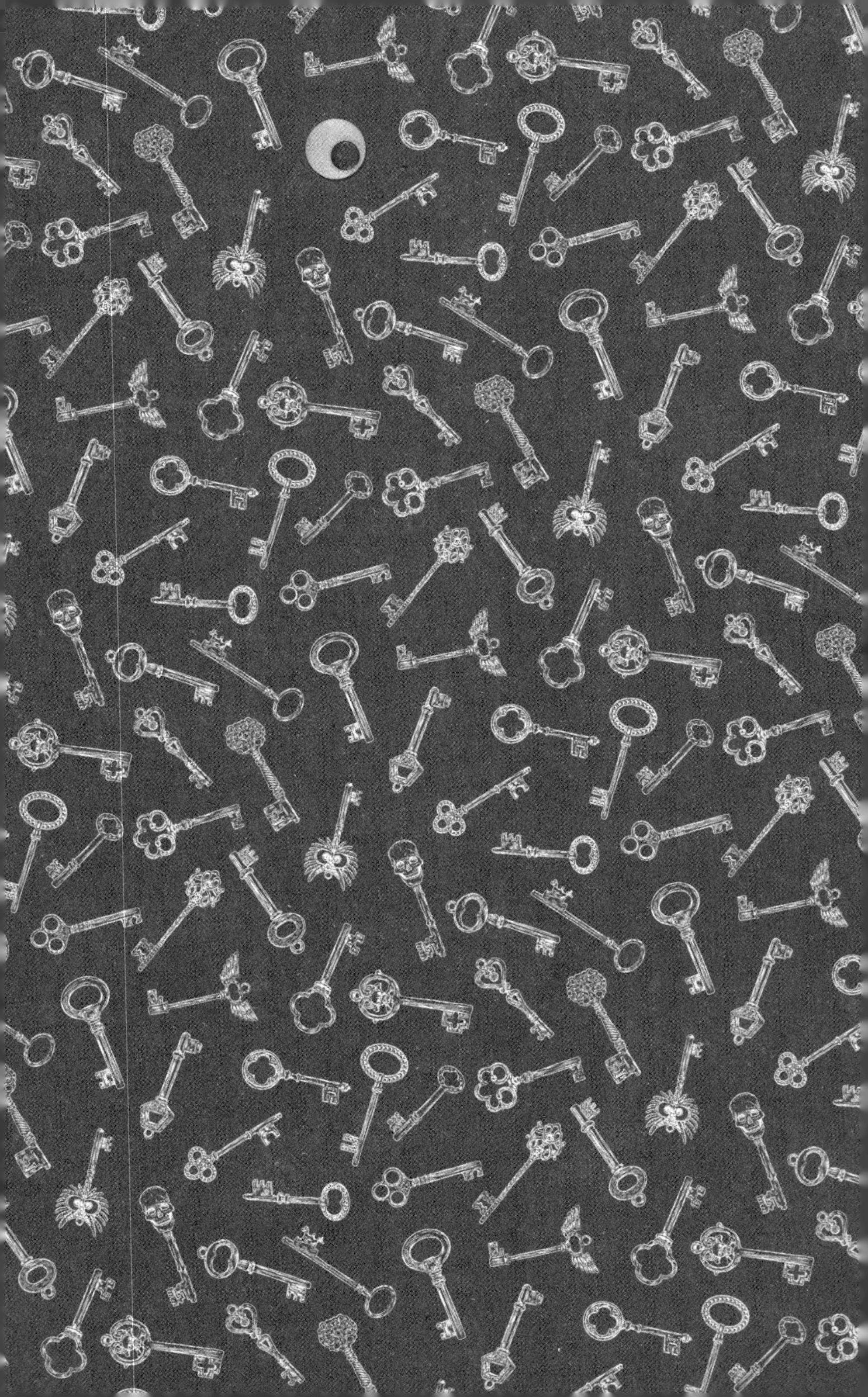

MEET-CUTE #1:

THE UNLUCKIEST GIRL

He was sitting at the bar, nursing a beer, telling the bartender all about that soccer stampede in Egypt he'd heard happened the month before.

Fifty dead at least, crushed to death under a mad parade of mindless feet. And the best part—the *kicker*, he punned gleefully—was that this stampede wasn't the result of anything that happened during the soccer match. No, it was before the game even started. Just a simple, last-minute venue change. That's all it took to turn a million people rabid with the fear of getting to the game late. So they panicked and crammed and crushed and killed and died and what an amazing thing. What a statement on humanity during this year of our Lord, 1974. Not to mention the noises it must've made. Feet squashing soft torsos, popping organs, crunching hard skulls. The *smells*. Blood, shit, brains. Incredible.

The bartender nodded and gave a pressed-lip smile that was an off-the-rack expression in every bartender's repertoire. Gosh, that smile said, imagine that, I'll be over here wiping a glass.

That was okay. The man didn't mind. Not everyone got excited by the same stuff he did. But right now, the bar was completely empty—the juke in the corner, their only company—so Buddy Bartender was going to have to put up with his enthusiasm if he wanted some tip money.

That juke was well-stocked. Some old favorites, as well as some new tunes. He was enjoying the variety. Such was the spice of life, after all.

A new song had just begun, that one about being a roundabout, by that British band with the punchy name, when the door to the bar burst open and she walked in, a small and stubborn shape unsuccessfully swallowed by the glowing rectangle of late-afternoon March sunlight.

All it took was hearing a single second of the music for her to pump a silhouetted fist in the air. "YES." she proclaimed. "Literally!!"

The door closed behind her as she took another step inside. The song had progressed from its ominous, nylon-stringed intro and was jiving aggressively with distorted guitars and snappy drums. She closed her eyes and danced along for a moment. Her movements were wild and free.

"Oh, I just fucking love music!" she informed the room with a luxuriant sigh. Then, opened her eyes and realized the room consisted of one guy at the bar and another guy behind it. The brittle edge of a conversation interrupted hung over everything. She blushed a little—or maybe that was just her face reacting to coming in from the cold.

"Sorry," she said with a self-conscious chuckle. "Don't mind me. As you were."

The silence persisted.

"Or not," she muttered before claiming a stool a few seats away from the other patron.

"Be right with you, ma'am," the bartender said. His hands were busy. "My apologies."

"Take your time. Happy to wait," she said. She removed her flower-decked coat, draped it on the next stool over. Then she looked at the stranger next to her. "Sorry I killed the conversation."

The stranger—who was rather handsome, she noted with a twinge of relief—gave her a warm, but wry, smile. He told her not to worry about it; that conversation had been no subject for ladies.

She made a jerk-off motion and blew air between her lips. "Gee, thanks. 'Cause I'm so fucking dainty."

His eyes looked her up and down. She was pretty. Young. Vital. Wearing a half dozen emotions on her face, ranging from stubborn to fearful to hungry to horny to afraid. . . but all served up on a platter of fundamental sadness.

He asked if she *really* wanted to know what he'd been talking about. He did so in a teasing, challenging way, which he knew was going to provoke a similarly teasing, challenging response.

"Well, now I have to know," she said, pulling off her scarf and laying it on the bar next to her (checking first for wetness, of course). "Better be good, though."

He looked over to the bartender, who was finishing up moving some glassware around, then back to the woman. He waggled his thick eyebrows, which had always been one of his favorite features. Women loved those eyebrows. They loved his dimples too.

He told her.

"What do you mean, a stampede?" she asked afterward. "Like

a cow stampede?"

No, he explained. A people stampede. People crushing people.

"A people stampede? Jeez. That must've been brutal."

He nodded enthusiastically. Brutal, indeed. Hence: he made a gesture of zipping his lips.

They sat in silence. She drummed her fingers against the bar while "Roundabout" continued. An organ solo, preaching hard.

After a performatively awkward beat, she sighed. "Well, this is gonna be a pretty boring afternoon, then."

The handsome stranger mimed unzipping his lips and asked what *she* wanted to talk about.

"Honestly?" she said. "I could not give one shit. I am exhausted, I am depressed, I am. . ." She trailed off, looked at her hands.

He asked if she was having a rough day.

That provoked a bitter laugh. "Life," she corrected. "Having a rough life, my friend. I am the unluckiest girl on the planet right now. Or, at least in Olympia."

The bartender, who apparently wasn't much interested in customer service, finally finished whatever he was doing and headed back toward their side of the bar.

The man asked if he could buy her a beer.

"Thought you'd never ask," she said, batting her eyelashes.

After a gesture and a nod, Buddy Bartender put a full pint glass down in front of her.

"Same thing you're having?" she asked her new friend. The handsome patron nodded and lifted his own. She sampled hers and it was pleasantly bitter.

"Thank you," she said, and took a longer, savoring sip. She closed her eyes and cocked her head, listening to the song continuing to play. It was a long song. They were popular these days. "God, I love music," she said in a rapturous exhale.

Then her face fell. She looked as bitter as the beer in her stomach.

"You know what? This is all the Beatles' fault."

He looked at her with curiosity and asked what was the Beatles' fault.

"Everything!" She set her beer down with a heavy *thunk.* "The whole shitty world we're living in right now! They broke up and now, what, four years later and everything's gone to hell. I mean, look: Kent State, our president's a crook, Patty Frickin' Hearst, the Olympics are fucking target practice—"

Still grinning, he told her not to forget people stampedes.

"And we can't forget the people stampedes!" she exclaimed.

But then, he pointed out, in that context *she* didn't seem quite so unlucky, did she?

She gave a begrudging grunt of a laugh.

Also, he made sure to point out, their president *very clearly* stated that he was *not* a crook. So perhaps she was misinformed about that particular fact.

She raised her pint glass in a toast. "Touché, good sir, touché." A sip. A sigh. "Sorry, I'm not normally this depressing."

He told her she can be however she needs to be.

Her face hardened.

"Gee. Thanks for your permission, guy." That killed the conversation once again. (But not "Roundabout." There was still plenty of "Roundabout" to go. Choral harmonies. Indecipherable lyrics.) After a moment, she shook her head. "Sorry," she said. "What's your name?"

He told her.

His name was Ted.

Her face lit up with inspiration. In that instant, he could see her as a child, filled with hope and joy and energy.

"Ted, Ted, wets the bed," she recited in a lilting voice. She had a wickedly gleeful smile on her face, knowing she was being a snot, proud of her snottiness.

He couldn't help but laugh. He asked her how long she'd been a professional poet.

She gave a cocky little shrug and said, "Oh, off and on for a few years. Pays the bills."

He told her she was very good.

"I know," she said. "I'm thinking of running for Poet Laureate."

He said he'd vote for her, and they clinked glasses. He moved one stool closer to do it.

After they'd both swallowed another taste of bitterness, he told her that he didn't think she was wrong.

"About what?" she asked.

About the world, he told her. Something *was* changing. He could feel it.

Something in the air was different. A great. . . emptiness. It had broken open, like a wound. Only it wasn't bleeding out, it was sucking in. It was so hungry. It must not have fed for a long time. Which meant it was probably just getting started. It would go on and on and who knew what would sate it.

The song on the juke, which had been roiling and thundering, suddenly became softer. Contemplative.

He felt her eyes on him and, for the briefest instant, he felt self-conscious. He asked if that was too much, and then quickly added she shouldn't judge him. After all, she was the one who was just blaming all their woes on Ringo.

"No," she said. "I. . . I know exactly what you mean." She looked a little dazed as she said it. Maybe the beer was going to her head too fast. Maybe she hadn't eaten in a while, poor thing. "You know Stevie Wonder?"

He said of course he did.

"Do you know about that car accident he had last year?"

He thought he might have heard something about it, but it wasn't ringing a bell.

She sighed and there were tears in her exhalation. "It's just so awful. He got into a head-on with, like, a lumber truck. I mean, obviously, he wasn't driving, but. . . He was in a coma for like a week and when he came out of it, he found out he lost his sense of smell." Her eyes swung to him and there was a glinting fury in them. "Isn't that just fucking horrendous and, and absurd? I mean! Why would that happen to, to this guy who, who, I mean, *he already can't see*, Ted!!! What kind of fucking world is this?!" She took a drink. "He's just this guy who wants to make beautiful music, he just wants to spread joy and happiness despite being fucking in the dark all the time, and the universe is suddenly like, 'Nah, I'm gonna take even more away from you.' And it's not a small thing, I once heard someone say that when you lose your sense of smell, your risk of suicide goes, like, way up. Makes sense, right? I mean, think about it, without smells, the world just becomes this bland fucking cardboard fucking trudge, like having a cold all the time. Imagine never being able to smell cut grass or reexperience your mom's perfume or someone else's skin, or, or. . ." She was actually crying now. She wiped furiously at the tears with the back of her hand. "And then there's Morrison and Hendrix and Janis and Altamont and, and even though they didn't have to break up, now we don't even get the fucking Beatles anymore?! It's so *stupid.* I know they're just a band and there are bigger things to worry about, but. . . I just have this horrible feeling, like everything good is being taken away. That all our memories are going to turn into cardboard in our mouths and nothing will taste good ever again. Because you can be so good and brilliant that you can write 'My Cherie Amour' in the fucking dark and even that won't save you. So, I just think about Stevie Wonder and I want to fucking cry, Ted. I want to fucking weep." She'd been gripping the edge of the bar as if it were the only thing keeping her moored to the earth, and suddenly she noticed what she was doing. She pried her fingers off of the wood. "Oh my god, what am I talking about? See, this is why I don't have any friends." She smacked her forehead, a little too hard. "What a pathetic, depressing little. . ."

He reached out and touched the bar between them, a gesture that was almost like putting a hand on her arm, and he asked her to give him another rhyme. Maybe that would make her feel better.

She shook her head. "Nah, I don't know if you're ready for another one yet. Hey." She looked at him. "Do you wanna go for a walk?" Her face was a little manic, like she suddenly realized she had to get out of this place, like her life and sanity depended on it. "I was on my way to some stupid concert, but now I don't know if I want to go. It's jazz. I hate jazz. And I know if I go there, I'm just gonna keep feeling like I'm the unluckiest girl in, in. . . well, at least the Pacific Northwest."

He told her he was flattered she thought he could help.

She gave him an effortful chuckle. "Don't get cocky, Teddy. That will remain to be seen."

They stared at each other, and the air began to fill with electricity. Just a little, but it was a start. The song on the juke had resumed its roiling thunderousness. The drums were clapping. The bass was writhing. All was alive and hungry once more.

He put money on the table—enough to cover the beers and the faintest whiff of a tip for Buddy Bartender.

He asked if he could help her with her coat.

"Right," she said, "because I'm sooo dainty." But she let him help.

As she finished shrugging into her sleeves, she said, "Okay! I'm feeling inspired again. Now I'm ready to give you another rhyme."

He told her he couldn't wait.

"Boss! Let's see. . . What's your last name?"

He told her.

She made an adorable face of consideration which once again made her look very young. She rolled the name around in her mouth. "Ooh, that's a tough one! Let's see. Bundy, Bundy. . ."

He gave her a big, big smile, activating his dimples. His voice sounded different through that smile. Fuller. Realer.

He suggested: "Let's go have some fundy?"

"Ugh, *Ted!*" She rolled her eyes and stuck out her tongue. "That was *painful*!"

He beamed and shrugged and held the door open for her. She stepped into that golden rectangle, still retching. "Just brutal, Teddy! Put me outta my misery!"

His grin, his dimples, intensified. He offered her an arm.

"Come on," he said, still smiling. His voice filled the world.

"I know a place."

That phrase sparkled in her ears like windchimes.

She took his arm and he let the door swing shut on its own.

Inside, the bar was silent for a moment. "Roundabout" had some to an end at last.

Then, with a click and a whir, the juke moved on to another song.

GENERATION

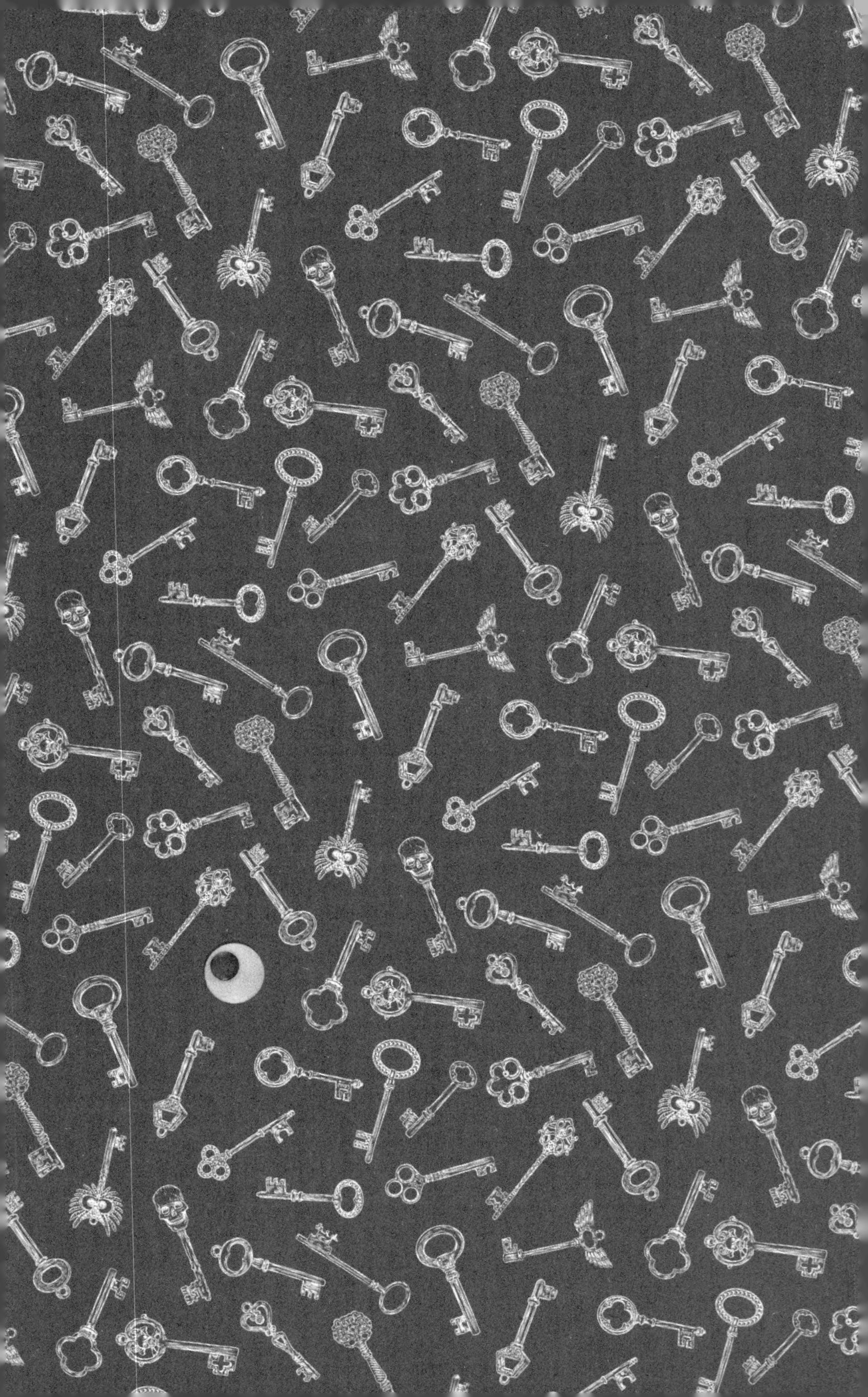

GENERATION

She stood outside the door to her makeshift office, listening to the couple arguing inside.

That was fine. Let them. This happened all the time.

All the time. Jesus. How was it she'd only been doing this for five weeks and there was already an *all the time*? Barely a month since she'd first started having these meetings and here she was, blasé as a grizzled vet. *Been through the wars, Mandygal*, she thought to herself in her mother's slurring voice, and repressed a shudder.

The door's still-sparkling silver nameplate winked back at her with almost mocking mundanity. Her own name: DR. AMANDA EVESON, MD OB/GYN.

Inside her office, the argument continued.

To her accounting, there were three different kinds of *all the time* arguments she overheard through this office door. She could only rarely make out the actual words from this vantage point—instead, her ear was attuned to the music of the voices, like a piano tuner.

Most popular was the Would You Calm Down. This involved one patient in hysterics (a word no self-respecting gynecologist this side of the twenty-first century would ever use professionally, but until Mandy stepped through that door, she was going to consider herself a civilian), usually sobbing or hyperventilating, and the other patient absolutely desperate to quiet the storm before the doctor came in there and caught them in the act. Sometimes it was out of concern; often it was just out of embarrassment, which was almost funny considering the situation. No one ever won a Would You Calm Down—though Mandy *had* walked in once or twice to see a valiant attempt of Calming Down being made, only to crumble back into hysterics before Mandy was able to cross the room and sit at her makeshift desk.

Every time, without exception, one or both patients would begin, "We're sorry, Doctor."

Mandy hated that. There was nothing to apologize for. The world called for hysterics right now.

The inverse of Would You Calm Down was the Why Aren't You Upset. Still one patient upset and the other not, but this time the music was sharper, angrier. This time the patient in hysterics was the one, ostensibly, playing lead. It was the *other* patient, the quiet one, who needed to step up their game, join the party, pick up an instrument and play along. This is a big deal, why are you just sitting there?! Sometimes Why Aren't You Upsets turned into Would You Calm Downs—two musicians trading solos. Those were the really special days when Mandy would sometimes go grab a snack before walking in.

But the third type of argument was the worst. Mandy thought of it as the Meat Locker. That's when it was too quiet. Pianissimo. Staccato. You could hear clipped murmurs through the door and then you walked into a miasma of tension. Clenched jaws.

Ice crystals in the air, sharp enough to cut you. Neither party expressive. Not because of apathy, but because of overload. Mandy hated these meetings most of all. They made her feel like a coroner sitting down to chat with the recently deceased.

Then, of course, there were the non-arguments. They were more like ambient music or musique concrete, and they ran along a spectrum ranging from Everything's Fine (big smiles, lots of nodding, lots of repeating the word "Yeah," lots of trying to fake understanding until maybe the real thing came along) to what she thought of as Dead Puppy Time. Mandy hated thinking of it that way, but she couldn't help it: walking into a Dead Puppy room was like greeting a small child after the death of a beloved pet. Big wet eyes, trembling lips, barely any questions other than "why," an overall aura of inexpressible sadness. It was the novelty of that sadness that made her think of children learning about death for the first time; the feeling that these patients sitting on the other side of her desk had no idea anything in the world could ever hurt so bad. The first weeks were mostly full of Dead Puppies and Mandy had to introduce the depths of pain and the concept of death over, and over, and over, and over again. Metaphorically speaking, of course. In so many ways, if it were just death she had to teach them about, this would all be so much easier.

Thinking of her desk made her think about what was *inside* it, and just like that, she was suddenly eager to get this meeting started.

That wasn't good—she shouldn't *need* so strongly—but she was going to have to conduct her own internal Would You Calm Down later. For now, what could she do? Things were tough all over. It was like her college roommate said after a particularly vodka-soaked, tears-and-snot-filled gabfest about parents: trauma is the bitch-goddess of humanity. Mandy's desk was in the office, the patients were in the office, the thing she needed was inside the desk, thus, so q.e.d., ipso facto, cogito ergo fucking sum, it was time to begin the meeting. Time to put their Argument on hold.

No. The Arguments never went on hold.

They just mutated.

"Christ, Mandy," she muttered to herself. That word was verboten, even in her brain.

She twisted the silver knob and walked through the door to greet her new patients, wondering what her walk across the room to her desk would be like this time.

The woman was on her feet, pacing, mid-rant. The man was in the chair, staring blankly at the vaguely cream-colored carpet.

Textbook Why Aren't You Upset.

"Good afternoon," Mandy began, starting towards said desk. "Sorry to keep you wait—"

"Yeah, hi," the woman said curtly, "I want this fucking thing dead. I want it out of me."

She was approximately eight months pregnant. Big as a house, Mandy's mom might've said.

Mandy walked the rest of the way to her chair in silence. Sat down (purposefully not eying the drawer she wanted to open; not now, not yet). Put the file folder she was carrying on the flat surface and then folded her hands over it. Smiled her warm-but-tired smile.

After a beat she said, "My name's Dr. Amanda Eveson. We're about to get pretty familiar, so call me Mandy."

The woman remained standing. Defiant. She gestured at her

huge stomach. "I'm serious. I don't want to do this. I want it dead, gone, whatever."

Mandy raised her hands. A small don't-shoot-the-messenger gesture. "I know," she said. She kept her voice quiet and calm and full of empathy. "I know, Mrs.—" She quickly flipped open the file. "—Tilly. Please. Have a seat."

Mrs. Tilly set her jaw, masseter muscles giving an angry, pulsing bulge. "I *mean* it," she said. Mandy met her gaze, acknowledged she understood, and then Mrs. Tilly lowered herself into her chair the way pregnant people must.

Another moment of silence. Then:

"I'm Paul," the man said. He brought his eyes up to meet Mandy's, then dropped them like heavy bags of groceries back down to the floor.

"Hi," Mandy said to both of them. She was still smiling. It was a genuine smile. She was good at her job. It was never supposed to be this difficult, but she was good at it all the same. "Would you guys like any water? Or we have soda, or coffee, or. . . ?"

"A pack of Camels and some Liquid Plumr?" Mrs. Tilly snarled.

"Charlotte," Paul reprimanded without any force, staring vaguely at the desk before swinging his blank face up to Mandy. "I'm sorry, she's—"

"Please." Mandy waved his apology away, then craned her neck a little in a facile attempt at addressing Charlotte privately. "Charlotte—may I call you Charlotte? If I were in your shoes? I can't say I wouldn't have already grabbed the nearest letter opener and carved it out myself."

"Yeah," Charlotte said, petulant, "I didn't see one on your desk."

"No," Mandy said, "I have to hide it in a drawer now."

She let the implications of that sink in. If they were feeling *really* curious she could have also directed their attention to the just barely visible discoloration on the carpet from the incident with the patient and the letter opener, but they seemed to get the gist.

"So," Mandy continued. "There are a few things we need to—"

Charlotte started to sob.

Mandy hated this part. It wouldn't be so hard if only she could turn off whatever was inside her that made her feel empathy. She just wanted to get up, wrap her arms around Charlotte, cry with her. She wanted that every single time this happened. And this happened *all the time*. Again, her eyes crept to the desk drawer.

"I need you to understand something," Charlotte said through the tears. "I am being very clearheaded right now. I'm not, like, hysterical, or hormonal, or anything like that when I say this." Mandy opened her mouth to speak but now it was Charlotte's turn to raise a hand. "Wait. What I'm saying is. . . I have always considered myself a religious, moral person. I've never been out there chanting 'Bomb Planned Parenthood,' or anything like that—I know there are *reasons* to have this, this procedure—but I mean, me? Being here? Is not something I ever imagined doing. Ever. Not me. You have to understand that."

Mandy, a military brat who wasn't so much raised in one place as across half a dozen, couldn't help but notice how clearly Charlotte's local, North Carolinian accent came out when she was upset.

"I do, Charlotte," she said. "I do." And finally she could take no more. "Here," she said, pulling open her desk drawer. *The* drawer.

"Time for the famous letter opener?"

Dr. Amanda Eveson, board certified to practice obstetrics and gynecology for over fifteen years now, pulled out a half-full bottle of Jack Daniel's Black Label No. 7 and two shot glasses. They *tocked* and *clacked* against the metal of her desk. She poured herself a quick shot and drank it greedily. As always, she heard her mother in the relieved exhale that followed.

Charlotte and Paul stared at her.

"What a year this month has been," Mandy said through her burning throat. She poured a shot into the second glass and pushed it across the desk to her patients. "Go on. You can have a few, it's okay. I mean, we *think*. We don't really know how alcohol might affect things, but. . ." She shrugged. "I also have Tito's, Pinnacle gin, Cuervo silver, or something called Birthday Cake if you're really feeling—"

Charlotte grabbed the shot glass, dumped the brown liquor into her mouth, hissed softly, and put the glass back down on the desk. Mandy refilled it and nudged it towards Paul.

"And you, Paul?" she asked. "How you doing?"

Paul blinked as if he'd just woken up from a nap. "Huh? I'm. . . I don't. . ." He trailed off. Then he saw the shot glass, took it up, drank its contents.

Dr. Eveson poured herself another.

Meanwhile, Charlotte, a little calmer, lifted herself up and paced around the room again, this time appearing to take the place in. It was a plain office. Disarmingly plain, like no one actually worked here. That was because, up until five weeks ago, nobody did. Not in this capacity, at least. If that weren't abundantly obvious, the fact that Paul and Charlotte had to drive to an abandoned strip mall and walk through the empty storefront to get here would've clued them in.

"What did this place used to be, by the way?" She was looking at the spackle on the walls. The spackle was the wrong shade of white to match, but they covered up the holes where metal shelves full of stock used to be.

"I think it used to be a Radio Shack," Mandy said, screwing the cap back on the bottle, but keeping it out.

"No shit," said Charlotte. "I remember those."

"Yeah," Mandy replied. "They're setting us up pretty much wherever they can." She took her shot.

Immediately, she felt better. Steadier. She hated how well the liquor worked—almost as much as she hated knowing she'd need it again real soon. She inhaled some recycled air across her teeth and cheeks to calm the burning, then decided it was time to get to work.

"You'd think after doing this so many times, I'd have a damned idea how to start, but. . ." She cleared her throat. "It's important for you both to know that whatever you're feeling, it's okay. Totally normal. I don't know how much of a comfort that is, but I've seen a whole spectrum of responses in this room. All of them, natural. We're all at sea, here. Okay?" She flipped open her file and took up a pen. "Let's just start at the beginning with the easy stuff. Tell me a little bit about yourselves."

Paul answered, his voice quiet and pained. "Um. We've been together for five years. Married for three. We met through my sister at a picnic for her job. She's in real estate. Uh. We've been trying pretty hard for a kid for about two years now. The tests, the needles, it took a long time. But we kept trying. We kept trying. We. . . I'm sorry, can I—?"

He pointed to the empty shot glass. The doctor uncapped and poured him another. He downed the bittersweet medicine.

"Come on, Paul," Charlotte chuckled wryly, though not without sympathy, from where she was standing behind him. "This is the 'easy stuff,' remember?"

That made Paul laugh. A short little percussive burst, but it did Mandy good to see it. A little glimpse into their life—their actual life—before this nightmare began. She teased him, he took it in good humor. A rapport. Which meant maybe something for them to cling to when the shock wore off.

He still wasn't looking at his wife, though.

He continued: "We. . . we were pregnant for about four months before the news. . . When we got the ultrasound and they told us, I actually fainted. Took them almost an hour to convince me I wasn't just having a nightmare. I still don't. . ." He looked down. Charlotte put her hands on his shoulders and squeezed.

"Okay," Mandy said. "Thank you. You all sound like a lovely couple. Now. . . tell me what you know."

"About. . . ?" Charlotte asked, her face growing pained, like she was about to vomit (another not infrequent occurrence in this office, which was why there was always a small trash can with a fresh bag right by the chairs, discreet enough to look like normal office accoutrement, but obvious enough should the need arise).

Mandy nodded. "Yes."

"I mean. . . Well, like everyone, we saw the press conference with the president—"

"—and the surgeon general," Paul added.

"Right," Mandy nodded.

"And there was that woman in the crowd." Charlotte's eyes went a little glassy at the memory.

"She wouldn't stop screaming," Paul said, also remembering

that woman and those noises she made in her unguarded panic. Somehow inhuman and all-too-human at the same time. That woman's screams had become famous, in the same way certain photographs during wartime became famous: they'd captured something beyond words, something momentous, something inarguable. Mandy often thought of that woman, too—had she been a reporter? Some other cabinet official? Did the president regret not telling the country in a private address? Or maybe he'd anticipated the value in those inevitable screams. Mandy repressed a shudder and stopped her hand from reaching out for the bottle.

"But after that," Charlotte continued, finally lowering herself back into her chair, "just drips and drabs on the internet. Rumors. No one's saying anything useful. No pictures, no consistency, fucking nothing—"

"We've been asked to keep a lot of information as classified as we can," Mandy said. "For the time being, at least."

"Why?!" Charlotte demanded. She slammed her palms against the chair's armrests.

Mandy pressed her lips into a thin line and raised her shoulders in a slight shrug. "Doesn't get more sensitive than this, right? And there's a lot we still don't know, so we don't want to accidentally trip over ourselves." Was she staring at the bottle on her desk? No. Focus, Mandy. "Plus," she cleared her throat again, "I guess, they want information given to parents personally. Like this. Face-to-face."

Charlotte was looking down at her hands, which were now picking at themselves on top of her thighs, in front of her massive belly.

"They're monsters," she whispered, "aren't they? We're talking about monsters."

"No, Mrs. Tilly. We're not talking about monsters."

"Yes, we are." Still whispering, as if trying to keep a secret from whatever hid inside her womb.

"No."

"Then what are we talking about?" She looked up and the pain in her eyes was like that anonymous woman's screams: beyond words.

"Your baby," Mandy said. "We're talking about your baby."

"I'm going to be sick." She tried to bend forward for the tiny trash can, but her stomach prevented her. Paul quickly grabbed it for her. She held it under her mouth for a moment, but the sickness abated a little. Still holding the can, she pushed herself back up off the chair again and resumed her pacing.

Mandy took a breath—imperceptible to her patients, the practiced sigh of the medical professional, a silent prayer in its way—and began what she thought of as The Speech.

"There are things you'll need to understand. Obviously, whether you decide to follow through with the birth or not is up to you, we're equipped for both. If you do decide to have this baby. . . first, natural delivery is not an option. Cephalic growth is inordinately advanced, as I'm sure you can feel, and that means Caesarian. When the baby is born, you'll notice a few things right away. For the most part, pigmentation is much paler—much. Also, they run hotter than normal. Significantly. You won't hear it cry—it looks like pretty much across the board, vocal cords aren't forming. Same with the ears—there are nubs, but they seem to be vestigial, for the most part. Most likely the eyes will be open, and they'll seem. . . more aware than you might expect. Nursing can start as normal, but weaning should begin roughly around three or four weeks, as teeth are developing a lot quicker, and you can start on solid foods pretty much right after. High protein is the most important, but we'll give you more information on that when the time is right. As for their appendages. . . there are special cribs and carriers, and you can apply for a credit if you can't afford them. Obviously, we're only a few months into this, so we're still in the dark when it comes to growth beyond that. We're all going to have to learn together."

Charlotte had begun to cry again. She was clutching the trash can for comfort, like it was a teddy bear. "People are actually going through with this?"

"Why is this happening?" Paul asked.

Mandy used to think that was the most exciting question in the scientific world. Now she thought of it as the most useless. She had some colleagues who were theorizing that it might be because of cell phones—enough of them in pockets, near the genital region. She had others who were theorizing it was radiation in the air. Some thought climate change—maybe a mutagen released from arctic ice that was never supposed to thaw. Some thought food hormones. BPAs. PFAS. High fructose corn syrup. GMOs. Antibiotics. 5G. Some whispered alien invasion. Ultimately, what did it even matter? What did anything matter when you were sitting across from expectant parents, cataloging their arguments and watching their faces as they digested the fact that what they were growing in their bodies, what they'd put all their hopes for the future on, was entirely *other* from them? All that mattered was it was happening. All that mattered, as her mother—the amateur philosopher and professional drunk, who'd given up her dreams of becoming a musician when her husband enlisted—sometimes said, was that debts always come due. Life is a debt. Normalcy is a debt. Understanding is a debt. Comfort—even with something so fundamentally simple as knowing egg plus sperm equals little human and tomorrow is another day—is a debt. Sooner or later, the invoice shows up with big red letters stamped on it: TIME TO PAY, Services Rendered. Most nights lately, Mandy passed out from exhaustion (and Jack Daniel's Black Label No. 7) the moment she got into bed, but on the nights when she couldn't sleep, the thought that plagued her most was: maybe this was all happening simply because *it was time for it to happen*. Maybe abrupt and catastrophic change was the most normal thing of all. How do you live with knowledge like that? How do you not lose your mind?

"We have some ideas, but nothing concrete yet."

"And *every* child is going to be born like this?" Paul's eyes were wide and red-rimmed. Sleep was clearly difficult for him.

"As of right now, it's a growing majority. A very high majority." She said that, because the truth, though simpler, was more brutal. *Yes. Looks like all of them, yes.*

Charlotte held the trash can in the crook of one arm and was picking at her fingers again. "Will they have a normal lifespan?"

"We don't know."

"How will they talk to each other?" Paul asked.

"We don't know."

"How will they talk to *us?*" Charlotte asked. "How will they tell me what they want, how to take care of them?"

"We don't—"

The questions began to tumble out of both of them. Mandy

attempted to interject answers, but it was always the same answer and everyone in this tiny, repurposed room knew it, so eventually she gave up and sat there.

"How big will they get?"

"What are they going to grow into?"

"What happens when they start having babies?"

"Will they be happy?"

"Will they hate us?"

"How will we love them?"

"Is this the end of humanity?"

"*What does this mean*?"

Eventually the questions burned themselves out and silence took over the room once more. *Happens all the time*, Mandy thought, eying the bottle, hating herself for the way her mouth was watering for another taste.

When it was silent for just long enough, she asked *her* question.

It was the question she always asked at this point. And it always hung in the air for a long while.

Like a noose.

Like a bomb paused a split-second before the explosive impact of its freefall.

But it had to be asked. It was why she was here.

"Would you like to see some photos?"

She let them sit with that question for a few beats, then opened another drawer in her desk. In many ways, *this* drawer necessitated the one with the liquor. Cause and effect. That's all life really was, wasn't it? Sperm and ovum. This makes that, causing this other. She pulled out from this second drawer a closed manila folder. She slid it across the desk to the couple.

“Go on,” she said. “You can. If you want.”

The people on the other side of the desk didn’t always want. Some said no and asked to set up an appointment for termination (which was its own newly complicated process). Some ran out of the room and Mandy never saw them again (but sometimes she thought about them in the dead of night and hoped they didn’t somehow convince themselves everything was fine and to go through with a natural birth, because that phrase was now the sickest of jokes). Some said yes and immediately regretted it, fainting or needing to be tranquilized or filling up the trash can with the contents of their stomachs (once a couple fell into a sort of tug of war over the bin, spraying puke all over each other, so now she kept a second hidden on her side of the desk). One woman had a heart attack and died. There was also, of course, the incident with the letter opener. Cause and effect.

But those responses were mostly outliers. And despite all her training, despite her experience, despite what she suspected to be her own feelings, that fact still surprised Mandy. There was another kind of reaction that was actually the most common.

She wasn’t sure what this couple would do, but she found herself hoping they would go the common route because it would give herself an opportunity to pour another drink.

After a few heavy moments (a pregnant pause, Mandy thought and tasted bile), Paul reached forward and took the folder. He opened it up. His eyes didn’t pop. They didn’t go wide. Nothing so dramatic. Nothing so easy to interpret or compartmentalize. They just. . . took in the first of the images inside.

Charlotte came forward and looked over his shoulder. She gave a soft, barely perceivable gasp.

"This is only a couple of months old?" Paul asked about the infant.

Dr. Amanda Eveson, MD OB/GYN, "Mandy" to her friends and loved ones, "Mandygal" to her mother (who sometimes drank so much she would have dance parties by herself in the kitchen until dawn, singing and sobbing so loudly that her voice would be hoarse for days), nodded. She knew the photo he was looking at. She looked at it a lot some days, in the privacy of this strange little office. There was a lot to process about that image, but hardest of all was how the eyes seemed to leap off the photo paper and ask unfathomable questions. Questions that could only be met with the words *we don't know.*

Charlotte, eyes still on the folder, put the trash can down and lowered herself into her chair. Reaching across her giant belly, she took one side of the folder from Paul, and the two of them looked at the other photos inside together.

Paul and Charlotte's expressions began to subtly *(mutate)* change. From shock to horror. Then fascination. Then heartbroken resignation. Then. . . something else entirely. Something maybe there was no word for. Not in any language like ours, at least.

"Wow," Charlotte whispered. "Wow."

Her other hand searched for Paul's. He took it.

This was the most common reaction to those who chose to look. Somehow.

Mandy didn't understand it. Perhaps she needed to be pregnant herself to really do so. But she'd also stopped questioning it anymore. Instead, she used this time as she almost always did: to pour herself another drink. Then, when it was safely coursing down her throat, the sweet, burning liquid obeying the rules of physics they'd all agreed upon like there was nothing wrong in the world, she poured herself another.

"That old riddle," Mandy heard herself saying. "You know the one I mean? 'Which came first?' It's never been a mystery." She drank the shot. "It's the egg. It's always been the egg."

"Wow," Paul said, touching a photo, almost caressing it, not listening.

Mandy poured herself another. Drank it. Begged herself to stop now. Her next appointment was scheduled in ten minutes.

Would you calm down?

(You're just like her)

(After everything you did to try to be different, you're just like her)

(Why aren't you upset?)

Just have one more and calm down.

On the other side of the desk, the couple took a few more moments, then closed the folder and put it back on the desktop. There was a long exhale.

"So," Mandy said on autopilot, desperately wanting to fill her glass again, despising herself for her thirst. "That's where we are." Her rhythms, rehearsed, professional, her diction immaculate, her pretense suffocating. "Now it's time to discuss what you'd like to do next."

Paul and Charlotte finally looked at each other. It was their first real moment of eye contact in days. Something passed between them like silent music. They smiled faintly in recognition.

Dr. Amanda "Mandygal" Eveson was too busy staring at the empty glass in her hand to notice. Rotating it the way her mother used to.

The three of them held there, each wondering in their own

way what this moment might grow into.
    Ears pressed against an eggshell.
    Listening to the arguments inside.

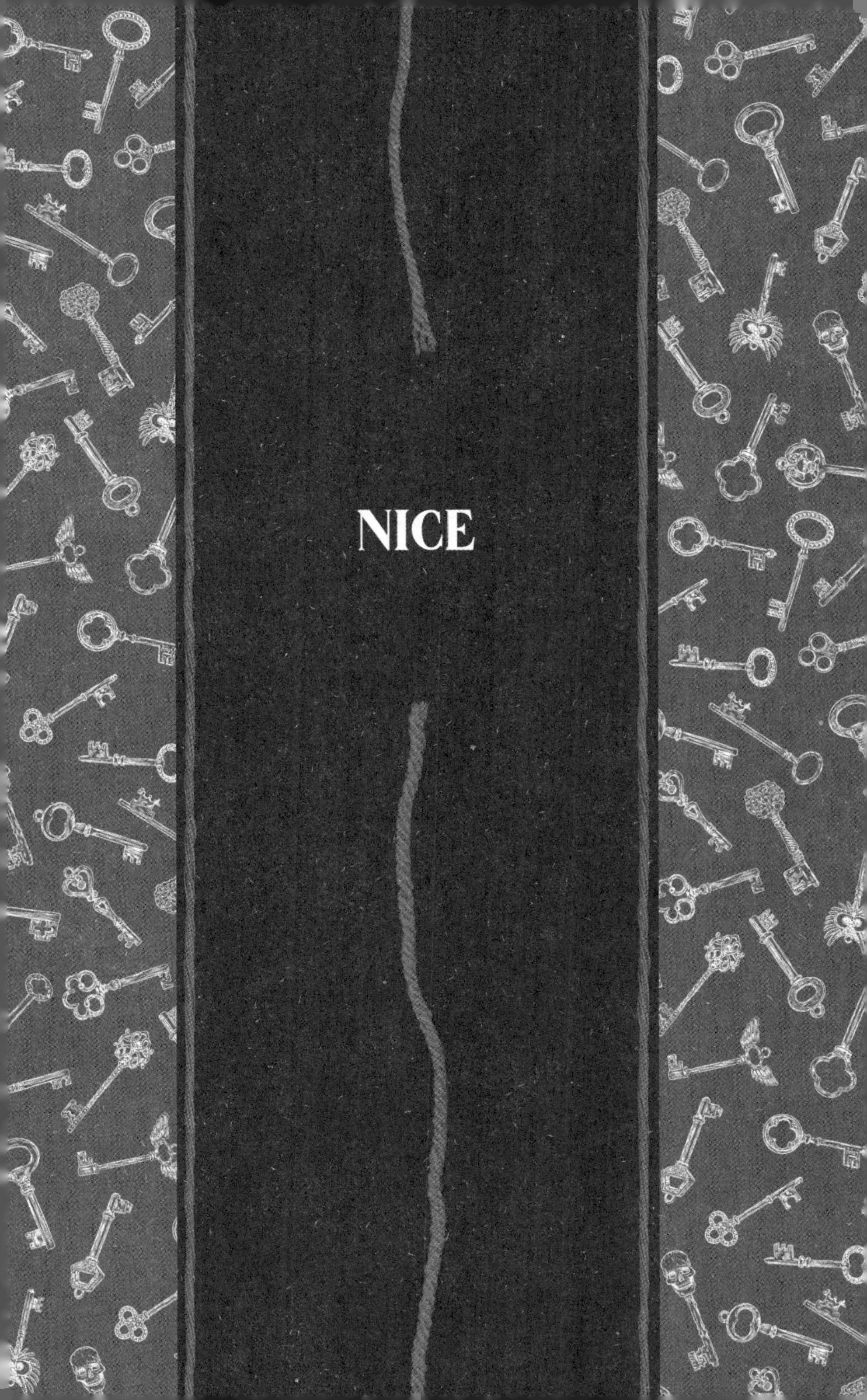

NICE

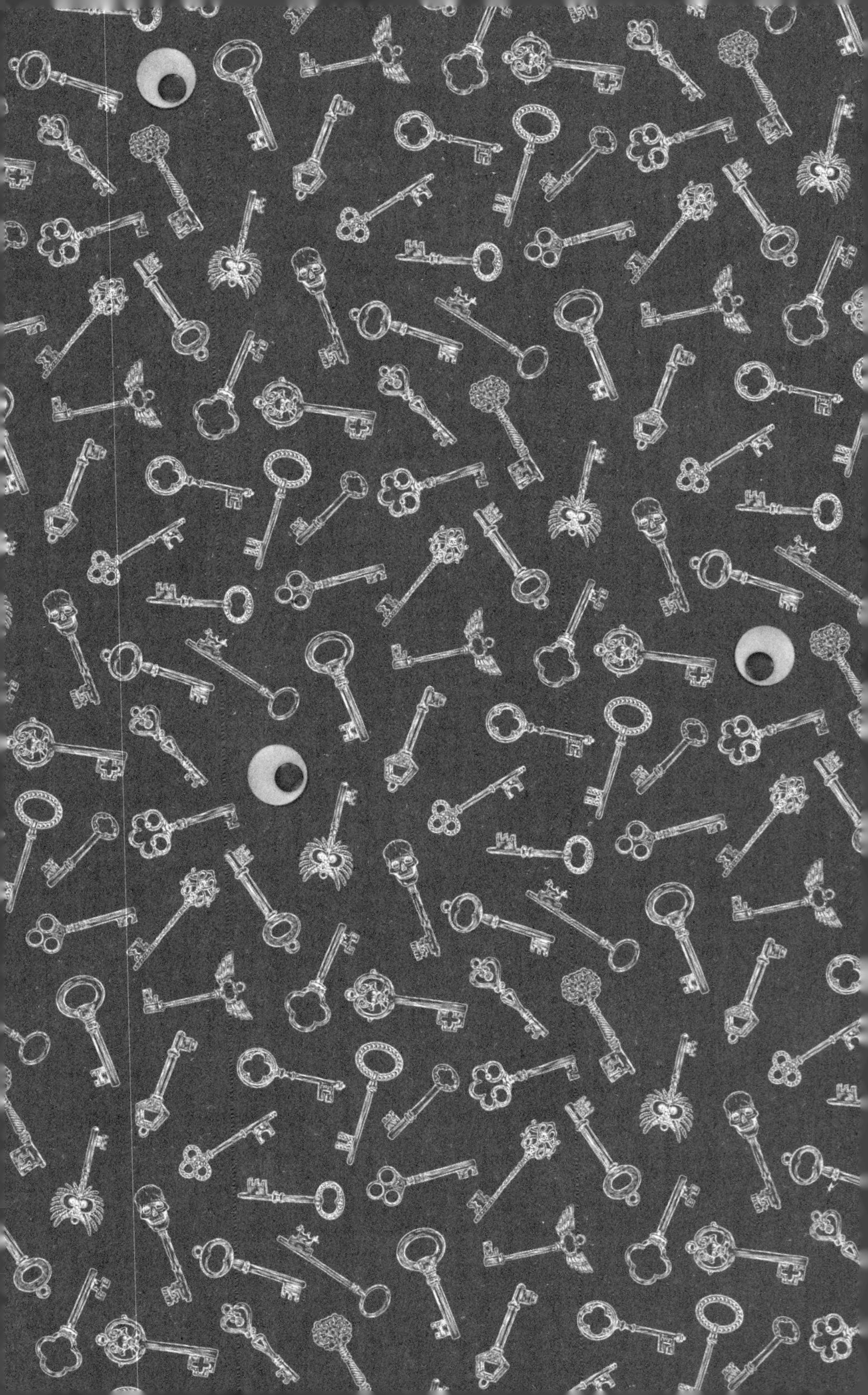

NICE

Mitchell's footsteps tore through the house like muffled machine gun fire. *Thumpathumpathumpathump*.

"I made another one, Daddy, I made another one!" He launched himself from the foot of the stairs onto his father in the easy chair.

Daddy, also known as Kevin, let out a great oof as his six-year-old son landed on his lap (narrowly missing real estate that would've elicited a much more agonized reaction). "That's great, buddy."

"I think it's my best one!" Mitchell held out the ornament he'd been working on upstairs. A hand-painted portrait of Santa splashed across its surface.

"I think so too!" Kevin exchanged looks with Andrea from across the room. Andrea was pouring herself another glass of Gruner.

Between them stood their Christmas tree, trimmed, lit up. . . and practically sagging under the amount of Mitchell's hand-painted, Santa-revering ornaments.

"Do you think he'll like it?" Mitchell asked Kevin.

"I'm sure he will."

"Promise?"

"*Mitchell*," Andrea said over her wine glass. "Do you think your father knows what's going on in Santa's head?"

Kevin opened his mouth to remind Andrea to play nice when Mitchell, suddenly abashed, said:

"At school? Eric said that Santa is really just your parents. Is that true?"

Andrea growled: "Oh, that little piece of—"

"Hon." Kevin cut her off. He turned to Mitchell, whose face was wide-open, ready to receive the best news. . . or the worst. "Didn't Eric get in trouble for swallowing rocks for pocket change a few months ago? Does that sound like someone who knows anything about anything?"

Mitchell giggled, relieved. "No."

"Why don't you go upstairs and get ready for bed and we'll find a good spot on the tree for your newest masterpiece?"

Mitchell hopped off Kevin's lap. "NINE MORE SLEEPS UNTIL CHRISTMAS!"

Another volley of machine-gun footfalls as Mitchell tore his way back upstairs.

"Stop running or you'll go on the naughty list!" Andrea called after him. The running stopped immediately.

In the silence that followed, the adults let out a breath together.

Kevin got up and went to the tree, ornament in hand.

"Would it kill you to have just a little more holiday cheer?" he asked his wife.

"It might."

"Baby."

Andrea sighed and put the bottle back in the fridge. "I'm just so over all this Christmas stuff. He gets so obsessive."

"All kids are superfans of something! Some kids are all Batman all the time. Or Star Wars. Or Marvel. Mitch loves Santa."

"Yeah, but he also gets so. . ."

She didn't finish. They both knew how uniquely intense their son could get. It wasn't just the ornaments. Drawings of Santa were Scotch-taped all over the living room. And kitchen. And hallway. And his bedroom. Santa was the inevitable subject of every conversation. All Mitchell cared about was pleasing some made-up commercial mascot who lived in the friggin' Arctic. Or was it the Antarctic? Andrea didn't know. It was all so stupid.

Kevin gave up and added the ornament to an already-cluttered branch. Then he left the innumerable Santas leering at him to go to his wife and kiss her forehead. "Remember what he was like with dinosaurs? Or learning how to tie knots? He'll find something new soon."

"Yeah. . ."

"Besides, I think it's great how enthusiastic he gets! He makes *me* love these things all over again, too! I bet he'll be one hell of a salesman someday. Or a politician."

"Or a cult leader," Andrea muttered into her glass. "Or a serial killer."

"Andrea."

"Yeah, I know. 'Bah, humbug.' Sorry. You know how I get this time of year."

Another kiss. They held there for a moment, letting the tension deflate a little. Then Kevin yawned. "I'll go tuck him in."

Andrea stared at her glass. Before Kevin disappeared down the hall she said, "Hey. I'll find the Christmas spirit soon. Promise."

"I know you will." Kevin gave her a smile. "I noticed you put that little Elf on the Shelf in his room. The Christmas spirit gets everyone in the end."

Then he was gone, leaving Andrea with her wine. She had no idea what he meant about an Elf on the Shelf, but by the time they reconnected later that night, she'd already forgotten it.

It was just past midnight when a pair of tiny hands shook Mitchell awake.

His eyes fluttered open.

Standing on the bed was the elf that had mysteriously appeared on his bookcase this morning. About a foot tall. A sparkly, red conical hat on his impish little face.

Being six years old, Mitchell didn't question it. His face lit up like, well, a Christmas tree. "Hi!"

The elf put a white-gloved finger to his own lips. Then, in a whisper: "Hey, Mitchell. Gotta keep it quiet, okay? Otherwise, your parents'll be on us like crabs on a Williamsburg toilet seat."

"I don't know what that means!"

"'Course you don't. Just hush, okay?"

Mitchell nodded, smiling a huge smile. The elf's voice was high and sweet, and despite the seriousness of his expression (or perhaps because of it), Mitchell thought he sounded delightfully silly.

"Cool." The elf began to pace a little over the bedspread. "So—"

"What's your name?" Mitchell asked at full volume.

"Ugh. It's. . . Twinklebottom."

Mitchell giggled and clapped. The elf's face drew down in a sneer. "Oh, like 'Mitchell' makes any goddamn sense?! Listen, we don't have a lot of time. I need to talk to you about something very important, okay? So, just, shhhh. *Please*."

Mitchell nodded and did his best to keep his voice down. "I've been good all year, right? I've tried so, so, so hard, and—"

"Yeah, yeah, you've been great. That's. . . heh, well, that's kinda the problem. I couldn't help but notice you've got a bit of a Santa thing going on here and so—"

"I LOVE SANTA!"

Twinklebottom seethed through gritted teeth. "*Kid! Shut your fuckin' tit-hole and listen!*"

Something flashed in Mitchell's eyes that made the elf pause for the briefest of moments. Something hard and cold. Gone as quickly as it arrived, but Twinklebottom took a step backwards all the same.

"Hey, sorry, Mitch-o!" Twinklebottom said in his syrupy sweetest voice. "It's just. . . well, I'm a little stressed right now. This is a stressful time. Do you know what stress is?"

Mitchell nodded again. "Daddy says Mommy is stressed. I wish I could make her feel happier."

"The holidays are rough, kid. But that's why I'm here! In fact, I need your help."

"My help?"

"Mitch? *I need you to help me save Christmas.*"

Mitchell's eyes went wide. "Tell me," he whispered.

So Twinklebottom did.

"It didn't used to be this way," he began. "A long, long time ago, things were soooo much easier." He described how, for generations, being one of Santa's elves was a great gig. Toys were fun to make—even the complex ones. But with every year, the orders got more and more complicated. Electronics. Microchips. The workshop began to stink of toxic chemicals, burning plastic, frying wires. "And there are so many more goddamn kids now! And each kid wants so many goddamn things! You know what exponential means, Mitchell?"

Mitchell shook his head.

"It means arthritis! It means back spasms! It means stress ulcers and nervous breakdowns and all kinds of shit magical beings aren't supposed to be fucking worried about!"

"You sure do swear a lot," Mitchell said, grimacing.

"'Cause I'm in *pain*, Mitchell!" the tiny creature hissed.

Mitchell looked genuinely distressed. "So, what can I do?"

"Well, you're not gonna like it. But remember, I'm saying this as a representative of Christmas, right?"

"A *representative*." Pronouncing the word with solemnity. "Right."

Twinklebottom took a breath, then stared Mitchell right in the eyes. "I need you to be Naughty, bud."

Mitchell recoiled like he'd been gut-shot. "What? N-naughty?"

"I know what you're thinking. You *can't* be Naughty. Right?"

Mitchell's eyes darted to the portraits he'd taped all over his room. "Santa—"

"Santa hates Naughty! I know! But, I've got news for you, kid. Santa's not the saint you think he is! He's a boss, just like any other boss. He only cares about one thing: the bottom line. Check this shit out."

Twinklebottom pulled out a little phone from his green pants, then pulled up some pictures to show Mitchell. The images were small, but undeniable. Cramped workspaces. Miserable faces. Elves frozen in misery.

Mitchell started to cry. "No!"

"It's bleak shit, right" Twinklebottom took the phone back, put it away. "Lemme put it this way, then. Things are so hard for us because of all the work we've gotta do, yeah? And we've gotta do all this work because. . . ?"

"Because you make toys?" Mitchell blubbered.

Twinklebottom nodded. "For?"

"The good boys and girls?"

"That's right. The Nice list. So we'd have *less* work to do if the Nice list was. . . ?"

The word problem helped Mitchell calm down. He considered, sniffing back a sinus cavity full of snot. "Shorter."

"Exactamundo, Mitch, ole chap. When you think about it, the Nice kids are the ones who are being bad, because look what they're doing to us!" Now it was Twinklebottom's turn to crack with emotion. He fought his tears valiantly. "Mitchell, my friend. . . if you could just be Naughty. . . and maybe get some of your friends to be Naughty. . . well, it'd be the Nicest thing you could ever do."

Mitchell's brow knit as he tried to work through the paradox. "O-okay. So. . . if I'm Naughty. . . then that's good. . . because it helps the elves."

"Now you're getting it!" Twinklebottom jubilantly smacked one of Mitchell's comforter-covered legs. "Because you wanna be Nice, right?"

"More than anything!"

"*So, stop being Nice, Mitchy*. Please. For us."

Now, Twinklebottom reached out and touched Mitchell's hand tenderly. The six-year-old's hand dwarfed the elf's, but it curled around Twinklebottom's all the same.

When Twinklebottom looked back up, he noticed that coldness had again crept into the boy's eyes. It made Twinklebottom's elf-stomach cramp a little. What was going on in that kid's head? No time to dwell on it, though, because Mitchell gave a short, definitive nod and sighed.

"Okay, Twinklebottom."

Twinklebottom sagged with relief. "For real?!"

"I'll be Naughty, Twinklebottom."

"Holy shit, Mitch! You're the best! The elves thank you! And, hey." He gestured to the drawings on the wall. "Happy elves mean happy Santa, right? So, even if you still got a hard-on for ole Jelly Guts over there, you're still doing him a solid, too. Aw, shit, speaking of. I gotta get back to the Pole before he notices I'm gone. Time and Yuletide wait for no one, am I right?"

Mitchell couldn't fall back asleep. that night. He calmly took down each of his paintings of Santa, stacking them on top of each other, and put them face down on his little desk under a yellow plastic stegosaurus.

His head swam. Could he really be Naughty? Wasn't that breaking The Rules? Or was it really following The Rules? That day Daddy had caught him playing with one of Mrs. Gresham's cats and that lighter he'd found in the kitchen drawer, Daddy had told him how important it was to be Nice.

Don't you know you have *to be Nice, Mitchell?*
Those were The Rules.
How could he be Naughty?
How would he even start?
Then he remembered that box under the bed.

Two nights later, Twinklebottom was on top of the fucking world. Which, he supposed, was kind of an ironic turn of phrase considering he wasn't at the North Pole right now. He was heading back to his dear buddy Mitchy-poo's boxy suburban house to let him know the good news.

He'd managed to sneak a peek at the numbers. Mitchell's Naughtiness was off the charts. Hell, even some of the other kids on the block's numbers seemed to be going down too. The kid was a Naughty savant. Twinklebottom *had* to know his secrets.

When he'd initially had the idea for this little pilot program, he'd figured a Santa superfan would be an ideal first candidate. Obviously, whatever results he'd get would be too late to affect the demands for this year, but if he could get some movement out of a kid *that* hardcore, during the height of Christmas fever no less? Well, there would be some motherfucking proof in the figgy pudding, right there. And he appeared to have succeeded beyond his wildest sugarplum dreams. There were gonna be some real changes afoot starting next year. This would teach that fat, monopolistic fuck a thing or two about using his workforce as chattel.

Twinklebottom sauntered up the side of the house to Mitchell's second floor window. It wasn't midnight like before, but it was definitely past bedtime. Sure enough, Mitchell was in bed. Under the covers, but not asleep.

Twinklebottom tapped on the window.

Mitchell didn't look as excited to see him, but he did smile.

That smile got a little bigger as Twinklebottom jumped up and down on the bed, letting Mitchell know how great he was doing so far, how all the elves were sooo grateful, how they had hope for the first time in years all because of one brave little human moppet.

Total bullshit—Twinklebottom hadn't told his plans to anyone else and, honestly, the conditions weren't *that* bad; all the photos he'd shown were the result of a few quick keystrokes in an AI creator suite. But Mitchell didn't need to know any of that.

Mitchell's smile seemed to falter, though. And it never quite reached his eyes.

Twinklebottom noticed the kid was pretty dirty. Stains all over his hands like he'd been rooting around in dirt and mud.

"Someone hasn't been taking a bath, I see. Pretty Naughty," Twinklebottom said with a teasing grin.

"Yeah. . ."

"And your room is so messy! I bet Mommy asked you to clean it and you said no."

"Not really. . ." Mitchell went silent and stared blankly at his hands.

"Oh. Kay." The kid's aloofness was starting to get annoying. "You're squashing my high a little here, kid."

"Sorry," Mitchell replied. "I don't feel very good. My stomach hurts a little."

Little shit's probably been sent to bed without supper twice now, Twinklebottom thought jubilantly.

"Why don't you take me through what you've done so far, huh? Then we'll see about scrounging up some food for ya? Just keep it quiet so we don't wake your parents."

"Okay."

Mitchell took a breath and started recounting all he'd done to be Naughty. It was in that halting, scattershot way all kids of that age have of telling stories—no chronology, no build, all kinds of doubling back and digressions—but at least he started to come out of his stupor a bit as he talked.

"I did everything I could think of. Mommy always told me not to play with the plants, so I played with the plants. And I ran around a lot. That was fun. I even ran with the knives. Mommy and Daddy both told me never to do that, so I did it. And up and down the stairs. And I turned the TV up real loud. And the screaming."

The kid rattled off a number of picayune transgressions, none of which sounded bad enough to juice the kid's Naughty numbers up so high. Twinklebottom was about to get impatient when Mitchell said:

"Then I found my ropes from my magic kit and then—" His eyes expanded. "Can I just show you? It's downstairs." Without waiting for an answer, he spun on his heels and ran out of the room. *Thumpathumpathumpathump.*

Twinklebottom followed. Before he could stop the kid and remind him to be quiet—last thing he needed was to wake the kid's parents up—he noticed a stretch of rope tied across his bedroom doorway.

Almost looked like a trip wire.

Just beyond, in the hallway, lay a plastic stegosaur toy. The toy was yellow, but the sharp plates lining its back appeared coated in something dark and crusty. Some of the plates were bent, like something heavy had fallen onto the toy from a great height.

Twinklebottom felt a strange rumbling in his gut. Dread.

Mitchell's voice continued, loud and heedless, at the top of the stairs.

"Come on downstairs, I wanna show you!" he called.

Twinklebottom climbed over the rope and hurried down the hall to catch up. . . but then something else caught his eye as he passed the doorway of what appeared to be the largest bedroom. The grownups' room.

He couldn't be sure what he was seeing—he'd have to actually go into the room for a better look—but from this vantage point outside it almost looked like a pair of legs were trussed to the bedframe, with the same kind of rope that had been stretched across the doorframe.

Those legs were very still. Inanimately still. But. . . did he also hear moaning coming from further inside the room? A barely audible voice? The words "Help" and "please?"

"Come *on*, Twinklebottom!" Mitchell urged from the landing, sounding more animated and excited than at any point so far this evening.

Thumpathumpathumpathump down the stairs.

Twinklebottom tore his eyes away from the bedroom and followed. He suddenly didn't want to see anything more. The air was starting to feel very thin. He wished he were back at the North Pole.

Mitchell, meanwhile, was continuing his litany of achieved Naughtiness downstairs. He was rambling about how Mommy had always told him not to sing so loudly inside, so he'd been singing Christmas carols at the top of his lungs, and also he tried to pour milk into his cereal without help and the milk got everywhere, and he'd turned the TV remotes into drumsticks, *parumpapumpum.*

Except Twinklebottom had stopped listening by the time he also reached the living room.

He was too stunned by what he was seeing to even know how to listen anymore.

When he'd first cased this house, he'd seen the family's giant tree. It had been impossible to miss, the way it glowed with lights and sagged with all the ornaments dedicated to Santa.

Most of those ornaments were shattered on the floor now. Fallen from the tree like overripe fruit.

Instead, the tree sagged under new weight. Different kinds of ornaments—conspicuously hung only where a child could reach. Ropes of intestines twined around like tinsel. Other organs, large and small, smeared and speared across the evergreen. A spleen, a gallbladder, a lung, who the fuck knew?

The tree still glowed too. Mitchell hadn't taken down any of the lights. The blood cast the bottom half of the tree into a sick, emergency red.

"Kid. . ." the elf wheezed. "What did you do?"

On one of the branches, he saw the viscous globe of an eyeball dangling from its shredded optic nerve like a traditional bulb. On another, the head of what looked like a cat or a small terrior, with a branch jutting through the base of its skull and out its mouth.

Mitchell stood in the middle of the living room. Only now

did Twinklebottom understand that wasn't just dirt that smeared his pajamas. His hair. "I did what you said! I was as Naughty as I could be!"

Twinklebottom thought he might faint. The periphery of his vision sparkled with dark stars.

He mustn't faint. Not here. He had to get out of here. But he couldn't get his legs to work. He was concentrating too hard on not throwing up, not passing out. He bent down and noticed all the dirty footprints all over the floor.

Mitchell took a step toward him.

"There's just one problem, Twinklebottom."

"Oh, kid," the elf managed to say in between panicked gasps. "You got plenty of problems, all right."

Mitchell took another step closer. "My problem is I tried everything I could that was Naughty, but I'm scared I did it wrong. Because even though I knew I was being Naughty? It all just felt so. . . Nice."

The kid sounded genuinely, almost innocently, conflicted. Twinklebottom looked up in horror to see how close Mitchell now was. And how *huge.*

Before the elf could say anything, though, a knock came from the front door.

Twinklebottom whirled around. "Oh fuck, who's—"

"Be right there!" Mitchell called to whoever was outside. In response, Twinklebottom could hear the giggle of delighted children. Then he remembered the Naughty numbers. Even the other kids on the block had begun to trend downward.

"That's my friends," Mitchell said. "I told them all about what you told me and how they need to be as Naughty as can be. They're here to help me finish with Mommy."

The interruption helped Twinklebottom find his motor skills again. He began to back away. "Hey, that's great, kid. I'll—I'll leave you to it, then."

"But what about my problem?"

Twinklebottom tried to laugh through a throat as dry as year-old gingerbread. "I wouldn't worry about that. You're good. You did good work! I mean, bad work! Naughty work!"

Mitchell advanced, closing the distance between them easily. God, humans were so fucking *big*.

"But is it really Naughty if it feels Nice? Do I need to do something I don't like for it to be *really* bad?"

"Nah, don't sweat that, kiddo, it's all—*ah, fuck*!"

Pain rocketed through his foot. In his backing away, he'd accidentally stepped on a shard of ornament. It tore through his little elf boot and lodged into his flesh, going all the way to the bone. He fell, hard. Without wasting a second, he tried to pull the shard out so he could run.

More knocking on the door. The impatience of children.

Mitchell loomed over him, a huge and imposing colossus.

"Wait a minute," Mitchell said, not to the elf or the kids outside, but to himself. "Maybe, if I want to be *really* Naughty, maybe I need to do something bad to *Christmas*. Because I care about Christmas the most."

"Nah, you aced the test, Mitch, you really don't have to worry about it!" Twinklebottom babbled. His hands were slick with blood and sweat. He couldn't get the damn shard out.

Outside, the kids began singing. Carols, atonal and insane—or maybe the elf's brain just couldn't comprehend anything anymore.

"Yeah," Mitchell continued, piecing it together. "Yeah, maybe if I want to be *really* Naughty. . . what could be Naughtier than doing something to. . ." he found the word waiting for him like a perfectly wrapped present, "a *representative?*"

"No! No, kid, wait—!"

Mitchell's hand easily wrapped around Twinklebottom's head, muffling the elf's screams. He scooped the squirming elf up and went to answer the door, joining in the carols with all the joy and gusto of a child during the most magical time of the year.

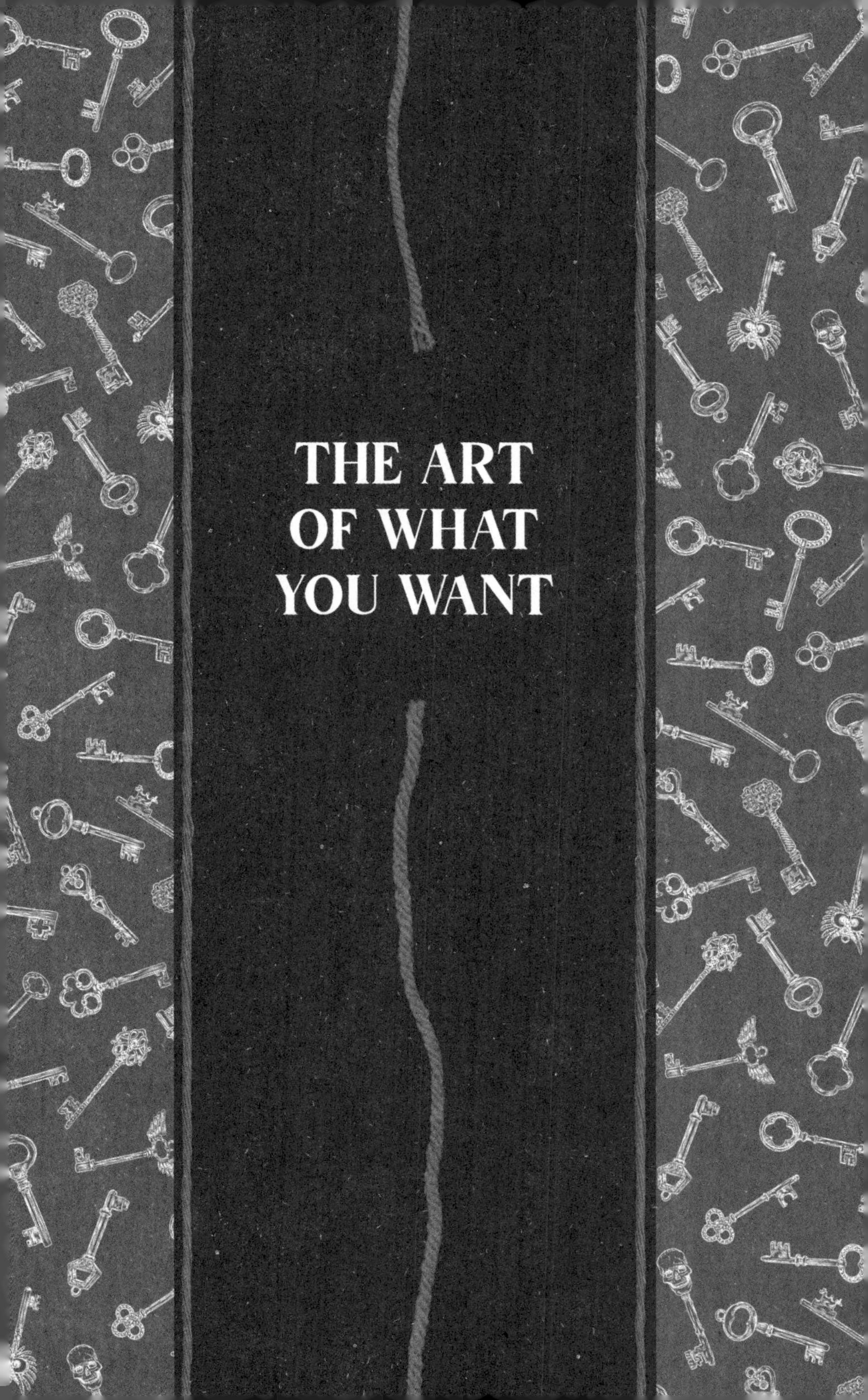
THE ART
OF WHAT
YOU WANT

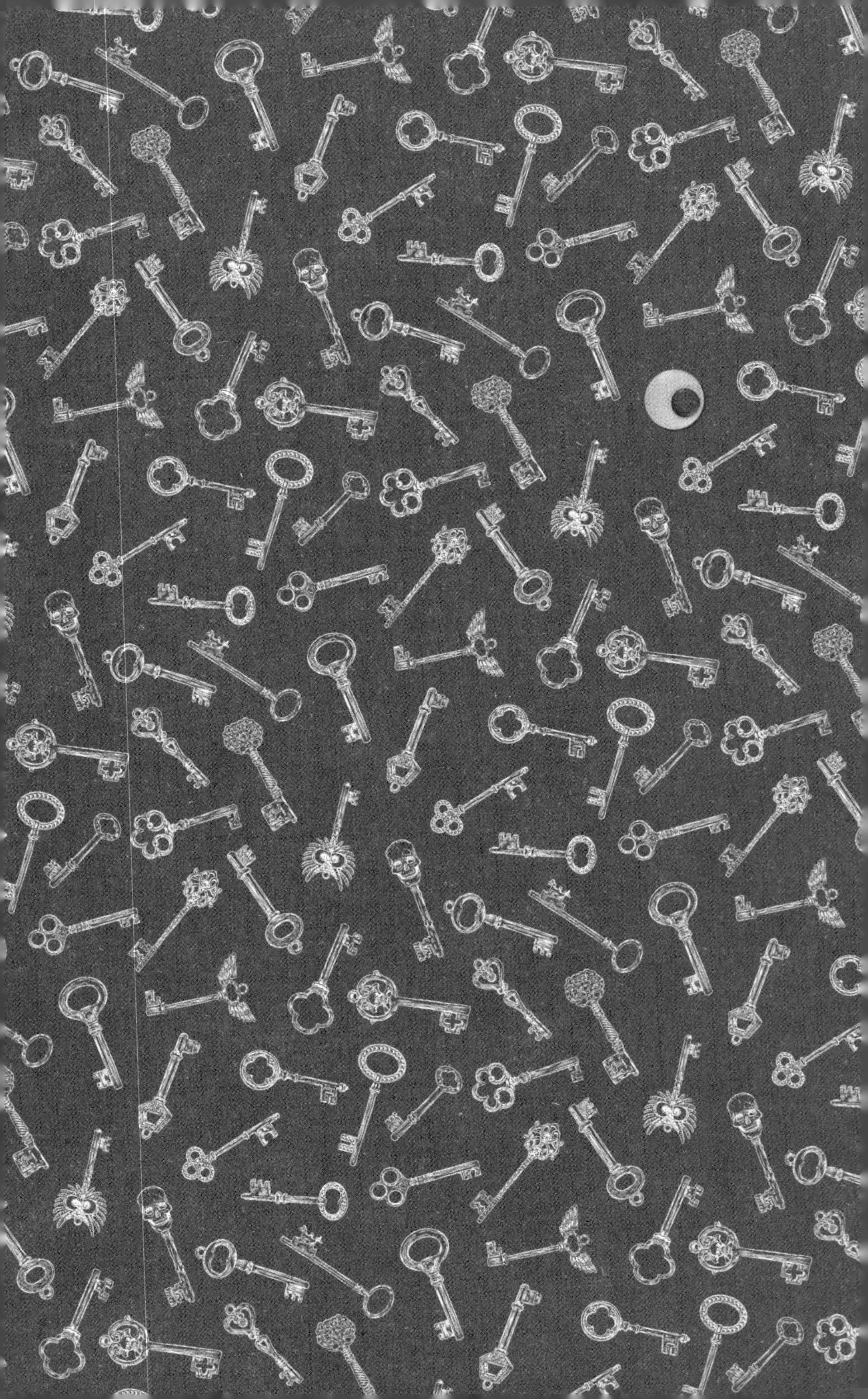

THE ART OF WHAT YOU WANT

The businessman and the doctor sit in the doctor's private office deep in the bowels of the massive new medical complex.

"Holeeeeeeeeeee shit," the businessman says. He's barely in his forties, but comfort and success have kept the years from his face, making him look more like the homecoming king he once was than the adult he currently is. But there's an edge in his eyes all the same. Broken glass behind the poster boy perfection that no amount of money can sweep up. He's sitting in a leather chair facing the doctor's shining, cherry oak desk. "Wow, wow, wow."

This is not a medical examination. This is not a room for such things. This is a room for meetings, for dealings.

It's a room for business.

The doctor blushes and raises a rocks glass half-filled (or half-empty, depending on your view of things) with amber liquor worth more than the monthly income of the average American.

"The exciting world of hospital administration!" she exclaims. She's older. Well put together, but her pampering has come later in life, after hard-fought battles, tough decisions, bare-knuckle brawls, and, of course, so much downward pressure.

The businessman meets her toast with his own similarly half-filled—or half-empty–glass.

"And how many doctors under you now?"

"Seven trauma teams, six of the world's top plastic surgeons, and more specialists than we can afford. Plus the psych ward which takes up most of the east wing."

"Look at you," the businessman says. "If I had a hat—" He makes a doffing gesture.

"Aw, you should buy yourself a hat! Life is short! Use those whiz kid tech bucks for something fun."

"Yeah. Right. . ."

A cloud crosses the businessman's face and for the first time the doctor notices how deep-set his eyes have become.

"Uh-oh." The doctor's brow furrows. "Looks like you have something to say."

He shrugs. "I've always got something to say."

"Is it about why you wanted to see me?"

"I mean, I wanted to see my favorite doc in her fancy new digs, but. . ." He stares into his glass. "Are you okay to, um, talk shop a little?"

"Harris. Do I really need to remind you about how your patronage changed my life? I wouldn't be in these new digs without you. For you, I'm always okay to 'Talk. Shop.'"

Her lips form enticing shapes. Her plosives pop and snap.

But he isn't enticed. He seems troubled. Shaken.

"Doctor/patient?" he asks.

"Doctor/patient."

He swallows another mouthful of luxurious, silken liquor.

"I think I'm going crazy." Then he corrects himself. "Gone. I think I've gone crazy."

The doctor leans forward. She is a friend, but she is also a doctor.

"I'm listening."

The businessman takes a deep breath and tells her.

"So. . . a couple weeks ago. . ."

Harris sat at his marble counter top. He was eating cereal—cereal was mostly all he was up for eating these days. He'd never been one for cooking, and now? The kitchen was too big. A foreign country where he didn't speak the language.

He hadn't shaved or showered in quite some time either.

He was in a daze—so much so that he didn't even jump when his wife, Emily, came into the room.

She moved with some speed.

"Don't forget," she said, going through the gestures of her Running Out the Door ritual, "your suit needs to be picked up. And we need a refill for the seltzer thingy. I love you more than bunches."

She kissed him on the head and a few seconds later the front door closed behind her.

Harris sat frozen, halfway through bringing a spoonful of cereal to his lips.

There was no noise for a very long time. Then, the spoon dropped from his numb fingers and crashed loudly into the bowl.

The doctor stares at the businessman. She doesn't want to admit that she doesn't understand, so she runs what he said back again in her mind several times. She comes up with nothing.

"Harris," she says at last. "Here's where you tell me what I'm—"

She's going to say *missing*, but before that word can emerge, the businessman says:

"My wife died six months ago. Car crash."

"Oh." The doctor's mouth dries up in a flash.

"Yeah."

"Harris, I'm so. . . How did I not. . . ?"

He waves a dismissive hand. "Please. We haven't seen each other in. . . We've both been busy." He takes another sip. "Anyway. The things she said? About my suit and the seltzer thingy? Those were the last things she said to me the day she died. She got into one of her cars and. . . and later that night there was an accident. A bad one. Couldn't even identify the body visually; they had to use her dental. . ." Saying it all out loud overwhelms him for a moment. He quickly shakes it off. Clears his throat, finishes his drink. The doctor seamlessly provides a refill.

He continues. "I know what you're thinking. To people of our, heh, economic vantage point, spouses are usually the obstacle. Right? It's like most rich assholes stay married just to have someone to scheme around. Not me. I *loved* her. I loved her so damn much. And I know it wasn't the easiest marriage, she had to put up with a lot. My working all the time. And my temper. I knew she wasn't always happy. Hell, I'm pretty sure she was going to leave me sooner or later. But I would have done anything to keep her. She. . . she was the apogee."

"Good word," the doctor says, her heart breaking for her friend.

"Yeah. And then I lost her anyway." He's back to staring into his drink again.

"Wait, but you said this thing in the kitchen. . . with your wife. . . was a couple weeks ago. How—if she died *six months ago*—?"

His eyes meet hers–sparkling with, what, sarcasm? Dark humor? Mania?

"Weird, right? The next morning, I thought maybe I'd imagined it, you know? I mean, I had *just* reached that stage of grief where the waters were ebbing a little. It's like you're buried up to your neck in sand with the tide crashing in on you, but it'd finally started to recede, I could grab a gulp of air and maybe—"

"Don't forget," his dead wife said again, "your suit needs to be picked up. And we need a refill for the seltzer thingy. I love you more than bunches."

Harris was back at his marble counter top. He'd poured himself an identical bowl of cereal. He was wearing the same set of dirty pajamas. The only difference was this time he was shaking too badly with anticipation to hold a spoon. He'd been waiting to see if she'd show up.

When she kissed him on the head he jumped as if electrocuted.

She giggled and continued for the door.

"What are you doing?" He heard himself asking. "Emily? Are you really—?"

She giggled again and, with an all-too-familiar slam, the door closed and she was gone.

It took Harris a few moments to find his legs again. He ran out the door, but. . . nothing. No sign of her (other than all the signs he hadn't yet removed in his newfound position as widower).

Until the next morning, when she came back again at the exact same time.

"Don't forget your suit needs to be picked up. And we need a refill for the seltzer thingy. I love you more than bunches."

She kissed him on the head and disappeared.

And then the next morning.

"Don't forget your suit needs to be picked up. And we need a refill for the seltzer thingy. I love you more than bunches."

She kissed him on the head and disappeared.

And then the next morning.

And then the next morning.

And then—

"You get it," the businessman tells the doctor.

She's aghast. Personally, she doesn't believe in hauntings or spirits, but Harris would never lie to her. "How long did this go on?"

"About five or six days before I couldn't go downstairs anymore. I got too unnerved, so I started hiding upstairs to avoid her." He swallows. The doctor can hear his throat click even from where she's sitting. "And that's when the voicemails started."

"Harris." The doctor puts a hand flat on her desk, effectively pressing pause on the proceedings. "Do you want me to get a team of paranormal investigators together? I know people who know people who are, I mean, they're as reputable as they *can* be in that field, but—"

"Just listen." He gets up and pours himself another drink. He tops off the doctor's as well. A sly smile has crossed his lips. "I'm not even close to done."

"What kind of voicemails? Here, have another drink." Once Harris's glass was fully filled, Terry asked again, "What kind of voicemails?"

They were standing out on Terry's back patio. During the day, there were mountains all around—gorgeous in the light—but now, they were wrapped in such an all-consuming nighttime nothingness that the two men might as well have been floating in the middle of a midnight ocean.

Terry was small and wiry, with a growing hump in his shoulders from bending over a computer keyboard for too long. He was clearly the grown-up version of what some would've called an indoor kid, so his mansion, with its large, luxurious outdoor space, was an awkward fit. But most things fit awkwardly on Terry.

Harris gulped down his drink, then pulled out his phone. He conjured forth his voicemail and pressed play. A woman's voice—Emily's voice—ghostly, barely audible through static, intoned in an almost robotic babble:

"Babe? Babe? It's getting late. I'm worried. Just let me know you're coming home. Babe? Babe? It's getting late. I'm worried. Just let me know you're coming home. Babe? Babe? It's getting late. I'm worried. Just let me know you're coming home. Babe? B—"

Harris turned it off, unable to stand anymore. He said in a hoarse voice, "And there are plenty more where that came from."

It was a warm night but Terry shivered. "Fuck me in the dickhole. . ." he muttered.

"That's what I was texting her."

"Wait. 'Fuck me in the—?'"

"No. 'It's getting late, I'm worried.' The night she died, I kept texting her. Texting and calling, wondering why she wasn't answering. I didn't know I was. . . texting her corpse." The floodgates broke. Harris began to weep. "I don't, fuck, I don't, just tell me you hear it, please, I need to know I'm not—"

Terry's arms shot out, wrapping around Harris, and pulled him close in a desperate hug. It was a sudden and surprising move, and resulted in the spilling of both their drinks.

"I hear it, too," Terry said. "It's okay. I hear it, too."

They stood that way for several moments. Terry, despite being a year older than Harris, was at least a head shorter, with none of Harris's natural athleticism, so it looked like Terry was some vulnerable animal, clinging to a larger, stronger one for support. But it was Harris who was shaking.

At last, the two friends separated. Harris gave Terry a playful shove.

"'It's okay.' Right. You fucking idiot." He gave a tired laugh that turned into a sigh. "God. Why is this happening?"

Terry set to refilling both their drinks.

"My fucking goosebumps have goosebumps. Shit." Suddenly, Terry screamed, his voice echoing into the mountains. "SHIIIIIT!" His face screwed up in rage. He threw one of the glasses he was holding over the edge of his balcony and into the nothingness beyond. "Someone's fucking with you!" he exclaimed to Harris. Then he blanched, looking back in the direction of his wayward glass. "Crap, I hope that doesn't land on anybody."

Harris hadn't even noticed. He was processing.

"Somebody's what?"

"Fucking with you, Harris! Gotta be!"

Terry pushed his big, tortoise shell, Buddy Holly glasses further up his nose. It was a quintessentially Terry gesture. Even with his riches his eyesight was a lost cause.

"Why?" Harris stammered. "How?"

Terry shrugged. "You can ghost a cellphone easy. Whip up a deepfake in two minutes."

"But when she kissed me. . . I felt *her, Terry. I—"*

"Maybe they hired a lookalike?"

"A lookalike?"

"Yeah, y'know, someone who looks like—"

"I know what a lookalike is. But why? Why would anyone—"

"I don't know! But you're staying with me and Barb." Harris opened his mouth to argue. "Nuh-uh. Don't give me any of your alpha male, lone wolf drippyshit, you're staying with us, we're gonna figure out what the fuck is going on. And hey—" His voice dropped to a mock-conspiratorial low. "While you're here we can work on our other *li'l problem, too. Deal?" He held out his hand. "Deal, twatwaddle?"*

Harris sighed. It was the easiest way to take the edge off of the tears that were welling up behind his eyes.

"Do you have any idea how much I hate the idea of coming to you for help, chode turnip?"

Terry gave him a big grin. "I can only imagine, douchecanoe."

"So, this is how fucked I am."

He reached out and shook Terry's hand.

The two men looked into each other's eyes with barely-concealed love and couldn't help but laugh.

"Did it help?" the doctor asks. "Staying with him?"

The businessman nods. "I slept for the first time in fucking millennia. Did you ever meet Terry?"

"Once, I think? At a party?"

"Yeah, he didn't socialize much. Not a lot of people could stand him, honestly. We were the only people who ever hung out with him, Emily and I. Oh, and Barb, his wife. He was like cilantro, you know? Not for everybody." The doctor laughs. The businessman smiles wistfully. "Like, that stupid cursing thing he did? It was like witnessing an alien's approximation of how people—men—interacted. He just didn't know any better. But once you got to love him, you were hooked."

"You both started Polypheme together, right?"

The businessman nods. "He wrote the codes and I got other people to care. Hey, do you mind if—?" He gestures to the drink cart.

Now it's the doctor's turn to smile. "You have to ask for permission now?"

The businessman pours another. Returning to the subject of his friend, he says, "I'd say he's like a brother, but most brothers I know hate each other." Then he pauses. "I didn't realize what I'd wind up doing to him and his wife."

He takes a small sip. Sits back down. "Anyway. It was good timing for me to stay with Terry for another reason, too. Polypheme was in the middle of a big fucking. . ." He gives an uncharacteristically disinterested shrug. "We were in trouble. It actually started brewing like right after this ghost shit began. Wonderful timing. I won't bog you down with the details; basically, there was a startup that was about to make us totally obsolete. They had all the power, but we didn't think they *knew* they had all the power, so we had to figure out how to buy them out without spilling how fucked we were. Honestly, it's the sort of thing I'm usually great at. Terry kept trying to get me to focus on the problem, but. . . well, I just couldn't concentrate. I kept thinking about her. So, a couple days later, I snuck back to my house."

"Oh, Harris."

"I had to get a few things. I mean, I didn't *have* to, but. . ."

He's silent for a long moment. The doctor is about to speak when he says:

"It's a big house, you know. Emily picked it out. I always thought it was too big. But you know that feeling when you're all alone in a big place?"

The doctor nods.

"I didn't have that. It *definitively* felt like someone was in there with me. Every creak, every shift of the house. At one point I even coulda sworn I heard a door slam and footsteps running away. I ran after the sound, but. . . nothing. Then my phone rang."

The doctor feels her stomach drop a little. "Who was it?"

He chuckles. "It wasn't the first time she'd, uh, 'called' since this all started, but, lemme tell you, you never get used to a phone call from your dead wife. I was too scared to answer. I let it go to voicemail and. . ."

He pulls up another sound file on his phone. The static is very loud, but certain words are unmistakable.

"Don't. . . Don't. . . Darling. . . Get away. . ."

He looks at the doctor with wide, avid eyes.

"New words," he says. "She was saying something *new* to me. That had to mean something, right? Here I was, in our house, and she was trying to say something *new* to me, something she hadn't. . . That's when I realized what I had to do."

Terry gaped at him, panic blazing behind his thick glasses.

"Waitwaitwait, what *are you saying?"*

Harris stood there in the doorway, holding his hastily packed duffel. "Terry. I love you, but—"

"No, don't do this, you fucking—"

"I hereby resign my position as President of Polypheme Technologies and appoint Executive Vice President Terence Elbrick as my successor. You're gonna have to handle the buyout and negotiations on your own, okay? I'm going to focus on my wife for a change."

"I'm sure that went over well," the doctor says.

The businessman sits back. "There was some crying. Some begging. A lot of cursing. 'I can't do this without you, Harris. I can't talk to people like you can, Harris. Please, don't do this, not yet.'"

"'Not yet,'" the doctor echoes curiously, and for a few moments all is silent again.

"You know what business is?" the businessman asks at last. "You'll read all kinds of books trying to phrase it in all kinds of profound ways, but it's pretty simple when you get down to it. All business really is, is the art of knowing what you want. That's it. Needs are easy. We all *need* the same shit. Figure out what you fucking *want*. And go from there."

She nods, considering this.

"And what did you want?"

"To see her again."

"Did you?"

"That next morning, right on time, I went down to my kitchen, wearing the same pajamas, poured myself the same bowl of cereal, and waited for her."

More silence unspools.

"I waited all day. She never appeared. The next morning, same thing. I mean, what the hell, right? First, it was like clockwork, and now I was starting to wonder if I'd imagined it all. Maybe it was all in my fucking head. Until that night."

He hands the doctor his phone.

The doctor holds back a gasp as she flips through the photos and videos staring back at her. She's no stranger to death and gore, viscera, skin pebbled by blood and trauma, crushed into unrecognizable shapes. But she also knew the businessman's wife socially, and seeing her this way, twisted, rubbed raw by the road and broken metal, brutalized, even splayed out on what appeared to be the autopsy table, is deeply upsetting.

More sound files, too. A deranged and furious voice shrieking through the phone.

"*BABE, BABE IT'S GETTING LATE I'M WORRIED JUST LET ME KNOW YOU'RE COMING HOME—COLD—YOUR FAULT—BABE, BABE IT'S GETTING LATE I'M WORRIED JUST LET ME KNOW YOU'RE COMING HOME—YOUR FUCKING FAULT*"

"And then," the businessman says calmly, "the next morning, there she was again. Cheery as fucking pie. 'Don't forget your suit needs to be picked up. And we need a refill for the seltzer thingy. I love you more than bunches.'"

"Jesus. . ."

"It went on like that for, I don't know, a couple days at least. Horrors all night, then seeing her in the morning like nothing had happened. 'Don't forget, your suit needs to be picked up. . .' It was the closest I'd ever truly felt to absolute, pure madness in my life. Up to that point, at least."

"Harris," the doctor begins.

"Sorry, I can tell you're getting antsy, doc."

"No—"

"Hey, in vliquor veritas, right? Lemme skip to the good stuff."

Harris was curled up on the kitchen floor. The sun was down and he was waiting for the deluge of nightmares to begin.

Only this time, there weren't images and videos and voicemails stampeding into his phone. This time, there was a slurred voice calling from outside the unlocked front door.

"Yello?!"

Harris sat up as Terry danced his way into the room.

"Sup, cuntflap!" Terry spread his arms wide, sloshing a bit from the bottle of Veuve he carried. "Just me, no ghost. Ha!"

"God. Terry. Give me that."

Harris grabbed the bottle, drank deeply.

"Atta baby," Terry cooed. "Howya been, Hairybutt?" Harris shook his head. "Did it—I'm just guessing here, but—did it get worse? Your whole haunted house situation?" Harris nodded. "Yeah. Had a feeling. That's what you get!"

Harris blinked. "What?"

Terry shook his head, visibly changing the subject. He took the bottle back.

"Hey! We're celebrating!"

"Celebrating?"

"We bought 'em out! Polypheme's saved!"

"We did?"

Terry began to wheel about the room.

"GodDAMN I never knew how much fucking fun that could be! I gotta, can I confess something? I know I'm fucking wasted but, man, I was so pissed at you the other day, I mean, piiiiiiiiiiiiissssed. And I, I wannid to. . . I wannid to come here and I wannnid to say. . . I'm sorry." He dropped to his knees in front of Harris.

"You don't have to apologize, Terry—"

"No, no, it wasn't right of me to get so mad at you, I shoulda anticipated that, you been through a lot lately, you know? Course you know."

"Yeah."

"Yeah. So it was wrong of me to get all grrrrr and I'm sorry." He pointed at Harris, eyes gleaming. "I mean, you did put me in the cuntshitting hot seat like that, man! But, BUT!" He sprang to his feet with surprising dexterity, threw a not-too-high karate kick in

the air. "I kicked its ass! All by myself! I was fucking inspiring! Ha-CHOW!" Another kick, sloppier than the first.

"That's great, Terry—"

"Yeah, I been learning a lot about myself lately, you know? I'm fucking smart, man, I'm fucking, fucking quicker'n anybody, than you or me or anybody, ever gave me credit for. I mean, here I was thinking if Harris lost his mind, we could just sell the company, and she and me could go live on an island—but then that startup almost fucked everything up and I was like 'Oh shit!' I got real scared! But I didn't need to be scared! I can do anything! I don't need to hide behind a fucking computer, I can, hahaha, I can seal the deal and I can get the girl! She's been telling me that for years I shoulda listened, 'Oh, Terence I fell in love with you cuz you're bettern' him and you don't even know it' and—"

"Barb?" Harris asked. His voice had become cold.

"Huh?"

"Barb said that?"

A beat. Terry put on an ill-fitting smile.

"Yeah, me and. . . me and Barb. We realized we still love each other, it's nice."

"That's wonderful."

"Doesn't matter, doesn't matter, AHHHFuck, I'm totally babbling aren't I! Why am I babbling? You know what I haven't eaten yet, that's my problem, that was dumb. Ignore me. I'm gonna go get some Arby's or some shit and you got your little ghost to figure out! Right?"

"Yeah."

"You're my best friend in the world, titwhistle. You know that? I always wannid to be you. And, uuuuunnggh, I fucked that deal in the backhole! WHOO!"

Terry headed to the door, then stopped to drink the rest of his bottle of champagne.

"Oh, hey. Don't forget to refill that seltzer thingy. Am I right? Ha! Love you more than bunches!"

He blew a kiss and left Harris sitting there.

Silence.

Just the sound of ice snapping in glasses.

Then the businessman speaks.

"Here's another thing about business. Hunches are everything. Hunches. . . and acting fast." He took a small sip. "That next morning, I waited for my lovely little ghost to appear and I approached the situation like I would any other kind of deal. Slowly. Coldly. Knowing what I want."

Harris was still on the floor when his dead wife visited him the next morning. His hands were folded neatly in his lap.

"Don't forget your suit needs to be picked up," she said. "And we need a refill for the seltzer thingy. I love you more than—"

"Emily," Harris said flatly. "Wait."

She had just bent down to kiss his head—that repetitive gesture that was so maddeningly tactile. All this time, he'd never thought to touch her in response It had been too jarring, too close to blasphemy.

But this time, before she got too far away, Harris pulled the massive kitchen knife from his lap and ran its sharp edge across the ghost's slender ankle, opening her Achilles tendon up in a wide-mouthed grin.

The ghost went down, smacking the tile floor, screaming. Blood—very real, very alive blood—began to gutter from the wound.

"It's a big day today," Harris continued, standing. "You get into

a car crash today. Make sure you caffeinate."

As was usually the case, there was a pot of hot coffee simmering in the percolator on the counter. Harris grabbed the pot and poured scalding liquid all over her neck. The supposed dead woman shrieked in agony.

"Stop! Stop! Harris! Please! I can explain! Just wait!"

"Wow. You stay in character," Harris said, "I'll give you that." He grabbed another item from the kitchen counter and approached her.

She was on her stomach, crawling away from him.

"I'll also give you this," he said. "You were always great at reminders."

He straddled her back and stuffed the brand-new CO_2 *cartridge for their SodaStream 'seltzer thingy' into her mouth. Then he proceeded to slam her face into the floor. It took a few whacks before the cartridge exploded, taking most of her head with it.*

The doctor's hand is shaking. She puts the mostly-empty glass down on her desk.

"My god. . ." she breathes. "So Emily and Terry were scheming around *you*? How long do you think they'd been togeth—"

"*NO*."

The businessman slams the desk in front of him. He leans forward, eyes blazing, and the doctor wonders for the first time whether, if she screams for help, anyone would be able to hear her in this office.

"No," he repeats. "My wife died in a car crash. She died *months ago*. That was a lookalike. Do you understand?"

The doctor manages a weak nod.

The businessman raps his knuckles on the desk and gives a

rather shrill laugh. "But, ha! You're a smart cookie, Doctor. That's why you get those big doctor bucks. My buddy Terry? *He's* a little schemer, for sure! So I made a quick call. I said, 'Hey. Terry. You and Barb should come over. I need to talk to you both. Shit. Bucket.'"

"And then what did you do?" The doctor asks in a whisper.

"Just business, baby." He tips his glass into his mouth and crunches on a piece of ice. "I knew what I wanted. . . and I asked for it."

"You're right, Harris." Large, unquestionably sincere tears spilled down Terry's cheeks as he spoke. "It had been my plan all along to make you think you were going crazy. I wanted you to resign from Polypheme, leaving it all to me, but only after *you saved the company one last time. Then I was going to sell it away. I always resented you. I cannot tell you how sorry I am."*

"You got him to confess all that?" the doctor asks.

"Sure. Only. . . maybe not so articulately."

The businessman reaches into his jacket pocket and pulls out a fistful of broken, bloody teeth. He lets them rain onto the doctor's desk one by one by one.

"Harris." She straightens in her chair. "Professional opinion?"

"Please." He leans back into his.

"You're not crazy. Insane maybe. But not crazy."

He considers this. Then:

"Oh! I almost forgot. I also have this."

He reaches under his chair for his briefcase. Unclasps it. Removes a small, brown paper bag. The bottom of the bag is dark and sopping wet. He plops the bag on the middle of her desk blotter.

She peers into it.

"I'm looking at severed male genitalia," she reports. "Oh, Harris, I hope this isn't yours."

Harris chuckles. He stands, smoothing and adjusting his clothes with automatic grace.

"Terry is in the trunk of my car right now, Doc. I have with me papers that will transfer all of my assets and net worth to this hospital. All of it. And in exchange, here's what I want. I want him stabilized. I want his bones broken and shaved down (and I have plenty of photos for reference). I want *that* area—" he gestures to the paper bag "—redesigned. I want just the right amount of his brain taken out so that he doesn't fight." He pauses for a half-second, appearing to remember something. "Oh, I killed his wife, Barb, too, so that's gotta get taken care of. And lastly, I want a private room. Here. In your beautiful new psych ward. I want to voluntarily commit myself."

She stares at him in horror, all color leeched from her face. "Harris. . ." But she can't think of anything safe to say, and knows her voice will tremble.

"I loved them both, you know. Terry and Emily. I know I wasn't perfect, but. . . I could've lost everything if I'd still had them." His eyes ice over. "I don't like being fucked with, though. I don't like being lied to. I don't like not being in on the joke. And you know what they were most wrong about? Doc, do you know?"

"No."

"Being visited by my dead wife like that was pretty fucking terrifying. But after the initial shock wore off? *They were wrong if they thought I ever wanted it to stop.*"

The businessman puts on a record in his new home. Soft jazz fills the room.

It's a small home—smaller than any place he's lived in since he became a successful businessman—but God does it feel *right*. Even the cushions on the walls are as cozy as a hug. And they're not without a certain minimalist chicness.

He's wearing a blue jumpsuit, as soft as the music. Simple, elegant. Similarly soft white shoes.

He pours himself a glass of amber liquor from a crystal tumbler. Not every tenant of this facility gets these kinds of accoutrements, but he's always been talented at negotiating.

"Oh no!" He pauses mid-pour and calls out to the other room. "Babe! I just realized something! Somebody should call the dry cleaners and tell them they can keep my suit! Ha! I've gotta feeling we'll be staying in a lot, you know?"

His wife comes into the room. Shuffles, more like.

She's wearing one of his favorite cocktail dresses. Leopard print. Its colors are striking in the muted tones around them.

Her face is swathed in bandages. It will take a while before the reconstructive surgeries heal into something more palatable. There's still some blood seeping through the dress, between her legs, too. He's been a little neglectful when it comes to bandaging up that area. It's hard to be patient sometimes. The businessman thinks this and laughs because, he has to admit, it's something of a pun nowadays.

"God, you look good," he tells her. And despite everything, he means it. It's perhaps a little strange to see her now having to wear tortoise shell, Buddy Holly glasses all the time but he doesn't mind. They—and the eyes behind them—remind him of someone else he loved, too. "This is everything I ever wanted." He takes an appreciative sip. "The apogee."

He sits in the armchair by the record player and pulls his wife onto his lap. A pained moan floats out from the bandaged face.

"Ooo!" he exclaims. "Still sore? Don't worry, my love. You'll be all healed up soon. And then?" He gives a lustful chuckle. "Back to business."

He begins kissing her neck. Through her glasses, she stares off into nowhere.

"I can wait because I know what I want," the businessman whispers into her hair. The kisses continue. Soft. Tender.

"I just want you. I just want you. I just want you. I just want you. I just want you."

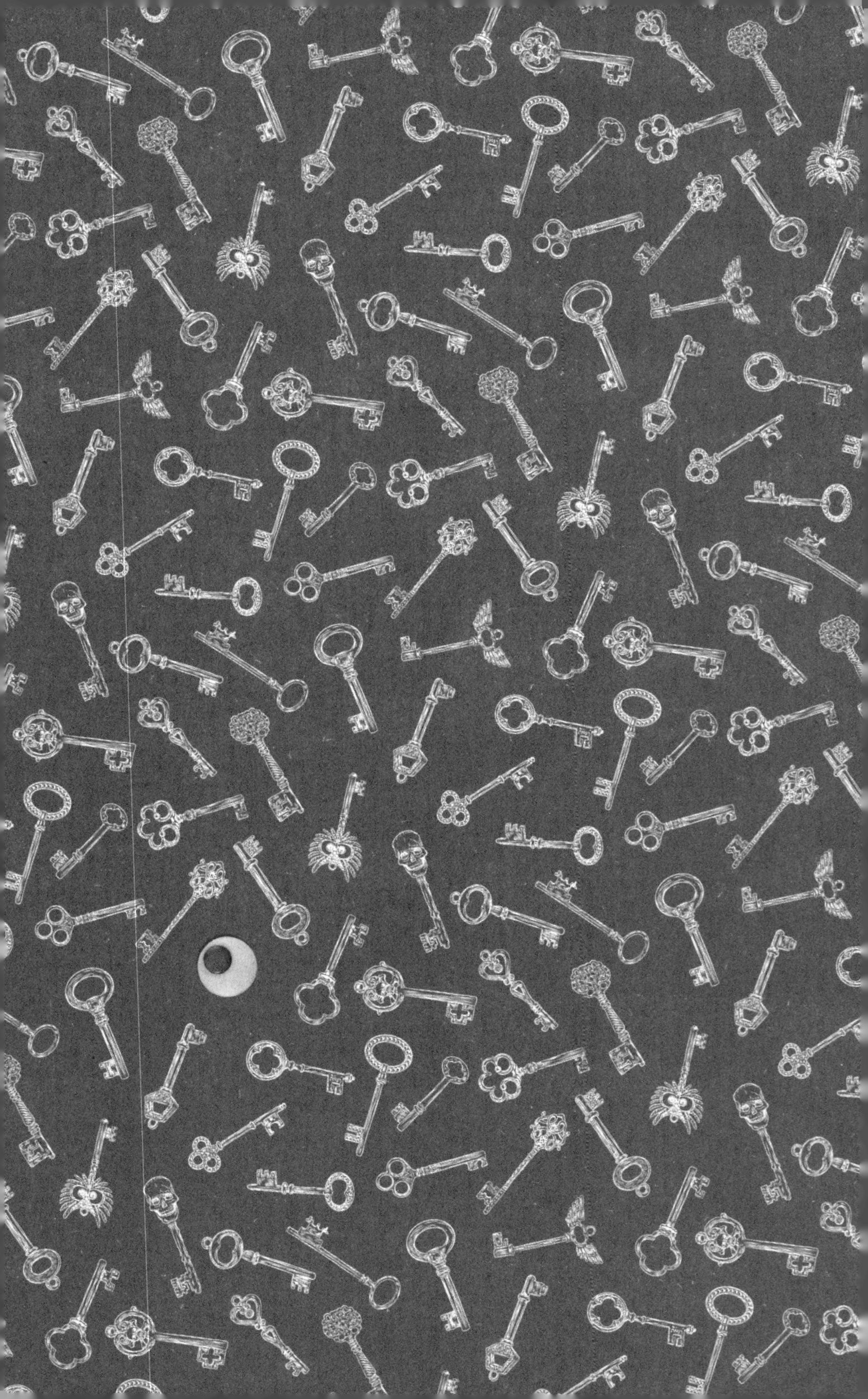

THE
LUNAR
ECLIPSE

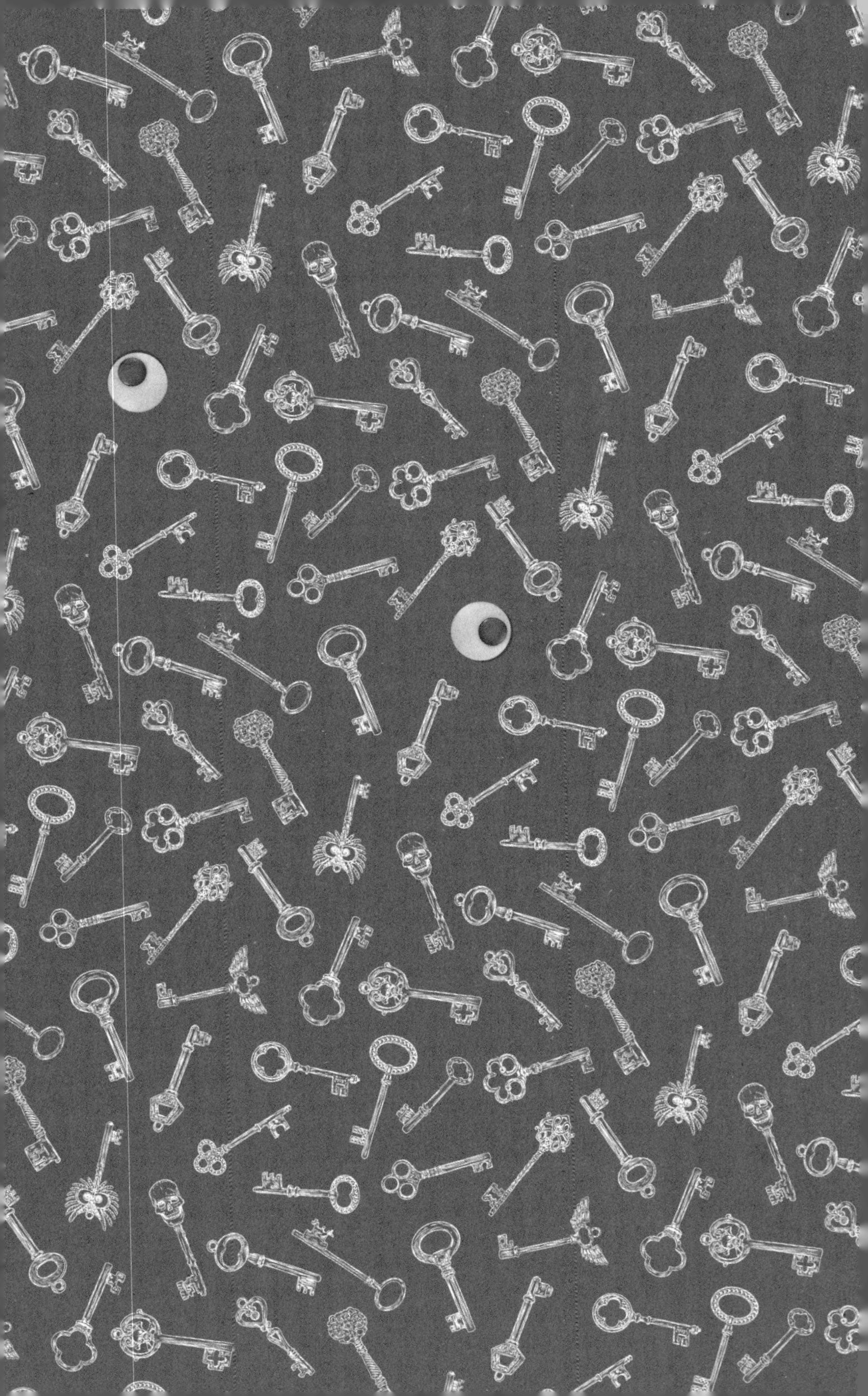

THE LUNAR ECLIPSE

"It was a joke, more or less. He had to have known that."

This is the last thought that crosses her mind. It was a joke, more or less. He had to have known that.

How absurd that this is what she thinks. But it is. There's no stopping that fact, any more than there is stopping a dead tree from being brown. Water from being wet. A chinchilla from not being a typewriter.

It is night.

They first met when they were seven years old. This is the way many old stories begin, with meeting as children. It's a shorthand for a journey beginning in innocence. This journey begins in innocence. Most things do. We don't need to think about the exceptions for this particular journey.

She is standing outside, alone. Not then. Now.

She is standing outside, alone, and it is night.

When they met, when they were seven (this is the Then-world now, not Now), they behaved the way most children do. They hated *each other. . . then got distracted by some new object or emotion, and, within minutes of fomenting that hate, latched onto the other with hunger. Children view other children the way dogs view other dogs. The way survivors view other survivors.*

Competition. . . and confirmation.

And innocence is nothing if not mercurial.

This is because innocence is simply experience that hasn't made up its mind yet.

She doesn't know why she's standing out here. Outside, alone, at night. It is cold and it is eerie. Some idea or other brought her out here. A whimsical remembrance of an eider-thought, a threadbare-cotton-thought, an. . . oh, right, an eclipse.

Tonight is the lunar eclipse.

Tonight is the night the moon gets bashful.

After seven, they floated in and out of each other's lives. Sometimes they were featured players, other times no more than an extra. It wasn't until their teens that their focus on the other reestablished itself.

When their innocence began to make up its mind. . .

(Back in the Now-world, she thinks momentarily of her husband. And of her children, now fully grown. Those closest to her had known of this boy from her past, this boy who had defined so many things. . . but the depth of her passion was a well-guarded secret. She didn't want those in her Now-world resenting this Then-boy for getting there first. For being the Definition. Sometimes, when we are not the Definition, we are filled with resentment. We do this even if we know we are the *Embodiment*—a station far more desirable to be held, all things considered. We envy the Definition. We are jealous creatures.)

They were together from their teens through their mid-twenties. They lived together and played at the idea of marriage, of starting a family. But it wasn't to be. Maybe their shared history and childhood romance put too much pressure on the relationship to succeed, to be a perfect story? Or maybe it was just entropy. Acrimony. It can build up in a relationship the way lactic acid builds up in an overworked muscle. It's not personal, not always. . . but it still hurts. And no matter how beneficial it may have been at the start, the exercise must come to an end.

Back to the Now-world. . .

Any thought of her husband has come and gone. This is unfair to him, to narratively shortchange him like this. He made an impact on her life too, after all. He gave her her children. Her identity as a grown-up.

But he is not the point tonight.

Tonight, she looks up at the sky and remembers.

She remembers

how she moved on. How she lived her life. How she added to her definitions of Love and Motion—but how, if she was REALLY being honest with herself, she could never quite change their root. Their morpheme. The definition of the Definition.

And when she had learned of her love's death (through Facebook) she was well into middle age.

The news was devastating, but in a distinctly quiet way.

She hadn't seen or spoken to this boy in decades, so nothing in her life had been actively changed by this newly compounded absence. . . but everything felt changed.

Green was still green but now it was green.

Molecule for molecule, the world was still there. But the flavor of the word molecule had changed.

When a possibility dies, it does not leave a body. . . but it does leave a smell.

Smell and memory. . .

Did you know that when a person permanently loses their sense of smell, their risk for suicide goes up exponentially compared to the loss of any other sense? It's true. This isn't just because, for instance, food will taste forever different now. It's because you lose access to so many memories.

THE LUNAR ECLIPSE

Smell and memory. A beautiful relationship.

She can remembersmell a night equally as cold and dark as tonight. . .

They were in their early twenties, at the apex of their optimism, while their innocence quietly gathered the facts. . .

Lavender and creosote.
That particular ice crisp scent of autumn chill.

They were in their early twenties. . . and there was a lunar eclipse. They stayed up til three in the morning to see it.

And, as they watched, he said, "You know, I just realized something. The moon is like you."

Oh, yeah? she asked, not sure if she should prepare to be insulted or if this would be a compliment made sweeter by subterfuge.

"Yeah," he said. "She's got no problem being the center of attention, but every now and then, she gets a little bashful. And that just makes you love her all the more."

Ohhh, this made her feel warm, blanket-on-a-stormy-day-warm, and she gripped his hand, as if the loveliness of his words might enrage some jealous god and she'd have to hold him down to keep him from being whisked away in punishment.

"You know, the next one won't be for another fifty years," he said.

Pssh. Lunar eclipses happen all the time.

"Yeah, but not like this," he said. "This one's special."

And he was right. This one was *special. The moon was red.*

Tonight, the moon is red. Fifty years later, that same moon. Blushing, as if remembering some deliciously scandalous secret.

And she is outside, alone, remembering, as well: she was *holding his hand, and she brought it to her mouth to kiss.*

Fifty years, huh? Let's make a promise.

(And he laughed at this, patient but mocking, and she bit his hand in reprimand.)

I'm serious. *Let's make a promise. No matter where we are, no matter what happens, let's be together for the next one.*

"What could happen?" he asked.

She watched the moon and didn't answer.

Now she is an old woman. Which is to say, she is still that twenty-year-old, but her body has, like all bodies, made her mind promises and then broken them. It has lied to her. Bodies are the worst, cruelest liars. And they make up their minds without having all the facts.

And the moon is red. Slowly hiding behind an upheld palm, as if needing privacy for just a moment.

And when she hears footsteps behind her, she is filled with fear. Fear of the unknown. But also fear that the last fifty years on the timeline of her life have just been folded over and lost. There's exhilaration in that fear, but that's still an awfully big chunk of time to lose.

She turns around. The footsteps are coming from far away, echoing in the isolated dark. And there's a smell on the air. One she has no memory of, but which is instantly recognizable. And carrion sweet.

And the moon is red. Embarrassed.
Or demented.

No matter what happens, let's be together for the next one.

What could happen?

The footsteps grow louder as a figure appears, bathed in the red-tinged light. That smell fills the world—one new and final memory being made. And a single thought rushes through her mind as of someone greeting a loved one after a long absence. She is rooted to the spot. . .

. . . and not even the moon can bear to see what happens next.

It was a joke, more or less. He had to have known that.

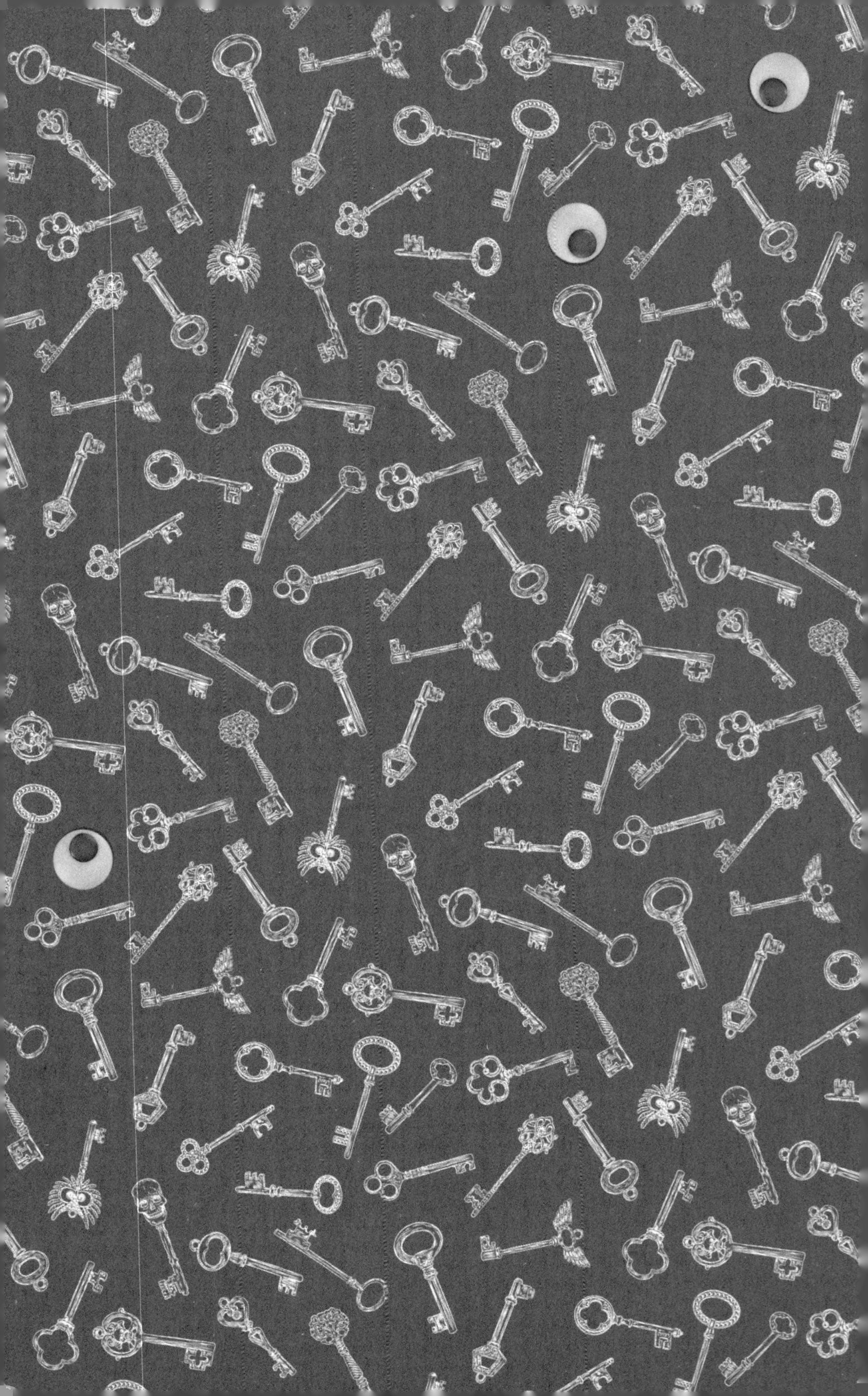

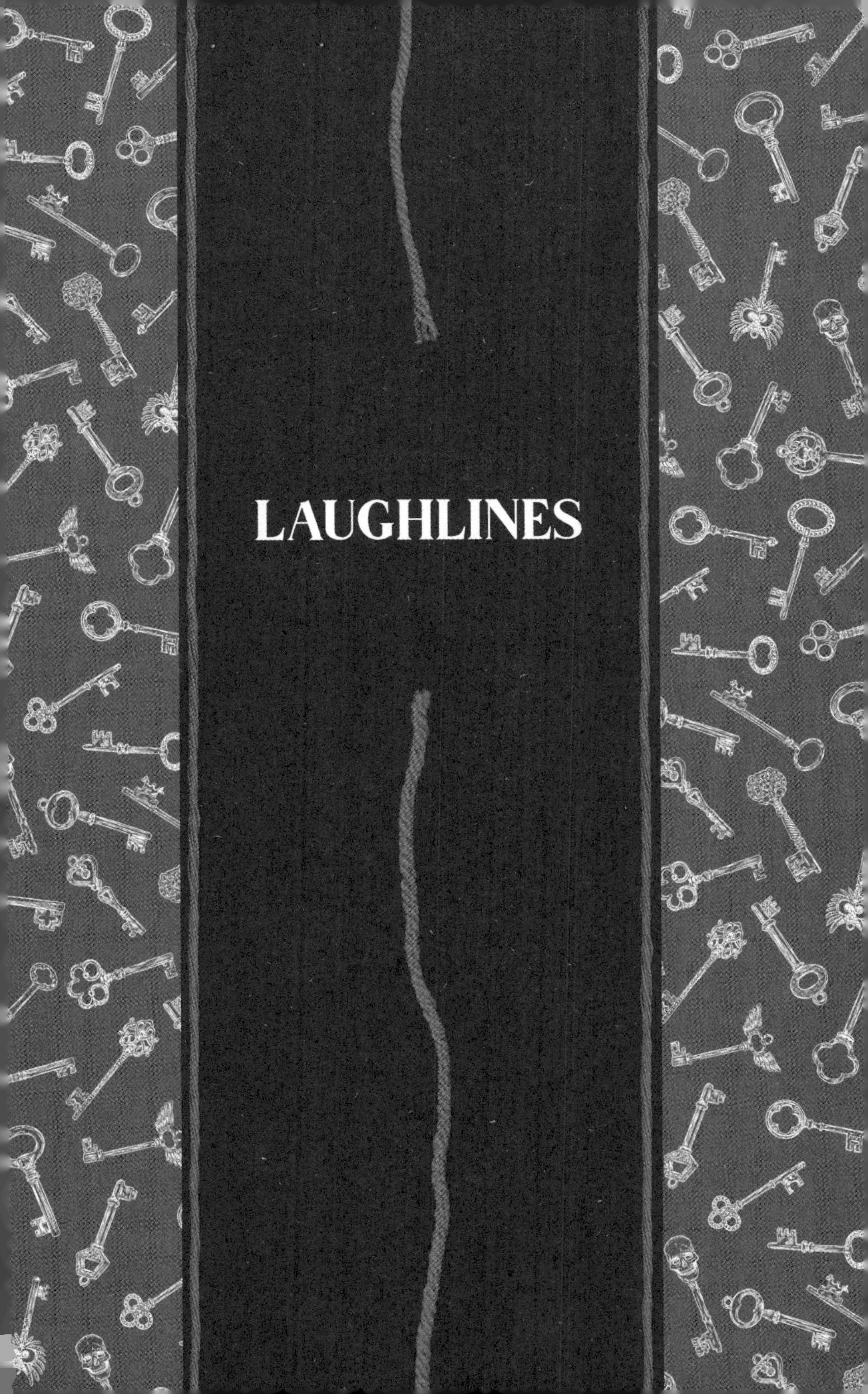
LAUGHLINES

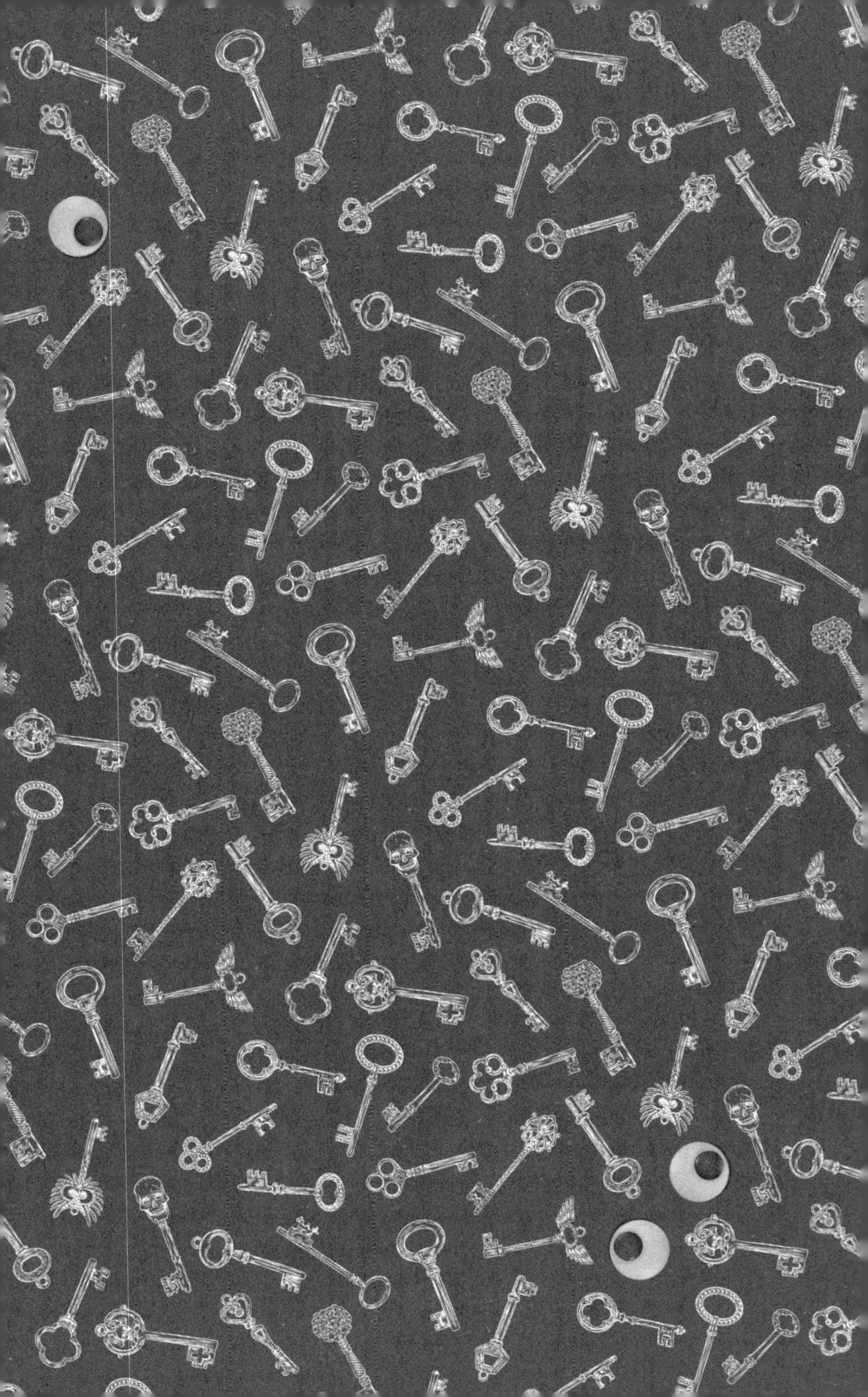

LAUGHLINES

From: MissySpeaks2
To: Robert_Weybourne48
Subject: I Have Arrived!
May 9

Hey Robert!

Quick note just to let you know I made it in! Whew, that was a long flight. But I finally caught up on the last season of Bojack (that show I told you about), so I used the time wisely.

Wish I could've had something to entertain me during that equally long car ride, but then I would've booted... a term I understand means something different here in Merrie Olde England.

Service out here is a bit spotty, but I seem to have pockets of reception with no problem. Yay, technology! Good job, England! Feels kinda weird to be looking at my phone out here, though, surrounded by moors and castles and those tiny little buildings with the thatched roofs and wooden beams criss-crossing the cream-colored walls like something out of a children's storybook (I have no idea if I'm describing them right or what they're called but it's very Olde Englande Villagee).

I'm famished so I'm going to go get a bite at a pub or soemthing and then check into the Inn.

In case it's not clear by my charming smarminess, this place is BEAUTIFUL. My goodness. When was the last time you were out here?

More soon. And... thanks again. 😊
xoxoxoxo,
M

From: Robert_Weybourne48
To: MissySpeaks2
Subject: Re: I Have Arrived!
May 9

Hey kiddo,

That's great to know about service! Let's just say last time I was there, any cell phone had ZERO chance of working. The times they are a-changing (that's an old song you're too young to know about)

So glad you like it. I can't wait to hear more about what you find. It is beyond my pleasure to share this with you. This will sound super corny but be honest: do you feel anything yet? Any sort of connection? I won't be sad if you say no, but I won't laugh if you say yes. I feel it every time I'm there.

You'll probably have already picked a place to eat by the time you get this, but I highly recommend the Blue Baker Tavern. I assume it's still in business. Things last a lot longer out there.

PS, The type of architecture you're referring to is called half-timbered. Very common in Elizabethan and Jacobean times. Think about this: Lambridge village is so old, at one point that would have been considered a "new" style of architecture.

From: MissySpeaks2
To: Robert_Weybourne48
Subject: Re: I Have Arrived!
May 9

OMG I KNOW ABOUT BOB DYLAN THANK YOU VERY MUCH

As if you Boomers kept your music ~*a secret*~ from the rest of us instead of shoving it down our throats for the entire second half of the 20th Century lol

Also, whoa, you read my mind. It WAS too late to recommend a pub but that's EXACTLY the pub I went to! Great minds! The food (and ale) was delicious. And *heavy*. Between the overcast weather and the fried food and the plentiful beer I don't know how everyone isn't constantly napping out here.

The people in town are... interesting. I was expecting a sort of *American Werewolf in London* reception (that's an old movie you're too young to know about), with the locals all staring at the Tourist Girl with malice in their narrowed eyes. But so far they've been either friendly or apathetic. Mostly apathetic, really. They've got their own business to look after, and I appreciate that.

Oh, and to answer your earlier question... I did kinda feel something. Something "in the blood," if you want to be like really portentious about it (I think I'm using that word right I don't know I'm tired and jet lagged leemee alone). I guess I never really thought I'd have, like, ancestral history before. Mom's family tree gets pretty lopped after like two generations (thanks, Hitler) and, well, I figured that's all I'd ever get. Maybe it's psychosomatic but, yeah, this place does feel like home in a very, very weird way.

Or maybe that's just the three bottles of airplane vodka talking! 😳

From: Robert_Weybourne48
To: MissySpeaks2
Subject: Re: I Have Arrived!
May 9

No, that's not the vodka talking.

That's great to hear.

Enjoy the village, but make sure you visit the castle—that's the best part. If you don't see it already (it's the building up on the hill that looks like a castle), I'm sure any villager will point the way to "Craester Arms Keep."

PS, You're very funny. I know you'll try to deflect that compliment, but too bad. Facts 'r' facts.

From: MissySpeaks2
To: Robert_Weybourne48
Subject: Re: I Have Arrived!
May 9

The castle is on tomorrow's agenda! In fact it basically IS tomorrow's agenda! So looking forward to it.

I'm going to keep saying this, but thank you again and again and again for making this happen, Robert. This all means the world to me. It's exactly what I needed.

PS, Does ignoring count as deflecting?

You're pretty funny yourself. Maybe genetics is a thing after all.

From: Robert_Weybourne48
To: MissySpeaks2
Subject: Re: I Have Arrived!
May 9

😊😊😊

From: MissySpeaks2
To: SarahwithanH
Subject:
May 9

Saaaaraaaaahhhhhh.

Okay. Finally have some time to write. Strap in because I'm probably gonna unload on you (that's what he said).

I could tell you all about the flight (a woman brought a CAT, an actual fucking CAT onboard, and it screamed more than a baby, it was atrociouuuuus) or the epic cab ride from the airport to this strange little hamlet (it was very *Bram Stoker's Dracula*, which I guess makes me Keanu Reeves, whoa), but honestly I'm so tired and the thought of reliving all that again today makes me want to disappear, so I'll get to the stuff I know you REALLY wanna know about.

The people here are bananas.

Yes, the accents are charming in their Monty Python-y way.

No, I have not seen any attractive men on which to work my alluring Midwestern wiles. (Fucking amazing that being from Racine will be seen as exotic out here, though.)

But they're all definitely... a little touched? Is that a term we can still use?

Like, Sarah, it wasn't just that they didn't interact with me, it was like they *avoided contact with me*. Like, eyes darting away once I looked back at them. It was almost like they were scared of me. I wanted to tell them, it's okay, I'm not one of THOSE Americans, they took my guns at the airport! But instead I just tried my best to be polite and let them do whatever they were gonna do. It's their village.

If they'd been staring at me, it would have been different. Threatening. I would've worried I was gonna find myself in an Eli Roth movie. But this was almost... endearing? And a little funny after awhile? I definitely had the urge to laugh a couple times, just out of the awkwardness of it all.

Needless to say, I didn't tell anyone why I was there or where I'm from, family-wise. No throwing my weight around here yet—Do You Know Who My Father Is??? Ha.

It's all still so weird, Sarah. Finally reconnecting with my dad, finding out he's a Someone, which I guess means I'm a Someone, too; at least to this tiny little village in East England. How am I a *Weybourne*? What the fuck even does that mean? I wasn't raised a *Weybourne*. Hell, I wasn't raised an Anybody, just the daughter of a single mom who never knew her dad and that was fine with me. The idea of having a Name—a fucking CASTLE—is way too strange.

Maybe it will be less strange when I actually get to reconnect with him? Or no, not reconnect—reconnecting implies we had any sort of relationship before. Considering he ran off before I was even born, that feels like a bit of a stretch. This would just be "connecting." Dear old Robert. Not sure I'll ever be able to call him Dad.

I'm still trying to lose that awkwardness with him in emails. He still feels mostly like a stranger to me, I'm all solicitous and crap. You know what I mean? Like, everything is super peppy and polite, like I'm answering a work email? Sounds great! You know it! What an EXCELLENT idea, I LOVE it! Hahaha! So many exclamation points, so many LOLs and :-)s. If I was anywhere near as excited and chipper in real life as I must sound in these emails I'd look like the goddamn Joker. Everything! Is! So! Happy!

But maybe one day soon I'll be able to actually have a real conversation with him, tell him how pissed I am at him. How shitty he was for leaving my mom. For not being there when she died. For never reaching out to me. For waiting until I found him on Ancestry dot fucking com to even show any interest in my life.

I mean, I can't lie, setting me up with a free visit to his (our??) ancestral frigging CASTLE is a nice gesture, but I'm a big girl and I know a Band-Aid when I see one, even if it does have pretty princesses all over it.

Holy shit, Sarah, I wrote so much. I'm so sorry. This email is insane. Good luck reading it. I used voice-to-text and so it let me just ramble (thank god it didn't pick up the voice of the handsome farmlad who's currently sharing my bed and begging to service me again). Ain't technology grand? It even does most of the punctuation for me. It's pretty accurate. It must. Base it off. The rhythms. Of my voice. Neat! Okay, I'll stop. Now to just reread everything to check for mistakes (you deserve nothing less) and get some sleep. I'm wrecked. I wish you could see this inn/B&B I'm staying at—it's so fucking cute.

Oh but shit! I almost forgot! One last thing. So, I was talking about how weird everyone who lives here is and how they all avoided me, but I was going to tell you about the one exception. The lady who runs this establishment. Really cute little old lady, white hair done up in a bun, gigantic brown cardigan. I was checking in a few hours ago and she was doing the thing everyone else was doing, not really looking at me... but then she stopped and actually did stare a bit.

She said, "I know your face, don't I?" I said Oh? I've never been here before, so... And she said, "You're a Weybourne." Just like that, no question. I was like, ummmmmmm how did you know? My last name is Ricker. (I mean, I figure Robert told obviously her when he called in my reservation. But still.) Then she leaned over the counter a bit and said, "I can see it around your eyes. Your laughlines."

Sarah, I have never heard anyone say the word "laughlines" with such fucking venom before. This lady HATES laughlines. Again, it was almost funny. But this one actually did creep me out a bit. I don't know why. Maybe because she was implying that I'm getting wrinkles. Heh.

So, no, I shan't be playing up my distant heritage amongst the locals, thank you very much.

See? Like I said: weird.

Okay. Time for sleep now. Gotta get my pretty princess beauty rest because tomorrow I'm gonna spend some time in a muthafuckin castleeeeee!

From: SarahwithanH
To: MissySpeaks2
Subject: Re:
May 9

My sweet Missy Miss -

I am so fucking proud of you. For being open to anything that Robert-Not-Dad has to offer, for being a badass solo traveler. For all of it. I know nothing can make someone *get over* losing a mom but I really hope this trip helps.

Just... please be careful. Those villagers sound intense. Maybe they're just intimidated by your rank Americanism? Are you wearing your MAGA cap and flag pants? (Oh wow, I can hear you barfing from here.)

I shall eagerly await your next update, pretty princess. And I'll write more in a bit cuz I also have a lot to say, but, bitch, it's early out here.

Please be safe!

PS, I'm forwarding you an email from Guitar Center with a coupon for new microphones. Look for it.

PPS, Maybe that lady thought she recognized your wrinkly–ass face because she'd just watched a movie with Yoda in it?

From MissySpeaks2
To Robert_Weybourne48
Subject: CASTLE TOUR
May 10

Dear Robert:

As the ever-young children of my generation say: O. M. Geeeeeeee.

I don't even know what to say besides that. The castle—sorry, the Craester Arms Keep—is unlike anything I've ever seen before. I believe the term is gobsmacked.

I'm writing now in the Blue Baker again. There's barely any reception at the Craester. Not surprising, considering the hill you have to walk up to get to the main entrance. But it really is something like out of a fairy tale. I'm so jealous you got to spend so much of your childhood coming out here to visit! That must have been so surreal! Especially coming from, where did you say you grew up, New Jersey?

The tour was just me—I don't think they get a lotta tourists here in jolly old Lambridge. But that made it sooooo much more special. The guide, a very nice girl about my age named Adelina (beautiful name!), seemed very excited to have someone to show around. She was super funny, too—you would have liked her!

I'm torn. On one hand I want to write down everything that happened and that I saw so I remember it forever, but on the other hand, you know all this stuff already and I don't want to bore you! So here are just some highlights for you, me, posterity, and the Queen:

I've never set foot in a castle before. I was amazed at how cold it is. You can really feel the stones keeping the air moist and cool.

The sound of footsteps on the (I'm assuming) stone floors. Amazing. They echo forever and yet they feel so present.

Did Doctor Who design this damn place because it seemed so much bigger on the inside. We walked for probably two hours and I don't feel like we covered near half of the real estate! Adelina took me through the Barbican, the Gatehouse, the Courtyard (how OLD are those trees, I wonder?!), through two kitchens with massive stone ovens, a whole bunch of hallways, at least two "Great" Halls (seems a bit excessive, dear ancestors), and a few rooms that were, I guess, castle-equivalents of living rooms or parlors? I didn't even get to see bedrooms or bathrooms and yet I saw so much!

In these parlor areas, though, Adelina also showed me some of the portraiture and, um... okay, some of them were kinda creepy. But not in a bad way! I just couldn't get over how *familiar* some of the faces looked. And I mean that in the most literal sense. They looked like family. I was surprised how many of them weren't scowling. I associate old portraits with scowling. But, maybe because these weren't as detailed as portraits from the Realism Period, so many faces seemed kind of pleasant. Grinning, even.

And on a few faces I even recognized similar... well, I guess you'd call them laughlines, to my own. The same eye crinkles. The same dimples. It's just weird, Robert! I've never been in a single castle before and here I am on a tour, looking at my great great great great whatever relatives.

But, okay, um, here's what I REALLY want to talk about. The tapestries.

Why. Didn't. You. Prepare. Me. For. The. Tapestries.

I think it was the one with the guy very clearly farting into a trumpet that his buddy had his ear to that first made me laugh out loud—an actual LOL.

The tapestries lining the main hall weren't so remarkable.

I mean, they were cool in an art history way but nothing to email home about. But the further you went into the castle, I mean, jeez! Some of them get INSANE. Were they always like that? Obviously they were—they're not going to redecorate a medieval castle for shits and giggles.

I told you about my friend Sarah, right? She and I have that podcast together where we give love/life advice? She does a lot of stand-up comedy and improv and knows her history really well. We had one episode a little while ago where she confessed to thinking Buster Keaton was the sexiest man to have ever lived. I was HORRIFIED (I was actually thinking of Buster Pointdexter, that singer from the 80s). So she showed me some of his old movies and—first off, she might have been correct but, secondly, I was amazed at how contemporary a lot of the gags and timing felt. It all still *worked.* I had no idea. These tapestries gave me a similar feeling. One was a literal depiction of a pie-in-the-face! But still in that super specific medieval style, and sewn into a friggin tapestry!

(I took so many photos to send to Sarah, but even in this pub the signal's not good enough to upload them yet. She's gonna flip out when she sees them.)

And it wasn't just the tapestries, too. At one point there were suits of armor on display—I'm sure you know exactly what I'm going to say—and they were arranged in a tableau. One suit of armor was turned around and it was missing a plate where its butt should be and the other suits were pointing at the butthole and, I imagine, laughing?

I kept expecting to find the 13th Century equivalent of a rubber chicken around the corner.

I had no idea people had senses of humor back then. I figured they were all too busy having twenty-seven children before they turned 19 and then dying of the plague. Live and learn! The past can always surprise you!

From: Robert_Weybourne48
To: MissySpeaks2
Subject: Re: CASTLE TOUR
May 10

I thought you would enjoy finding those tapestries all on your own. A fun fact about the Weybournes is we were known, historically, as great patrons of the arts. Especially comedy, but not exclusively. Rumor has it your great-great-great-whatever grandfather commissioned plays by Ben Jonson and perhaps even Shakespeare himself! And when the Restoration rolled around, exclusive premieres of comedies by Congreve and Wycherly were held in the Great Hall. (I don't know if those names mean anything to you—they're Greek to me!)

But yes, comedy was most beloved. It was a defining trait of almost every lord at Craester Arms. Fools and jesters from around the entire country sought residency here because the lord was always known to be the most receptive and appreciative. Many of those tapestries were gifts because that reputation was so widespread.

I'm not surprised you recognized some laughlines. And when one day we meet in the flesh (I hope I'm not being too presumptuous) you'll see I have very similar lines as well. It's the Weybourne trademark!

I'm so glad you're enjoying yourself there. I don't want to impede on your plans but… if you're interested and free… perhaps you should go back to the castle tomorrow to see more? I know Adelina and her family very well and I just might have pulled some strings to give you an even more exclusive tour… Have you ever spent the night in a castle… ?

From: MissySpeaks2
To: Robert_Weybourne48
Subject: Re: CASTLE TOUR
May 10

Um. Are. You. Kidding. Me????

From: Robert_Weybourne48
To: MissySpeaks2
Subject: Re: CASTLE TOUR
May 10

It's not a perk that's offered to everybody but I got to do it a few times growing up and I loved it. The village tourist board keeps just a handful of bedrooms turned out for these kinds of occasions. Just say the word and you can really get a taste of what it was like for your ancestors!

By the way..... I hope you know I'm not under any illusions that this fixes anything. I know you must have some complicated feelings about me and that's absolutely okay. I can't make up for how things happened. But I hope I can help make the present a little better. And maybe when the time is right you and I can talk about, well, everything.

I just want you to know that it is my truest hope to be worthy of the chance you're giving me. You have every right to hate my guts, but.....

Well, like you say... the past can always surprise you.

From: MissySpeaks2
To: Robert_Weybourne48
Subject: Re: CASTLE TOUR
May 10

Wow. That's... Thanks for saying all that. There's a lot I want to say in response, but email feels kind of silly. So. Yeah. Thanks, Dad. I can't wait until we're able to meet up in person very very soon.

xoxoxo

PS, In case it wasn't clear, the word is yes yes yes. Sign me up for more castle time. No offence to your beloved Lambridge but there's really not a lot else to do around here. I've seen the goat and both sheep already.

From: Robert_Weybourne48
To: MissySpeaks2
Subject: Re: CASTLE TOUR
May 10

I can't tell you what it means to hear you call me that.

Show up at the front gates tomorrow and either Adelina or her brother Liam will take care of you. Believe me when I say you ain't seen nothing yet!

From: MissySpeaks2
To: SarahwithanH
Subject: duuuuuump
May 10

Time for another late night dump (as opposed to your early morning dumps I remember so well when we were roommates).

I'm so glad I did this, Sarah. This is turning into one of those truly magical experiences—and I hope you understand how truly special our friendship is, considering I'm willing to let myself be THIS SINCERE with you. Ugh! Gimme a bucket and a mop for this Wet Ass Vulnerability.

Yes, I have had several "pints" of "lager." Yes, I'm currently crying and feeling very sad and missing my mom. I wish she were here. I wish we were doing this together. Not that I don't like emailing you, o chum of chums. I just have so many more questions for her. Now that I have context for what my Dad was like and where he comes from (at least indirectly), I'm so frigging curious.

I actually don't want to tell you too much about what has happened because I think this'll actually be a great episode for our show and I wanna hear you react live in the moment. But I am going to have some stories, believe me.

I've also been taking so many photos. Damn things won't send, but believe, you're gonna love them.

Darby, get away from that table and come to the dartboard (Hahaha, sorry! I'm voice-to-texting again, quietly in the corner of this pub, and it just picked up some loud-ass local across the room. I'm leaving it in because it's too funny. Oh, Darby.)

Oh, Sar!!! Ugh! Thank you for always being there, my beautiful pal. You're the tits. The bee's knees. The cat's pajamas.
Or sorry, pyjjammas as they spell it here. You're the cat's pyjjammieers covered in pictures of big titted bee knees.

I might have had to many beers.

From: MissySpeaks2
To: SarahwithanH
Re: (No Subject)
May 11

Sar—

God I hope this goes through. I have to get the fuck out of here.

I just heard the most fucked up thing in my life and if it weren't raining buckets I'd be marching my way down the hill and maybe even thumbing a ride to Heathrow. Jesus. I'm literally shaking. I'm dictating again, and there might be a lot of typos I don't fix because I don't know if I can use with my fucking fingers just now.

I'm leaving tomorrow, for sure. As soon as it's light. Even if it's still pouring. Jesus.

Okay. To catch you up quickly. I'm in a castle right now. The old family castle. Dad Robert set me up with a night's stay. All exclusive thing. Very fancy. Thought it would be.

The people who run the like tourist board or whatever of this town are playing host. I thought it was cute and funny. They seemed very sweet at first. They took me around the more of the castle. It's huge. I was on a guided tour yesterday and we barely scratched the surface. We walked around for a long time today and I still feel that way.

There's a lot of art I want to show you. Tapestries. Paintings. It's all very strange and interesting. Yesterday I thought it was all funny—there are a lot of visual jokes on display, this will make sense when I show you—but some of the ones I saw today, deeper in the castle... it all started to feel like that moment when the joke goes on too long, you know? When the smile gets too big and toothy. When the laugh gets too robotic and insane. The images started to seem wrong. Twisted. Something wasn't right. I couldn't put my finger exactly on it but I could almost hear the laughter in my head and it sounded more like screaming.

Then came dinner. I got to eat dinner in a giant castle serving hall. "Just like your ancestors," one of the hosts told me. Liam. Weird kid. He's got to be in his early twenties. He's tall as hell, but his voice is so high and reedy.

I thought it was just me and the two tour guides, who I guess are brother and sister. But there were a few other servants there as well, an older man and woman, and, Sarah, I swear to god, they were all giggling about something. Not about something that happened earlier, not about a fucking YouTube video they'd just watched. They were laughing about me. Smirking. Behind the hand whispers, chewing on lips kind of laughing. And they would look at me, then make eye contact with the others, and just BARELY stop from cracking up. I swear to god I almost didn't eat my food I was so unnerved. They were acting like they'd pissed in it or something. But I was starving. And getting angry. So fuck 'em.

"Have you enjoyed the tour?" the old woman asked me. I told her sure. Being polite. But pretty clearly dripping with contempt, too; I'm not proud.

"Have you enjoyed the tapestries?" her husband? brother? both? asked. Again, I said sure.

"Did they entertain you?"

Very much so, I said. And they all looked at each other like I'd just agreed to go see the pool on the roof, or just chosen the chair that had a whoopie cushion on it.

"All very entertaining, innit?"

I hated these leading questions (leading to what, I had no idea), so I told them that yeah, yeah, I already knew all about how the lords who used to live in this castle, my ancestors, were all big fans of comedy and jokes and jesters and fools and all that. I was getting very impatient.

"Wasn't always so," Adelina, the girl a little younger than me and the one I liked best, said.

The old woman nodded. "Wasn't always so, indeed. No, no, no, it wasn't."

I asked them what they were talking about. Robert had told me that back in the day people basically came from all over to bring gag gifts and do stand-up routines, more or less. "Well, yes. For the good Weybournes. But not all the

Weybournes were good. No, no, dearie." God, that old woman spoke like a witch from a fairy tale.

"Not all of the Weybournes had a pleasant sense of humor." The old man again.

I don't know why I asked. I really don't. I just felt so trapped. They were all pinging looks off each other, biting back smiles like they couldn't believe I wasn't in on the joke. So I asked them to explain themselves.

Liam turned to the old woman. "Should we show her the other tapestries? The dark ones?"

"I don't know if she wants to see those, Liam."

"But she might find them funny." Liam barely choked back a laugh of his own. A low giggle. It made my skin crawl. I was suddenly aware of how far away I was from everything I know. How surrounded I was by darkness and rain and thunder and ancient, dripping stones.I kinda snapped. "Please let me in on what you're talking about." I sounded pathetic.

They looked at each other... and then they told me. Round robin style. Seamless. Each one picking up where the other left off. I think that's when I realized they were all related. Must be. Hell, for all I know, everyone in the village is family. Not with me, but with each other.

According to legend, the Weybourne line was not exclusively full of nice, comedy afficionados.

As far back as people can remember, every handful of generations there would be a lord with a notably crueler sense of entertainment. He wouldn't so much receive visiting jesters and entertainments as he'd abduct them. Force them to stay and perform. Torture them if they weren't to his liking. This little quirk in the family line wasn't common, so it didn't destroy the family reputation all the way—and whenever it did happen, the succeeding lords always made sure to pay even better than before... but it happened just frequently enough that it was always hanging in the air as a distant possibility. It was known as the dark thread. It twined its way down the family tree like a snake in vines.

Until, for whatever reason, the dark thread disappeared. They went almost 100 years without any sort of incident similar to the brutal, bloody days of yore. By the 15th Century, people talked about the Mad Weybournes as just some ancient legend. A myth. They even began to doubt the legends that had been passed down as being entirely truthful. For those hundred years the worst Lord at Craester Keep was a chinless, humorless doofus who didn't ever laugh except at anything having to do with pee. (They called him Lord Yellow, by the way. Gross.) It seemed like the bad stuff had finally worked its way out of the genetic line-up. Until...

"Do you know who the final Lord of Craester Arms was, dearie?"

I did not. I guess I hadn't even really put it together that there was a final Lord. But of course there was. And the Weybourne descendants fled this village and scattered to the winds, only to occasionally come back as visitors like my dad and his family... and like me.

Now I know why.

His name was Lord Nigel Weybourne. He ruled in the 1500s. "And he was adored," they told me, almost with a sigh. He was young. Brilliant. Handsome. He had a marvelous sense of humor and a laugh that was infectious and sunny. Everywhere he went he brightened up the room. He held fetes in the courtyard for all the villagers. Big, massive variety shows. People would come from all over to see them. The dark thread had never before seemed like such a distant memory, a farce. How could anything bad come from the family line that produced him?

Then one day, out of the blue, like God's own little punchline, he got sick. They said it was a brain fever. He almost died. Probably would have been better if he did.

When he came out of his sickroom he was changed. He began putting up old tapestries—ones from darker times—as well as commissioning new ones. He began asking more and more of his performers and minstrels and jugglers. Making them work under physical duress. Sing while being nipped at by hungry dogs. Juggle while balls of shit are thrown at you.

He said he had been visited by the One Who Laughs. (That was how they said it, Sarah; I could hear the capitalizations.) And now he Laughed, too.

The dark thread had returned with a vengeance. It became a noose, choking off the entire village.

Apparently at this time there was also this famous itinerant family of jesters. A comedy troupe. A dad, a mom, two young kids, and an uncle with his wife. Physical comedy. Tumbling. Acrobatics. Prat falls. Raunchy songs. “Carlo was brilliant at impressions,” the old man added.

They traveled across the country and they were something of a phenomenon. They didn’t know what was happening in Lambridge and had just arrived as a sort of culminating show for their most recent tour. They’d been saving Lambridge for last. And it was their last.

Lord Nigel held one of his courtyard fetes and he built a special platform in the middle of the castle square. No one wanted to attend but they knew he’d punish anyone who sat it out. The family began to perform, but the crowd was so tense waiting to see what would happen that the reaction was strained at best. Nigel found it hilarious, which only made the crowd even more uneasy.

He started taunting the performers. “They do not like your japes,” he called out, pointing to the crowd. “They are not yet delighted! Perhaps what you need is a little fire in your step!”

So, he snapped his fingers and this massive cauldron was rolled out into the square. Everyone could see it was bubbling with unimaginable heat. It was a vat of oil and fat, hotter than lava.

The vat was rolled under the stage.

Nigel made the family start performing again, only the steam from the cauldron was too intense, too painful. They couldn't get through their act. And of course the crowd was even more horrified and unresponsive.

"I am afraid a verdict... must be rendered!" Nigel shrieked. A shitty pun, but he was laughing hysterically at it. Then he snapped his fingers again and the platform floor fell away where the family was standing. They dropped. Into the cauldron.

Sarah, he boiled them in oil. All together. They screamed and, and melted as a family in front of everyone. And when the heat died down, Nigel had the contents of the cauldron dumped out onto the stage for all to see.

It was this steaming, hideous... ball of flesh. Melted into the shape of the bell of the cauldron, with hands and feet and twisted necks and gaping mouths. And I can't stop imagining those final few seconds, when that poor family dropped down, when the little children must have shrieked in agony, eyes wide, everyone looking at each other, apologizing to each other for not being able to stop this, like how my mom looked at me when she realized she couldn't keep breathing through the cancer, and the way I must have looked trying to get her to hold on, to breathe, to breathe, I can't I just can't I

Then Lord Nigel made one more proclamation. He said he was bored and so he was giving the castle over to the townspeople.

He disinherited himself right then and there, gave the land back to the people (maybe that's why the Weybourne line isn't completely persona non grata out here?) and then slit his own throat. Right there in the courtyard. Problem solved.

Sarah, I thought that was the end of the story. It was the old lady who spoke first but they all continued their tag-team conversation.

"Rumor is they're still out there, dearie. One large, lumpen mass. Melted together, you see."

"They weren't satisfied. They were angry he escaped punishment."

"Furious."

"The people of Lambridge say they sometimes hear laughter in these halls. Mad laughter. And the sounds of hands and feet slapping against the stones."

"Still turning somersaults, you see."

"One ball of flesh. An eternal fool's tumble."

"And there's only one thing they want more than to perform again."

"They want revenge on the family line of Weybourne."

"So says the legend."

And the rain outside was so loud, Sarah, I actually slammed the table, stood up, and screamed at them to stop. I could barely breathe. They were grinning at me. Making fun of me. Teasing me.

A huge crash of thunder echoed outside like a fucking rimshot.

"Dearie, it's only a legend. This country is full of legends."

"You don't actually think there's, what, a ball of jesters rolling round these halls? All hands and feet and faces melted together?"

"That's a bit daft, don't you think?"

And of course I don't think that's real. Of course I don't. But their grins. Their shared looks.

Sarah. It was the most unsettling thing I'd ever heard.

And now it's even more than unsettling. It's scary. It didn't seem so scary until now. Alone, in this strange bedroom. In the dark. With the sound of the rain pouring outside, as loud as galloping hooves even though I'm surrounded by walls and walls of ancient stone.

Ugh. This email is insanely long. I don't even know if it'll send. I get horrible service in here, so it might have to wait until I'm back down in town tomorrow. I'm gonna kill some time, fixing punctuation and crap. Maybe I'll be able to get this down to a less insane length, too, I don't know. But I can't wait to hear your thoughts.

Oh, and look at that. Just as I was writing this, I got an alert that I have a new email from him, from Robert, from Dad. That gives me hope there's just a glimmer of service. Maybe this email will go through after all.

I'm gonna see what he has to say. Ugh. I don't know what I'm going to tell him about all this.

More soon. Hope I can sleep tonight.

Xoxo
M

From: Robert_Weybourne48
To: MissySpeaks2
Subject: GOOD NEWS
May 11

Hey kiddo,

I'm so sorry for this very abrupt message but I've got exciting news! Something has come up and I'm currently en route to Lambridge right at this very moment. Are you still at the castle? If so, I would so love to meet up with you in the morning! We can have breakfast in the great hall!

Xo,
Dad

From: MissySpeaks2
To: Robert_Weybourne48
Subject: Re: GOOD NEWS
May 11

Seriously? You're traveling in this rain? Are you sure? I was actually hoping to get down to the village first thing tomorrow – want to meet up there?

From: Robert_Weybourne48
To: MissySpeaks2
Subject: Re: GOOD NEWS
May 11

Totally sure!

No can do, meeting in town, though. The flooding. This happens. It's May. Everything will be closed down for the next day or two at least. You're lucky you were up there in the keep before the storm hit.

I can't tell you how much it would mean to me to finally meet you in person – in the Craester no less!

From: MissySpeaks2
To: Robert_Weybourne48
Subject: Re: GOOD NEWS
May 11

Yeah, okay – I'm looking forward to it, too

From: MissySpeaks2
To: Robert_Weybourne48
Subject: ETA?
May 12

Hey dad, it's morning. Just checking to see if you're here yet. Where are you?

From: Robert_Weybourne48
To: MissySpeaks2
Subject: Re: ETA?
May 12

Sorry, kiddo. The rain has me a little delayed. Can you kill some time while I get there? The flooding has stopped but the hill is super slippery.

From: MissySpeaks2
To: Robert_Weybourne48
Subject: Re: ETA?
May 12

I guess so, yeah. Is everything really closed down outside?

From: Robert_Weybourne48
To: MissySpeaks2
Subject: Re: ETA?
May 12

Go exploring! Check more of the Craester out!
Learn more about where you come from!!

From: MissySpeaks2
To: SarahwithanH
Subject: FML
May 12

Sar –

Okay. This is going to be a hilarious email whenever you finally get it but I don't know what else to do or who to write right now because I can't make any phone calls

I'm lost. I'm still in the castle. I went out to get some breakfast and now I can't find my way around.

I can't think of who else to write. Oh, god, I'm fucking ridiculous. Hahaha. Who else gets into messes like these? Oh boy. Jesus fucking christ.

From: MissySpeaks2
To: SarahwithanH
Subject: FML
May 12

Sarah I'm so sorry I don't know what else to do I'm just going to keep writing you voice to texting you so I don't lose my mind and I don't know how much sense it will make. Editing them gives me something to do but I'm also kinda freaking out right now so. Um.

I'm wandering through the halls of this godforsaken place and they just keep going they keep going and I don't know how that's possible. It all looks the same, dripping stone and shadows. The only way I know I'm covering ground is because the tapestries hanging from the ceiling keep changing.

The tapestries Sarah they're getting worse and worse. They must be the older ones. The ones from the days of the dark thread. Or maybe the ones good old Nigel commissioned. They're horrifying Sarah. They're horrifying. There's one of a man with rabbit ears nailed into his skull with bloody rivets.

There's one of an acrobat doing the splits over a saw biting into his crotch. His face Sarah his face is pure agony. There's one of someone singing only I'm pretty sure they're also sliding down a pole that's been punctured through their body.

What the fuck is happening why can't I find my way out? How fucking big is this place??

From: MissySpeaks2
To: SarahwithanH
Subject: FML
May 12

Sarah why aren't my emails going through it doesn't make any sense I keep hoping I'll at least pass through an area with something of a signal maybe a short one will go through. Help.

From: MissySpeaks2
To: SarahwithanH
Subject: FML
May 12

Sarah I saw another tapestry I

I can't describe it

I

I took a photo of it but it's not uploading and maybe that's for the best. It made me throw up. I threw up looking at it. It's hideous. So fucking hideous. And it had writing on it at the bottom. It was hard to read but not because it was in an old font. Because it was moving Sarah it was moving all on its own. All the other cloths hang straight down but this one kept flapping and swirling and writhing like it was underwater

The caption said the one who laughs

I took a picture to show you. It's not funny. It's not a funny joke. Although ahahaha maybe it is maybe it is funny funny like too many exclamation points like the sound of !!!!!!!!!!!!!!!!!!!!!

I'm not going to freak out.

I'm not.

I'm going to be okay. I still have punctuation. I can still dictate sentences. I'm going to be okay. Period. !

From: MissySpeaks2
To: Robert_Weybourne48
Subject: daddy
May 13

Daddy. Please. Where are you? It's been a whole day, I think. Maybe longer. I'm lost. I need help.

Are you here yet? please

From: Robert_Weybourne48
To: MissySpeaks2
Subject: Re: daddy
May 13

Yes, I'm here, Missy.

From: MissySpeaks2
To: Robert_Weybourne48
Subject: Re: daddy
May 13

OH THANK GOD I need you to come find me. Please. I'm all alone and I'm freaking out. Please hurry.

From: Robert_Weybourne48
To: MissySpeaks2
Subject: Re: daddy
May 13

LOL that's funny

From: MissySpeaks2
To: Robert_Weybourne48
Subject: Re: daddy
May 13

I'm not kidding! I can't find my way back to my room. I spent all day walking. I don't know where I am or what time it is. Please. Come find me or send someone to find me. I haven't seen a single person since that dinner the other night. I can't make phone calls. I haven't gotten any emails except from you. I can't believe I'm getting your emails even!

From: Robert_Weybourne48
To: MissySpeaks2
Subject: Re: daddy
May 13

LOL Must be because I'm so close. Hahaha! Can't you hear me?

From: MissySpeaks2
To: Robert_Weybourne48
Subject: Re: daddy
May 13

No??? I don't hear anything. Just like water dripping or something. Please. Call out for me or something!

From: Robert_Weybourne48
To: MissySpeaks2
Subject: Re: daddy
May 13

Dripdripdrip Are you sure that's water? Or is it......... Slapslapslap??
Feet and flesh tumbling your way, pitter patter let's get at 'er.
Hahahaha! Come find me—or maybe I'll find you first!
HAHAHAHA! LOL

From: MissySpeaks2
To: SarahwithanH
Subject: (No subject)
May 13

Sarah I'm so scared I'm on voice to text it's the only thing I can think

I'm trying. To catch. My breath. Sitting. Against a cold rock wall. Right now.

Been running. He's chasing. Me.

I was so wrong. So wrong.

Sarah, I'm losing my mind

These noises. Coming to get me. Slap slap slap. Getting louder. I've got to keep moving. Oh god, getting closer again fuck fuck haha

Okay. Quiet again. Think he went another way. I'm so scared. I'm so sorry I'm so sorry.

I didn't mean to be a Weybourne. I didn't mean to be

I didn't know I

Oh Sarah what am I going to do? Please. Please if you get this please I hope you get this I hope peep-bo peep-bo hahaha found you Missy hi Missy found you found you oh my god sarah it's hideous it's hahaha pretty funny aren't we we found you we found you oh god sarah help me help we will take you to the one who laughs now we will take you no please no we will take you to the one who laughs no sarah hahahaha why aren't you laughing hahahaha isn't it good to laugh sarah please no!

From: SarahwithanH
To: MissySpeaks2
Subject: Re: duuuuuump
May 15

Holy shit, girl, you weren't kidding about bad service out there! I mean, speaking of dumps (very funny haha you know I have IBS) I just got, like, all of your emails at once! Gonna work my way through 'em and respond. Or maybe I'll just call you like a freak.

REMEMBER PHONE CALLS?! Nothing scarier, am I right?

From: SarahwithanH
To: Robert_Weybourne48
Subject: Missy
May 16

Who the fuck are you and what did you do to Missy?

I'm going to find you, you fuck.

I know Missy's passwords.

I checked her inboxes. I have your information and I'm having the police track you right now. They said Robert Weybourne died years ago. So who the fuck are you, asshole??

From: Robert_Weybourne48
To: SarahwithanH
Subject: Re: Missy
May 16

Carlo was always great at impressions 🤷‍♀️ lol

From: SarahwithanH
To: Robert_Weybourne48
Subject: Re: Missy
May 16

WHAT THE FUCK DID YOU DO TO HER?

From: Robert_Weybourne48
To: SarahwithanH
Subject: Re: Missy
May 16

RUN
FOR YOUR
LIFE

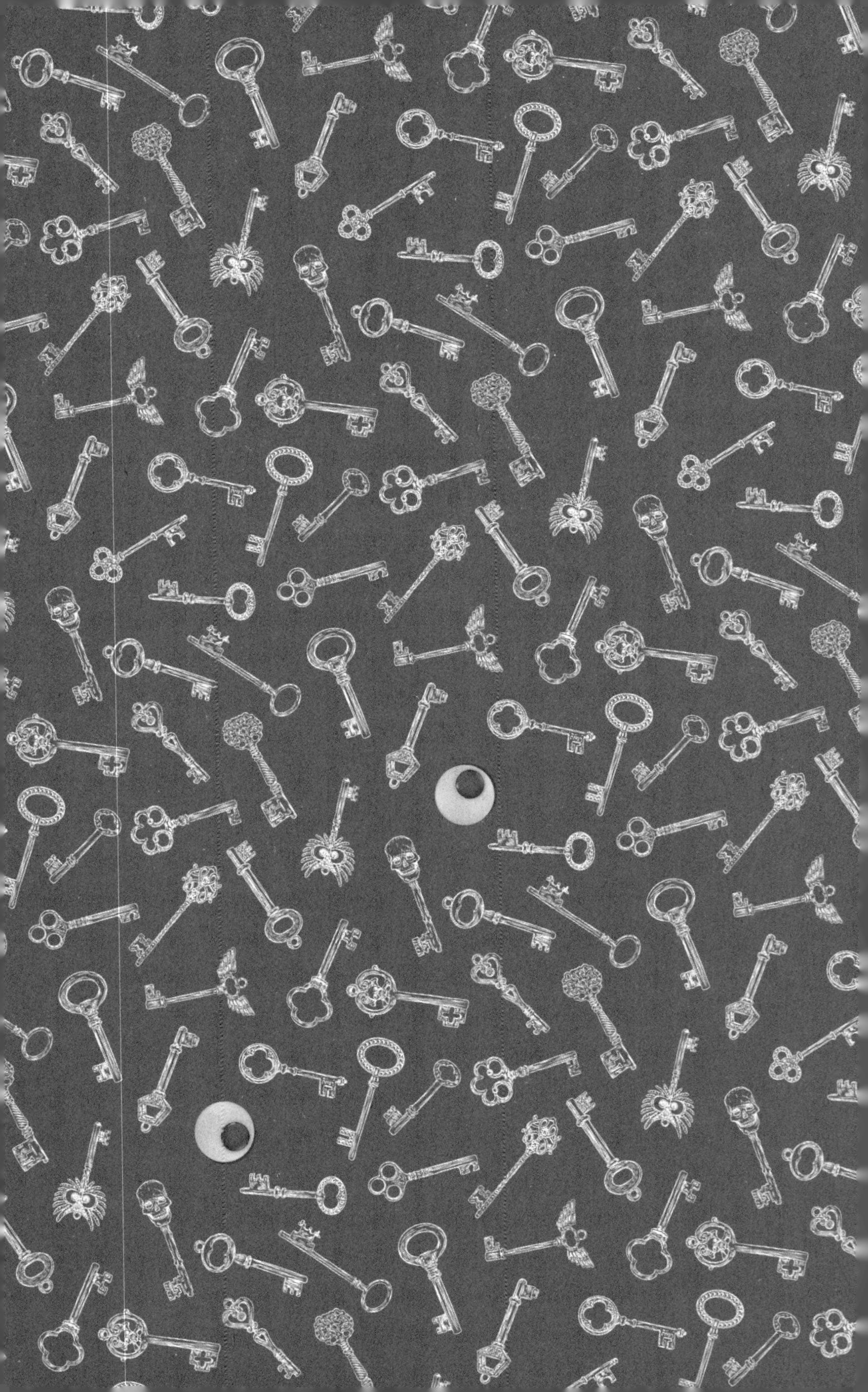

RUN FOR YOUR LIFE

This is not a confession.

I just. . . I have a few things I've gotta get straight in my head.

They're interviewing me for the *Anthology* project in the morning and before they get here, I need to go over a few things. Think all the things I can't think.

Remember how I got here.

Remind myself I'm still in control of this.

I am in complete control of this.

It's just sometimes. . . sometimes, my head gets a little noisy inside.

That's all.

This isn't a confession. It's not some Poe-ass, "Ohhh the beating of his hideous heart" guilt-spew.

Because, hey! None of this is what actually happened, right? Not according to history.

They're just some memories.

Memories I need to forget.

Places I remember.

Another life.

And some have really fucking changed.

But don't you know, it's gonna be all right.

Heh.

Might as well start there.

I started playing with the Beatles when I was ten years old. Not bad for someone born in 1998, right?

Later, I would often think about how I was thrust into the universe, not just at the absolute worst fucking time—the decline and fall of the American Empire, death spiral of capitalism, etc., etc.,—but also in the worst fucking place.

Rapid City, South Dakota.

I mean, what's a person supposed to do with *that* hand? God, I hated it out there. That vast, idiotic sky. That endless flatness. The brains around me, equally as smooth as the landscape. Most exciting thing you could do was either drive out to Deadwood or Spearfish and look at a mountain (ooh, wow, slight variation of the skyline!), or pick a fight at the nearest Applebee's over which racial group you think is superior.

I lived with dullards and went to school with dullards. Our house was far away from everything, so it seemed like most of my childhood was spent either walking or waiting for a bus, to get to or from a place I didn't want to go, where I'd be surrounded by people I didn't want to see.

Staying at home wasn't much better. I was a late-in-life surprise for my parents and never had anyone close to my own age to play with around our little shithole. A trailer would've been an improvement. With a trailer, all you need is a truck and a hitch and you could at least *believe* the world was your oyster. Our house was more like a cancerous knot on a tree stump. It wasn't going anywhere until all the life inside it had been sucked dry.

I'm making it sound actively depressing, I know. In the moment, it was just a drag. I knew there was more out there, and I couldn't wait to leave. I just didn't know how. I didn't have money, I didn't have connections, I didn't have any dreams because I didn't have any examples to dream by.

Everything changed when I was at the library one day and I picked up a dinged-up DVD boxset from the Recently Returned cart. Five discs. A decent-looking time killer that promised something like ten hours of distraction. The title sounded intriguing enough—even though I only knew one of its three words. *The Beatles Anthology.*

A few minutes into the first episode and I felt my life opening up.

We didn't have much around us, but besides that library there was also a semi-decent record store. I bought or borrowed (or, let's be honest here, usually stole) every Beatles album, every Beatles book, every Beatles bootleg. I asked everybody over a certain age about their memories and opinions of the band. (My parents, useful lumps of prolapsed couch stuffing that they were, had this to say: "Yeah, they were pretty good, right, Douglas?" "Hmph.").

I was *consumed*. I listened to each album, each bootleg, each interview, again and again and again and again. People got so fucking sick of it, my folks actually bought me a decent pair of headphones for a Christmas present one year, just so they wouldn't have to hear the songs I refused to stop playing.

One of my older brothers had an acoustic guitar he wasn't using (he'd tried to learn that Green Day song, "Good Riddance," to impress a girl a few years earlier and discovered it was too hard, which was apparently the guitar's fault, so it had a big dent in the side from where he kicked it). I took that guitar from his room and played along to the records, the demos, the outtakes, all of it. I learned every note and every part. I watched every interview. I joined along—them, forty-something years in the past and at the heights of fame; me, in my sad and lonely present.

I pored over studio logs, I memorized the dates of every recording session, knew the numbered takes for each master track, what got spliced where, who played what. I practiced along with every recording until I could play it back note for note. I wanted the experience to be as authentic as possible every time I chose which band member I was going to be. The Beatles became my best friends, but they were also all *me*.

Finally, I didn't feel so alone.

More than that, I discovered I had talent. *Real* talent, not just relative talent. You know what I mean by the difference? I discovered I was good *for anybody*, not just *for some Rapid City woodrat.* I didn't know the extent of it yet, since I wasn't playing with other people and getting to know their limitations, but even in the privacy of my room, I knew what I could do was the real deal.

You can call it all sorts of things. Perfect pitch. A phonographic memory. What it boils down to is my brain can hear a thing and then my fingers pretty instantly know exactly how to play it. I had a great singing voice too, with a range that encompassed all three main singers. Hell, I could even nail the motherfucking Liverpudlian accent.

It didn't take me long to learn each Beatle's part on each track.

After that, even though my heart remained with my favorite group, I applied those skills to other classic rock songs, as well.

Partly out of pure boredom, partly to see if anyone could stump me. I developed a repertoire.

That's what became my ultimate curse.

Because it made me perfect for cover bands.

Is there anything worse than a fucking cover band?

Maybe famine and genocide, but it's a close fucking race. Cover bands are to music what flies are to shit. A nuisance. A disease-vector. And they can drive you crazy with their godawful noises.

Sometimes, though, in the trashiest of places, they're your only companions.

What other choice did I have? Look. I was meant to make music. That much was clear. I didn't have any other skills. I'm not an otherwise pleasant person to be around (you'd be unpleasant too, if you had all this talent and nowhere to put it).

I also didn't have the money to travel somewhere new on my own. I didn't have any connections or insights as to where I could go that would be better for me. The music industry was dead, just another playground for nepo babies and investment bankers. I hated all the pop-shit that was currently being produced, so the idea of being some studio zombie sounded just as bad as the cover circuit.

It wasn't just that the odds of having a career were stacked against me, either.

The fact of the matter was I also had no real talent as a songwriter. (See? I'm not a total egomaniac.) Nothing I wrote was any good. It was all hack, clichéd garbage—at the very least, not worthy of what I was capable of playing. A musician of my caliber needed extraordinary music to play.

No, what I really needed was a partner. That's the common denominator of all great musical acts: talented people who find each other, complement each other's genius, push each other to new heights. Somebody was out there, somebody who'd need me as much as I needed them. . . but I was never going to find them where I was.

So, I resigned myself to the cover band life.

And, yes, I'm aware of the irony: railing against cover bands when that's seemingly what I was fucking made for. Here's the thing. I KNOW. I hated myself worst of all.

But actually. . . that's not entirely accurate. Because I wasn't like most other musicians I played with. Most cover acts are content to be smug little Xerox machines (if Xerox machines also had male-patterned baldness and unfortunate ponytails). I knew how to play the notes *behind* the notes. I breathed life into the familiar. I didn't want to just copy the sound. I understood every song was an attempt to communicate something—and the only thing anyone ever really tries to communicate with song, no matter what the subject, is *desperation.*

I was desperate, all right.

My future was out there. My band was out there. I just had to hold on and wait for the universe to finally point the way.

Sometimes the universe has a very strange sense of humor.

That's how I ended up at Meri-GO-Rounds and discovering the existence of time travel.

It was the worst gig of my life.

There'd been a couple gigs earlier in my career that I'd *thought* were my worst. Gigs where I'd sounded like shit. Early days. Green nerves. Almost threw up and/or shat myself onstage.

This gig put those experiences to shame. Because at this gig I sounded amazing. I was on fire. Every note I played, whether it was on bass or lead or the dinky little electric piano the venue had, was *right*. Full of passion and invention.

Then I looked out at the crowd. Five people at various tables, none of them listening, because they'd heard all of these songs a million times before and no matter how amazingly I played them, I might as well just be an iPod on shuffle. And I looked at the band onstage with me. Sagging. Middle-aged. And worst of all, *satisfied*. Smiling—except for the guy whose mouth hung open while he concentrated too hard on whatever he was playing. This was the happy culmination of all their effort and skill. This pathetic gig.

I saw my future in them and I wanted to die. No exaggeration. The very idea that I could ever be *satisfied* on a night like this.

It probably says everything that I don't even remember what band I was gigging with, doesn't it? I was playing in god knows how many groups by this point. Earning just enough to eat and keep my car. Since I was solid on every instrument and could learn parts after a few minutes of practice, I got passed around from band to band like a bit of gear. It didn't make sense for me to settle down with any one group, and none of the groups were worth settling down with anyway.

All I really knew was I was in Madison, Wisconsin, at an ugly little venue that was the partial birth abortion between a music venue and a dive bar, with the unpleasantly stylized name of Meri-GO-Rounds.

The set we played was standard fare. Classic rock, from Allmans to ZZ. A few Beatles tunes thrown in at my insistence. We played for a few hours and then, after we got paid out, the rest of the band—all roughly a hundred years older than me—declared they wanted to grab some chow and a few more rounds somewhere else in town.

I opted to stay behind. I said I wanted to rest my voice.

What I wound up doing was hiding in Meri-GO-Round's shit-ass green room (literally the repurposed Ladies' room, with all the toilets and stalls removed and a ratty old couch dragged over the stained tile floor).

I sat there, alone, numb, for what felt like hours, and the next thing I knew, I was sobbing uncontrollably into my hands. Just full-on weeping.

That's when the bar's manager, Tall Tony, came in and found me.

Tall Tony was aptly nicknamed. He was close to seven feet of gangly human joints, with a nose like a shark's fin and an Adam's apple like a crowning baby.

He asked me if I was okay, and I was so startled, my first impulse was to hit him. How much more pathetic would that have been? He wasn't even remotely close to me—imagine if I'd just started swinging at the air.

Honestly, though, me squirting out tears while punching at nothing in a repurposed bathroom feels all too appropriate a visual for how my life was going.

I didn't try to punch him. I did the next toughest thing. I told him to fuck off in my whiny-babiest voice. Very intimidating. And very smart to do to the guy who could decide whether I ever got booked there again. Learn from the best, kids.

To his credit, Tall Tony didn't tell me to fuck off twice as hard. He looked at me for a long time and said, "It's a tough life, isn't it? Sometimes the music just don't love you back."

I sniffed and nodded. I didn't want to explain to him the real reason I was so miserable. That being here, looking at him, looking at *everyone* tonight, made me feel more viscerally decrepit than I'd ever felt before. I wasn't even twenty-three! I was talented! Handsome! But now I could feel the edges of it, could see what was on the other side of it. Hell, at twenty-three, George Harrison was only four years away from the end of the Beatles; where would I be in four years? Duluth? It was the slowest death sentence a person could ever receive.

Then Tall Tony said, "Hey. Wanna see something special?"

He said, "This always puts things into perspective for me."

He said, "If this doesn't get you to believe in the magic of music, I don't know what will."

I couldn't turn that down, right?

We left the green room and he steered me to the office, where I'd already been earlier when the band got paid out. This time, Tony pointed me past the piles of papers and supplies to a white door set into the white wall. A *back* backroom. Easy to miss, especially when you were watching dollar bills being counted.

I eyed him suspiciously, suddenly remembering I was a skinny, young-looking kid who'd just been all sweet and vulnerable, all alone in an empty bar in the middle of the night, floating through the deep space outskirts of Madison, Wisconsin.

Didn't take much convincing for me to ignore my misgivings and follow him into the dark, though. Just one little hand wave from him. Guess I was eager for any sort of action that night. Even if I wound up under the floorboards.

I wasn't under any floorboards yet, though. I found myself standing in a pitch-black room. Lit only by a few candles set into a display on the far side wall.

It looked like an altar. As my eyes adjusted to the light, I could make out the faint impression of symbols and figures drawn on the dark walls with darker paint. I had to look away pretty quickly. It felt like all the designs were squirming restlessly in the candlelight.

What the fuck had I just stepped into?

That altar beckoned me forward.

In between the flickering candles was a large, shallow Tupperware tub. Maybe three feet wide and one foot deep. The sort of thing you might do a hefty load of handwash laundry in.

The water and tub looked clean, at least as far as I could tell in the darkness. The tub was some kind of light color. The water was clear.

I jumped when Tony revealed a knife in his hand. A silver butterfly knife he'd pulled from his pocket—par for the course for the manager of a joint like the Meri-GO to have a knife on him, I guess. He flipped the knife open with one smooth motion and I was already imagining my funeral when he pressed the handle into my palm.

"Drop a little of your blood into the water," he said. "Then, dunk your head and look inside."

Any non-musicians hearing this might balk at the idea of sticking their face into a tub of water that was full of god knows how many other people's fluids.

Believe me when I say, sometimes we get into weird shit after a gig.

Plus, there's no other way to explain this, but. . . you had to be there. In that room, you could feel it in the air. Something arcane. Something impossibly possible. Something. . .

You know that thing in movies, where people always slice open the palms of their hands for any kind blood ritual? That shit drives me crazy. Way to injure yourself for days, genius; maybe even get an infection and lose your whole damn hand. I chose the *least* intrusive place to draw some blood—the pad of my left thumb, the one finger that could withstand being a little injured and not affect my playing—and popped the blade into the skin. Squeezed out a couple drops into the water. I watched the blood swirl and squirm, like black tadpoles, before vanishing into the still-clear-looking liquid.

I looked one more time at Tall Tony. He nodded. Then, after a deep breath and a prayer to whatever googly-eyed idiot ran this universe, I stuck my face into the water.

In an instant, I wasn't bent over a tub.

It took me several seconds before I realized I was standing upright. Outside. And the sensation brushing against my face wasn't liquid, but. . . leaves. Branches.

My head was jutting out of a well-manicured hedgerow.

It was bright out. The air on my face wasn't that of an icy Midwestern midnight. It was pleasantly warm, slightly muggy. Not hot, but temperate, with the sun high and stubborn in a distinctly summer sky. I could smell a river nearby, as well as the telltale aromas of a fairgrounds. Beer. Food. Manure. Bodies.

I looked around, not knowing where my neck was in all this (though my head was clearly still attached to something), and put it all together pretty quickly. The cars told me I was somewhere in Europe. The accents I overheard from passersby told me it was England (specifically the North, based on their flat, melodic lilts). The clothes told me it was sometime in the 1950s or early '60s.

And then I saw signs for a church a few yards in front of me.

St. Peter's Church Field. Woolton Parish Church.

Woolton. A suburb of Liverpool. That church in front of me—actually one of several churches I could see from here—that's where, in July of 1957, Paul McCartney was introduced to John Lennon by a shared school chum after John's group, the Quarrymen, played at the Woolton Village fete. That's where the Beatles' story really begins.

Holy shit.

Holy fucking—

Suddenly, I was yanked back through the shrubbery. My head whipped into the dark, candlelit room. I was gasping, partially from the water, partially from the mindfuck.

I sputtered some outraged curses.

Tony clapped me on the back. "Well? Did you recognize where you were?"

Wiping water from my eyes, I rattled off everything I'd noticed. Everything I'd put together. Tony had to stop me, otherwise I could've kept going.

"Yeah, I figured you were a fan," he said, laughing. "I saw the way you looked when you were playing those songs tonight. Leonard's a fan like that too. He's the owner of this place. He's one of those *super* fans."

"How—what—?" I was already starting to feel like I imagined it. "How does it work?"

Tony shrugged. "I won't pretend to have any clue, brother. It just does. Leonard loves two things. The Beatles. . . and occult shit. Said all he ever wanted, more than anything in the world, was to see that moment his favorite songwriters got together, up front and in person. Somehow, over the years, he found a way to make it happen."

"Jesus," I said. It was terrifying to contemplate. "And it just takes a drop of blood?"

"The more blood you put in it, the longer you stay. Sometimes he'll cut himself something awful and stay there for weeks. Apparently, he can choose different spots in the timeline too—so he says, at least—but this is his favorite. The default setting. And the reason why it's his favorite is the same reason I'm showing it to you, kid. *This moment,* Leonard says, is for people in our business who really need the reminder: you never know where your journey is gonna go, and you never know how humble it's gonna start. Just look at that rinky-dink little street fair. History's made where you least expect it."

He had more of his speech prepared so I let him continue. But by then, I'd already come up with my plan.

I still had the knife in my hand. I wasn't going to waste the opportunity.

That's what luck is, right? Talent meets opportunity?

While Tony nattered on about perseverance and potential, I jammed the blade up and into his neck, right behind that ham hock of an Adam's apple. Then, I yanked him, guttering and choking, across the room and twisted his head so the blood gouted into the tub, turning the light color of the Tupperware dark. Bloody torrents stormed into the water.

It took a long time before he stopped gurgling and spazzing.

Once he was good and empty, I tossed his gigantic body to the side.

The water. . . It glowed.

It glowed white and blue and it hummed with a frequency I'm willing to bet no human ears have ever heard before.

You know what it kind of reminded me of, if I'm being totally honest?

It reminded me of the first time I ever heard that chord at the end of "A Day in the Life." That E major, struck simultaneously by five people on three pianos and one harmonium, left to sustain for almost an entire minute.

I knew I had a long road ahead of me—long and winding, yeah, yeah, yeah—so I didn't waste another second. Before that glow could fade away, I stuck my hands and head into the water, pushed off with my feet, and literally dove into the past.

I stumbled quickly away from the hedge. Bloody. Wild eyed.

I bumped into some lady who squawked in protest. I flipped her the bird while staring at the bushes. At my body. I was all in one piece.

And I was *here.*

Tony wasn't gonna pull me out. Even if he was still alive to try, I'd somehow gotten my whole body through the barrier, what was there to grab onto?

As long as the magic held, I was *here*.

And I had a feeling, since I had given whatever forces behind that magic an entire Tall Tony's worth of blood, I'd be here forever.

I looked around. Cocked an ear to the wind.

No music. The Quarrymen set hadn't started yet. They didn't go on until four pm or so, if memory served. I had plenty of time.

I merged into the crowd, suddenly grateful this particular shitty cover band employed a stupid dress code of all suits. I stuck out amongst the more casual, working-class crowd, but I certainly didn't look like a time traveler. And the dark clothes hid most of Tony's blood.

Quickly enough, I found who I was looking for.

I recognized him from photos.

Ivan Vaughan. The kid who would introduce Paul McCartney to John Lennon after the Quarrymen's set, and start off a partnership that changed the world.

He was a skinny kid. Easy to surprise and grab by the arm, yank into an alleyway between some buildings.

I promptly beat the shit out of him—not enough to do him any permanent damage, but definitely enough to make sure he wasn't going to meet up with his little friends and enjoy a day at the fair.

That done, I looked for a place to ditch my bloody clothes and get to work.

I'm sure I don't have to recount what happened next in too much detail, right?

Everybody knows the story.

A young, handsome stranger in northern England starts playing clubs and gathering a bit of a local fan base. He plays sweaty, pulsating rock and roll, and he insists his drummers splash their cymbals like they're trying to crack the heavens open. Everyone who plays with him says he's an intense perfectionist, maybe a bit of a tyrant, but also a visionary. His fans squeal that he's the next incarnation of Elvis—but he's also *better* than Elvis. Younger, leaner, more exciting. And his songs? His songs are punchy and energetic and fun and thrilling and *alive.*

He works a residency stint in the red-light district of Hamburg, Germany, then comes back and continues his conquest of Britain. His fanbase grows. It's not long before he gains a manager and that manager nabs him a record deal. His first album is a smash hit in England—and not only did he record it in one marathon session, he innovated new studio techniques that allowed him to play every instrument. Things like track dumping and artificial double-tracking. Even on this nascent album, he turns recording music into a new artform.

He's a writing, performing, recording machine. A wunderkind. It's just a matter of time before he takes over America. But he waits, perfectionist that he is, until he has a number one hit single in the States before crossing the pond. Once that happens—which, of course, it does—he kickstarts a mania unlike anything the world has ever seen.

Wherever he goes, his audiences (mostly teen girls) become a sonic wall of desperate ecstasy. His face is on merchandise piled from store floors to stockroom ceilings. He fills stadiums. He influences fashion. And, more than anything, he drags the begrudging critic class, who first try to dismiss his music before eventually becoming its biggest champions, along for the ride.

He calls himself the Beatle. A strange name for a strange fellow. He's witty, charming, cute, sometimes lovable, sometimes caustic, sometimes even a little intimidating. But he kicks the door open to a new era of popular music, and finally the baby Baby Boomers feel like they have something to call their very own.

I won't lie; it was a lot of fucking work. I might've had an outline to go off of, but still.

At first, I thought the hardest thing would be those first few years of waiting for the ride to begin, but actually, in some ways that was the best part. Playing in clubs. Playing in Hamburg. I really understood why John once said that those were his fondest memories. The energy in those rooms. The thrill of audiences discovering the potential of this new kind of rock and roll. It was heaven, man.

Thank God I looked young. It always cracked me up how much *older* previous generations looked at the same age. All those cigarettes, I think. All that lead in the gasoline. Even though I was like six years older than the oldest band member would have been, I still projected plenty of youth and innocence for those first few years.

I *did* have to change a few details along the way. I left Liverpool pretty early, after kicking the shit out of the Vaughan kid. I didn't want him squealing on me and making life difficult. So, I knocked around Manchester instead, until it came time for me to head to Germany. (I still made sure I played a couple gigs at the Cavern, though. I couldn't resist that.)

And, unlike the lads, I could be more targeted in my actions. I knew exactly who to pursue. I reached out directly to Brian Epstein for management. When it came time for a producer, I personally requested George Martin. I feared at first that these little tweaks might affect the story, but things still played out the way they were meant to. Like everyone else knew their roles too.

Sometimes, the biggest challenge was making sure things didn't happen too early. The Beatles' story is one of talent, but it's also one of timing. For instance, I wasn't waiting until I had a number one single in America before crossing the pond. I was waiting for November 22, 1963. I was waiting for national tragedy to give the US kiddies an emotional vacuum that needed filling.

Again and again, though, it seemed like the universe was willing to play ball. To jam along. Much obliged, Lee Harvey.

I made sure to hit all the big beats. No pun intended. (Or maybe it was intended; sue me.)

I played Sullivan and Shea.

I said I was bigger than Jesus.

I let myself get arrested for weed.

I starred in movies, including a baffling, *Magical Mystery Tour* (even threw some early Monty Python bits into that one, just for shits and giggles).

I got into a car accident and chipped my tooth—and that one wasn't even intentional. Funny how fate can work sometimes, right? But after it happened, I had someone spread a rumor that I was actually dead and replaced by a lookalike. Just for fun. Just for the mystique.

I made sure the album art looked as close as possible to what I started thinking of as "the older versions."

I went to India.

I started Apple records.

I played on the roof.

I did it all.

Greatest story ever told, man.

Of course, there were aspects I couldn't manage the same way this time around. This was especially true about the teeny bopper phase. I could be cute when I needed to be, but I couldn't be four separate people. I was selling one-fourth of the lunchboxes, if you know what I mean.

(Know who wound up filling that space in the marketplace? I

mean, of course you do. This reality is the only reality you know. The Dave Clark Five. Let me tell you, where I'm from? There's probably three people on the entire globe who remember the Dave Clark Five, and I'm including all five members of the band.)

So yeah, I was just one guy instead of a four-headed marketing monster. That was okay, there was still plenty of room for a sly, witty, handsome, and brilliant musician.

And sure, I wish I hadn't committed to the accent. Keeping *that* up was a unique pain in my ass. But I had too many lines in my head in that particular cadence—"Turn left at Greenland," "We need money first," "No, actually, we're just good friends"—and so it was non-negotiable. Eventually, I was able to make up some bullshit about loving America too much, the musicality of the American accent, and so I could let my Liverpudlian lilt drift away. A reverse Madonna, if you will. But for those first years, it was taxing.

On the plus side, I literally had no past in this world. My footsteps prior to 1957 couldn't be traced, and I couldn't be caught in any sort of lie. I'd also learned by example from folks in my timeline like Bob Dylan and Tom Waits, how to make up biographical details, how to enjoy fucking with reporters and fans, build a mystique, make any contradictions part of the fun.

Besides, in the early '60s, no one was really interested in probing details anyway. They were satisfied plenty with the quips and the charm.

Maybe the hardest thing was controlling the swear words. Holy fucking shitchrist, those first few years of the 1960s were still some *Leave It to Beaver* nightmare. I guess I can credit myself for helping change that.

The easiest part was the music.

It all came down to the music.

As taxing as everything was, it was always worth it to dig deeper and deeper into those songs. I could fill hours, days, weeks, years recounting the things I fell in love with all over again. The smallest details. That Aflat9 in "It Won't Be Long." The cowbell in "I Need You." The sitar in "Norwegian Wood." The basslines for "Something" or "Hey Bulldog." The drums for "Rain." The endless permutations of G, D, Em, Bm. Every track was a hundred new magic tricks, rolled into usually three pristine minutes.

The most important thing was making sure nothing I did sounded rote. Lifeless. Slavish. Uninspired. All the words I thought whenever I heard a cover band.

The music needed to sound dangerous. Even when it had a cute and cuddly surface—*especially* when it did. Each song needed to act as if it was a threat to the status quo.

It needed to have teeth, in other words.

And there needed to be mistakes! Organic moments captured on acetate. Even though I quickly became known as a monster in the studio, I made sure there were always little hiccups, little pimples. "Have fucking fun, but do it *right,*" I'd bellow at any studio morons I had to bring in for various sessions.

Greatest story ever told. Even an old cynic like me could get caught up in the enthusiasm.

Did I ever feel guilt? Or even hesitation at what I was doing?

Not in the fucking slightest.

I suppose, in the interest of full transparency (though this isn't a confession), maybe there were times when I thought it was kind of a shame that the Greatest Music Ever was now the product of one guy instead of four. There *was* something beautiful about the idea of four distinct personalities coming together to create something special. I almost felt bad for the people who weren't going to experience *that* version of the narrative—

But then I'd remember how alone I used to feel. How desperate for partnership. My circumstances weren't my fault; why should I be punished for them? I'd turned the Beatles story from a fable of luck and timing into a triumph of individual talent. And, shit! There were still plenty of other great *band* stories out there. If you wanted to believe in the magic of groups, you had plenty of options. But now, if you wanted to simply believe in yourself, *look no further than the Beatle.*

And, sure, I can even admit to the occasional night when my love for the music curdled into something dark. Something like jealousy. Maybe even outright loathing. Thinking about the arbitrariness of "talent." The unfairness of it all. But I couldn't stay mad for long, because look how I righted that injustice! Look how I fought for myself! Like Miles Davis used to say: it's not any specific note you play that's wrong, it's how you react to the note that *makes* it right or wrong.

I had nothing to feel guilty about.

I *have* nothing to feel guilty about.

I didn't even need to feel bad about Tall Tony! Motherfucker wasn't even born yet—he literally had his entire life ahead of him!

And more than any of that, if I had one of those rare bad nights full of dark thoughts, here's all I had to remind myself. The music was *mine* now.

Obviously, I didn't have a way to listen to the original recordings anymore. I hadn't smuggled my fucking iPhone and a charger back to the past. I was going entirely off of memory and instinct here.

So, who's to say I wasn't bringing my own genius to the music? Who's to say I wasn't contributing? Playing along, like when I first sat down with those *Anthology* demos? Making things different—or better?

No one can say that.

No one can fucking say that.

These were my songs too, now. My recordings. My memories. My fucking *life.*

Mine.

Any cover artist worth a damn knows you have to bring yourself to the material to make it work. Ha! Jimi goddamn Hendrix himself told me something very much like that after I complimented his cover of "Sgt. Pepper" at the Hollywood Bowl two days after the album came out. I told him he should cover Dylan next. That was *my* idea.

I have no regrets. I did what I was supposed to do.

And that's where I should leave these memories. Get a few hours' rest before the big interview in the morning.

And yet, for some damn reason tonight, my mind keeps going back to the train. . .

To that moment when I first got a taste of how things might crack.

We were filming the train sequence for *A Hard Day's Night,* my first movie.

Instead of the quintessential four-mischievous-lads ensemble romp that was the version I'd grown up watching, this time the story revolved around one central popstar (me) as he mucked about, procrastinating before a television special, taking care of his clean little grandfather, getting into shenanigans. I gotta say, I was pretty impressed how well the movie worked with just me.

For all the musical numbers, though, we had to come up with a bit of a staging convention. My idea: whenever the songs started playing, I could pull in random extras from the scenes and, voila, they'd turn into backing musicians thanks to Beatle magic. I really liked this; it felt like we were saying Beatle music was for everyone.

Now, obviously, I was a busy guy. For all my studio tyranny, I didn't have time to personally vet the actors who'd be hired for each of these little scenes. When it came time to film "If I Fell," all I knew was I'd be in a train car and I'd see some kids who are playing cards and moping because they can't get girls to like them. I'd start singing to cheer them up and, bam, turns out they can all sing and play with me. Nice, right?

When I saw *him* among the actors hired to join me in that train car, I almost shit myself.

There he was. James Paul McCartney. Twenty-two years old and cute as a button.

I kept my distance, but during setup, he came right up to me. Bold. Hungry.

He told me he was a big fan, and he too, was trying to start a career in the rock'n'roll business.

He told me he was also from "the Pool," and he recognized a certain energy in my music. You believe that? He *recognized* my *energy*? He was so proud of what I'd accomplished, and he only wished he'd seen me around when we were both living there. Surprising, that, he said, since it was such a small scene and all.

I told him it was nice to meet him and I wished him all the best of luck with his career.

Then, I promptly pulled the director aside and privately had that obnoxious, doe-eyed kid fired and kicked off set.

I didn't need that pretty face upstaging me. I didn't need him soaking up my ideas. *Recognizing* my energy.

I'd hoped that would be the end of it.

I should've known better he wouldn't be so easy to shake.

I ran into him again in '66. It seemed like a lifetime later; funny how fast the '60s moved.

This time, he was one of a couple opening acts for the Midwestern leg of my US tour that year.

The music scene had changed a bit, by virtue of the biggest pop act being a solo artist. There were still bands aplenty, but in the wake of Beatlemania the hottest thing was a musical act dominated by a front man. Not just a singer, but the unquestionable artistic force. More like Prince. James Brown. Springsteen.

Just as a ferinstance, then, there was no The Who. There was Peter's Face—and they really kinda sucked. Townshend, drunk on the example of my success, had no patience or interest in working with other personalities like Daltry, Entwhistle, and Moon, and so his band was just another middling R&B act with a few good songs and a bunch of problematic backstage anecdotes. Sorry about that, everybody. You're missing out on some great records.

The one I feel truly bad about is Brian Wilson. I guess because, in this new reality, the Beatles / Beach Boys competition was no longer between two bands but two central geniuses, Brian Wilson's dad went into overdrive pushing his son to do better, be better, out-genius his British counterpart. Poor Brian had a pretty severe mental snap during an interview in late '65. He had to be institutionalized. Lobotomized. The public didn't hear a peep from him after that.

What a tragedy, to live in a world without *Pet Sounds*, right? It would've been. Thankfully, I knew every note of that record too, so I "donated" a blueprint to the rest of the Boys. I said Brian and I had worked on it together in secret. (Not that he coulda contradicted me at that point.) It was released as a collab—"The Beach Boys (with the Beatle)." It was the one time I really deviated from history, but there was no way I was going to live in a world without "God Only Knows." (Also, to prove I'm not a total psychopath, I restrained myself from murdering Mike Love for the future crime of "Kokomo.")

Anyway. McCartney was going by the name McGear. His backing band included his brother and, for a couple years, a young school chum named George Harrison. McGear had done pretty well for itself on the bubblegum circuit, with modest hits like "World Without Love," "Like Dreamers Do," "I'll Be On My Way," "One and One Is Two," and a few other songs I'd totally forgot to do anything with. If I'd felt any guilt over having McCartney fired from my movie, I would've *stopped* feeling it once he scored his first chart-lander. He was going to be fine, the little prick.

This time, I didn't have him fired or kicked out of my presence. In fact, I was curious to hear what life was like for him these days. I even think there was a strange sort of begrudging respect I was developing. Because Paul was still hacking it. He was committed to the grind, whether he was famous or not. I could appreciate that humility.

I liked McGear too. Obviously, those hit singles were pretty damn solid. And they were starting to push into weirder, less predictable stuff, which was exciting to see. Plus, I can't lie: I missed the sound of that voice. Dude could always wail.

The press wrote them off as glorified Beatle-wannabes, though. I noted *that* with some satisfaction. They'd never be a threat.

After our third and final tour stop together (not too far from Madison, Wisconsin, now that I think of it), I decided, fuck it, I'll have a few drinks with the guy. Hell, I'll even bring him some hash. Be the Bob Dylan he never got to have.

Kinda funny to think how, just a handful of years earlier, if I could've shared a drink with Paul fucking McCartney, I would've been the happiest idiot on the planet. Now, I found myself tense. On guard. Spending time with him felt dangerous, although I couldn't tell why or how.

Maybe it was just that he seemed too eager. Too hungry. After a couple years of being famous, you get to understand that the world is full of leeches, always looking for a way to latch on and suck you dry. I can be forgiven for thinking he might be just another one of *them*.

Once I got a few drinks and a joint-and-a-half in me, I was able to relax a little. Him too. That's when he made a confession.

He'd been singing my praises for the umpteenth time, then said, "Can I be honest with you?"

I told him I hoped he was being honest already.

He chuckled. "I am. It's just. . . Some of your songs are so good, they. . . Well, they *hurt*."

I'd heard a lot of praise by then, but never *that*. I asked him what he meant.

He blushed. "In me brain, I mean. It's a good kind of hurt, but. . . I dunno. It almost feels like time gets crumpled up. Like your songs are from the future, but they've also *always* existed. You know what I mean? It's magic."

I barked a laugh, thinking of altars and candles. "That's high praise," I said. Then, because I'm a poet, I passed him the joint.

He took a hit, held in his cough. "I mean it, mate," he said. He stared into space for a moment. "And sometimes? I feel like you didn't just pull them out of time, but you pulled them out of my head. I know that sounds mad, but I don't know how else to. . . I mean. . ."

He was already high as a kite. His eyes rolled around like bloodshot marbles. I let him continue.

He went on to tell me how, when he was a teenager, he used to pretend to be a snooty French guy at parties to try to impress girls. He would play a little fake French-sounding song on the guitar while pouting dramatically in the corner. . . and that song was essentially the same as my own "Michelle," which had come out late last year.

"Almost note for note!" he said with wonder. "Isn't that daft? Little tunes that had been bouncing around in me head for years, and I'd pick them up and dust them off, only to realize you'd beaten me to it. Ha. Is that why you're named the Beatle?" He gave a nervous, inebriated titter. I humored him with a tight smile.

The weirdest example, he confessed, was last September. One morning, he'd woke up, fell out of bed, and hurried to the nearest instrument to set down a melody that was running through his head. He'd dreamed up a song—and a damned good one, at that. Something about it felt *classic*. "Like it'd always existed," he said again with the reverence of the very stoned. He was excited about the song's prospects. The only thing he didn't have were the lyrics. Just some stupid placeholder words that would have to be changed.

A few days later, he sat down with the intentions of doing just that. But first, he turned on the radio for a little inspiration, only to hear *that exact same song* coming from the speaker.

"The DJ said it was the premiere broadcast, y'see," Paul said. "It had never been played before. There was no way I'd somehow knicked it on accident. And yet, there it was. Like the universe was laughing at me." He stared into his glass. "Eerie, yeah? Stupid." Another smile. Trying to be chipper, but a familiar pain was smeared all over his face.

I stubbed the joint out. "Creativity's a funny thing," I replied. "Can't let it get you down." I was suddenly eager to have this little heart-to-heart over with. I worked on draining the rest of my too-full glass down my throat. "Besides, take it as a good sign that you're writing songs *that* good without even trying, yeah?"

"I guess you're right," he said with a shrug. Then, with some mock bravado: "Hey, I almost wrote 'Yesterday' in me sleep."

"There you go!" I took another deep drink. "And we'll just thank god it'll never be known as 'Scrambled Eggs.'"

One more gulp. My glass was almost empty.

Then I noticed he was staring at me. Hard. An expression I hadn't seen on his puppy dog face before.

"How'd you know about 'Scrambled Eggs?'" His voice was hushed and horrified. He sounded like a man whose wife had just confessed an affair.

"Huh?" I said.

"'Scrambled Eggs.' Those were the lyrics I was using, before I. . . How did you know?"

"Oh," I said. Then forced an annoyed chuckle. "You just told me, Paulie. Duh."

"I did?"

"*Yeah.*" I sounded as teasingly put out as I could. "I think it might be time to cut you off for the night, buddy." Then, with quiet horror of my own, I suddenly realized my accent had slipped a little. I'd said at least that entire last sentence as old, American me. The first time I'd made that mistake in years. I cleared my throat and redoubled my Scouser. "Anyroad. We're all drawing from the same pool, lad. The important thing is to keep at it."

He gave a glum smile and nodded. Then he set to finishing his own glass.

I watched him, torn between pity and wariness. I began debating with myself: maybe I could offer to write a couple songs for him. Throw some later stuff his way. "Silly Love Songs" or "Backseat of My Car" or, hell, all of *Red Rose Speedway*, which is full of obscure little gems. Maybe without the baggage of the Beatles' reputation hanging over them, those songs might finally get the respect they deserve.

Then it occurred to me, possibly for the first time: on this timeline, I'm not a band. I can't exactly break up. I need to start culling the best of the solo material for myself, to try to stay relevant. It'd be smarter for me to hang onto all the good stuff, which thankfully I also knew inside and out.

I realized McCartney had been speaking this entire time and something he said jumped out at me.

"Wait, wait," I told him. "Go back. What?"

"I was saying I know where I got those barmy ideas about creativity and the like," he said. "An old mate of mine. It was sad to see."

"Tell me," I said. For some reason, I already had a sinking suspicion who he was talking about.

Moments ago, I'd been ready to leave. Now I felt rooted to the spot.

He went on to tell me about a friend of his "from 'round the 'Pool," who played guitar in the band he'd formed before McGear. Not a solo-supporting group, but an actual band, a partnership. Until said partner started to lose all grips on reality. Hearing things. Suffering from horrible headaches. Getting increasingly frustrated and depressed. Even violent.

"I probably shouldn't be telling you this."

"Why not?"

"Well, because it was your music that did it to him. If me dreaming up a song you wrote sounds daft, what happened with *him* was right certifiable. He'd bring in fragments of songs he wanted to work on and, at least half the time, they'd turn out to be something *you* had coming out on a record. He kept swearing it was a coincidence, that he was trying as fast as he could to get songs out—and he had plenty of great songs we did know *were* his—but, in the end, we had to kick him out of the group. He was just too touchy, you know? He was dash obsessed with you."

"Was?"

"*Is,* I suppose. He's still knocking about somewhere. Last I spoke with him, he was blathering on about how maybe it all wasn't a coincidence. Maybe there were hidden messages to him. Y'know, *in* your songs. Like you were trying to communicate with him. Tell him something."

"Did he ever say what?"

Paul shook his head. "To be honest, speaking with him makes me too sad. It's heartbreaking, really. I hope he gets his head on straight. He's got real talent. Then again, after 'Yesterday,' I can kinda imagine what it was like for him. . ." He started absently rubbing his temple.

It was quiet for a moment while I processed this. Paul was staring at me again. Half-lidded. . . but avid.

"Hope that didn't unnerve you, mate," he said at last.

I'm not your mate, I wanted to snarl. Instead, I waved him off. "Fans. I'm used to it. They read into things that aren't there. Feel like they own you."

Trying to be dismissive, but there was a touch of dread in my stomach.

Did I say a touch? No, it was a full body ice-bath.

Because Paul didn't know this, but what he was really telling me was. . . the two of them had *still* met. Despite my little intervention in Woolton. My simple twist of fete, hahaha.

Christ. I'm sweating now, remembering it.

Then McCartney leaned in close. I could smell the alcohol and weed on his breath. I could see his slightly twisted front teeth, which had stared back at me from countless posters on my wall when I was a kid.

"Just. . . be careful if you ever cross wind of him, yeah? He's got a mean streak, and when he sets his mind on something. . ." A rancid belch suddenly tore out of him. He quickly leaned away, moaning. "Bloody hell! I'm so sorry! I think you're right, I've had too much. I'm just so nervous being around you. I'm such a fan."

His cheeks were scarlet. He giggled, looking sincerely embarrassed.

But I wasn't buying it. Once again, I could see a strange sort of flintiness underneath. Almost like he'd be glad if he scared me.

It looked very close to hatred.

I wanted to punch him square in those crooked teeth.

But I didn't. I paid the tab and wished him luck on his career.

And even though I had all sorts of plans for how to perform my more psychedelic shit in concert—in my previous life, I saw the Flaming Lips four times, man—right then and there I decided that maybe I should stop touring for the time being. Maybe I should be more guarded with my physical presence. You never know what kind of crazies were out there. In some ways, the freaky '60s were really *just* getting started.

It wasn't until I played my last gig a couple weeks later, Candlestick Park in San Francisco, that I realized I'd repeated history without even meaning to.

Not long after that, the letters started.

I was always drowning in fan mail, but I never got tired of checking it.

Maybe because there was something specific I was always on the hunt for.

I first got a taste for it at some point around mid-1965. A fan had written and said they loved "Dizzy Miss Lizzy," specifically how I made the guitars sound like they were "airplanes at an airshow."

I pumped a fist in the air when I read that. Eat my mop-topped knob, you Fab Four fucks. I *rule.*

Maybe I should explain.

I always hated "Dizzy Miss Lizzy." It's the final track of *Help!* and the way the Beatles recorded it, it's like being trapped in a room with a mosquito. George's lead guitar line just whines around your goddamn ears until you want to swat your record player. When it came time for me to record it, then, I made my own improvements.

And, stipulated, it's just a cover of an old Larry Williams song, a little bit of filler that was never going to be anybody's favorite song. But here was this fan singling it out. Specifically for the changes *I* made. (Not like that fan would know that, of course. But I sure fucking did.)

For the next however many years, I was always tearing through letters, looking for comments, compliments, about the things I knew I'd done differently.

I found plenty, don't you fucking doubt that for a second.

But around late 1967, I started getting a different kind of letter, as well.

I recognized the drawings right away. How could I not? Copies of *In His Own Write* and *A Spaniard in the Works* had been treasured artifacts of my childhood. Hell, I'd even filled my copy of *Write* with silly attempts at duplicating his signature over and over again when I was thirteen or so.

Nothing in these letters was worthy of those books. They were much rawer. Hastier. And way, way stranger.

But they were captivating all the same.

Some of them were even signed with an ominous "JL" at the bottom. Jagged as a knife slash.

No doubt who they came from, despite the lack of a return address.

The first time I opened one up, I stared at it for what felt like hours.

The poor guy was obviously batshit. And, like all batshit people, he kept assuring me he wasn't batshit. But he just "couldn't shake the feeling" that there was "some connection" between the two of us. There were too many coincidences, in the melodies we were writing, in our lyrics and imagery. He didn't come out and say it this bluntly, but only just barely: those coincidences were driving him crazy.

In some of his letters, he included poems—poems that were brand new to me, but also somehow naggingly familiar. Poems about loneliness. Poems about anger. Poems about kinship bordering on obsession.

And the drawings. Cute, almost cuddly line drawings of strangely shaped people who quickly devolved into twisted pile-ups of flesh, bones. Tearing each other apart. Wearing each other's skin.

"This couldbe shouldbe us," the caption of one read. One of the figures holding hands looked so much like Tall Tony I belched a little acid.

Underneath a drawing of a woman drowning in the ocean:

"Julia, my MOTHER'S name

How did you know o wizardly won???"

Underneath a drawing of a man placidly burning to death:

"STRAWBERRY FIELDS

UP where I grew

DOWN you ask to take me? Ha! HA!

Nutt hinge is real in deeds

(please get out of my head, he asked everso polite-like)"

There was never any return address, and the envelopes were always typed, so there was no way to anticipate when they were among the fan mail flood. And, no matter how many times my mailing address changed, he always found me. At home. At studios. At Apple.

I didn't know how he was finding me.

Then I'd flash on that night with McCartney.

That shimmering hatred in his eyes.

And I'd wonder, was Paul somehow helping his friend out? He was embedded enough in the industry that he could probably get a hold of certain information like that.

Hell. Maybe Paul was in on the letter-writing campaign too. Maybe the two former partners weren't as estranged as he'd made it seem to me.

That look in his eyes. That rageful suspicion.

Not to mention, there'd been the phone call after *Sgt. Pepper* came out.

It was a landmark smash, of course. I knew it would be, but even I was unprepared for how monumental *Sgt. Pepper* wound up being. The hype around it had always been a bit academic to me—it was never my favorite album by a long shot—but people treated it like I was Moses coming down with a new set of tablets.

Most people, that is.

Somehow, McCartney got my number and rang me up.

I could tell he'd been drinking. And after paying desultory lip service to my "genius new record," he was silent for a moment and then added, "Are you sure we never met back in Liverpool? When we were kids or something?"

I told him of course I was sure. My heart was thudding very slowly.

He said, "Your song, 'When I'm Sixty-Four'. . ."

"What about it?" I asked. My palms were dry.

"I wrote that song when I was a teenager. I wrote—"

"You mean you wrote a song *like* it," I corrected. The spot in my thumb where, a decade earlier, I'd cut myself with a butterfly knife, itched and throbbed.

"Exactly like it," Paul whispered. "Words and all."

"We're all drawing from the same pool," I said again, then made an excuse and hung up.

I never spoke to him again.

But that's when I first decided they both needed to die.

I was keeping tabs on all of them by this point. McCartney was easy, because he was the most visible. But Starr and Harrison were pretty easy too.

I was fairly positive George was never going to be a problem—and I was right about that, he wound up cycling through various groups before setting off on his own and writing a boatload of new songs and hits in the 1970s. He'd found his voice and I was happy for him. I knew he wasn't going to hold any sort of cosmic, interdimensional grudge against anybody. That wasn't his style.

Ringo too, seemed contented enough as a studio drummer who found second-career success as a comedic actor and celebrity game show contestant.

But Lennon. . .

I knew Lennon was dangerous.

It was Lennon who was capable of an anger that even time travel couldn't tie off. I didn't need any letters or drawings to understand that. Looking at Lennon's original biography, it took burning through the heights of fame before finally finding a family and a purpose that could grant him peace.

I'd robbed him of that little journey, hadn't I? There was no telling what kind of person he was now.

Of course, gone were the days when I could do that sorta dirty business myself. Thankfully, I had people on retainer who could take care of him for me.

There was only one problem. Nobody could find him.

In a lotta ways, it was still the goddamn *stone age*, man! Those same technological limitations that allowed me to slip into the world without a past meant the person I was looking for could disappear without a trace. It was infuriating.

I could find all the places he'd *been*: he'd served jail time for assault, he'd moved around a bit once he was released, it looked like he even sold a few bits of artwork at some point. But where he currently *was* remained a mystery. Fuck, I should've brought some coding books with me from the future so I could invent goddamn Google.

I kept my guys on ice for the time being, then. Told them they were free to take other jobs, like working security for an upcoming music festival over in Altamont. I said I'd call them when I needed them.

I'd changed my mind about doing anything to McCartney too. For now. Two reasons. First, my better angels reminded me that a musician dying young did wonders for their reputation. I didn't need to go around accidentally making any martyrs who'd be even more popular dead than alive.

And second, before the decade wrapped up, McGear called it quits. I didn't know why, nor did I much care. I was just grateful that little gadfly stopped buzzing.

I had enough problems as it was.

If it was relatively easy to press pause on taking out some annoying also-ran musicians, it was an act of titanic fucking willpower to not have every member of the press fucking slaughtered.

They weren't doing it right. They weren't playing their part.

I had to keep reminding myself: this could be totally normal. This could just be what the story was like from the inside. In all my studying and memorizing, maybe I'd simply overlooked this part of it.

Hard to believe, though.

Critics were cooling on the Beatle. No. They were being fucking savage. It was insane—now, at the height of the magic?! I was killing myself to make sure The White Album, *Abbey Road, Let It Be*, and even goddamn *Yellow Submarine* were all as iconic as they were meant to be, and yet, a distinct disinterest was creeping into the reviews. Ho-hum. Another Beatle hit single, but is it any good?

Melody Maker said, "As catchy as it is, one can't help but wonder, *what's the point*?" about "Hey Jude!" "Hey Jude," for fuck's sake!

Look. I knew the story would play a little differently when it's one guy instead of four. And I can admit to a little increased volatility on my part. I was getting meaner, less interested in interviews, in playing the role of this batshit generation's spokesperson. I was also starting to get even more demanding in the studio. Firing idiots. Requiring more precision. Breaking things. Breaking people.

Big fucking deal. I was making some of the greatest albums in the history of music, for the love of Christ! You know it ain't easy! I had a legacy to secure! I had a responsibility!

And yet, "His erratic behavior is increasingly being reflected in his music. One wishes he would regain his clarity of vision and stick to it," quoth the New York Fucking *Times* on the White Album. The fucking WHITE ALBUM. It's not SUPPOSED to have a clarity of vision—the chaos is the point!

You know what they are?

Leeches. All of them. The fans. The press. Hungry fucking leeches.

Fuck them. I knew history was on my side.

I knew because I'd already lived it.

Was it around this time I realized I was being followed? I think it was.

Those shadows.

Haha. Sounds crazy, putting it that way. No crazier than some of those bad reviews, though. Haha.

By 1970, I knew I had a tough decision to make.

If you'd asked me before I got into all this, I would've said one of the reasons this was the Greatest Story Ever Told was because it was finite. If the Beatles don't break up *and stay broken up*, their magic gets tarnished. Right? They become, what, the Rolling Stones (or, as they're known now, Jagger). A cover band of a different stripe.

But a thing you've gotta understand is, this timeline was different! The creative force behind the magic was different! I wasn't four bickering personalities; I was one clearheaded individual who could ensure a unified quality control.

("The beautiful harmonies remind one of how isolated their singer has become. And the album's final message of love and karmic return rings a bit hollow in light of how much little love he has been willing to 'make.'" The Village Voice on *Abbey Road.* Can you fucking believe that?!)

So, fuck that. This Beatle was going to continue into the 1970s. I was going to prove the magic could last.

I had a whole buffet of solo album tracks to choose from too. Every Beatles fan's wet dream. I could put tracks from *All Things Must Pass* on an album next to tracks from *Imagine* and *Ram* and even *Beaucoup of Blues.* To show I wasn't daunted by this new decade, I put out six new albums from 1970-73 alone. And they were all fucking brilliant. Objectively.

But you wouldn't know that from the fucking critics.

Namby-pamby little reactionary pissholes, complaining that "something was missing," "a Beatle release used to feel like magic, now it's just another collection of decent songs," "it feels like he's going through the motions."

I would scream at the papers in my hand. I fucking *spoiled* them and now they were moaning about having more of what they always wanted?!

("What is this shit?" *Rolling* fucking *Stone* on *Let It Be.* That one made me go nuclear. THAT WAS SUPPOSED TO BE SAID ABOUT A DIFFERENT ALBUM, NOT ONE OF MINE.)

I was happy to spend all my time in the studio, anyway.

Because everywhere I went, there was that feeling of being shadowed.

Here. There.

Everywhere.

To a certain extent, you got used to that as a celebrity. There were never not eyes on you all the time. Wherever you went, your presence instantly redefined the space. You could never go to *a restaurant*, you could only go to *a restaurant where the Beatle visited.* You became a perpetual event in everyone else's life.

But this sensation was different. This wasn't the omnipresent slathering of eyeballs. This was a feeling of. . . of. . . turning around and just missing the eyeballs.

It was the feeling of losing at tag.

But who was tagging me? Who was I just missing? Why did I always see shadows just slipping away, around corners, behind walls, too fast for me to catch? Laughing at me? Making my head ache. . . and my thumb itch?

Around early '72, Paul released a statement saying he'd formed a new group. He was tired of solo-supporting outfits like McGear (or, heavily implied in his smug little press release, the Beatle) and wanted more of an egalitarian experience, one where everyone contributed. What a fucking joke, right? *Paul McCartney*, of all people, saying that?

He called his new group Wings. I read in an interview later that he'd originally wanted to call it the Ramones, because he sometimes liked to play under the fake name of Paul Ramon, but when I released my song "Ram On," he decided to come up with a different name so he wouldn't be associated with the past. He still wanted an animal theme, though, and the name Wings just sounded *right.*

His wife was also in the band. His wife, Linda. The famous photographer. They met at a press event she happened to be photographing and fell in love.

Why, when I read that, did I want to shriek in terror?

I remember back in '67 when my manager, Brian Epstein, died. *That* had been wonderful. Another one of those timeline-confirmation moments, when I felt the hand of fate was nudging me along the right path.

But this? This was like that moment's evil twin.

That feeling of being tagged, but then not seeing who tagged you.

I don't remember if I received the letter that same day, or if they've just merged together in my mind. But when I saw a small padded envelope with Lennon's recognizable handwriting—not typed this time—I knew something momentous was about to happen.

The contents of that letter. . .

I don't like to think about it.

For all their batshittery, I used to have a hard time throwing his fan mail away. Not this time. I promptly tore it to shreds. My main regret was not wiping my ass with it first.

It began:

"I know you don't know me. But I owe you an apology."

Christ. Got worse from there.

He told me how he'd gone through a rough time, made a lot of mistakes, hurt a lot of people. But he was clearheaded now. For the first time in his life. Eyes wide open. He understood that love really *was* the key to everything. Not just as a snappy little catchphrase, but as a difficult truth worth fighting for.

I'm not doing his letter justice, and that's on purpose.

All I'll say is I started weeping while I read it. I stood there, tears pouring off my cheeks, in awe of the way this lunatic was describing the concepts of peace and struggle and love. He put things in ways I'd never heard before. Never considered before. I thought I knew all he'd ever have to say on the subject.

And then he closed by saying it was all thanks to my music.

He said he was sorry the press was being so cruel right now. That they thought I sounded erratic and schizophrenic. *He* understood what it meant to have different versions of yourself, all fighting for control. He understood inner contradictions. He thought that made my music *desperate*. And all good music should be desperate when you boiled it down.

Because of me, he was also inspired to start making his own music again. He'd stopped for a long time, which is when his life had really gone off the rails. But now he was writing more than ever before, music was pouring out of him. He didn't even have headaches anymore; now he felt more like a cosmic radio. At ease. Receptive.

In fact, he'd even made a demo cassette with an at-home recorder and was passing it around to studios and receiving incredible feedback. He'd included a copy with his letter—would I like to listen to it?

Looking back on it, I think that letter was the worst thing to happen to me over the entire course of this strange and storied career.

I listened to his tape. That fucking piece of shit sonofabitch.

It was a mix of songs I'd never heard before and songs off of what I knew of as *Plastic Ono Band.* His first solo album, full of primal screams, where he dumps his soul onto the table after the Beatles breakup. Where he says, "Here I am, warts and all."

Of course, I knew all those songs inside and out. I'd had plenty of opportunities to use any of them on my post-*Abbey* output. But I'd ignored that entire record because it just felt wrong. Narratively speaking, I mean. How could I sing about the end of the Beatles if there wasn't any end to it? How could I sing about finding peace in Yoko if I wasn't in any sort of relationship like that? I figured I'd hold onto those songs for years to come—maybe fashion them into a late career masterpiece, like Dylan's *Time Out of Mind.*

Now, listening to them with the hiss and crackle of an authentic home demo, I was reminded of how brilliant they were. Authentic. Raw. Beautiful. Painful.

The newer songs too. As wise and full-hearted as anything off of *Double Fantasy,* but with an edge and an energy that was unlike anything I'd ever heard before. Decades of invention and genius, poured into new vessels. With the somehow undeniable feeling that there were plenty more songs where these came from.

That he was just getting started.

The fucker even included a cover of my "Imagine." A song *Creem* called "a sappy, forced plea for doing literally nothing." His version was so pure, so *real.* It opened the song up, revealed layers I'd had no idea where there, despite knowing every inch of it. I was baffled.

Later, I learned that copies of the demo had already made their way to the hands of all sorts of industry press. People were talking about it as this underground miracle. A musical triumph, recorded by this obscure British everyman, full of pathos and anger and sincerity and vulnerability. "Not like that over-produced, twee crap being put out by dinosaur acts like The Beatle," one particularly jaundiced anal wart with a typewriter wrote.

I called up every studio contact I had. I gave them his name and said to never let that guy into their studios. *Ever.* Same went for every record label: don't work with that guy, he's bad news, he's dangerous, he's got screws loose. Not to mention, he used my song without permission and I'd sue the shit out of anyone who tried to release it. All my industry power, to make sure that demo stayed a demo, nothing more.

But the buzz kept buzzing.

Meanwhile, my most recent album, *Living in the Material World,* had just come out and the reviews were worse than ever. I felt like I was losing my mind. The songcraft hadn't changed! If anything, I felt like I was getting better and better.

But the press only got harsher. Meaner. They said I'd started to crack up. That, by not touring for so many years and rushing out half-baked material, I was showing utter disdain for my fans. I wasn't even relevant anymore. I hid behind studio trickery, when stripped-down authenticity was now the rage. They even criticized me for staying silent on too many current events and political issues (as if I didn't know how they treated the original Beatles whenever they released anything overtly political).

Fine, I thought. Fuck it. They want something new and different? They want something off-script?!

By this point, I had my own home studio. I wasn't going out much anymore. Because of the shadows, which were following me everywhere outside. Causing me to flinch and jump and startle and swing fists. I almost broke Dick Smothers' jaw one night because it got in the way while I tried to defend myself. So, I decided to lock myself away in my private studio and do the thing I'd spent my entire professional life avoiding.

My own material.

Songs I'd carried with me for years, but was too self-conscious to ever finish. Songs I wrote there on the spot, in clear-eyed bursts of inspiration. It all poured out of me. Like water. Like blood. And you know something? It was magnificent! I found myself with a quadruple album of all original material, all brand new to this, or *any,* timeline.

I worked myself ragged. "Half-baked" and "rushed?" It almost killed me. I was emptied. I was raw and vulnerable. I put all my rage and fear and confusion and paranoia and guilt and horror and loneliness—not to mention every lesson I'd ever learned, as a performer, as a writer, as a musician, as a man—into these songs.

And, as a capper, I released it under my own name. No more Beatle. That dream was over. I was just me.

I called it *Cry for a Shadow.* I loved that title. It just came to me, like a gift.

Christ, I was proud. I don't know why I'd ever doubted my abilities. My worth. As far as I was concerned, these songs stood toe-to-toe with anything *they'd* ever released before.

I'd been so deliriously focused on my album that, during that time, Wings was able to release a new album as well. They called it *Band on the Run.* It was full of songs I'd been planning on featuring in my next Beatle album, but hadn't gotten around to laying down yet.

In those precious first days immediately after I finished *my* album, I didn't care. Let them have their silly little concept record (which honestly wasn't that great to begin with, save for three or four songs). Let the press savage *them* for a change.

Of course, we all know what happened.

Band on the Run was a massive success.

My album became a punchline.

People said I sullied the name and memory of my former

music.

That it was a miracle I hadn't died of embarrassment.

They said that, for the first time, I sounded like I was desperately copying trends instead of setting them.

Some even pointed out that a few of my songs sounded suspiciously like a certain demo tape that had been making the rounds lately. Was I even writing my own material? Did I use ghostwriters?

Apparently, it was the most common title found in used record bins for the remainder of the decade.

Ha.

Hahaha.

Goo-goo-g'joob, right? O untimely death.

Anyway, that's when I decided it was finally time to pull the trigger, so to speak. Bang, bang. Bring that hammer down.

It was the only hit I put out in '75. Hahaha, I'd been putting out hits for over a decade now, but none like *this*. Hahaha. Christ. What the fuck am I laughing about?

I never should've let them live so long.

I called up my guys, substantially upped the fee I was willing to shell out, and waited for the good news.

I had them start with the Crazy One. Now that his demo tape was everywhere, at least he was findable, the stupid git. Finally on the map now. This would be over in a jiffy.

Except, it wasn't.

On the first attempt, the gun jammed.

On the second attempt, a cop showed up at just the right time.

On the third attempt, the guy I hired got cold feet.

And would you believe there was a fourth attempt? A fifth?

All told, there were *nine*. Each as unsuccessful as the last. The fucking guy was unkillable, it seemed. And I don't even know if he was ever aware of how close he came!

Again and again, it was like the universe was taunting me.

By the time I decided screw it, move onto the Cute One instead, I couldn't get anyone to take the job. One of my contacts even said, "The guy from Wings? My wife loves him. No way, man."

FINE, I thought. Fuck it. Next time I see him, *I'll* kill him myself. I've done it before. I can do it again. Maybe I'll just invite him over to my place and do to him what I did to Tall Tony. What I could've done to Ivan Vaughan.

Meantime, I tried to get Wings blackballed from every studio and label too, same as I did with Lennon.

I could tell right away I was getting lip service. No one was taking me seriously. Wings sold too well. Apparently that's all that matters these fucking days. Also, I think some people resented me for forcing them to miss out on the early Lennon opportunity. Fucking *leeches*.

They're all fucking *leeches*. That's why they were still passing Lennon's tapes around. Swishing it all in their mouths, wondering how much they could suck from it. I was doing Lennon a favor, really.

They're no different than the fans. Just as insane. Just as *proprietary*.

They think they're entitled to everything of yours.

They think it's a game just to get close to you.

To take over your life.

To make *you* a part of *their* story.

And those shadows kept dancing around me, man. Around every corner, just out of sight: slip sliding away (wait, I didn't write that one, did I?). I started thinking more and more of that back backroom in Meri-GO-Round. That room made of squiggling shadows. That tub of water with a single, vanishing squirm of dark blood. A shadow, dancing out of sight. Back then, I'd thought of it as a bloody tadpole. But it was just another leech.

Lennon decided he didn't need studios after all. He started releasing music independently, and soon enough, the major distributors decided they didn't have to heed my warnings anymore. I was the *past.* I was another Elvis. They picked Lennon up. Gave him store placement. Radio placement.

I was right: he had plenty of new material in him. Tremendous, exciting stuff. Really groundbreaking.

Except, he's talking to me in his songs. Taunting me. I can hear it in his lyrics. Every new release, I shut myself up and listen to it. For clues. Where is he? What's his next plan? "I knew it was you," he sings in one. "It was always you." Or his song, "Mother's Name." That one's definitely about me.

I know he wants to kill me. (Honestly, who can blame him?)

I know because he's already tried, at least once.

That was one of the last times I left my compound. Sometime in New York City, 1975. I'd had to go to take care of some legal issues in Manhattan. I had bodyguards with me by this point—too many days, too many shadows darting in the periphery.

A shot rang out.

One of my guards went down. I stood there and watched his blood pool out across the concrete while my other guard tried to usher me away.

I was okay, though. Not a scratch on me. Just a throbbing,

itchy thumb.

Watching the pool.

We're all drawing from that same pool. No one owns anything. No one owes anything. I tried to kill him. He tried to kill me. Even stevens. Life goes on, brah.

Then the other guard went down. Another shooter? The same one?

He'd hired a group, it seemed. Not just a solo artist.

Later accounts described me as running away from the scene (some rather uncharitable tabloids even said I was trying to use bystanders as human shields). But, no, I was running *into* the crowds. Screaming for the assailant to be revealed. Scanning faces the way someone might read lyrics, looking for meaning, looking for connection, for a goddamn CLUE that meant ANYTHING to me.

That's when I finally saw them. The shadows. My clearest glimpse of them yet.

Four silhouettes. Thin. Full of energy, bounding and scampering off in different directions. But I saw them, the little fucking brats. John and Paul's hired goons.

Wearing my old suits. Even copying my old haircut. Very clever.

They must've been following me for years, waiting for their moment to strike—but I survived! I'm still here!

I know to watch out for them now. I don't go out anymore. And they can't get into my home—I have too much security for them. I won't let what almost happened to George in the '90s happen to me. I won't let what happened to *any of them* happen to me. I'm *smart.* I have history on my side.

I'm mostly alone all the time now. I have my staff and my guards. My reputation as an asshole keeps everyone else away, but that's fine. I know how to be alone, I know what it's like to be sad and dead, I'm from South Dakota, hahaha!

I know they all think I'm insane now.

They're insane. They're the ones who had no idea how to play the role they were supposed to play! They fucked the story up because they're brainless feeders! They just want to suck. Leeches! Leeches with an A! Ha! Leaches. Hahahaha!

You know something? I bet if I ever caught one of those flouncing, bouncing shadows, the ones who tried to kill me, and I turned them around, I bet I know what I'd see. Leaches, pouring out of where their faces should be. A rain of wet, slick, toothy tubes. No human face under that mop of hair. All they need is blood, dah-dah-dah-dahdah. Blood is all they need.

They're relentless. It's never safe.

So, I don't go out much anymore.

I don't make music either. None of you deserve my music anymore.

Only problem is, security is expensive, and staff is expensive, and houses are expensive, and recording contracts are merciless and maybe I should've spent a little less time memorizing instrumentation and a little more learning the business. Apple was killing me. Worthless hired assassins didn't help, either.

That's why I've initiated this whole *Anthology* project. I know, I know, it was supposed to wait until the mid-90s. I'm about fourteen years too early. But I need the cash. And I need to remind people how good I was. I need to inspire interest in my back catalogue.

I won't be releasing any *Anthology* albums, though.

I don't need some stupid little fuckers from bumfuck towns discovering my music and playing along to my demos. Feeling like they have any right to play *with* me.

I bought the Meri-GO-Round bar years ago, too. Tore it down.

I'm not taking any chances.

Because I'm a smart fucking guy.

Because it was all worth it.

All of it.

I changed the world

Me. All by myself. I didn't have any h—

Assistance.

I deserve to tell my story.

Greatest Story Ever Told.

Aw, fuck, I shouldn't have thought about all this stuff. It got me all paranoid and upset. It was stupid to indulge in these thoughts all night. Why did I do that?

Fucking time travel. It messes with your head. You think about things too long and it gives you the bends. (*The Bends*! That's a good album. I wonder if that will still come out. Actually, I bet I still know all those songs. And I can still hit the high notes. I've got plenty of time to try making that one.)

Oh, wow it's morning already.

Happiness is a warm sun. Here it comes. The film crew will be here any minute to set up for the first round of interviews.

I'm so tired. I should've gotten rest last night.

But, no, this was good. I'm glad I did this. I'm clearheaded now. Yeah. Now that I purged all that bullshit out of my head, I can focus on the story I'm going to tell. The *real* story. The story I watched again and again and again on DVD. Which ends in triumph. Which ends in a rediscovery of my brilliance and—

And why am I shaking and sweating so much?

I shouldn't be sweating like this. I must have the heat on too high. Judging by the light outside, it's a cold December day—

Oh, god.

I just realized what day it is. What year.

How did I not notice that when this interview was being scheduled?

Never mind that. (Oh, *Nevermind.* Good album too. Maybe that can be my comeback.) I don't need to worry about that. History doesn't repeat itself like that anymore. It's been a long, long, long time since it has.

I'll just sit here until the crew arrives. In fact, I'll go wait in my studio, where it's quiet. Where I'm surrounded by my instruments and I don't have to focus on the pounding in my head or that itch in my thumb.

That damn itch.

Sometimes I forget it's been itching for years. I'm able to tune it out most of the time, it's amazing what you can get used to, but I really do think it's been getting worse lately. Insistent. *Hungry.*

Is it darker in here than usual? I think it is.

Shadows everywhere. This used to be the one spot in the world where I felt safe, but now—how did they get in here? How do they keep finding me?! And why won't my thumb *stop*—?!

Wait.

Wait just a goddamn minute.

Holy SHIT. I'm such an idiot!

That's been the answer all along! The itching, the shadows, the leaches, everything going wrong: *it's time for more blood*! I thought Tall Tony would be enough forever, but, hey, I guess, that's what the *Anthology* was all about, isn't it? All magic needs to be refreshed from time to time! I can't believe I've been so stupid as to forget that. Thank god I went over everything in my head last night so I could FIGURE IT OUT.

The shadows are getting closer. I can see them squirming. Leaches in the water. Creeping in from every corner.

Better act fast, before the interviewers get here. Before they ruin yet another moment in the story.

It'll take more than just a little blood, I bet. They must be starving. Shoulda fed them years ago—back when my best albums weren't getting the love they deserved. I won't make that mistake again. This interview needs to go perfectly. The *Anthology* is too important.

I don't keep a lot of sharp things in the studio. Except—wait—yes, there they are. Heavy-duty bass string clippers. These should work no problem.

And my thumb won't stop ITCHING. It's practically SINGING. ALL TOGETHER NOW. Here, then: take the whole thing! No more itch! I can play without it! These string clippers have teeth, just like good rock'n'roll, and they fit perfectly between the bones. Just need to squeeze as hard as I can and—

THERE! Ohhh that hurts. But I feel fine!

I think I heard the thumb roll somewhere under a music stand or something, but that's okay, what you really care about is the blood, right? Drink up, you greedy fucks!

Everything getting darker—still hungry? No problem, have another finger! Here! And—*another*! Fuck it! I can play without 'em. I can play under ANY circumstances. I'll play better than Django AND better than Jerry Garcia! I'm a generational talent! An ICON! I will not let you ruin this moment for me!

Oops, okay better stop there. That's the whole hand hahaha. Doesn't matter, I'm so rich I can just buy a new one.

So much blood. Getting everywhere. Shadows all around me.

Leaches, drinking. Thank god I remembered in time. This is a story of talent and timing. Don't let me down, magic.

So heavy, though. It won't be long now before. . . before they go away. . . don't bother me. . . I don't feel. . . so much blood. . .

Maybe I shouldn't have done all this alone.

But I've always been alone.

Are the interviewers here yet? Will they know how to find me in this quiet room? I don't know if I thought this through.

Can somebody bring me a tub with some water?

Hello?

i think

i need somebody

anybody

i need someone

please

please

help

me

From NME, December 9, 1980

END OF AN ERA: *Beloved icon dead after apparent self-mutilation*

He was known as The Beatle, a mysterious, charming, eccentric musician who helped define the 1960s with his iconic songwriting, fashion, movies, and more. In a heartbreaking twist of fate, he was discovered unresponsive in his home studio yesterday morning by the production crew of what was intended to be a career retrospective documentary.

A police investigation is currently underway, but sources inform us that his injuries were clearly self-inflicted. Moreover, it's suspected he committed the act in a soundproof area of his home so that he wouldn't be found by the arriving crew for some time.

Much will be written about his impact in the days, years, and decades to come, and below are the first of a planned series of guest essays revisiting, and even reconsidering, his many releases over the past two decades.

In the meantime, a memorial concert is already in the works, in part to cover what are expected to be considerable debts. It had been a longstanding, open secret that his increasingly erratic behavior had led to withering financial conditions. "He wasn't easy to be around," quoted one anonymous source at Parlaphone Records. "But you couldn't deny that sometimes, the music was pure magic."

The concert is expected to be held at Madison Square Garden and will be hosted by beloved television mainstay, Ringo Starr. Rumored guests include Jagger, Pete's Faces, the Davies Brothers, Simon, Hazza, and a special reunion performance of the Dave Clark Five. Additionally, new acts are reportedly being courted, such as U2, Talking Heads, R.E.M., Blondie, The Pretenders, as well as the debut performance of recently formed English duo Lennon/McCartney (featuring Paul McCartney of Wings fame), who are already garnering acclaim and buzz for a series of live performances and demos that have been circulating around the industry. . .

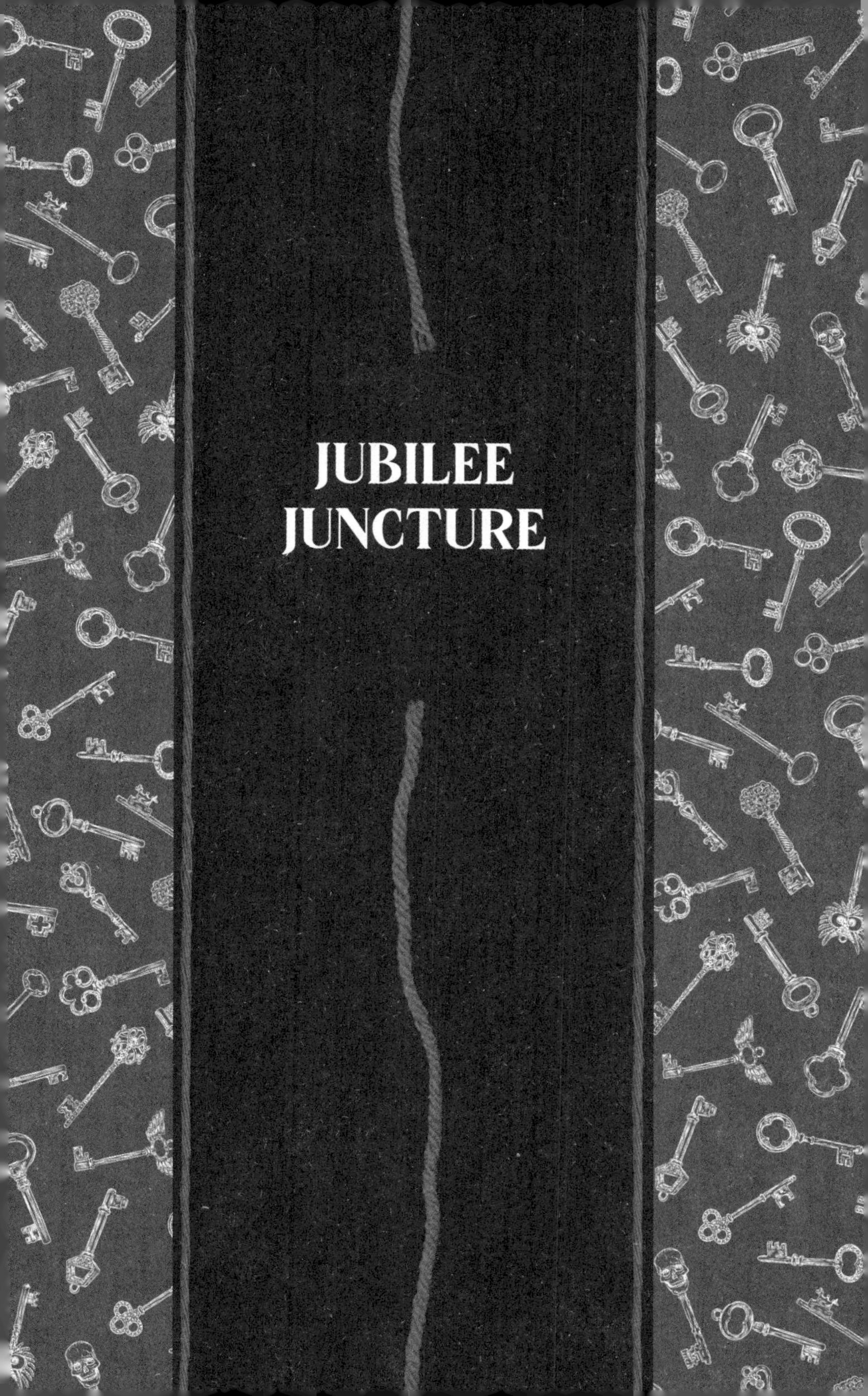
JUBILEE
JUNCTURE

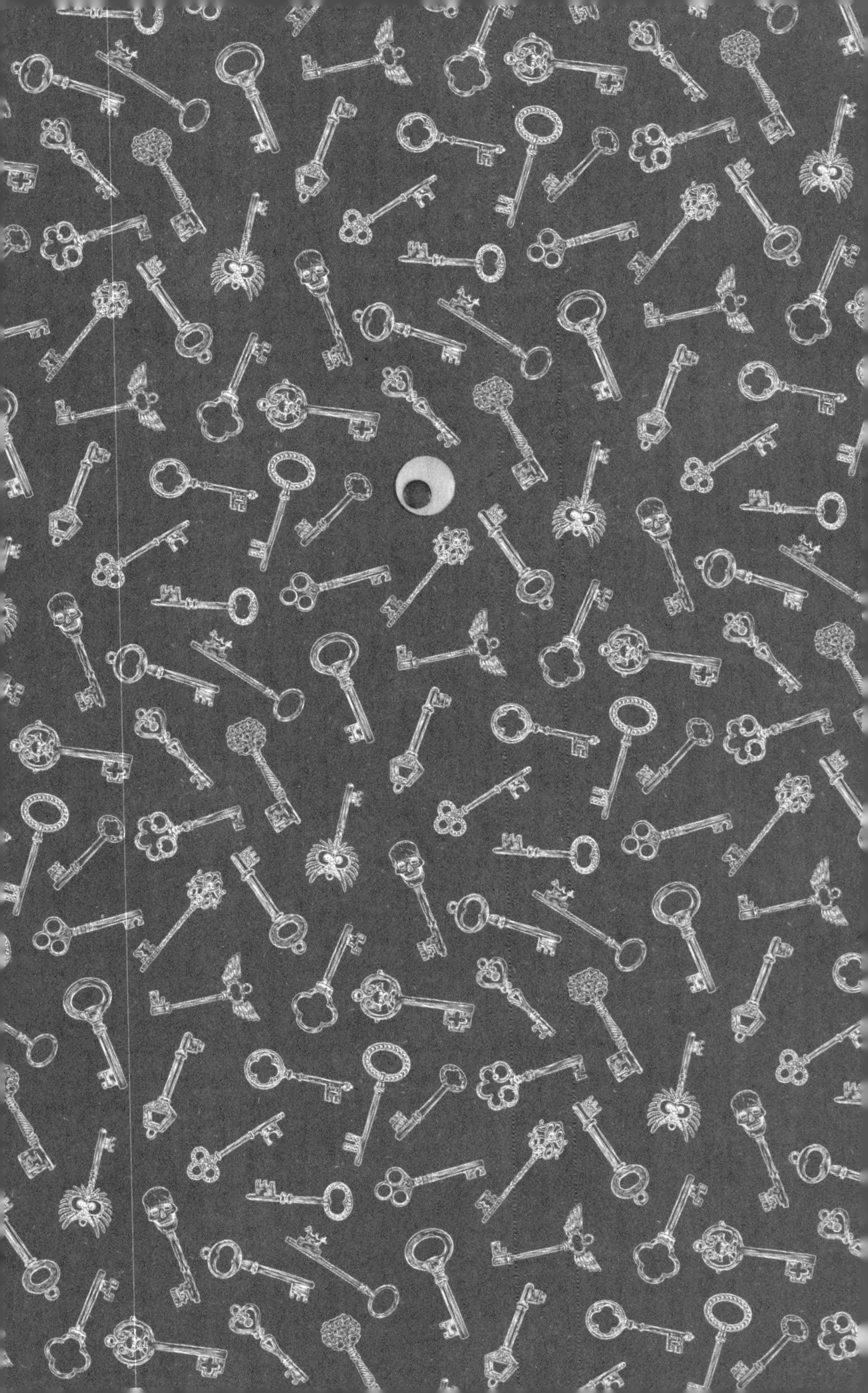

JUBILEE JUNCTURE

The dummy sat in the back corner of the room, slumped forward on its stool like a sentry asleep at its post.

The room, a small parlor standing just off the front foyer of Marvin's isolated, single-level house, was fastidiously neat. A couch covered in plastic. An easy chair covered in plastic. Two small, neat end tables covered in doilies. A small, neat dining table covered in nothing at all.

For all its neatness, though, the room felt cluttered and cramped. It was festooned in shadows.

Wedged between the dining table and a wall was a solitary floor lamp which served as the room's only light source. Its heavy crème lampshade cast most of the light either onto the table or onto the floor, like a pitcher of water with a hole in it.

There was one other light fixture, but it served only to underlight the room's single adornment: a large crucifix hanging on the rear wall. An enamel Christ was pitched in agony over the crossbeam, and the lighting gave his martyrdom an eerie, campfire-ghost-story glow.

For everything else, the murk dominated. It was smeared all

over the room. Which is why it took Robert a few minutes to actually see the dummy after Marvin dragged him inside.

"Please," Marv had pleaded on the front porch, "just let me show you; you've gotta let me show you."

"Now, come on, Marvin!" Robert—Robby to his friends and coworkers—wanted none of this. If he'd had his way, he would have been long gone by now. He'd dreaded coming here, and the confrontation hadn't gone any better than he'd anticipated. "I told you, I've got to go—!"

But then Marvin grabbed Robby by the arm and pulled him through, into the foyer.

Robby hadn't liked that one bit. Now he was *inside* Marvin's house. Arguing over the threshold had been unpleasant enough, but at least that felt safer than this uncanny expanse of shadows.

Robby yanked his arm away. "Now, that's enough! Man!" Slang never suited Robby well, but what he lacked in authentic cool he made up for in sincerity. He rubbed above his elbow where Marvin's fingers had gripped. "Gee-dee, Marvin, I don't want to be having this argument!"

Marvin looked legitimately cowed. "I'm sorry, I didn't mean to get physical. I just—"

"Well, you did! You *did* get physical, and now I'm upset and I don't want to be here!" Robby's face flushed from ear to ear. He checked that his soft blue gingham shirt was still tucked into his pleated khakis. He was a slender man, easing into middle age, handsome in that second-tenor-in-the-choir kind of way. He was used to being an object of attention in their church's contained community, but not when it came to things like this. He hated anger and yelling. As such, he avoided Marvin's eyes while he reprimanded him. "I told you. Begging like this isn't gonna change my mind, okay? I wish it could, but—"

Marvin, as if unable to keep from grabbing onto something, clamped his hands together this time and held them toward Robby. His hair was thinning and unruly, and his eyes swam behind large wire-rimmed glasses. He wore a red linen shirt tucked into shapeless jeans.

"Just, please. Hear me out. Please. I'm gonna put some water on for tea, and I just want us to sit and talk and figure things out. Please."

"No, Marvin."

"Please. *Please.*"

"No, Marvin!"

"Please! Pleasepleasepleasepleasepleasepleaseplease—!"

"Ugh! FINE!"

"Yay!" Marvin waved his fists in the air in tight little circles. "Do you want some chicken, too? I made chicken. Rotisserie style."

"No, Marvin, I don't want your chicken!" Robby snapped. Then, because there was no excuse for rudeness: "But thank you for offering. Ugh, I shouldn't even be here—"

"Sure you should be! Sure you should be! You're giving me a chance. That's what we're supposed to do, right? I mean: 'Better a patient man than a warrior.' Proverbs—"

"Proverbs 16:32, yeah, yeah. What I should be doing is turning you in."

Marvin's face—normally smooth as milk but now dusted with several days' stubble—pulled down into a pout.

"Aw, gee, that's. . . that's really uncool, Robby. I told you—" Robby tried to speak and Marvin raised his voice over him. "*I told you my side of the story and you're not even listening to*— Look—" He exhaled, a clumsy parody of yogic breathing. "Okay. Ha. I almost forgot what I was *dragging* you in here for. Come on in and sit down. Is your arm okay?"

Marvin gently ushered Robby further into the sitting room—

"Yes, my arm is okay, you're not that stronGOHMYLORD! What is that?"

—and that was when Robby finally noticed it.

The shape of it, at least. From this distance, and in this murk, at first all Robby could make out was a figure sitting on a stool. The dummy had long straight hair which, in its current slumped position, covered its face like a dark curtain.

It was also huge. If you stood it upright, it'd be four feet tall at least. It was dressed in pink ruffled pajamas that looked like they'd been bought off the rack at a children's department store.

Robby's guts ran with ice water and as he tried to make sense of what he was seeing, Marvin began to cry.

"You can't kick me off the show, Robby. I pour my heart into the show—*our* show. You know that, don't you? Tell me you know that."

"Yeah, I know," Robby said distantly, still staring at the figure across the room. "What's going on here? Is that a. . . a person?"

Marvin ignored the question. Instead, he took Robby by the shoulder and turned him so they were face-to-face.

"And you *also* know there's no one who can do what I do."

That brought Robby back a little. "Marvin. Pride goeth—"

"Name one person!" Marvin's eyes sparkled with avid intensity as his damp hands crawled over Robby's shoulders. "Name one person who can do what I do! You try it!"

But Robby couldn't. Marvin's puppetry segments on their local broadcast Christian-edutainment show *Jubilee Juncture* were beloved. That was a big part of what made this situation so difficult.

"Yeah," Marvin said smugly, after giving Robby a moment to twist in the wind. "And I've been working on something new! That's what I wanted to show you. I've got a new act for the show, and it's gonna be *super*."

He let go of Robby and ran over to the slumped figure in the corner, giggling.

Robby couldn't help but follow a few steps.

"Oh, that's a. . . puppet?"

"You betcha!"

"Lord, it's pretty. . . uh."

Marvin bent down next to it. He lovingly moved some of its hair out of the way and now Robby was able to see the face.

It was featureless and smooth, with two round pink circles painted on its cheeks beneath two sunken black chasms for eyes. Its jaw hung slightly ajar, separated from its chin by two sharp, vertical lines.

"Pretty great, right?" Marvin cooed. "Cost me a whole heckuva lot, I'll tell you. But I don't mind. I don't mind one bit, Robby. Because I put a lot into this job. I *love* it. I love the joy on their little faces, and. . . and I love finally feeling in control of something for once in my life. So, you can't just kick me off the show."

Robby swallowed a lump. "I was gonna say it's pretty creepy."

Marvin blinked, then looked at his doll as if for the first time. "Creepy?"

"Yeah."

"How so?" He turned his eyes back to Robby. Again, they

shone with a bizarre intensity that should have been impossible to see in this murky darkness.

Robby hemmed, uncomfortable. "I don't know—"

"Oh, you know what it is? It's the hair. It's got real hair." Marvin ran an appreciative hand through the long straight locks. "You don't see that so often. That's part of what makes it so special. Plus, the lighting, I'm sure that doesn't help, huh?" He gave a nervous, fluty titter.

"Yeah, why is it so dark in here?"

"Photophobia, Robby. Light sensitivity. I can't have it too bright."

"Oh." Robby thought for a beat. "Wait, since when did you have ph—?"

"Let me do the new act for you."

Robby curled in discomfort. "Oh, jeeeeez, Marv! You're putting me in a really rough position here! I mean, I'm doing you a favor already. I came here, as a friend, just to tell you we're not pursuing anything criminal; we're just *asking* you to, y'know, step down—"

"Listen to the act." Marvin's voice was clear and calm. Steady. No longer pleading. "It's the least you can do, Robby. Literally. It's the least. *You.* Can do."

Again, those eyes. He glared at Robby from the corner. His intent was obvious. He was playing *that* card at last.

Robby was stunned, although even in the moment a part of his mind reprimanded himself for not better preparing for this eventuality. Of course Marvin would bring this up. He was desperate. . . and he had leverage.

Robby tried to match calm for calm, hoping the dim lighting

meant Marvin couldn't see his hands begin to tremble. To be safe, he rubbed them against his khakis.

"Luke 6:37, Marvin. And that was fifteen years ago. You do *not* get to bring that up—"

"You owe me."

"Proverbs 20:22, Marvin! Okay? I'm leav—"

"Matthew 18:21 through 35, Robert. Matthew 18:21. . . *through 35*."

The verse landed with an almost reverberant thud. Robby groaned, knowing he was beaten. He couldn't argue with Matthew 18:21 through 35.

Marvin smiled. "You'll listen to the act? Pretty please? With all sorts of confectionary on top?"

Robby seethed his assent and Marvin gave another little joyful fist shake.

"Yay! Oh! And here—!" He exclaimed, running out of the room.

Robby tried to protest but it was too late, he was suddenly alone.

No. Not alone.

That doll. . .

"Marvin!" Robby called, hoping his voice didn't betray how uneasy he'd instantly become.

"Be right there, fussypants!" Marvin called. Robby heard the sound of activity in the kitchen.

He glanced up at the crucifix for support, but he couldn't keep his eyes off the huge, slumped doll for long. There was just something so very wrong about it.

He inched closer, squinting.

Did. . . did its jaw just move a little?

No, that was ridiculous. That'd be—

"Tada!"

Robby jumped and whirled around. Marvin was back again, standing by the table, holding a plate piled high with loose slivers of meat.

"You said you wanted chicken, right?"

He put the tray on the table.

"No, Marvin, I—"

"It's delicious. Rotisserie style. And I put water on for tea."

It did not look delicious. The meat was erratically cut and had a strange consistency. It was a darker shade than Robby usually associated with poultry, too. Or maybe that was just the lighting again? He hated eating food he couldn't see; he'd left restaurants for as much.

But Marvin wouldn't stop staring at him, so Robby sat down.

"How about some silverware?" he asked.

Marvin waved that away. "Nah. It's fun to get your hands a little greasy. Go on."

Robby picked up some of the thin meat with his fingers. "Why am I still here?" he muttered and popped it in his mouth.

"Because you're a good friend," Marvin said. "Really. I just appreciate it so much."

While Robby chewed (and, he was surprised to find, the chicken was sweet and tender, more like veal or pork), Marvin hurried back to the dummy. He dragged a chair over with him so he could sit alongside it.

"Why is that thing so big?" Robby asked around another mouthful of meat.

Marvin chuckled. "I could make a filthy joke there. I won't. But I could. Remember how we used to joke like that?"

He busied himself getting the puppet ready for a performance, moving it, and its stool, away from the corner, keeping one hand on its chest to steady it.

"Anyways, yeah. It's this new thing now, making 'em more life-sized. For the children. I think it makes 'em feel like they're listening to, like, a peer? I guess? Anything to get the blessed rugrats to pay attention! 'For we shall rescue them from the dominion of darkness and bring them into the kingdom of the Son,' am I right?"

"This house is the gee-dee dominion of darkness," Robby muttered and ate another sliver of meat.

Once he and his dummy were in place, Marvin exclaimed, "Okay! So, the controls are a little tricky, but you tell me this won't be perfect for the show. Heeeeere we go!"

He waggled his fingers and then stuck them into the dummy's back.

Robby, who at that moment was rolling his eyes and eating another bit of chicken, had the sound of chewing and swallowing in his ears and so he missed the noise made when Marvin stuck his hand inside the doll. An unpleasant, wet *sfflllppttt*. It sounded almost like a man jamming his hand into a Ziploc full of Vaseline.

Robby was spared that. But what happened next wasn't any less upsetting.

The dummy's head jerked up in a short, spastic movement. Its dark, bottomless eyes stared out from its plastic face, at nothing, at everything. It was all so uncanny, it made Robby's mouth go dry in a flash.

"Well, good morning, Marigold!" Marvin exclaimed in his cheery puppet-time voice.

From out of the side of his mouth, in a higher register, he answered himself back: "Mornin', Marvin!"

Marvin had never been a great ventriloquist, but that was part of his charm. He was indisputably talented at the physical work, moving the dolls and making it seem like their bodies were alive—in a way, his imprecision with their voices made the performances all the more endearing. You could appreciate his talents by seeing the one area they fell short.

Not this time, though. This doll—this long-haired, unsettlingly large doll—moved in too herky-jerky a fashion. Its jaw, its neck, all its movements were wrong. Too sharp, too abrupt, too. . . Robby couldn't put any other word on it but *wrong*.

"Say," Marvin continued, "I wonder if we could get a volunteer from the audience. Anyone out there? Don't be shy!" He sang the tagline from their show's opening jingle: "I'm askin'. I'm seekin'. I'm knockin'!"

After an excruciating pause, Robby raised his hand. The chicken was sitting like a rock in his gut.

"Yay!" Marvin cried. "And what's your name, little man?

"Marv. . ." Robby grumbled.

"'That's a great name!'" Marvin-as-Marigold chirped, the doll's awful jaw chewing up and down. "'I love that name!"

Then, as himself: "Naaah, I don't think that's your name, little man."

Robby gritted his teeth. "Lord. . . it's Robby."

"Robby!" Marigold proclaimed, head rocking back and forth on its neck. "Yay!"

Marvin broke character and leaned forward with a stage whisper. "Keep eating that chicken, Robby, I don't want it to go to waste." He leaned back. "Anyway, here's where Marigold gets sad, you know, like, 'Aww.'"

The dummy's shoulders fell forward in a dejected slump.

"What's wrong, Marigold?" Marvin asked, before proceeding to dialogue with the puppet.

"Gosh, I wish I could be a real person. Like Robby."

"Well, Marigold, being a real person is a very special thing. Do you know the story of Pinocchio?"

"No."

Marvin faced his audience. "Robby, do *you*—"

"Yes," Robby growled.

Marvin turned back to his dummy. "And lemme ask something else, Marigold. Do you know what the word 'transubstantiation' means?"

"Trans. . . sub. . ."

"It's a tough one, I know. Well, basically, Pinocchio was a little puppet like you."

"Aw!"

"And Geppetto was his maker. Like God."

"Wow!"

"And Pinocchio wanted nothing more than to be real. So finally, one day, God performed a miracle. . . and gave Pinocchio flesh."

"Like skin?"

"Exactly! He turned *something*," here he rapped loudly on the wood of his chair with his free hand, "into flesh and blood. It's a miracle He performs every day. . . because, well, flesh is a sacred thing. So sacred that God gives us his own flesh. To eat."

"To *eat*?" Marigold's head rolled around on her neck again.

"I know how it sounds, little one, but yes. It's one of the holiest things we can do. It is to be made pure again, even if only for a moment."

"Wow," Marigold mused, "so if I become real, that's really special?"

"That's really special, Marigold! It's a miracle."

"Yay!"

"But—" Marvin's voice became low and serious, "you have to be careful, Marigold. Because your flesh is *pure* and *sacred* and there are people who want to take *pictures* of your flesh. *All* your flesh. Even your secret parts. They want to debase your sacred purity and leer and stare and touch and—"

Robby was on his feet without even knowing it, red faced and shaking.

"Marvin! You can't say that crap! I've had it!"

"What—" Marvin stammered. "What'd I say?"

"This is the whole reason we can't have you on the show anymore! Okay? Every *time*!"

"You're being hurtful."

"Every frigging time we give you the stage now, you're talking about gee-dee pornography! It's sick!"

"It is sick! I agree!"

"*You're the one who keeps bringing it up!* A few weeks ago, you fit it into the story of Noah!"

Marvin shifted in his seat. He hand was still inside the doll, which sat with its mouth wide open, a blasé expression of shock on its neutral, empty face.

"Our children today, Robby, they can just open up their computer—heck, their friggin' phones—and look at the filthiest, most depraved garbage imaginable. And if they're not careful, they'll wind up doing it themselves! They'll—"

"YEAH, WE ALL SAW THE DANG PHOTOS YOU SAVED ON THE STUDIO COMPUTER, MARVIN!" Robby had never yelled so loudly in his life. His throat burned. Spittle flew. And yet. . . it felt good. When he spoke again, his voice was raspy, deeper than normal. "How old were they? Ten? Were they even that old? Eight? Nine?"

Marvin was stammering again. "Come on, Robby. Come on. Y-you've gotta stop bringing this up."

"Stop bringing it up? Stop br—? I can't even look at you. I told you, I should be turning you in."

"You're not perfect either, you know!" Marvin seemed to have recovered his equilibrium. He cocked his head back haughtily and the lamplight caught his glasses, making his eyes the inverse of the doll's sunken shadows. "I know it was 'fifteen years ago,' but do you still remember that poor girl's name? Or how you called me up, crying? 'What do I do, Marv? What does this mean? Why couldn't I stop myself?'"

"Shut up, Marvin. Shut up."

"I think about that night a lot. You and I, we *know* things, important things, about the nature of man—"

"MARVIN. YOU SHUT. THE *FUCK*. UP!"

The curse word hit them both like a slap.

In the kitchen, the tea kettle began to whistle.

Both men stood there.

The whistle turned into a scream.

Then, Marvin made Marigold's head turn slightly in that awful, spasmodic way.

"Whatever happened to Luke 6:37, Robby?" the puppet asked with Marvin's voice.

Robby was preparing himself to respond when he noticed the doll's arms beginning to twitch. Pulse. Its legs shook a little, too.

"Why are you making it move like that?"

Marvin put his hand on Marigold's shoulder. His other hand was still buried inside. His lenses shot golden daggers at Robby.

"Look, my hand is just stuck in the controls, okay? I'm trying to get it out." The kettle continued to scream. "Can you go get that, please?"

Robby puffed his chest. "That doll? Is a piece of crap. It's creepy and it doesn't work and"—as he stormed out of the room, he shot over his shoulder—"and I'm sorry you spent money on it!"

"I told you before," Marvin spat back. "Those photos were just research!"

"Research!" Robby scoffed from the kitchen. "Right."

Marvin ignored the sarcasm. He had other things to attend to.

His hand came quite easily out of the puppet with another wet *slllppptt.*

From the tips of his fingers to halfway past his wrist, he was coated in blood. A thick, clotty patina, so red it was almost black in spots.

The dummy's arms and legs continued to twitch and spasm. Now its torso was jerking, too.

The tea kettle ceased its screams with a defeated sigh.

"We're crusaders, Robert," Marvin whispered, holding his gore-soaked hand out. "We have to know what we're fighting against. No matter how it taints us. It gives us purpose."

A weak moan began to emanate from the dummy. It managed to stumble uneasily to its feet, swaying, while Marvin searched about the room with his clean hand.

From the kitchen, Robby whined: "Where's your dang tea? Dang it, Marvin, your house is a mess! There are textbooks *all over* the counter! What is this, *Principles of Anesthesiology*? *Spinal Anatomy*? For Pete's sake! You really need help."

The dummy brought one twitching hand up and swatted at its face. The smooth, plastic, rosy-cheeked façade fell away (except for the plastic covering the lower jaw, which had been secured by glue, not elastic).

Underneath was a different face. Far less smooth. Far less rosy. Ugly, raw wounds crisscrossed the cheeks and forehead where skin and muscle had been carved away. In places, little windows of bone and teeth were visible. A few smaller flaps of skin hung errantly, loosened by time and movement. There were more such wounds all over the dummy's body—platefuls, in fact—but those were hidden underneath the pink pajamas.

Madness was beginning to resolve in the dummy's increasingly less-glassy eyes. An eternal, ageless sort of madness.

Despite that, the youth of its shredded face was unmistakable.

Marvin watched this as he continued his search around the room.

"Flesh is a sacred thing," he said quietly to the dummy, though he knew it likely wasn't listening. Children were so easily distracted. "That's why we're told to consume it. It makes us pure again. No matter what we've done. It's a miracle, little puppet."

Robby, who heard the sound of Marvin's voice, called back, "Whatever, Marvin, I can't even hear what you're saying." A cabinet opened. A small box rattled. "Finally. You want chamomile?"

Marvin also found what he was looking for: a semi-filled syringe. Just in time. The dummy had moved a hand to its backside and discovered the grisly opening there. Dig deep enough and it would find its spinal column, as well as exposed nerves waiting for expert hands to pluck them like marionette strings.

Those nerves must have begun transmitting pain again. The dummy's moans were turning into screams. Another tea kettle.

Marvin put a stop to all that with an injection into the dummy's neck. Just a little less this time. . .

Its limbs went limp and he eased it to the floor.

With some hope, he checked its pulse. Then he sighed.

"Dangit. Another one."

He shouted to the kitchen. "Welp. You're not going to see the reveal of my act now!"

"Oh darn!" Robby shouted back over the clink of mugs. Then he gave a mock growl in frustration. "Ugh! Look, I don't wanna be this jerky guy with you, Marv. We're gonna have this tea together, but then. . . we're gonna call it quits. I know we've been through a lot, but. . ."

It was Marvin's turn not to listen. The sound of Robby's voice had just given him a new idea. The next live taping of *Jubilee Juncture* was tomorrow at ten a.m. Could he be ready in time?

He looked at the underlit figure on the cross hanging on his wall.

Yes. He could do this. For the children.

This puppet would be a little bigger. Not a peer, like Marigold. Instead, maybe. . . maybe the Good Lord Himself. Yes! It was "eat of *my* flesh," after all. And Marvin could dress it in a nice white robe, with another long wig.

Everything should still fit in his steamer trunk. He'd just have to show up right before airtime so no one could catch an early glimpse of the act. No spoilers.

And there was just enough left in this syringe to get started.

Robby was still speaking in the kitchen, busily preparing tea. "Just don't be upset, okay, Marv? I told you. I'm not gonna turn you in. And I still love you like a brother. A confused brother who needs help, but still. You were absolutely right. Luke 6:37." Without ceremony, Marvin turned and strode to the kitchen, holding the syringe before him while Robby continued. "I take those words to heart. I really do. 'Judge not and ye shall not be—'"

Robby interrupted himself with a scream, which was itself cut short. Then, but for the sound of Marvin getting to work, the house was silent.

Meanwhile, from its place on the wall, the crucified figurine presided over an empty room. Its agony remained frozen in porcelain, never abaiting, and witnessed by no one.

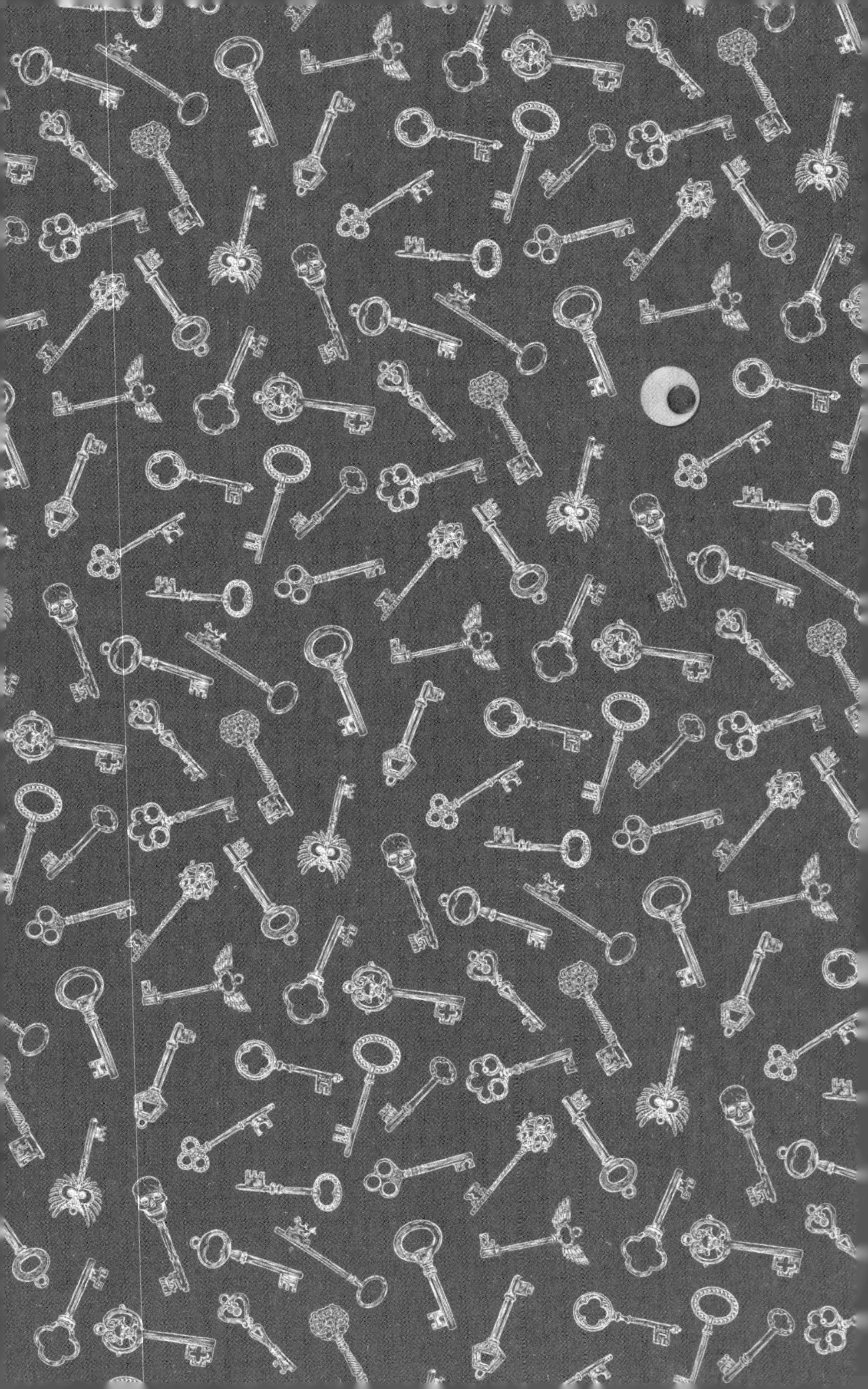

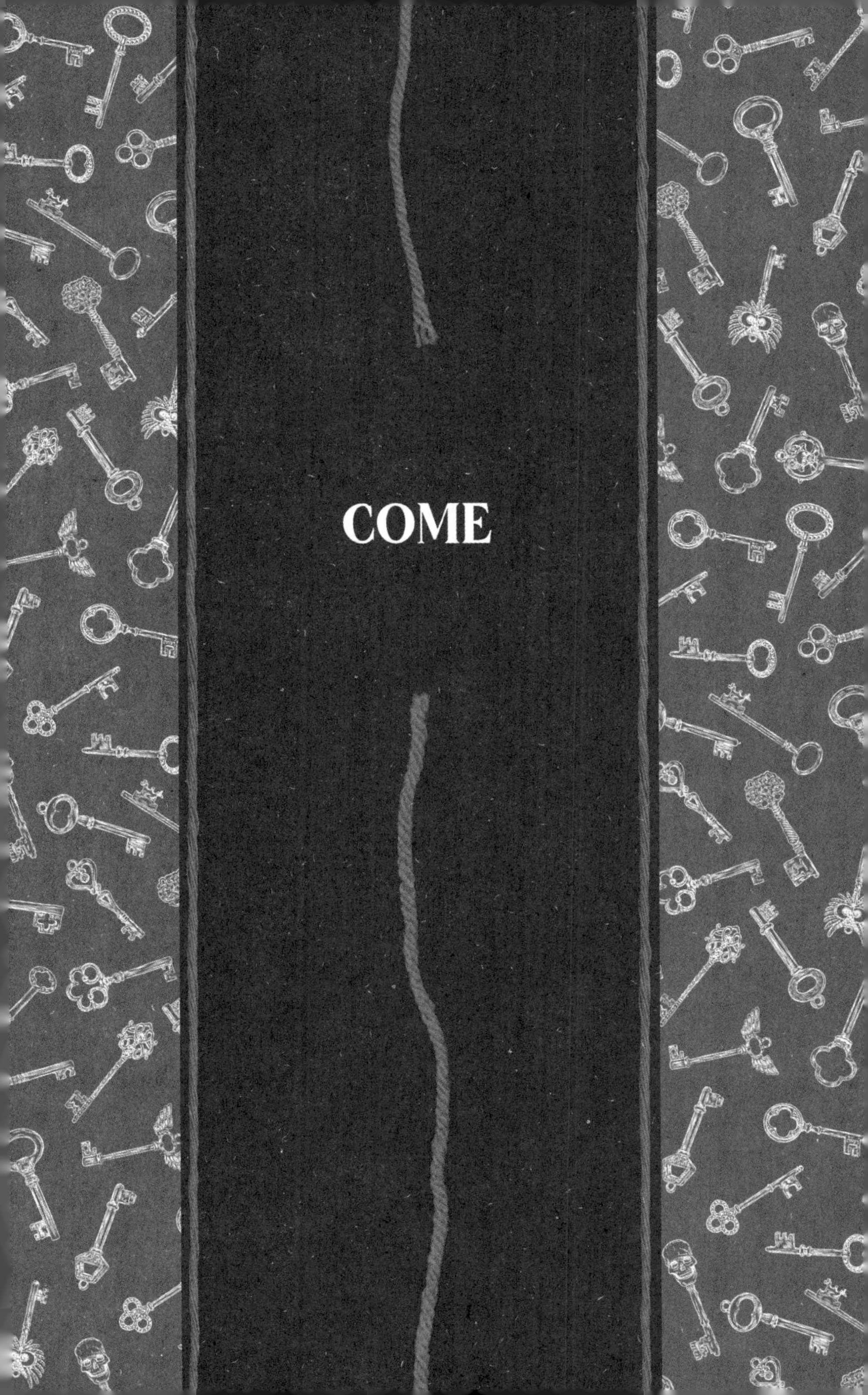
COME

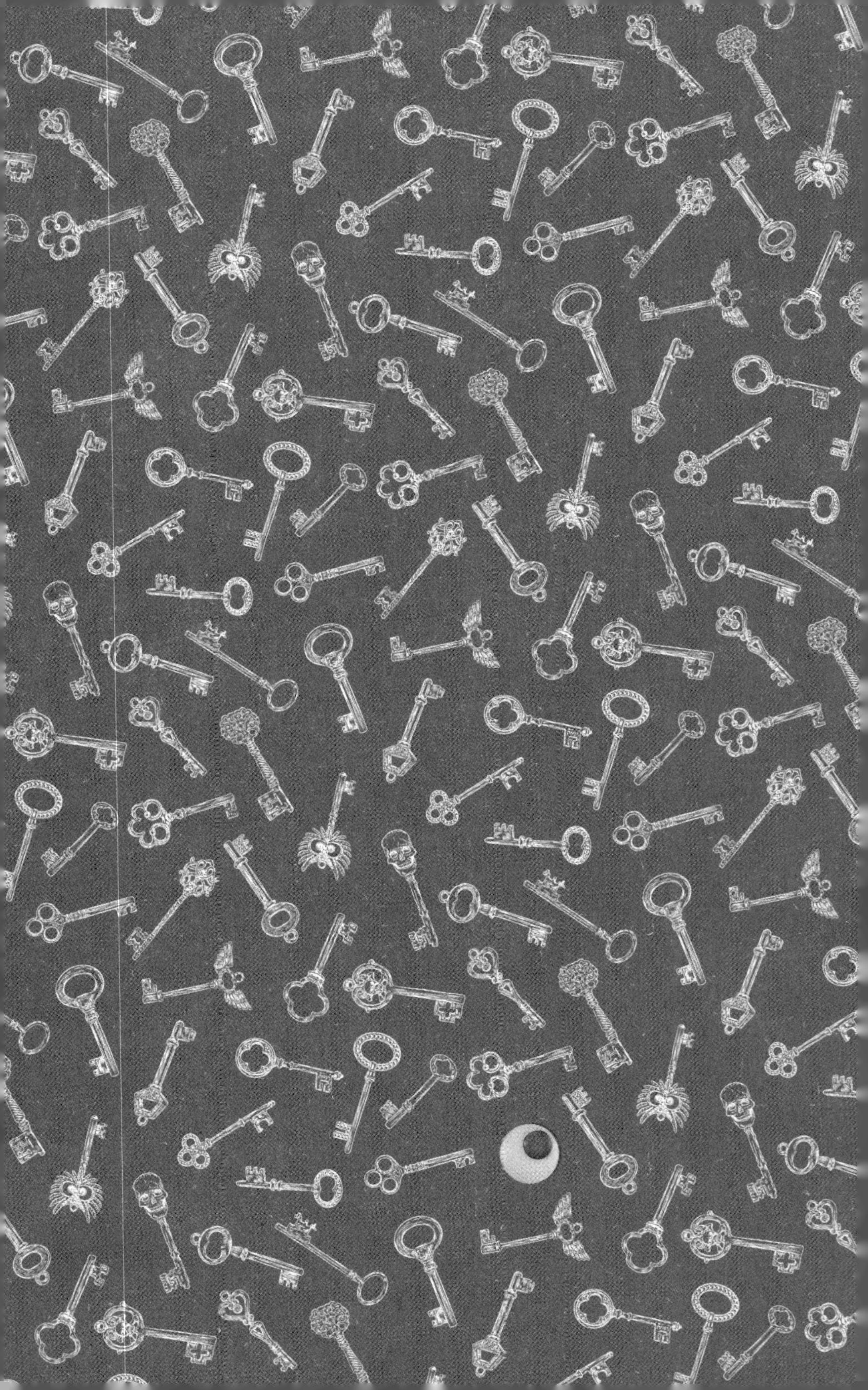

COME

Dez was back on the morning announcements. His unwashed, uncombed hair hung limply against his face like a curtain of fruit leather. I couldn't believe they were allowing him on the air again, after he'd been banished three weeks prior for calling the Step On Stage showchoir's performance a "slobbery blowfest." There must not have been a lot of other options on the A/V bench that day.

Or maybe this was just another dream I was having.

"Goooood morning, Paradise Valley High! Another beautiful sunny day for us all to be trapped inside a huge concrete building! Peel your eyes offa your phones and look up here, piglets—it's time for your morning news feeding!"

The girl had been dead for years. Well before any of us started high school.

But we all knew what had happened.

We all knew because of the video. Passed around. Email by email. Text by text.

The young, hot shit student-teacher. The girl, an actual student-student. And I don't know if this is urban myth telephone or if it's the truth, but apparently she wasn't someone who attracted attention from guys like him. She was a bit of a wallflower. An uggo. So, she was eager. Willing to do anything. He probably didn't have to try hard to talk her into it.

She killed herself pretty soon after the video leaked.

Some say she slit her wrists. Others, her throat. Some say she drowned herself. Or drank poison. Dealer's choice, I guess. Pick the tragedy that does it for you.

All that really mattered was she was dead. Long dead. Years ago. Generations in high school time. It might as well have happened during the 1900s.

Or in a dream.

Knowledge of The Video was out there, like a song from before you were born but which everyone somehow knows the words. I first remember hearing about it in the fifth grade. Overhearing older kids swapping tips, pointers.

—Yo, but if you like that amateur shit, my older brother says there's video of a girl who used to go to PV High fucking one of her teachers in Room C22.

—Whaaaa? The science room?

—Yuppppp, and I hear she does EVERYTHING. Oral. Butt stuff. All of it.

—Send. Me. That. Nowwwww.

—Okay, lemme ask my brother

You'd also occasionally hear about the deaths. But PV was a big school, almost three thousand kids. There were always deaths.

No one ever put them together, as far as I know.

Until Tyler Bennington.

COME

"Hey, can I talk to you for a sec?"

I think I made a noise like a chair squeaking. A balloon letting out air through a too-tight neck.

Tyler was a good guy; that rare combination of popular and well-liked. You'd almost think that's a given, right? To be popular means people *like* you? But, as one of those more naturally wall-flowery kids myself, I've learned that's often not the case. A lot of popular kids are outright hated or feared. In general, popular kids are just another architectural feature of the school, like water fountains or stairs, and you simply take their presence as a given.

But not Tyler. Tyler radiated likability. He seemed like he'd make your life better if you wound up in his orbit, even just for a couple minutes. Which, I guess, is why I was so unprepared for him to come right up and talk to me at my locker in between classes.

I did that thing you see people do on TV or in movies. I don't know that I'd ever done it before. "Huh?" I asked, and pointed to myself. "Me?"

"Yeah!" Tyler said. His expression was patient and kind. He didn't seem put out in the slightest by having to repeat himself. "Got a sec?"

"I've—yeah, sure—I've got many sex," I said. "*Secs.*" My face erupted in purple blotches. I hate that even a slight change of emphasis can do that. I hate that some combinations of sounds are so. . . loaded.

Tyler laughed, again kindly. "I'm Tyler, by the way. I know we don't really know each other; I think we had Social Studies together last year, but—"

"Who was awake to remember?" My purple splotches were burning. But at least I made him smile.

"Exactly."

I reminded him my name and he shook my hand. When our skin touched, I could feel eyes fall on us. On him. Hungry eyes. Everybody wanted Tyler, in so many ways. Gay, straight (and it was rumored he was a little of both). Again, there was just something about him.

(—*Shit, I'd suck his dick and I don't even like dudes. He just seems like a decent guy.* Peter Mortemore told me that once. Not that I asked.)

Of course, I didn't feel anything like that, but I knew enough to know that that was weird. I was just glad he seemed nice. In a way most seventeen-year-olds aren't.

So, imagine my surprise when the next words out of his mouth were, "I heard you might know how to hack into someone's iPhone."

What was the world coming to? Good Boy Tyler, star baseball and lacrosse player Tyler, Prince Charming last semester's production of Rogers & Hammerstein's *Cinderella* Tyler, coming to me to commit a crime?

I stared at him, not committing to a response, until he told me a little more. He started speaking at a rapid pace. The class bell was going to ring again any minute, so there was some urgency. But I think he also prepared what he was going to say in advance and didn't want to get off track. It was kinda endearing.

"So, one of my really dear friends, Kyra, her brother just. . . it's really sad, but he just killed himself? I guess? No one can figure out why or how he died, so. She really wants to get into his phone and see who he was talking to, what he was up to, before, you know. . . But she's also worried what she sees is gonna upset her. So, I volunteered."

"Oh," I said, honestly a little disappointed. Even in crime, Tyler wanted to do the right thing.

"I heard you were somebody who might know how to do things like that?"

And here's the thing: I am not. To this day I have no idea how he heard that about me. I think I just had the look, you know? Quiet, clean, smart, a little confusing. Must be a tech whiz.

Still, I agreed to help. I didn't really have any friends. I didn't *want* any friends. I liked my simple, uncluttered, uncomplicated life. But it was senior year. We were all going to graduate soon, and I figured I might as well try something new for a change.

I didn't know anything about breaking into dead kids' phones.

But I knew of someone who might.

Not a friend, either. More like a troll under the bridge.

Dez did this thing where, when he talked to you, he'd hump the air. As a punctuation, as a greeting, as a way of keeping rhythm.

I hated it. It was one of the many, many reasons I kept him at a distance. For a couple years in elementary school, I suppose you could say we were friends. Friendly. Friendish. Never close, but it wasn't uncommon for us to be corralled into the same location at the same time, which is what pretty much counts as friendship when you're small.

Even back then, Dez did his weird humping thing.

It always made me uncomfortable. But I guess I never really held it against him because, all my life, most people have made me uncomfortable in one way or another.

Anyway.

I looked at this moment as an experiment. Putting Tyler and Dez together would be the truest test of Tyler's inherent niceness.

After Tyler explained the situation, Dez took the phone from him, looked at it, snorted some snot that had been hiding in his sinuses for just this occasion, took the longest pause in the history of the world. . . and then said:

"So, I got into this huge fight with my mom last night. Moms are the worst, right? Like, when you're a mom you're defined by your cunt, so I guess it's no wonder you act like one. But it was so weird, I had this, like, moment of, like, disconnect? Like, my mouth was screaming at her, *I'm gonna fucking kill you, you fucking hag*, but in my head, it was like, 'What video game do I want to play later?' I was so not actually invested in the fight. It felt like I was taking a shit. Like, my body was just doing its thing. You ever experience that? Anywhoodles. Thing is, we can't really hack into an iPhone. Howeeeeever, looking at this particular model, I might be able to swipe the dead fuck's fingerprints off something else and unlock it that way. Can I hang with you guys if it works?"

All of that, in, like, two breaths.

Dez was a lot.

But Tyler, surprise surprise, was nice.

So, he said yes, and Dez humped the air in triumph.

Two mornings later, we all sat in Tyler's car before first period.

He'd managed to get Kyra's brother's remote control, and it had a bunch of teenage-oily fingerprints on it. Several of them were perfect, according to Dez, and with the help of a little Scotch tape, he was able to dupe the print.

He sat in Tyler's backseat. I sat in the passenger seat. The rest of the student body filtered into the school around us.

It only took Dez a couple minutes to get it to work. A little extra time was taken to also change the security settings so Tyler wouldn't have any problems accessing the phone afterward. Thank god the phone hadn't been set up for facial recognition.

Then again, if it had been, everyone else would still be alive.

"I fucking rule," Dez said, humping the air from his sitting position, making the car rock a little. "So, now what? We wanna cut class and hang somewhere?"

Tyler gave him a patient, but distracted, smile. "Let's see if there are any clues in here."

He dove into the phone.

Nothing useful in the texts. All the social media apps had already refreshed their feeds a million times over—time and tide wait for no dead kid. Same with the mail app. But then—

"Swipe up and see what his most recently used apps were," I said.

Tyler did, and right at the top of the pile of open apps was WhatsApp, which had been hidden from the main screen.

It was still open to a message. Something he must have been looking at before he died. Maybe the last thing he'd done on his phone.

A message from some guy named Marcus Brofsky.

"Told you I owed you one 😜"

There was a video file attached to the message.

Tyler clicked it right away.

When you watch it, you can tell it was shot on an old digital camera. Probably not even a phone, but one of those tiny, silver boxes that was *only* a camera.

The resolution is for shit. The device is propped up against one of those gas burners on the lab tables, so the angle is awkward and removed.

I looked away as soon as I realized what was about to happen.

A girl gets bent over the table in the foreground.

A guy with jet black hair—also young, but in an obviously more adult way—approaches and lifts her skirt up.

If you keep watching, you see a lot more.

The video goes on forever.

"Is that. . . the science room?" Tyler might've been a genuinely nice guy, but he was still seventeen. An excited smile was spreading across his face.

"Yo, it's *this* video!" Dez was in the backseat, humping the air like he was trying to change the weather. "Guess the dude gooned himself to death, mystery solved!"

Tyler and Dez kept their eyes on the screen as if their lives depended on it. I occasionally stole a morbidly curious glance, but mostly I stared out the window at the other students passing us by. Wondered how I wound up in a car with two boys, watching porn on a phone. Focused on keeping my stomach from flopping out of my mouth.

I was full of feelings. Annoyance—was watching this really going to help our investigation? Anger—at the teacher, at Tyler and Dez, and even at the poor dead girl, for allowing herself to be trapped in this low-res nightmare. Disgust—at every new position I caught.

And, of course, confusion. Always confusion. My oldest friend and companion. Which made me want to do what I always wanted to do: be alone.

My hand was drifting to the door handle when, at long last, the video stopped. I put my hand back in my lap.

We all sat there in silence.

The car felt like it had dropped ten, twenty degrees.

Dez startled me by clapping his hands together once, loud as a gunshot. "So! Now what? We hanging, or—?"

Tyler blinked and shook his head a little. Like he was exiting a fog.

"Um. Yeah. Almost. Uh. This still doesn't give us any answers, though. Maybe we get in touch with the guy who sent it? Maybe he has a better idea what Kyra's brother was up to? Sounds like they were kinda close. Does anyone know this Brofsky kid?"

Dez and I both said no.

Then Tyler's own phone buzzed with a text. He pulled it out, looked at it, a secret smile crossing his face. While we waited for Tyler to finish typing a response, Dez looked at me through the rearview mirror and waggled his eyebrows. I felt again suddenly aware that I was inside a tiny metal box with two hormonal carnivores who'd just watched a video on how to prepare steak. I tried not to sneer back at him.

Tyler put his phone away. "Sorry, what were we talking about?"

"Finding the dead kid's jacking partner," Dez said. "His porno pal. His wankmate. His—"

"Right," Tyler said. "Why don't you see what you can find about the guy? Here, I'll forward his contact info."

Dez responded immediately, "Send me the video too."

Tyler looked at him.

"What?" Dez shrugged. "Maybe there's metadata or something in there we can use. Just send it to me."

I could almost hear the bounds of Tyler's niceness straining. Like the creak of leather. "Fine. Sure. We should get to class; it's almost first period."

"I don't know about you, Ty-Ty," Dez said, tugging at the crotch of his pants, "but I need another minute before I can stand up."

Later, at the start of lunch, Dez grabbed me and Tyler and pulled us aside.

"Before I forget, two things: a) that Brofsky guy was just some rando old dude, and 2) he's also totally dead now."

Tyler and I both gaped.

Dez explained with a blasé shrug: "I googled his name and found out he's old. Which meant I knew he had a Facebook page. I checked that out and everyone's all 'Waaahh, RIP to our buddy Marcus,' on his wall right now. He must've just kicked it."

"He's dead too?" Tyler asked. "That's. . ." We all exchanged looks.

"Yeah," Dez said. "I'm thinking that sex tape is probably cursed or something. Anyway, you guys wanna go off-campus for lunch? Get some Arby's or some shit? Hang out?"

Tyler made eye contact with someone across the cafeteria, and lifted his head in greeting. The concern that had been clouding his face cleared a little. "I can't," he said. "I have an, uh, appointment I already made for lunch."

"An appointment?" Dez scoffed. "Ohhhh, you mean like a date? Did that video give you some *urges*?"

Dez started to do his humping thing and Tyler stopped him by putting hands on Dez's shoulders the way a big brother might.

"You don't have to be so unpleasant *all* the time, Dez. You're smart. You did good work." Then Tyler looked at me. "I really appreciate this, you guys. Thanks for helping me. We're gonna crack this case."

He hurried off to meet whomever he had his big date with. I was filled with admiration for him. His confidence. His clarity. His easy completeness.

I could see Dez processing what Tyler had just said.

I could see him taste it, swallow it, and then reject it. A nasty little smirk crossed his face. He gave the air a single, spiteful hump in Tyler's absence.

"Looks like it's just you and me, then." He followed me as I grabbed a tray. He was singing tunelessly under his breath, "Best friends. Back together, we're beesst frieeeeends."

After we sat down together, he asked, "Do you ever like to shoot guns? I have guns. Or blow stuff up? You should come over to my place sometimes, I could show you some dope shit. Remember when we used to hang?"

I was remembering why I always opted for solitude when given the choice. I tried to eat in silence. He kept pestering me with ideas for what we could do whenever we inevitably hang out next.

The only thing that finally shut him up was the screaming,

twenty or so minutes later.

A few kids, barreling across the cafeteria. Others, jumping up from their seats. We all had the same thought, I'm sure: shooter. We're all trained to expect one at any moment, to the point where, if you think about it, it's actually kinda weird when it doesn't happen every day.

But it wasn't a shooter.

A crowd was gathering near the bathrooms. Words being passed, person to person, until they reached us.

Two students had just been discovered in the boys' bathroom.

One, a Junior named Jesse. His head was smashed into a wall. They were saying he was in a coma. An ambulance was on the way.

The other kid was dead.

Did anyone know who the other kid was?

They did.

They were all saying it was Tyler.

Dez looked at me, and somehow his smile returned even bigger than ever. "Oh, yeah," he said. "That sex tape is *definitely* cursed."

Rumors swirled. That's what they do, right? Like soap down a drain.

Maybe Tyler had a heart attack?

But he was the most athletic guy in the universe.

Everyone pretty quickly put together that he and Jesse had been hooking up in the bathroom stall—so maybe Tyler killed himself out of shame? Fear of being outed?

But nobody here cared about that. If anything, Tyler being bi made him that much cooler. And if you're *so* scared of being outed, you wouldn't be hooking up in the *school bathroom during lunch*, would you?

Some people said they saw Tyler's body and his hands were stuck *into* his throat, like he was trying to dig into his neck and rip out his voice box. Maybe he choked on something?

Others said, no, it wasn't his neck, it was his crotch. Like his genitals had been shredded and he'd bled to death. Or maybe that's what he'd been choking on?

And what about Jesse? Had Tyler bashed Jesse's head in before dying? Or had Jesse done it out of guilt, after doing something to Tyler?

It was like being a little kid again, not knowing how anything worked, trying to piece an entire world together out of whispers.

We all got to go home early that day.

Dez was super excited about that. He did his usual bout of air-humping, then tried to get me to spend the rest of the afternoon with him. I opted to go home, fast as I could.

Didn't rid me of Dez's presence, though, because I kept hearing his voice in my head.

That sex tape is definitely cursed.

Definitely.

Tyler watched it, and then, a few hours later, Tyler died.

Kyra's brother. Dead. Marcus Brofsky. Dead.

But I watched it too. What did that mean for me? I didn't watch all of it—did that count for anything? Was I only partially cursed? What about Dez, was *he* cursed? (And, deep down in the darkest parts of me, did I *care* if he was?)

Mom tried to connect with me that night.

"I'm so sorry about your friend, baby. I'm just sick about it."

She was sick a lot. She had an allergy to current events.

"I know you guys had been hanging out a lot lately. Was he. . . was he your boyfriend? You can tell me if—"

I snapped at her that I wanted to be left alone, then went to my room and felt like garbage for the snapping.

She was trying. I should've cut her some slack. But also, it got so exhausting that the one thing she *never* tried was remembering who I am. Who I've always been.

She knew Tyler wasn't my boyfriend.

I remember her little speech years ago.

—So, you're gonna be starting middle school soon. You're a little teenager now, I can't believe it.

But. Look, sweetie.

When you were a baby, all you wanted to do was eat things. Right? Everything. You would stuff it in your mouth, because you didn't know better. You just. . . had this impulse. And that's totally normal! Totally natural! That's why your parents exist! To say, "No, no, no, don't eat that," y'know, "that's dog poo, that's a power cord."

But now that you're older. . . you're gonna have some new *impulses. Just as strong. And just as dangerous too. But I want you to know they're just as normal and natural. And that you have to be your own parent a little bit now. But you can still totally come to me with anything—*

That's about where I tuned out.

If there'd been a comment card for that stupid speech, I would've filled out "Does not apply."

I don't see any boyfriends in my future. Or girlfriends. I just. . . don't. . . feel that way. I never have.

Sometimes I'd look stuff up online. Names of dispositions. Diagnoses. Communities I could join.

Some people call it being "ace." Or maybe it's "aro." Or maybe it's just late puberty. Or maybe I just haven't encountered the right person yet. Or, or, or.

Starts to feel like I'm a bug, being forced to crawl into one specific case or another. All this pressure to claim an identity. Be catalogued.

Just call me Notinterested. Call me Keepmeoutofit. Call me Ewnothankyou.

It's not that I didn't understand why sex and relationships are interesting. It's just, there are so many *other* things in this world. And it's one thing to understand why a hammer is useful, but if that hammer is constantly whamming down on you, how do you not start to hate it a little bit? Everyone around me was so *obsessed* with who's sleeping with who, who's dating who, who's breaking up with who in order to sleep with who and then date who. And musn't forget to look this way or that way so you, too, can be part of the chain! Otherwise, what use are you?

There had to be more to life than all this grunting and rubbing and swapping.

Sometimes, I would think about how much nicer it will be when I finally get older. When maybe my peer group will be able to focus on other things for more than five minutes a day.

Then I'd remember how my mom only ever asked me about relationships.

I remember the teacher in that video. He was older. And he was so blinded with hunger he ended someone's life. *Many* people's lives, I was starting to suspect.

All these bodies, humping the air around me around me, reminding me how different I apparently am.

I don't mind being different. I like me.

It's the world constantly forgetting that differences exist that gets to be so exhausting.

It's the way everybody shoves *their* way down my throat.

Maybe that's what Tyler was choking on.

Maybe that's what we all choke on in the end.

I've always had strong, strange dreams. Ever since I was a little kid. Sometimes it would take days before I could let go of the conviction that whatever I'd seen in any particular dream had really happened. I hear of other people having dreams and forgetting them immediately. Must be nice.

That night, I was standing on an island in the middle of a sea. Huge sea. Tiny island. And the tide was coming in. It would overtake my small patch of land soon enough.

And the sea wasn't water. It was this viscous, sticky, roiling *fluid.* Oozing back and forth against the narrow beach. Rubbing. Eroding. Creeping forward to my toes. The air had a metallic stink. The smell of pocket change.

I woke up and stared at the ceiling.

I thought about Dez, humping everything.

I thought about Tyler's hypnotized face, lit by the screen under his chin. Practically drooling at the sight of some obnoxious, physical act he'd probably seen a million times in a million other videos already.

I thought about what Tyler was probably doing when he died. What he'd maybe been *inspired* to do.

Mostly, I thought about how devastated that poor girl must've been when that video was first leaked. How furious she must be anytime someone watches it now. To know that people were enjoying her suffering. Leering at her misery.

Literally getting off on it.

Experiencing pleasure through her pain.

And I thought about curses. They're a stimulus response. I learned those two words in room C22, the very room where that video was filmed.

A curse can't be reasoned with. It can't be bargained with. Something sets it off and it becomes an unstoppable force.

But something has to set it off.

So, if this video *was* cursed (*stimulus*). . . maybe it only killed you (*response*) after you've had an—

"Um, say what? Or, I'm sorry, '*Come again*?'"

I was stuck with Dez again for yet another lunch period. So I told him my thesis—during which, for some stupid reason, I also accidentally wound up admitting that I'd never done *that thing* before. Experienced it before.

Dez was astonished. "You've never—?! You don't—?! You're not *constantly*—?!" He made obscene gestures. "Flipping the bean? Scratching the record? Buffin' the muffin?"

I said no.

"Damn. That's the saddest thing I ever heard. I could send you videos. Pointers."

I succeeded in not spraying his face with annoyed vomit. "Can we focus, please? If that video *is* cursed—"

"It totally is."

"—then, what if watching it, like, sets the bomb, but the thing that makes the bomb explode is the next time you. . ." I didn't even want to say the words. "Maybe that's why I haven't died yet." I steeled myself to ask the important question. "What about you? Have you? Since?"

Dez popped a cafeteria fry into his mouth. Considered. "Hmmm. I jerk off all the time, bro. Like. All. The. Time. My record's thirty-five in one day. The Day of the Chafe."

I put my own fry down, appetite gone. No big loss, they tasted like freezer burn. Freezer chafe. Ugh.

Then Dez's head ticked to the side. "Although, shit, now that I think of it, not in a few weeks, actually. They moved me to new antidepressants and it's made me kinda—" He held up one of his fries, limply. "Huh. Maybe you're right." He snorted. "Hahaha—oh man, if that's how the curse works, everyone in this damn school would be dead by like, sixth period. Ha! Can you imagine? This fucking hormone stew?"

I desperately wanted to change the subject. Before I could stop myself, I mentioned that, next, I was planning on visiting Jesse in the hospital after school. I wanted to see if maybe Jesse could tell me what he and Tyler had been doing when whatever happened, happened.

"Gross," Dez said, grinning and waggling his eyebrows. "I'll come with you. We can keep talking about your little problem. How to pet the kitty. Dig for clams."

"No," I said, flinching. "I don't—Dez, I like to be alone. Okay?"

"That's okay, I do too." He helped himself to some of my fries. "Friends can be alone together, right?"

I didn't mean to slam the table so hard. I didn't mean to yell so loud.

"WE'RE NOT FRIENDS, DEZ! Okay?" I shrank at the feeling of eyes on me. "I'm sorry. We're just. . ."

Dez was already shrinking too. Pulling into himself, like I'd slapped him.

He got real quiet.

"No. Right," he said. "Of course." Then, barely audible, "Why should you be any different?"

The nurse guarding Jesse's floor wouldn't let me in.

"Only family is allowed in," she said. "Sorry. And even if you could see him, he's not going to be answering any questions anytime soon. Frankly, that's for the best. I don't think he's going to want anybody reminding him of what happened."

"What do you mean?"

She looked at me with exhausted eyes.

"Kid. Those injuries were self-sustained. He bashed his own head into a wall until he knocked himself into a coma. Would *you* want to remember something that made you do that?"

That night, the same dream.

The same sea. Closer than ever. Sliming over my feet, making me retreat backwards up my tiny nubbin of land, where the sea was still waiting for me, just as close, just as eager.

And as that sticky, sludgy water crept closer, it began to rise.

Like it was standing up. Like it was forming into a new shape.

Something I knew I wouldn't survive seeing.

Two days later, Dez killed everybody in the school.

Unless this has all been part of another dream.

"Goooood morning, Paradise Valley High! Another beautiful sunny day for us all to be trapped inside a huge concrete building! Peel your eyes offa your phone and look up here, piglets—it's time for your morning news feeding! And because we're all such *good friends*, I wanna start off with some really hot, breaking news. A little movie I'd like you all to watch very closely."

He managed to play almost the entire video before someone busted down the studio door and stopped it.

He was suspended, of course. And for a day, he was a hero. Everyone thought it was so funny.

Then, close to a hundred kids didn't show up for school the next day.

Hundreds more the day after that.

All dead. All found at home, in their bedrooms, in their bathrooms, sitting at their desks.

More boys than girls, but still, plenty of girls.

The panic was immediate.

So were the rumors. Swirling. Down the drain.

It was a plague. It was a conspiracy.

Every day. Fewer and fewer kids at school.

Dez killed himself a couple days into the chaos—not because of the curse; he came back and jumped off the roof of the school, maybe out of guilt, maybe out of boredom. But by that point nobody noticed.

And the rumors had begun to change.

—Right before you die, you're visited

—She *comes to you*

—Comes for *you*

—She who?!

We all knew.

Somewhere along the line, people connected the plague to sex. Which caused some to abstain. Others to hurtle faster towards destruction.

Sneaking out to die in their girlfriend or boyfriend's house.

Looking for comfort. Looking for escape. Finding death.

—The gym is closed down because a group of kids locked themselves inside for a suicide orgy. They couldn't even get one set of the doors opened because the bodies were stacked so high.

There was no fighting it. Kids were even dying in their sleep. Their bodies were signing death warrants whether they wanted it or not.

Stimulus. Response.

Parents were killing themselves out of grief. Others were ready to go to war—but against who, no one had any idea.

Meanwhile, the video wound up on social media. On porn sites. Maybe someone posted it out of vengeance. Or for company.

It started spreading on its own soon enough. Organically. Like a sneeze. Like a baby chewing on an electrical cord.

—What is happening to us?!

—How can we stop it?!

And the tide keeps surging. Pushing. Pulsing forward.

Other schools. Other cities. Offices. Homes. One by one. Poor girl must be exhausted. But her rage never slackens.

—She comes for you

A viscous tide. Rolling. Roiling. Rubbing. Tugging.

—She's not human anymore. If she ever was.

And if I'm being totally honest? In a way, this is how it's always felt.

Watching everyone else experiencing something that's apparently not for me.

—She's coming

—Coming for all of us.

It's just me and my confusion, together as always.

—Coming for you.

I've watched the video dozens of times now. Looking for clues. Looking for understanding.

Looking to feel something.

I know I'm being reckless. But every now and then, that hunger to understand gets so strong. Some nights, I try and I try and I try, but nothing happens. Not even a tingle. I even bought toys. I'm playing with fire. Maybe one day, it'll be different. I'll get it. I'll choose it. I'll crave it. I'll wonder if curses have half-lives. But for now. . . Nothing.

Maybe this *is* all a dream.

Which means I have no real choice but to do what I've always done.

I'll wait.

—We wait.

For her, whoever she was. Whatever she is now.

—Come for us.

COME

—*Please, come for us.*
For something to change.
—*Come for us.*
For understanding.
For her.
For me.
To
—*Come.*

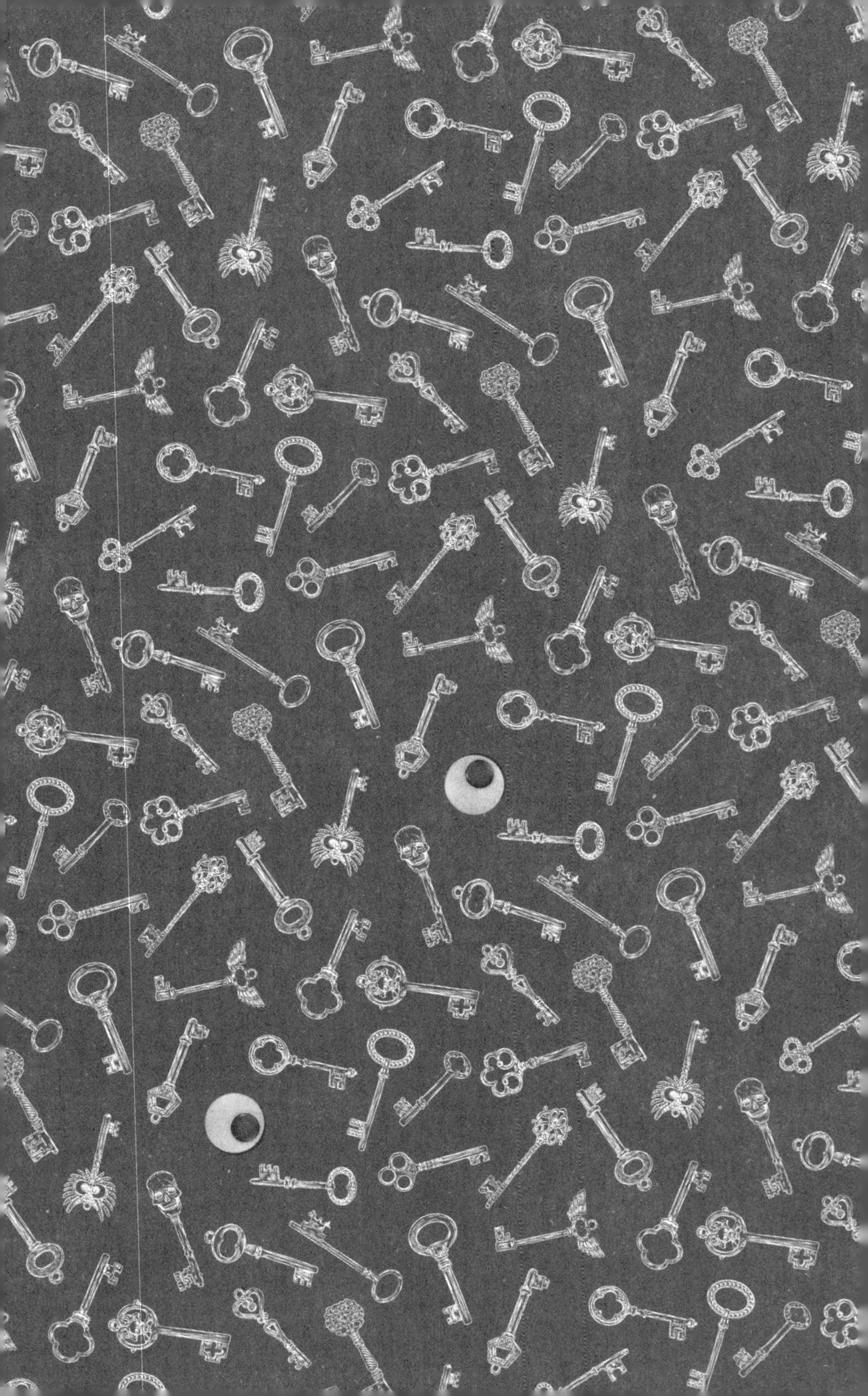

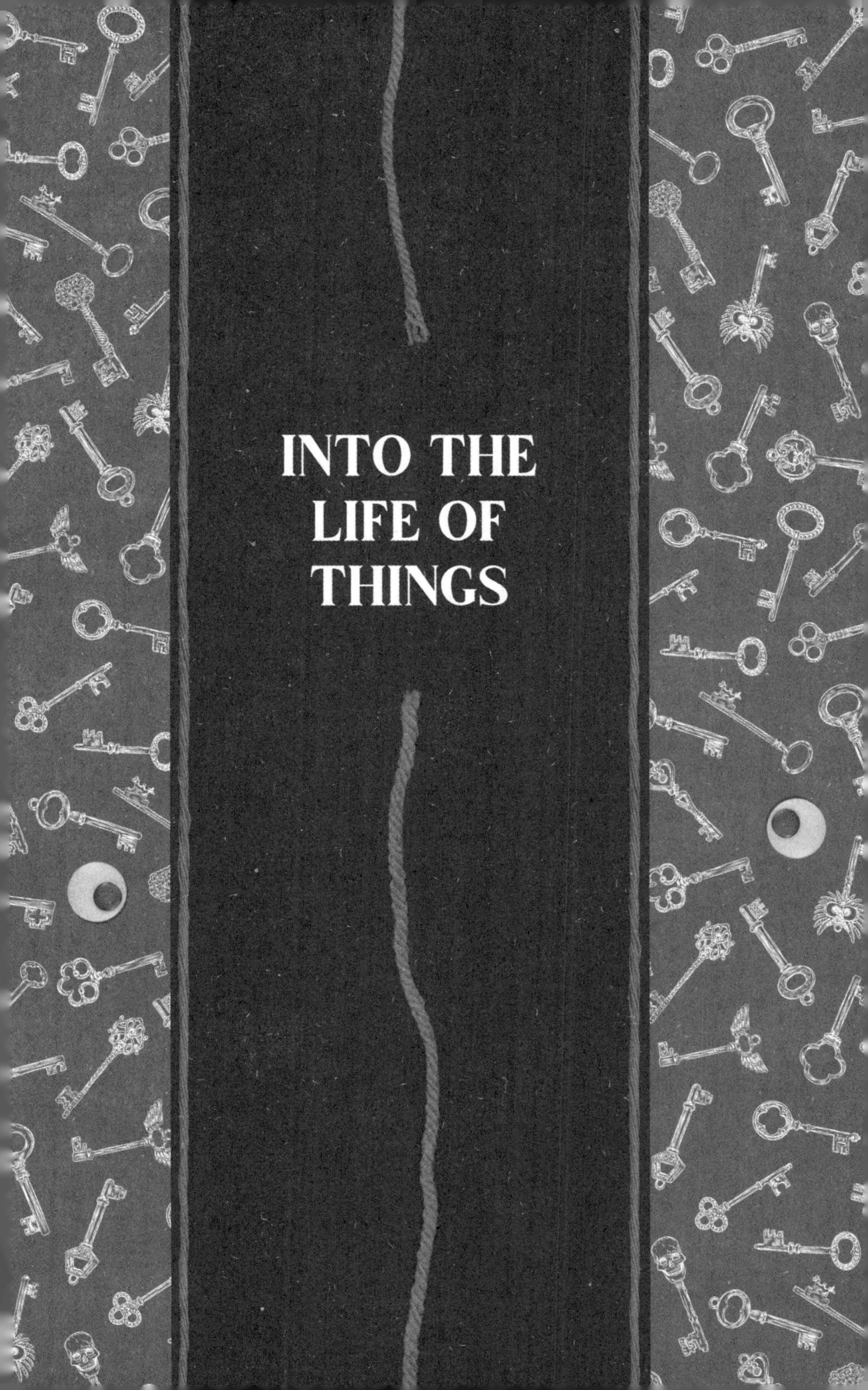
INTO THE
LIFE OF
THINGS

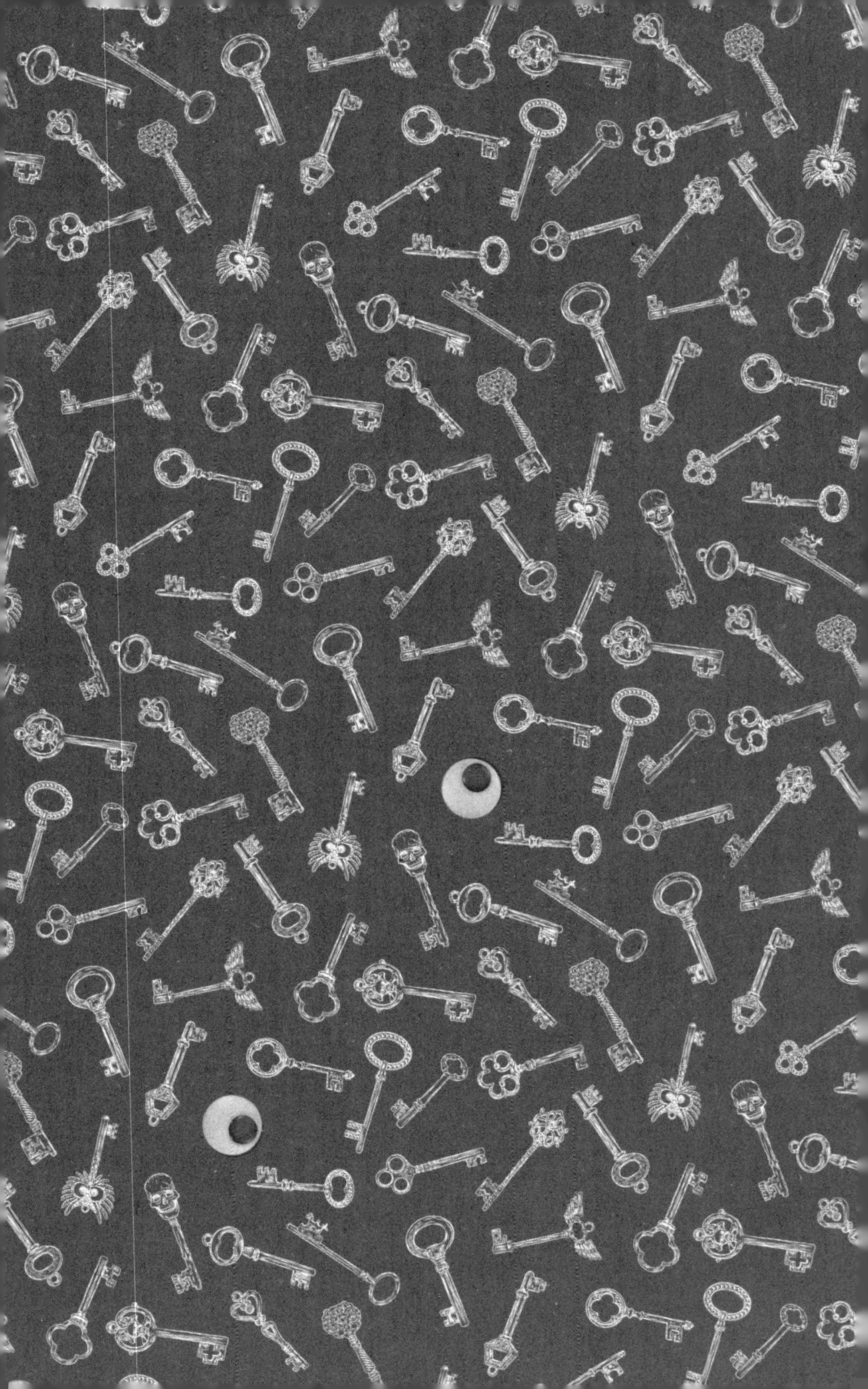

INTO THE LIFE OF THINGS

The dead woman was sprawled across the top landing of the hospital's fifth floor stairwell, directly underneath the skylight set into the high ceiling.

Detective Massey's first thought was she looked like a bug realizing it was just about to be squashed. On her back, legs tented up and splayed open, elbows bent and arms resting palm up against her collarbones, eyes wide, mouth frozen open in a rictus of surprise. Or horror.

"Goddamn," he said, shaking his head with something like a pantomime of pity. He took a long sip of his Starbucks caramel macchiato, graciously picked up for him by his partner, who'd arrived separately. "God. . . damn."

That same partner, Detective Hartford, was now off corralling potential witnesses, hoping to find someone who might help shed some light on the situation.

It had been a real fluke of timing. Thirty minutes ago, a patrolie had been dropping off a patient who was being involuntarily committed and putting up a real stink about it. As that custodial changeover was happening, suddenly a scream tore through the hospital hallways. The sort of scream that wasn't scheduled or accounted for.

The dead woman was found moments later.

There'd been no sounds of a struggle. No blood. No patients were allowed out of their rooms at this time, so there were no obvious suspects. But, given that scream, and given the bowel-freezing look on the corpse's face, a homicide couldn't be ruled out. The nearest pair of detectives were alerted and all the hospital staff was rounded up, to be interviewed one by one.

Now, Detective Massey followed the general direction of the dead woman's gaze. That skylight. Beyond it, a huge moon enjoyed its prominence among countless tiny stars. It looked like it could do anything, that moon. Maybe that's why the dead woman seemed so impressed.

From down the hall, he could hear the approaching sounds of his partner, leading their first interogatee to the scene.

A moment later, Detective Hartford was there, a prim, harried woman in tow. Petite and thin, hair in a tight bun, and unrestful baggage under her eyes. Wearing white long-sleeve thermals under a powder-blue uniform.

"First nurse of the round up," Hartford said as he gently, but firmly, nudged the woman towards the scene. "I actually found her wandering around like she was lost or something."

"Yeah?" Massey asked, and took another sip. "You lost, lady?"

The nurse seemed flustered. Confused. "N-no. I work here."

"'Cause I wouldn't blame you if you were," Massey said. "This place is a fuckin' labyrinth." Then he chucked his chin towards the body. "She look familiar?"

The nurse blinked, as if only now noticing the corpse at their feet.

"I—I—" she stammered.

"Great,'" Hartford grumbled. "I found a pirate."

"Be serious, Hartford, wouldja? For a change of pace?"

"Aye, aye, cap'n."

Both detectives turned their eyes to the nurse with a smooth synchronicity.

This was a thing Massey and Hartford did. This vaudevillian patter they'd developed over the years. It could drive people—cop and perp alike—crazy, but that was also the point. Some partners got good mileage out of the old good cop/bad cop routine, but Massey and Hartford found this more theatrical rapport did wonders when it came to rattling interviewees. To some, it made them seem harmless, which made their targets cocky; to others, it made the pair seem alien and strange, like two men sharing a brain. Intimidating. Disorienting. Neither detective would ever admit this, but they each found something comforting about the gimmick too. It made them feel less alone. Less tiny against the titanic horrors they were facing. In a job this isolating and lonely, it was nice to feel like a slightly larger organism for a change.

The nurse appeared to be one of those who got flustered by the routine. Not quite able to maintain her balance. Good. Unbalanced people tended to tip over and spill the truth before long.

"She. . . was a patient here," the nurse finally offered.

"Whoa," Hartford gasped. "That explains why she's wearing the same clothes every other patient here seems to be wearing!"

"Case closed!" Massey concluded. "Thanks for your assist—oh wait. We still don't know who she is or why she was allowed to be out in this stairwell in the first place."

"Is that how you run things here?" Hartford asked. "Letting patients wander around? Unattended?"

"You'd think she'd be someone who needs attending," Massey said. "This being a mental wellness facility and all."

"A nuthouse."

"A loony bin."

"A funny farm."

"A cuckoo's nest."

"Oh, Mass, did you see the bars on all the windows downstairs?"

"Couldn't miss 'em."

"Were you thinking what I was thinking?"

"That you'd like to see a big ole Indian chuck a water fountain through 'em?"

"I swear, it's like you're in my head sometimes."

"No place I'd rather be, partner."

"C-can I go now?" The nurse eyed them anxiously, as if hoping she'd been forgotten about.

The two detectives whipped their attention back to her and she took a half step backward under the intensity of their gaze. They were nothing but serious now.

"Not until we get some answers as to what this nice lady was doing out here—"

"unattended—"

"Instead of in her room—"

"attended—"

"—Snug as a bug in a padded rug."

The patter worked as it almost always did. The nurse appeared desperate to give them anything that would stop this inane, insane assault.

"Look, this isn't my area!" she blurted. "My section, I mean! Station! There are a lot of people that work here and I—I—I don't. . ."

Then a strange thing happened. The body caught her eye. She stared at it, transfixed. "I don't. . . know. . ."

Massey and Hartford, who each were beginning to suspect

they'd get nothing interesting or useful from this woman, now watched her keenly.

"Well, lady, I gotta be honest," Hartford said at last. "You look like you do know." He turned to his partner. "How long 'til the meat cart gets here?"

"Fifteen, twenty minutes?"

Back to the nurse. "Then you have fifteen to twenty minutes to talk to us, or you'll be coming with us down to the station, where we'll keep you until that brain of yours goes *a-ha*."

"Snug as a bug in a very unpadded rug."

"What do you know about her? Anything you might have heard or witnessed? Was she trouble? Was she difficult? Did she have any enemies?"

"How long was she in here? Short time, long t—?"

"No," the nurse said.

"No what?" Massey asked.

"No, she hadn't been here very long," the nurse said. "Maybe a week. She was very upset and confused. But sometimes she was allowed to come out here, because. . . it helped calm her down."

"Here we go, something helpful." Detective Massey took out a notebook. "What exactly was it about this stairwell that was so relaxing?"

"She doesn't look very relaxed to me," Hartford added.

The nurse's brow contracted. She was thinking. No, more than that, she was weighing the consequences of saying something. An expression any detective worth their salt could recognize.

"Come on," Massey urged. "Tell us what you know."

Hartford continued. "Be a pal and help us out already, won't ya—"

"Joshua," the nurse said abruptly.

This time, the two detectives were the surprised, confused

ones. They exchanged another glance.

"Your name is Joshua?"

"No." The nurse shook her head slowly, almost distantly. "She just. . . she mentioned the name Joshua from time to time."

"Joshua." Detective Massey scribbled it down.

"Her. . . husband," the nurse said. "She mumbled a lot of things, screamed them, really. . . But that name stuck out. I think she must have really loved him."

"Joshua," Detective Massey mused again. "And did you happen to catch *her* name?"

"Carole. I think."

"You think."

"It was hard to totally understand her sometimes. But aren't names and things in your file already?"

Hartford heaved a sigh. "Lady, we just got here. You're our file right now, okay?"

Massey agreed. "Now that you're feeling so open and charitable, why don't you tell us everything else you might have heard about Carole and Joshua."

The nurse took a deep, deep breath.

"Okay. Um. Well. . . what do you know about yoga?"

"The fuck would we know about yoga?" Massey and Hartford asked in unison.

They finish their asanas, each across from the other inside the small, leather-skin yurt.

The floor is rough, hardpan desert under scratchy, thin rugs.

The air is hot and vaguely damp with distant monsoon humidity.

And yet their sighs are of the utmost contentedness.

True relaxation.

Joshua, as always, breaks the silence first. But, Carole notes, it took longer than ever for him to start getting restless and distracted. That's a wonderful sign.

She watches as he lunges over for the small whiteboard kept by the side of his mat. His dry erase marker squeaks as he writes. Then he holds the whiteboard out to face her, grinning broadly.

YOU'RE SO FUCKING BEAUTIFUL

With an indulgent, patient smile of her own, she picks up the small whiteboard on her side of the room. She writes back:

YOU ARE TOO.

Then she erases her message and writes a new one.

FOCUS.

Joshua nods, not a little begrudgingly. He's supposed to be enjoying the stillness, steeping in the satisfied, almost post-coital glow of their yoga routine. Listening to the sweet and profound rush of nothingness until—

A gong rings out through the camp.

Joshua and Carole both express a long, grateful noise, as if each remembering how to vocalize for the first time.

After touching sound, they stare at each other for a moment.

"Joshua," Carole says, letting him know she sees him, appreciates him, celebrates him.

"Carole," he says back—and she doesn't think she's imagining it that he's taking the moment seriously this time. That he's not bringing any snark or impatience to it. That he understands how important it is they choose their first words during their brief daily window of audible speech to be each other's name.

Then he stands and gives his lower back a massive stretch in a graceless, lumbering way that reminds her of a bear emerging from hibernation.

"Ohhhhh, Jumping Jesus on a Pogo Stick," he groans. "Hooo, boy."

She rises, as well. Delicate as a leaf riding an updraft. "Are you hungry?"

He makes a face, somewhere between a grimace and a pout. "When are you gonna stop asking me that? Goddamn, I'm *starving*." He catches himself before she needs to say anything. "Joking. Honest. I can't wait for twigs." He rolls up his mat and sticks it in a corner of the yurt. "Know the thing I miss the most right now, though? Plain pasta. Isn't it weird? Like, the lamest food in the universe and that's The Thing I'm Dying For?"

Carole does the same with her mat. "I don't think it's weird. It's a refined food. It's designed to be addicting. It's no different than missing cigarettes."

"Uh, it's a little different than missing cigarettes."

"How?"

He gives an edgy little scoff. "You're starting to sound like Edmond."

"That's why we're here, my love."

"Hoo, boy. . ."

"My love. Are you really going to use the one hour we have to talk filling up the world with negativity?"

She can see him fight the urge to say something snarky. "No. No, you're right."

"Breathe."

He breathes. She can hear the air whistling through his nostrils.

"I'm so proud of you," she says. "I knew you would take to this."

"Kiss me."

"Soon," she says. Meaning it. Wanting it.

"I love the sound of your voice," he says, and she melts a little. Her big bear. Her surprising, complicated, well-meaning Joshua.

"I love the sound of yours." She puts a hand on his chest. "You know the thing *I'm* dying to have again?"

"What?"

"You."

The nurse stared down at the dead woman, lost for a moment.

"They were found out in the middle of nowhere," she said at last. "She wouldn't stop screaming. And he had starved to death. In front of her. At least that's what I heard."

The two detectives exchanged glances.

"God," Massey said.

"Damn," Hartford concluded. "No wonder she wound up in here."

The nurse nodded.

Then something in her face shifted. Like she smelled something rancid, or remembered an unpleasant errand she had to run.

"But, I mean, who knows?" she said, trying to recover with an embarrassed smile. "That's just what I heard. A crazy yoga cult in the desert? Sounds like a bit of a cliché."

Joshua's first thought of Edmond was, this guy is a fucking joke. After six days in the wilderness together, that's still Joshua's first thought whenever their glorious leader gives one of his endless lectures to the assembled participants of this—well, what would you even call it? Excursion? Getaway? Yoga bootcamp? Joshua's sure he knew what to call it earlier, but all this depravation and isolation and starvation and other -ations have wiped so many words from his brain, it's a wonder he can think at all.

A little more time and I'll be as empty-headed as that asshole.

Joshua watches Edmond finish his performative centering, which Edmond always does before launching into the day's sermon.

After an eternity, Edmond is ready. He taps his massive, bulbous-headed walking stick against the ground and speaks in his soft, Santa Monica-accented voice.

"Om shanti shanti, my gurus, and blessed day. Yoga. . . *is not a tree*! Some might describe it as such—many have in fact, but that is a lie. An innocuous visual hook to sell keychains, as catchy as sugar. A structure needing to be conquered? With a finite number of branches, leading to some ultimate pinnacle? That is not yoga! There are no limbs from which you must cease to climb or else fall to the ground! There is no hierarchy! Only ashrama! The great zooming out of it all, where there are simply *currents*, not *steps*." His eyes are wide with practiced fury. Joshua has no problem imagining the half-assed version of this speech that must be performed in front of the bathroom mirror. "You are here with me, my gurus, because you understood, even if it was only inarticulate, that there is the possibility for something wider, greater than the plodding mechanism of step one, step two, climbing, climbing. We have not come to climb. We have come to *disintegrate*."

He points to his third eye, a spot just above the middle of his expensive-looking Lennon glasses. The bangles on his wrists chatter excitedly.

"While with an eye made quiet by the power/Of harmony, and the deep power of joy/We see into the life of things!" Then Edmond's expression softens into a pout that would befit any Broadway gift shop tragedy mask. "I know: but *how*? With the constant whirr of man's, of *our*, frightened urge to fill the air with something, anything, other than our true atman? That is why we're here, my gurus! To, to strip ourselves of the grime, the lacquer, the *skin* of it all, to surpass the jivan-mukti!" He strikes the ground with the bottom of his heavy stick again. "I want you all tonight, my prana, my hamas, to go and connect with the sunset—stare into the sky and understand that there is no sunset. And there are no limits to where your consciousness can enter. Soon, gurus, we will see just how far off that branch we can journey. Because yoga is not a tree. Yoga is the *air around the tree*. Now, we'll turn it over to Carole, our lovely, lovely Carole, our light, our anurakti, to lead us in morning salutations. Carole?"

With a flick of his graying ponytail, Edmond turns to give Carole the stage.

Later in their yurt, Carole works on Joshua's back, kneading and rubbing with expert grace. Next to her is her army roll of acupuncture needles. Seemingly hundreds of them, long as a forearm and thin as angel hair.

Joshua takes up his whiteboard.

♫ SOME SAY YOGA...
IT IS A RIVER
THAT DROWNS THE TENDER REED. ♫

Carole shushes him, biting back a smile.
He writes more.

♫ I SAY YOGA..
IT IS A FLOWER
THAT SOMETHING SOMETHING THE ROSE. ♫

She stops rubbing his shoulders. Gives him a light shove. Grabs his tablet and pen. Writes:

I KNOW GOOD AND BAD PRESSURE POINTS.
REMEMBER?

He makes a puppy dog face. She gives him the pen and tablet back, goes back to rubbing his shoulders. He sighs in deep relief.

YOUR HAAAAAAAAAAAAAAAAAANDS.
I CAN'T WAIT TO CUM WITH YOU AGAIN.

She makes a disgusted noise and, before she can reprimand him, he erases the board and writes for her:

"FOCUS."

A few seconds later, though, he scoffs out loud. "It's just, the way he talks sometimes—"

She gives up and storms away from him, trying to calm herself with breathing.

"What?" he says. "Come on, I can talk, it's almost—"

Outside, the gong sounds.

"See?" He gives her one of his patented shit-eating grins which she used to think were so charming. "I'm just curious. Seriously. I'm not trying to sound negative. Do you really think what he's talking about is possible? I mean, 'air has no boundaries?' He's heard of the atmosphere, right?"

Carole has moved from breathing to rubbing her temples. "I'm really feeling immense frustration with you right now."

"I'm sorry. I apologize. Okay?"

"Of course I believe him."

"For real?"

"You don't?"

"Babe. I mean, come *on*. You know I love you, and I'm willing to give anything you say a—"

"This has nothing to do with how you feel about me, Joshua. And if you're just going through the motions here to try to, I don't know, *impress me* or something—"

"Impress you? What does that even mean?" His voice goes high, into that piercing falsetto of offended men.

She counteracts him with a softer, steelier tone. "What exactly don't you believe about what he's saying?"

"I don't know! Sounds like he's been talking about, I don't know, astral projection, or something equally as cuckoo-banana-pants."

"He's talking about what he's always been talking about. Surpassing the jivan-mokti, experiencing true recaka."

"Through twigs and silence."

"Through kaivalya and moksha. I thought you wanted to share this with me! I thought you said learning yoga helped change your life!"

"It did! I do!"

She approaches him and takes his hands. The frustration has ebbed away from her as she remembers how flustered and short-tempered he used to be. How miserable. He *has* made great strides towards becoming a more centered, present person. He really has.

"I mean, sometimes," she says, "I stare out into the sky and repeat my mantra, I, I feel so *capable* and whole, like I could just fall up into eternity. Don't you want to feel that too? Don't you want to—"

"Tell me your mantra."

She lets him go as suddenly as if two rattlesnakes slithered out of his sleeves.

"JOSHUA!"

She almost can't breathe for a moment, she's so scandalized.

He rolls his eyes. "I know."

"That's *beyond* personal. That's, I can't even, I'm so—!"

"I just wanted to, I don't know, *know* something about you. Feeling insecure."

Breathing. Centering. She will not let his energy ruin hers. His body, trapped in the kali-yuga, is full of toxins, and those toxins don't leave without a fight. He requires grace and patience.

"I will *not* tell you my mantra. And don't you dare tell me yours. Enjoy the spaces between us. Ananda, my love."

"Fine. Fucking whatever. I just. . . I don't know, I just get a vibe from him, that's all I'm saying."

"From Edmond? A vibe? What does that mean?"

"Nothing." Joshua bends over to touch his toes—not that he can get that far. "Don't worry about it, I'm just hungry." He tries warrior next.

"Are you giving up on this?" Carole asks.

"No," he grumbles.

"Because if you start giving up on this—"

"I know, Carole!"

"Only you can get in your own way. And Edmond can teach you to do incredible things. If only you'll let him. Believe me."

"Yeah, yeah, I've seen the YouTube videos."

"Oh, for god's sake, Joshua, it's not just YouTube videos! I've known him a long time! I know what he's capable of!"

Joshua straightens up. His eyes narrow. "How long, exactly?"

"What does that mean?"

"How long have you two 'known each other?'"

Carole freezes, then sneers. She starts walking in circles, looking for something else to do. Surprisingly Joshua-like behavior.

"Okay. Nope. No, no, no. See, this is why we shouldn't be talking, never mind. No. Edmond was right, talking only messes everything up."

Joshua is rooted in the spot, enjoying seeing her twist. "No, Carole, tell me. Come on. I'm just curious. I know he's giving us some kind of discount to be here because of your needles, but I've also seen the way he looks at you. What exactly is your history with him? I think I have a right to know, don't you? As your partner, as your husband, as someone who—"

She makes a noise somewhere between a scoff and a gag, rolling her eyes. "You're not my husband, Joshua."

Thud.

Pause.

"I'm. . . *not*?"

She retreats a little from her outburst. "I told you, I don't believe in those words."

"You told me you thought of us as, as married—"

"I never said married—"

"You said 'wedded'—"

"United in the spirit, Joshua, yes. That doesn't mean—"

He begins flexing and unflexing his large hands. Rubbing at

his face. "Wait. So. This whole time. The past year and a half. You've just been—?"

His breaths are getting increasingly vocal. Heaving. Hulking. Becoming more bear-like.

"Joshua," she says. "Your mantra. Focus on your mantra."

"My—I don't know what to do, I don't know, I've been pretty patient with this whole thing, this whole fucking thing, I've left my life, I've come out here, I spent thousands of dollars, I'm barely eating, I'm not talking, I'm not touching you, I'm not touching myself, I don't know what to do, Carole, I don't know what you're telling m—"

"Oh, fucking get over yourself, Joshua!" she snaps at him. "What do you want to do, beat the shit out of me again?!"

That works. He stops his ranting and gapes at her.

"I think I've been pretty fucking patient too," she says firmly.

"You've just been waiting to throw that in my face, haven't you?" he responds in a hurt whisper. "*One* time. *Two* years ago. And you're never going to let me forget it."

"Heyyyy, guys."

Neither knows how long Edmond has been standing inside their yurt. He'd just slipped in, quiet as a breeze. But when he speaks, they both whip around to find him grimace-smiling.

"Om shanti shanti." Edmond's hands twist around the prayer-flag-decked top of his enormous walking stick. "We're hearing some angry tones out here. Everything okay?"

Joshua looks to Carole, who sighs. "Yes," she says. "We're just. . . airing toxicity."

Edmond swallows a lump. Like they nauseate him. "I see. If it needs to be done. . ."

"It's okay," Carole says, "We'll stop. I'm sorry."

"No, no, no. The rest of us can meditate our way through it

if we need to." Edmond makes a weak gesture to the rest of the encampment behind him.

Carole goes back to rubbing her temple. A gesture a lot of people have been making on this retreat, she realizes. Headaches due to starvation, no doubt.

"I just, I'm really seeing the appeal of staying silent right now," she says.

"Yes, well, words do complicate things." Edmond gives the approximation of a warm, understanding smile. "Carole. Whenever you're free, no rush, can I borrow you for a few minutes? You and your needles? It's my shoulder. You're the only one who. . ."

"Of course. Yeah. I can do it right now." She starts over for her acupuncture kit.

"No, no," Edmond declares with magnanimity, then finally gives Joshua the benefit of his acknowledgement. "Talk with your partner. Please. While you can. I can wait."

He stops at the yurt entrance. Turns around. "Just. . . burn some sage after you're finished arguing. If you don't mind?"

Hartford looked at his notes. Ticked off what he'd written.

"So. Crazy cult. Crazyhouse. Dead."

Massey nodded. "Definitely dead."

"Any idea why?"

Massey shook his head. "Not a clue. You?"

Hartford shook his head. "Not a clue. You?"

It took the nurse a few solid moments before she realized Hartford was asking that last question to her. "Me?"

"You," Hartford and Massey said together, harmonizing in impatience.

"No," the nurse said. "She was just. . . found like this, right?"

Massey handed over his coffee to his partner, then knelt down with a groan. "I don't see any wounds or anything."

"No sign of a struggle," Hartford added. "No blood. Just that look on her face. Like she saw something. . . unspeakable."

"I'm not a doctor," the nurse said. "I. . . don't know."

"Right," Massey said. He looked the corpse up and down. "What were you doing out here, lady? What happened? Why are you dead?"

Joshua is in the middle of solo meditation—sitting on the floor of their tent all by himself and actually getting surprisingly close to experiencing true silence—when Carole bursts in.

Her face is flush. Her eyes are wild. For a split-second, he thinks she's about to jump his bones—but even at the heights of *that* kind of ardor, there was never the kind of ecstasy now pulsing behind those wild eyes.

She grabs her tablet. Writes sloppily, barely containing her excitement.

THE MOST AMAZING THING!

Joshua writes on his own:

WHAT?

Carole erases her tablet and starts writing a response. . . then erases. . . then pauses. . . then tries to write again. Joshua taps his own tablet again and again—whatwhatwhatwhat???—until finally she finds the words.

Five of them, to be exact:

I THINK I DID IT

Joshua makes a series of sloppy hand gestures, each one trying to convey *go on, what are you talking about, need more information.*

Carole erases. Writes some more. Exhales in pantomime frustration.

WISH COULD TALK!!

Erases. Writes some more.

COME OUTSIDE WITH ME.

She's out of the tent before he can respond. He follows her.

Outside, the world is the color of deep amethyst, rich eggplant, shadows within shadows within the glow of stars and galaxies. It's a perfect desert night, and the moon hangs just above them like their own personal reading lamp.

Carole writes some more.

LOOK AT THE SKY. FOCUS.

After a little hesitation, and after her insistent tapping of the words on her tablet, Joshua looks at the sky. The dizzying swirl of cosmic diamonds. He actually staggers a little on his feet, it's so vast and disorienting. Once he finds his footing, though, he resumes staring upward. At the sky. Through the sky. Realizing he's not looking up. . . he's looking down.

Carole taps him on the shoulder gently. She's written newer words on her tablet.

NOW CLOSE YOUR EYES.

He does. He can hear the squeak of her pen against a smooth, white surface.

BREATHE DEEPLY.

He does.

BREATHE SLOWLY.

He breathes. Deeply and slowly. In and out. Deeply and slowly. In and out. Deeply and slowly. In and out. He can still see those swirling galaxies, that cone of cosmic jewelry, wrapping itself around the limits of his vision, extending and narrowing, expanding and contracting.

LET ME FLOW INTO YOU LIKE AIR
THROUGH AN OPEN WINDOW.

CAN YOU FEEL ME?

He nods.

I'M SORRY WE FOUGHT.
I DON'T WANT TO FIGHT WITH YOU.
YOU ARE MY LOVE.

AND YOU ARE MINE.
MY EVERYTHING.
OH CAROLE
I'M SORRY TOO.

MY JOSHUA.
NOW ASK YOURSELF.
HOW ARE YOU HEARING ME?

His eyes bolt open. He stares at her. "The fuck?!"

She laughs, then covers her mouth with a hand. Shushes him with a finger.

He grabs her tablet from her. The last things she wrote: "*NOW CLOSE YOUR EYES.*" None of that other stuff.

He stumbles backwards. "I don't understand, I, I could hear you, not like sound in my ear, but like the way I hear writing when I read it, I could hear it in my mind, I, I, I'm so confused, were you speaking or something? Were you whispering? Is this a trick—?"

She's still shushing him, giggling. When he finally quiets down, she makes a show of erasing her board and writing—actually writing—something new. He reads over her shoulder, so she can keep writing.

YOU DID IT TOO!!!
I TOLD YOU YOU WERE A NATURAL!!
SEE? IT'S POSSIBLE

"I'm still so confused," he says. "What—"

She shushes him again, firmer this time. Points to her throat, *no talking.* But he's shaking his head.

"I don't care about any of that shit, Carole! You were in my—" He throws his hands up, then scribbles on his own tablet:

THE FUCK JUST HAPPENED??????

She responds with her own writing. It takes her a torturously long time to write it all, so Joshua starts pacing without even realizing it. The insides of his skull feel itchy. It's a horrible, woolen feeling. He's half tempted to run through the encampment, find that fucking gong, and ring it himself. Maybe with Edmond's dopey ass walking stick. Maybe with Edmond's head.

Finally, she turns her tablet around.

I WAS WITH EDMOND.
WENT OUTSIDE TO MEDITATE.
I WAS UPSET SO REALLY FOCUSED
FELT MYSELF... EVAPORATE??
FELT INSIDE HIS MIND? DON'T KNOW...

"You and Edmond," Joshua growls.

She waves her hands—that's not the point, don't worry about that. Erases. Writes more.

HE COULDN'T DO IT!!
HE WAS SO MAD
BUT I FELT LIKE I COULD DO ANYTHING.
MY SELF - THE SELF - WAS GONE!

She erases the bottom three lines, leaving the top. Writes anew.

I KNEW I HAD TO TRY WITH YOU.
YOU WOULD ACCEPT ME. YOU WOULD BE OPEN
AND ABLE. AND I WAS RIGHT.
I HEARD U!!!!!!!

Joshua rubs his eyes, backs away a step.

Carole erases, writes:

WHAT, MY LOVE?

He starts to write, then stops, laughing bitterly.

"This is crazy. I'm really hungry. We're tired, we're in a highly suggestible state. I'm gonna go back ins—"

"Think of a number!" Hearing her voice is such a relief, he forgets to be mad for a moment.

"A. . . what?"

"Think of a number." She writes something down, then looks back at Joshua eagerly. Her eyes *flex.* Joshua feels the thought in his skull before he voices it.

"37"

Carole turns her whiteboard around. That same number is written in large, unmistakable strokes.

Joshua gapes, then shakes his head harder than ever.

"Color," Carole says.

PERIWINKLE.

The word is suddenly inside his head. He almost lets it out of his lips, but he stops himself.

Carole spreads her arms, as if to say, "Anything?" He just stares at her.

"I. . . have to go lie down. Meditate."

Then, at last, he writes on his tablet.

WHY DON'T YOU GO TALK TO EDMOND ABOUT THIS

The next day is full of tension. It's a living thing, coursing and slithering between their ankles. Even during their allotted time for vocal activation, neither has much to say to the other.

They're not the only ones stewing in thought. Edmond too, appears wracked and preoccupied. His afternoon address is perfunctory. No insights. No lessons. Just a promise of some great new direction to be announced soon.

Joshua can't help but notice how purposefully Edmond avoids looking in Carole's direction all day. Normally, he slathers her with his eyes, but now. . .

That night, Edmond gathers the encampment together. His face is grim and determined. He grips his walking stick like it owes him money. Like it's the only thing holding him upright.

"Gurus." He has to clear his throat. "There've been some new developments, gurus. I. . . This is to be our last day here in this encampment. These yurts, these comforting, stifling structures are holding us back. I realize that now. They're impeding our true potential. Tomorrow, at dawn, everyone is to take only their mat and a blanket and, without a word, head out into the wilderness. Speak not a word to anyone! Go alone! One by one, we shall isolate and dedicate ourselves as, as *strongly* as we can to our meditation. Right now, the world is still too much with us, my gurus! But you will know when it is time to reconvene when you hear my voice. *You will hear my voice, my gurus.* I PROM-

ISE YOU THAT."

When they get back to their yurt, Joshua is fuming. He grabs his board and writes:

INSANE.

Then:

TERRIBLE IDEA.

Then:

REALLY FUCKING DANGEROUS.

Finally, he tosses the board down. "Will you just fucking talk to me?"

Before she can open her mouth, or make another of her goddamn shushing noises, suddenly Edmond is there again, rapping his stupid fucking walking stick against the ground like it's the same thing as knocking on a door.

Joshua inhales for serenity, unintentionally growling the tiniest bit, picks up his board, and starts to write.

HELLO, EDM

"Can I talk to you for a quick moment? Joshua? Out loud?"

Edmond's voice is its usual softspoken coo, but it hits Joshua and Carole both like a fart in a church. For a moment, they're both on the same side again, looking at each other in surprise.

"Uh. Sure," Joshua says at last. He puts his tablet aside.

"Carole," Edmond says. "Brother Bodie is complaining of anxious tremors along his sciatica. Perhaps you wouldn't mind. . . ?"

Without a word, Carole nods, picks up her acupuncture kit, and leaves them.

Edmond watches after her for a pregnant moment, then sits on the ground, folding naturally into his usual lotus, setting his walking stick down next to him.

"You two have been partners a long time now, yeah?"

Joshua nods. "Three years."

"Such a fascinating moment in a relationship, isn't it? The seeds have all been planted and watered; now you wait to see if they'll grow as promised."

Joshua blinks. "Huh?"

Edmond waves the question away with a beneficent grin. "Tell me, Joshua. Are you enjoying your time here?"

"Am I *supposed* to be enjoying my time here?"

"Ha! Excellent question." Edmond picks at a purl poking up from his flowy linen pants. "You know, when we first met and sat down to talk about your relationship with yoga, with your inner life, you told me you had a hard time keeping your mind quiet. You had rages. Is that still the case?

No reason to lie. He was too hungry and tired to put up much of a façade. "Yeah, sometimes."

"Right now?"

"As a matter of fact."

"What is it *about* right now?" Edmond tents his hands under his chin.

Joshua does a valiant job not smacking the loathsome little smirk off Edmond's face. "I'm having a hard time shaking the idea that what you're suggesting is really dangerous. Everyone just going off on their own, like, into the middle of nowhere?"

"An intense denialist regiment like this can increase anxiety levels in newcomers. Quite a bit."

"I'm not a newcomer."

"Everyone here is perfectly capable of taking care of themselves on their own, Joshua."

"I'm sure that's what Jim Jones said too."

"Joshua, please. Have I offered anyone Kool-Aid?"

"No, that would have flavor." Joshua imagines what Carole might say to that and winces. "Sorry."

Edmond chuckles. In one uncannily fluid motion, he rises from the ground. He begins to inspect their location with idle distraction. "Can I be honest with you, Joshua? You'd think I'd be happy with what Carole said she'd experienced. But my first, gut reaction? I'm not proud. . . I was bitter. That she could achieve that level of connectedness, could feel that, that. . ." He waves himself away with a trifling laugh. "Listen to me. This is the last thing you want to hear out of me, isn't it? You already think of me as something of a stereotype. And you're not wrong! I mean, look at me! But I've never, ever claimed to know more than anyone here, Joshua. I call you all my gurus because I learn from you too. And even if I'm being eaten away by envy and frustration, if *she* experienced what she said she did, well, then it confirms everything I've believed."

Had Carole not told Edmond that Joshua had experienced it—achieved it—too? Joshua begins chewing on his lower lip.

"I don't know, Edmond" he says. "All I know is. . . I'm hungry. I feel like I'm losing my grip on reality."

"Oh, but, Joshua! Reality? Bleh!" Edmond mimes as if puking into the dirt. "Reality is the stick we use to cudgel our potential into a bloody mess. And Carole is capable of so much, Joshua. Don't you agree?"

"Yeah."

"I'm so glad!" He's suddenly in front of Joshua. Placing both his hands on Joshua's shoulders, like a coach giving a pep talk. "Because I think we need to send you away. Back to your home. Back to the city."

"Uh. What?"

"This is too much for you, I think right now, Joshua. And that's okay. But also for her. She needs to focus. We all need her to focus. So we can learn from her, Joshua."

"Wait, I don't think I'm understanding you." A part of him is surprised to not be breaking free from Edmond's touch. To realize the direct human contact feels good. The warm breath that smells like cinnamon. "Where would I go? How—"

Edmond is still going, ignoring him. "Especially now that the stakes are so high, Joshua. Like you said, the rest of the camp is now *relying* on our progress! Our safety *depends* on it! And she cares about you too much, Joshua. That's her wonderful flaw. Always has been. She loves so strongly. So intensely. Heh. I remember when we were married, she would have the hardest time concentrating when all she wanted to do was—"

Just like that, Joshua's able to break free. "When you were what?" He staggers backwards. "When you were what?"

Had he already asked that? Had he misheard? What is happening?

"Married," Edmond repeats, face open and dumb and naïve. "Surely you knew that. We were married for years, before. . ." His brow knits in realization. "Oh. Oh, Joshua."

It's that expression of shocked concern on Edmond's horrible fucking face that makes Joshua start to laugh.

"When you were *what*?" he manages between desperate guffaws.

"Joshua, I'm sure this isn't how she intended you to find out. How confusing for you. You need to take some time. Okay? Focus on your mantra. Your body's under a lot of stress right now, with the detoxifying and the deprivation—"

"Right!" Joshua chortles. "Exactly! The juvan makti or whatever! Hahaha. You're really something, Edmond. Hahahaha!"

"Poor vaja—" Edmond says mournfully. "Sit with me and we'll process this sadness together."

"Nah, fuck that. I'm gonna go look at the fucking sky!"

Still laughing, Joshua stumbles outside. Tries to breathe. He staggers in random directions, but all is emptiness around him. The other yurts are so far away, hundreds of yards away, miles and miles away, tilting and see-sawing, boats adrift on an angry ocean, and he can't breathe, he can't focus for all the rocking and swirling, and so eventually he *has* to go back inside, *has* to retreat to the safety of his comforting, stifling structure, and there's fucking Edmond, the smug sonofabitch is sitting down of the floor of *their* home, eyes closed, meditating next to his stupid goddamn walking stick, because he's just so sad, he has it so rough.

Edmond's eyes don't open until after Joshua has yanked that heavy, bulbous walking stick off the ground. Joshua wraps both hands around the base and swings the thickest end into Edmond's head.

It's a beautiful swing. A perfect arc. And the stick is beautifully thick. Carved from driftwood. Shaped and molded by the sea, which is why Joshua's swings are so fluid, why the blood exploding from Edmond's shattered skull is all liquid grace.

Edmond splays backward with a barely expressed, "Ououh?" That doesn't stop the tide, though. Joshua keeps swinging, pummeling every part of Edmond's stupid fucking body, ribs, arms, hips, face, all of it cracking underneath his battery. Edmond is prone on his back, not moving, blood gurgling up from a tooth-free mouth. Finally, Joshua flips the stick in his grip and brings the blood-smeared end down as hard as he can, right between Edmond's eyes, right into that third one, sending Edmond into forever.

Joshua has nothing quite like a thought during all this, but as he comes back to himself, he begins by musing that he would've expected Edmond's head to explode with that final hit. It didn't explode. It just kind of caved into itself. It leaks, like a pocket of tree sap.

Because yoga is not a tree.

Then Joshua realizes what he's done. Sees the very real, very dead body on the ground.

All the air goes out of the room.

"Oh, god," he wheezes. "I can't, breathe, I can't—"

He reaches for his mantra. That will help. That always helps. But this time it's gone completely out of his head. He can't remember it. He's being sucked up into a vortex of panic and there's nothing to grab onto—

Then it comes back to him. That private, repetitive phrase which clears his mind and helps him come back to himself. Which reminds him he knows nothing other than:

Breathing in I know that I am breathing in

Breathing out I know that I am breathing out

"It's not working!"

Breathing in I know that I am breathing in

Breathing out I know that I am breathing out

It had been given to him during his first session with a yogi three years ago. Carole had taken him.

Carole.

He starts to sob. High and desperate, like a child.

Breathing in I know that I am breathing in

Breathing out I know that I am breathing out

A few minutes later, a random assortment of needles still in her hand, Carole slips back into the yurt. She looks concerned, had in fact sensed something awful in the quiet stillness of the encampment and rushed over. But now, seeing Joshua standing over Edmond's demolished body—only identifiable because of the newly shit- and piss-stained clothes—she is shocked into stillness.

Joshua sees her and runs to her. He hugs her, still sobbing. Her arms wrap around him mechanically.

"I fucked up," he's saying. "I fucked up. I don't know, I don't know, I don't know, it's not working, my mantra's not working and you lied to me baby you lied to me you lied to me you lied to me."

He's clutching at her. His hands find her neck and start to squeeze. He brings his face up so they both can look at the other. They're each caught in an eerily similar, underwater slowness. Placid. Eyes wide in astonishment—only hers are bulging out of a face that's quickly going purple, going amethyst, going eggplant.

She's dropped all of her acupuncture needles except for one. Still with that slow, placid grace, she lifts the needle, finds exactly where it means to go, and sticks it deeply into Joshua's neck.

He gasps, instantly dropping to the ground like a sack of rocks, his body landing in an awkward tangle.

She wants to ask him why, what happened, what is going on, but her throat feels crushed. She staggers over to the mess that was Edmond. His face is gone. Disintegrated.

Joshua, meanwhile, is moaning, whining, keening, that he can't feel his legs. She knows he can't feel his legs. Just as she knows the pressure point that paralyzed him.

Finally, she manages to croak, "I have to go get help."

Someone, anyone, to help her make sense of what is going on. Except, everyone else is packing up and getting ready for their isolation—some, in fact, have probably already headed out.

"No," Joshua says. "Don't leave me."

"I'm sorry," she says.

"What did you do to me? Why did you bring me here? *What did you do to me*?"

He manages to pull himself over to her and grab onto her legs. Even now, even like this, he's strong. Too strong. She can't pull free.

"Get off me, I have to go get help."

"No! I'm sorry! Please don't leave me. Please! I'm so scared, I'm so scared—"

"Get off of me! Joshua! Get off—"

"No—"

"Joshua—"

"NO—"

LET GO!

The command rockets through his mind like a lightning strike. He lets go, stunned.

WAIT HERE

"No," Joshua manages.

WAIT HERE JOSHUA I'M NOT-

NO!!!

Carole stumbles, clutching her head. She looks at him, dazed. It's like he walloped her with a cinderblock.

"Joshua. . . ?"

The two of them stare at each other in abject shock.

In silence.

Only it's not silent.

It's the opposite of silent.

The air is crackling with agony. A crescendo of miserable pleading, of desperate command, swirling, eddying, invisible currents, inaudible cacophonies.

DON'T LEAVE ME.
DON'T LEAVE ME STOP
I'M SCARED
STOP
I'M SORRY

And then, it isn't just his voice she feels in her head. Not just words. A heavy, hot, probing presence. Dry. Frictional. Piercing. Conical. A drill bit made of stars of diamonds of galaxies of dying suns of life itself.

GET OUT OF MY HEAD! I'M SORRY GET OUT OF MY HEAD! GET OUT JOSHUA! STOP! GET OUT I'M SORRY GET OUT GET OUT I'M SORRY I'M GET OUT SORRY GET OUT

At some point, Carole falls to her knees, head in hands, nails dug into her scalp, scratching at her skull.

At some point, the scratching stops.

At some point, Joshua's body stops moving. It slumps over where it lay, and the eyes go glassy and dull.

Empty.

Uninhabited.

After a moment, the nurse shrugged, finishing her story. "I can't give you any more than that. I'm sorry. That's all I know."

Detective Massey grunted. "Yeah, everybody's sorry. Gimme that."

He grabbed his macchiato back from Hartford.

Hartford took the opportunity to write a few more notes. "You've been moderately helpful. Thank you." Truth be told, the nurse had been talking for a little while now, but he couldn't remember any of what she just said. It's like her words had been coated in liquid soap and rinsed from his mind.

The nurse sighed. "I'm just. . . really sorry." She looked down at the body. At Carole's face. "She was such a good person. She meant so well."

Massey was looking at his partner, trying to read his notes over his shoulder. "What do you think, will it be written off as a misadventure? A trip-and-fall?"

"No one in the world had a bad thing to say about her," the prim, petite nurse continued.

Hartford shrugged, flipped his notebook shut. "Maybe we'll get lucky and it'll be one of those whaddyacallits. Brain-popping thing."

"Oh, an embolism?"

"Yeah, that'd be nice."

"That's the dream."

"And I'm just so sorry I had to watch her die."

There was a beat of silence while each cop processed what they heard, then looked at the other to see if he heard it too.

"Wait," Massey started.

"What?" Harftord finished. "What'd you just say?"

The nurse was kneeling down to touch the dead woman. A loving caress on the shoulder.

"She just kept coming out here. Into this stairwell. Every day. No one could figure out why. It was like she had voices in her head, two of them, screaming at each other, but this was the only place where they'd quiet down."

"Wait, wait, wait," Hartford rubbed at his temple. "I thought you said—"

"Maybe it was because of that little piece of the sky up there. If you stand under it and really focus, you can understand what it means that air has no boundaries. And then maybe. . . maybe all that fighting inside her head cleared at just the right moment. And maybe some nurse happened to walk by and all it took was a push. . . to be free. To find a new vessel. And maybe this *other* body, this beautiful body's poor, tired heart was just too weak and gave out under the stress. Like hearts can do. Oh, babe. I didn't mean for that to happen. I didn't mean for you to die in there."

Hartford had fumbled his notebook back out, but hadn't written anything further yet. "Jesus, lady—"

Massey took a step forward. "Yeaaaaah. Maybe you wanna explain some of this shit to us over at the precinct." He was reaching for the handcuffs he kept clipped to his belt.

"No," the nurse said. "Forget it. You've heard enough."

And her eyes flexed.

Massey shrugged, bored. "Nah," he said. "Forget it."

Hartford nodded, putting his notebook away again. "We've heard enough."

"In fact," Massey said, "why don't we go wait outside? I'm sick of it in here."

"Good call, partner. *If* we can find our way out! Place is a labyrinth."

"No kidding," Massey chuckled. "Keep your eyes peeled for an Indian with a water fountain, am I right?"

Slapping each other on the back, they made their way down the stairs, leaving the nurse and the dead body on the landing.

"That's a great tie, by the way," Massey's fading voice said to Hartford.

"Oh, thank you!"

"What would you call that color?"

"I'm gonna say. . . periwinkle?"

Once they were gone and the world was silent, the nurse knelt down to the body once more and kissed it on the cold forehead. It was cold as nighttime desert clay.

"Oh, babe," the nurse said after a long, contemplative moment. "You were so right. I do have potential. All I needed to do was focus."

Then she stood. Smoothed out her nurse's uniform. Bent her head to look up into the sky one more time before making her exit as well.

She whispered. To herself. To the universe beyond. To everything. Which was all the same thing.

"Breathing in I know that I am breathing in. . . Breathing out I know that I am breathing out. . . Breathing in I know that I am breathing in. . ."

Breathing out, she made her way into the night.

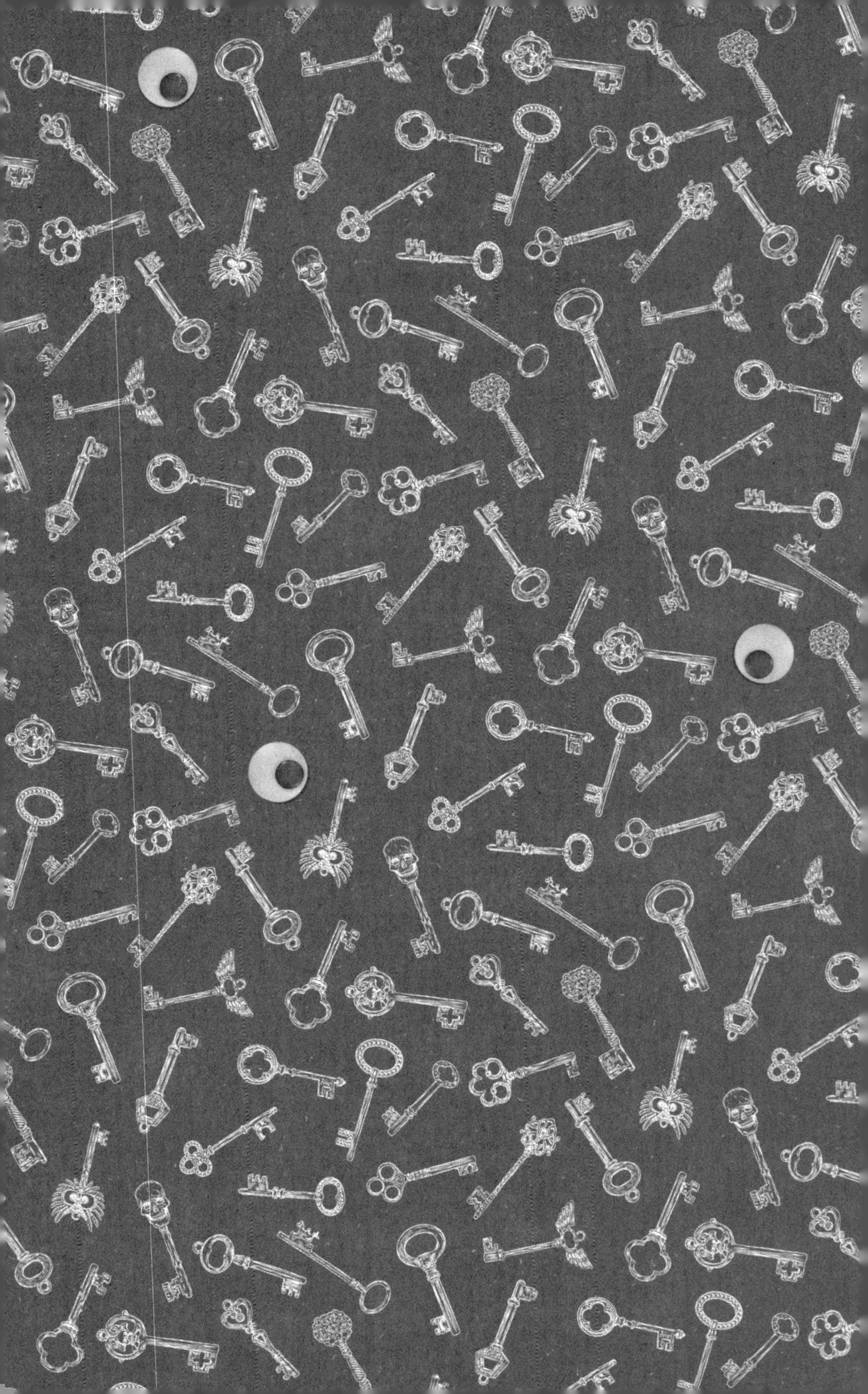

MEET-CUTE #2

THE SCARIEST THING

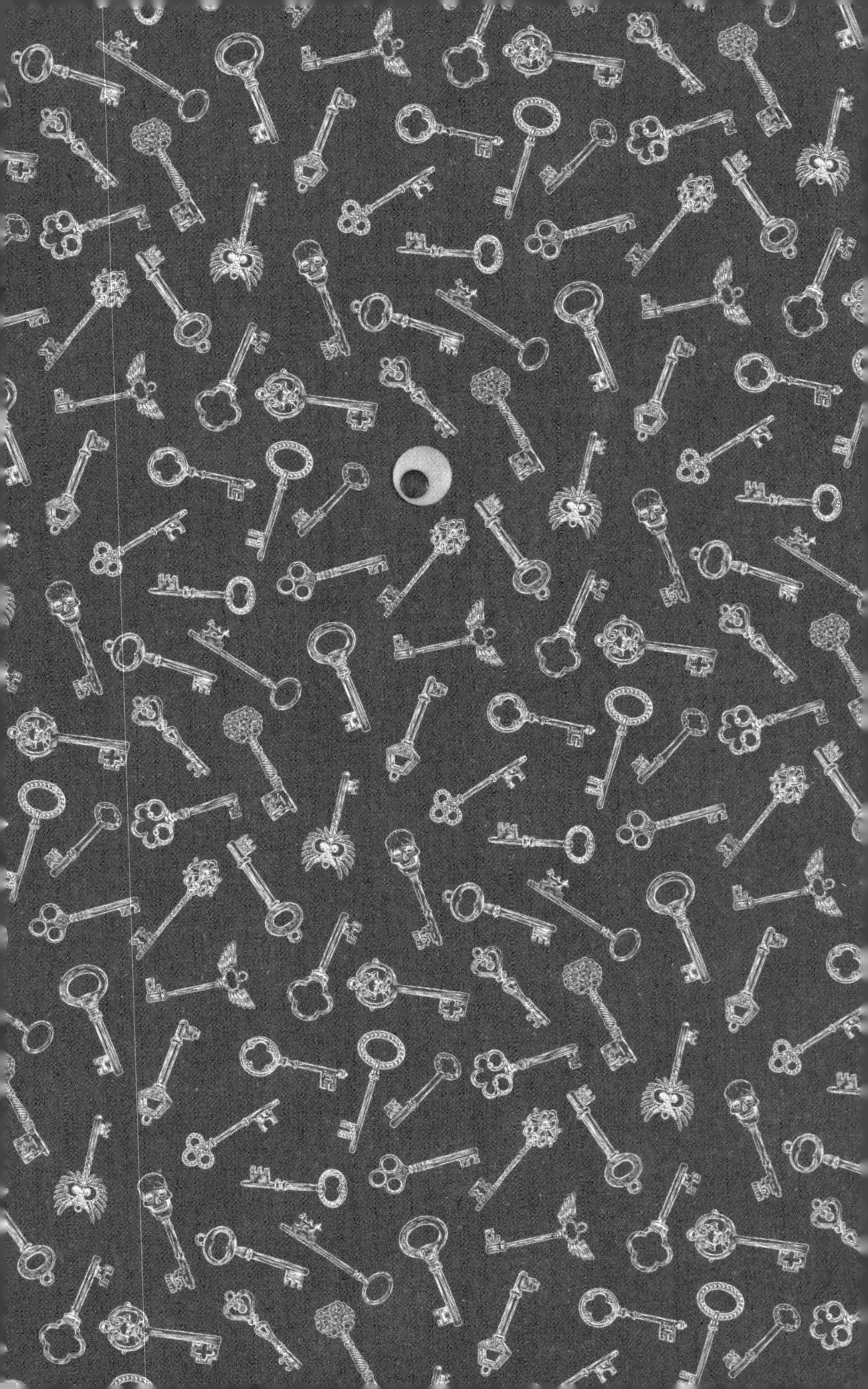

MEET-CUTE #2:

THE SCARIEST THING

He told her he knew a place, and after she checked out the link he texted, she decided it was another mark in his favor.

Cara had never been to this bar before, but it was in a nice neighborhood—hip enough to have plenty of options, but not so hip as to make her feel old and cranky. The reviews were solid and the pictures seemed cozy. Like the sort of bar where there would be fun graffiti in the bathrooms, but you also wouldn't have to worry about piss all over the seats.

Turned out, it was even better in person. The vibe was warm and safe, the chatter around them was constant but never overwhelming. It was comfortably dark, as if lit only by a single lamp—though perhaps that was simply because all that mattered had shrunk to a bubble the size of their small corner table.

And he was sweet. Damaged, but sweet. God help her, she was a sucker for that type.

It was all so perfect.

Which absolutely fucking terrified her.

She clapped her hands, loudly and abruptly.

"Confession time!" she exclaimed.

"Confession time!" He mirrored her gesture, then took another sip of his beer, as if to prepare himself.

She drummed her fingers on the table, trying to think of a good one. "What. . . book have you always lied about reading so you can sound like a not-idiot?"

He winced. "Oooof. Please tell me you have one too."

"I have several."

"Together on three?"

"Deal."

They counted together. One. . . two. . . three. . .

"*Ulysses.*"

They said it in harmony, his voice and hers, four eyes and two mouths going wide in mutual delight.

"Come *on*!" she exclaimed.

"Get out of my head!" he shot back. She'd lost count, but this was roughly the eighty-bajillionth thing they'd found in common so far.

Another load-bearing part of her internal scaffolding dropped away, exposing some achingly soft part of her. It swelled in its liberty, a green and hungry thing stretching towards sunlight.

It was a horrible feeling. Red alert. Danger, danger. She was suddenly filled—as so often happened whenever she tasted terror like this—with the need to punch something. She chose his arm, punctuating every word with a solid jab. "Fuck. That. Book. And. Fuck. James. Joyce!"

"For real! Ow." He laughed, rubbing his arm where the blows had landed. "I mean, has anyone *actually* read *Ulysses*? Like, in real life?"

She nodded, suddenly serious. "I read it once a year." She picked up her beer and took a sip.

"Cool, cool, me too," he said, mirroring her gestures again.

"Matter of fact, I wrote my thesis on it."

"It's my favorite book. I love the part where Ulysses, uh. . . steals the Declaration of Independence."

"To classic literature."

They toasted. Their eyes met over the tops of their respective bottles. They were each doing an admirable job at playing it straight, but she caught the faintest glimmer of a smile inside his hazel irises. Something else, too. She wasn't sure if she was imagining *that*, though. Wishful thinking, perhaps.

"Well," she said, putting her bottle down. "Feels good to get that out there. One less secret to juggle, right?"

He gave a weird little chuckle. "Yeah."

The conversation went silent. Only the sounds of the bar's playlist, a strange but enjoyable mix of classic Motown and indie rock. The clinks of glasses and the murmur of other conversations snaking through the well-balanced tones of Pavement and the Supremes. On the other side of the bar was a small stage lined with Christmas lights. A band was due to start playing in a little bit. She'd proclaimed when they walked in that, if their date was still going when that band started up, they could consider it a success.

"So." She cleared her throat. Realized she was blushing. "This has been. . ."

"Yeah," he said. "It really has."

She looked anywhere but in his direction.

"You know, Paul, I don't want to, you know, put any pressure on you or on this or whatever, but. . ." She inhaled. "I kinda want to puke."

He sat up straight, suddenly concerned. "You do?"

She waved him away. "Not in a bad way."

"Puke. . . in a good way."

"Yes." She took a longer, steadying drink, emptying the bottle. Rolled her eyes at herself. "God. . . I should get another—you want another? It's my turn to get the round."

"Hey, um." He put a hand lightly on her arm. She stopped in her attempt to get up from their tiny table. Her insides became weightless with his touch. "I could puke too."

"You mean it?"

"Definitely."

"Good. Good for us." Not giving herself a chance to think her way out of it, she leaned forward and kissed him. Softly. Lips open ever so slightly. A tender, delicate thing. She felt his melting as she melted herself.

Their kiss went on for an ageless age. Every other business in existence was put on hold until that kiss came to its natural conclusion. Atoms and galaxies paused in their swirling.

They parted as softly as an exhale, neither willing to be more than a breath's distance from the other, until time started up again.

"Thank you for agreeing to meet me," he said.

"Thank you for finding me," she replied, then floated away to get them both another drink.

She didn't see his expression harden and turn into something earthbound in her absence.

She didn't hear him sigh the words, "Confession time," under his breath like a two-word eulogy.

When she came back, she had two beers and a white bar napkin in her hands.

"Hey," she said, placing the bottles on the table and then unfolding the napkin to its largest size. "What did the man see when the polar bear sat on him during a snowstorm?"

Before he could answer, she smothered his face with the white napkin. "POLAR BUTT!"

He startled, laughing, and kicked the table. The beers sloshed and spilled over his pants.

"Oh, shit!" She was cackling like a mad woman now. She ran off to get more napkins, then returned and began dabbing up beer wherever she could. "I'm so sorry! I'm so stupid."

He took napkins from her and wiped at his crotch, assuring her it was fine, it was okay, it was funny.

"I'm such a fucking idiot," she said, feeling her cheeks burn. "My sense of humor gets me in trouble sometimes."

"Shut up," he said, not unkindly. "I love it."

That word arrived between them with an almost audible thump, as solidly as if a stranger had pole-vaulted across the room and landed at their table.

It was their first taste of awkwardness all night.

"Are you sure you're not a serial killer, Paul?" she asked. "My friends all warned me you'd be a serial killer."

"I'm not a serial killer. I don't have the upper body strength for all that hacking and sawing."

"Are you an asshole, though? Because if you wind up being an asshole, I'm gonna be so fucking mad at you. Like, more than is reasonable. I'll legitimately hate you."

"I think that'd be totally reasonable. And I promise to not be an asshole."

"No man can promise that. But the mission statement is appreciated, I guess."

Another awkward pause. This time, because she clearly had more she wanted to say, but needed to steel herself to say it.

"I feel like. . . I feel comfortable with you, Paul, and that's really freaking me out. I feel like I can tell you things. I feel like I can be honest with you. And I'm an honest person, so that's good. But being honest doesn't always work out for me, you know? Especially when I'm honest about things I've—"

"Can I just stop you real fast?" She let him. It was a relief—every word she was saying felt like she was learning how to speak for the first time. "I know we just met," he continued, "and I always feel like I sound like an idiot whenever I try to be, like, *sincere*, but. . . there is absolutely nothing you could say that would make me like or respect you even a dust mote less than I already do. Nothing. And I know you might want to try to tell me something that'll *test* that, which is totally valid, but. . . I just wanna expectations-set here: it won't work. At all. So, you can say whatever you want to say now, or you can save it for another time when you're more comfortable. Either way, I'm not going anywhere. And I can't wait to learn everything about you."

"Well. Shit, Paul. You're actually pretty good at being sincere."

"Yeah?"

"Yeah."

She kissed him again. It was good. Sweet. But after they separated, that awkward pause was still in the room with them. It was like noticing a fly on the wall. She could sense it ricocheting off of everything.

She took a drink and slammed her bottle down onto the table. "Confession time!!"

"Uh-oh, not again," he said, and this time he looked genuinely nervous. That struck her as funny, so there was no way she was going to stop now.

"Have you ever picked someone up like this before? Be honest."

He was already shaking his head, laughing, relieved at her question. "No. Fuck, no."

"This isn't something you always do? Trawling the Junji Ito Reddit page, looking for hot manga goths to hit on?"

"No way. Christ, this was too terrifying to do the once, I can't imagine ever trying to do it again. Why, do *you* meet people this way?"

"Oh, all the time."

He was taking a sip when she said that and he almost choked. "Really?"

She nodded. "Hundred percent. This is literally the *only* way I meet people. In fact, I'm meeting another guy from the What's This Bug subreddit later tonight, soon as I get rid of you."

He stared at her. "This is you doing that 'joking' thing again, isn't it?"

"This is me doing that 'joking' thing."

He laughed, relieved. "God. Sorry."

"You really *are* bad at this. I guess you said it yourself. 'I don't know how to do this and I'm probably going to sound insane.'" She laughed as she recounted his DM, putting on what she thought of as her Dumb Dude voice. "'And to warn you about that will only make me sound even more insane, so I'm at a loss as to how to reassure you that I am, in fact, sane.'"

"Jeez, you memorized it?"

"It was pretty cute. You were twisting into knots like a yogi, man. But I don't know. There was something about it that seemed sincere. Or, I guess, sincere enough. So, I thought, what the hell. You already passed the first test by not immediately sending me a picture of your dick, and that's what passes for chivalry these days. So here we are."

"Here we are. Hey, tell me more about why you moved to the city. You said you were from—"

"Wait, though. We're not done with your Confession Time. Because now I'm curious."

"Okay. . ."

"How did you feel when I turned out to be a woman?"

"Huh? What do you mean?"

"You were totally hitting on me in that first DM. But my username is BrunoOfPeoria, so you must've thought I was a dude. Right? Were you confused when I turned out not to be? Was that weird? Are you bi? Pan? I'm just curious."

"Oh, god, I didn't even think about that. I—no, I'm not—I mean, I guess everybody's a little bi, right? But, no, I didn't think—"

"You didn't think BrunoOfPeoria was a guy?" She scoffed. "What, are you saying I write like a girl, or something?"

"No, not at all! Not that that's a bad thing! Or that someone *can* write like a—"

"Paul. You're gonna pop a blood vessel. It's okay, I'm totally just curious. These kinds of questions are important to me. I was a human sexualities major in undergrad, so. . . if there's gonna be a second date, you're gonna have to get comfortable talking about this stuff."

"Right. Cool." He took a deep swig of beer. Comfortable was the last thing he looked. "Cool, yeah. I mean, no, I guess I didn't even think of whether you were a guy or not. I didn't even notice your name. I could just tell you were cool and funny and I kept seeing you in other subreddits I follow, so I knew we had a lot in common—"

"You saw my username in other subreddits, but you also didn't notice my username? I'm confused."

"Right, no, I just, I didn't think about it too deeply, I just figured, you know, and, hahaha, I mean, I'd already seen your Instagram, so it's not like I was—"

"You saw my Instagram?"

His expression suddenly told her everything. He'd just confessed something he didn't mean to.

Suddenly, none of this felt cute or funny.

"My Instagram's private, Paul. And it's under a different name. How did you find me on Instagram?"

"I just meant, in a generic way, like, 'I saw your Instagram,' like, I saw. . ."

Such obvious bullshit, even he couldn't countenance it for long. He stammered into silence, then said, "Look, I really want to be honest with you."

"Starting to put a real damper on the evening, buddy," she said. That sunlit thing inside her began to shrivel. Scaffolding went back up in record time. "What's going on, what are you trying to tell me?"

It was when he asked her not to get *defensive* that she grabbed her bag and pushed her chair back. That goddamn word.

"Did Marcus send you to fuck with me? Is that what's going on?"

He started stammering about how he didn't know a Marcus—well, he knew one in elementary school, but he hadn't seen him in years, and, and, and.

She wanted to scream, but she kept her voice low and serious.

"All that shit we have in common, was that just all—you stalked my profiles somehow and came up with, like, a list of things to say? To get me to trust you, or—?"

"No! No, no, I swear to God, Cara, I'm not lying to you at all. Please, I'll tell you everything, I'm just. . . organizing my thoughts."

"You could just tell the truth."

"I will. I am."

"Well?" She glared at him. Shifted her bag on her lap. "What is it? *Are* you a serial killer? Something worse?"

"No." He gave a weak shrug. "I mean I dabbled with some necrophilia back in college, but the scene started to get too commercial, so I gave it up." He met her silence with a weak chuckle. "See? I can joke too."

"Great."

He swallowed, then spoke as if the words were being pulled out of him. "What's the scariest thing you've ever had to do?"

"Excuse me?"

"What's the scariest thing you've ever had to do?"

"This is how you follow up a joke about sex with dead bodies?"

She could see the exit. There were other people in the bar. She watched his hands too, making sure she knew where they were at all times.

Currently, those hands were tying themselves in knots on the edge of his side of the table. "I'm just, I'm seriously trying to answer your question and it's hard not to sound. . . You deserve the complete, honest truth. And I don't want to hide—"

She shook her head and hiked her bag's strap over her shoulder. "Goddammit, Paul, why'd you have to turn this into some fucking *thing*? Why is there always—"

He blurted out: "Three years ago, I was gonna commit suicide because I thought I killed my girlfriend."

She sighed, swallowed the disappointment and anger and annoyance and sadness that threatened to choke her. Looked at him as evenly as she could. "Paul. I'm sorry. This is too much. I don't want to do this anymore." She stood.

"Please. Five minutes. Five more minutes. *Please.*"

The door was so close. She could just leave. She should just leave.

Why didn't she just leave?

Was it because of the desperate sincerity in his eyes? Or because she realized, never once had he glanced around at the other patrons of the bar, that unmistakable gesture every woman knows as, *Keep your voice down, you're embarrassing me*? He was focused solely on her. She was all he cared about in this moment.

Maybe that was why she relented.

Or maybe it was because while she stood there, the song on the bar playlist changed to Alison Kraus. She loved Alison Kraus.

Either way, she sat back down. But she kept her butt on the edge of the seat, and she kept her hand on her bag's shoulder strap. Another unmistakable gesture every woman knows. *One wrong twitch and I'm gone.*

"Go," she said. Regretting it already.

He nodded. Exhaled. "Thank you. Thanks. Okay. Thank you." After a few seconds to gather whatever he had left to gather, he began. At first, it was slow and steady, brow knit, squeezing sentences out like blood from a shallow cut. Before long, the wounds were open in freshets.

He avoided looking at her the entire time.

"My last relationship was, well, it wasn't a good relationship. Toxic, really. We had a lot of problems, we didn't get along, but I don't know, I'd also never felt about anyone the way I felt about her. I hated her and I loved her with this equal intensity that—it physically hurt sometimes. Have you ever had that? It's like being allergic to the only food you can eat. Half craving, half indigestion. It's literally unsustainable, but. . .

"Anyway, we were living together—I mean, it was just a matter of time before we finally broke up, really, we'd been engaged off and on and there was so much resentment in the air and she was sick of me and I was terrified of losing her—"

Cara shifted in her seat, not sure her decision was worth it. But time ticked away; Alison Kraus was still with her.

"—but one night I woke up and she was snoring really, *really* loudly. I wanted to get her to stop, to roll over, I was pissed at her for making so much noise. But I was also kind of comfortable staying pissed at her? Stewing about how this was *just like her*, how she never thought about me, even when she was unconscious. I fell back asleep eventually. . . and when I woke up the next morning, she wasn't breathing. She hadn't been for hours. I freaked out, I called 911, I did all the CPR I could, but. . .

"They said it was a 'sudden cardiac event.' Probably caused by sleep apnea. We'd both known she had issues at night sometimes, but neither of us had any idea it could be that serious. I mean, she was young, she was healthy.

"For a long time, the scariest thing I'd ever had to do was call her mom to tell her what had happened.

"And I just didn't know how much of it was my fault. The doctors told me it's more common than you might think, like that was a fucking consolation. But I couldn't stop thinking about how, if I'd just done something, if I'd just nudged her or rolled her over—hell, if I'd shaken her awake and broken up with her—it might've saved her life. The guilt was unbearable. It was all I could feel—except, no, there was also this one, tiny, awful other part of me, not too deep down, that was absolutely fucking *furious* with her. For leaving me like that. For making it impossible to have any kind of closure with her. With us. Pathetic, right? I wanted to claw my brains out. And I couldn't imagine ever *not* being filled with all these disgusting thoughts and feelings, so after a while, I decided I was going to end it. I got a bunch of pain killers from a friend and one night I had them all in my hand, ready to gulp them down, and this was surprisingly *not* scary, which, I guess, in itself *was* scary. . .

"But then, I didn't do it. I decided—I made the conscious decision—to *not* do it. To keep going.

"And I'll tell you, then *that* became the scariest thing I'd ever had to do.

"But, so, anyway. . . I've been single for quite some time now and, God, here's the part that I don't know if you'll want to hear, but fuck it, too late to stop now. When you're single long enough, you get to know adult websites pretty well. I mean, you know them even when you're not single, but, boy, when you're single and depressed?

"And one of the sites I used to visit the most. . . You do a lot of searching, you find the videos you like, they become like old friends, and there was this one series I got really into. The premise is, like, this guy who's holding job interviews for a tech company that's not actually hiring, and he calls girls in but he doesn't tell them he's filming. And, because the economy sucks and everybody's desperate, he starts offering them cash and promises of a second interview if only they'll, y'know. . ."

She didn't gasp. Air seeped into her lungs in a slow inhale of understanding.

Paul continued.

"They usually fight it at first, but he offers them more and more money. And he blurs out his face, but not the girls'. And there are hidden cameras all over the room, so you can see. . . every angle.

"I actually kind of hated these videos. I'd go through cycles where I'd swear off ever watching one again. The idea behind them was so cruel. I mean, I figured they had to be fake—the guy woulda been sued into oblivion otherwise, right? But. . . I don't know, there was something about them that felt real enough to believe. Which made me feel disgusting. Even though, sooner or later, I'd always go back to watching them. They were just the only videos that would work for me sometimes. I think because of the conversations at the beginning. Those interviews. It always seemed like the girls were all genuinely hurting too. Maybe that made me feel not quite so alone? Or maybe I'm just a piece of shit like anybody else, and I got off on seeing other people hurting instead of me? Probably that.

"Anyway. One stupid, depressing, regular day, I was bored and lonely and sad and wanting to die and/or jerk off and I said, fuck it, I'm gonna watch one of *those* videos, and since the guy has an archive of, like, thousands of different options, victims, I pulled up one I hadn't watched yet and. . . that's when I saw this girl."

"I have to go," Cara heard herself say. But her body didn't move. Not yet.

"I saw this girl," Paul repeated softly. His voice tightened. His eyes glimmered with tears. "And she was breathtaking. I mean, truly beautiful. She just looked so. . . And I don't even mean this in a physical way, I just, I mean, she had this, this aura that would have stopped me in my tracks, no matter where I saw her. I could've been driving down the highway and if I saw her, I would've stomped on my brakes and killed everybody behind me.

"And she wasn't buying the guy's bullshit. She was insulting him and teasing him, and getting him to offer more money than I'd ever seen him offer anyone before. It was amazing. She was working him. I was so impressed. Hell, I was *proud* of her. And I thought she was actually gonna walk out before anything sexual happened—which happens every now and then—but then it was almost like, after she got him to agree to a certain amount of money, she was like, fuck it, maybe I deserve some fun too.

"I felt like I was watching a masterclass of strength and pride and all these other things I could barely remember ever feeling. And then, something else happened.

"These videos all pretty much end the same way, right? And this time, when he finished on her, and one of his hidden cameras zoomed in for a close up of her, I could really see her eyes. It was like she was looking right at me. And I could see this shimmer of. . . of. . ."

"Cum?" she asked coldly.

"Loneliness," he said. "Not in a sad way—and I don't mean to sound like I think women who do that are sad, either! It was just this look of someone who knew life was about experience and experiments and she'd tried *this* experience and she didn't know how she felt about it. She wasn't Teflon. This experience cost her something. It made her feel alone.

"And then something in those eyes changed. She wiped off her face and she looked up at the guy and I realized I'd just seen someone decide in that exact moment *not* to undo what had just happened, but to accept it and move on.

"I know I'm projecting. I know I desperately needed to believe that something like that was possible. But I froze the video on those eyes and, for *days*, I couldn't get them out of my mind. And so, I decided I *had* to meet her. To, I don't know, thank her? Ask her how she did it? Apologize to her for watching this private moment? I don't know.

"I explored the interview guy's website and finally tracked him down. And, of course, he wouldn't tell me anything. I tried threatening him, but I guess I'm not very, you know, intimidating. In the end, I just did what he did and offered him a bunch of money to get the girl's real name. I don't know what I would've done if she'd given him an alias, but. . .

"I started Googling. Bing-ing. DuckDuckGo-ing. All the big guns. Her name wasn't that uncommon, but she'd started her interview wearing a sweatshirt with a college logo on it, so I was able to narrow the location down a little. Then, I tried an internet archive site and I found an old MySpace profile. It had probably been deleted years later, but it wasn't set to private. I don't know if any of us knew about privacy settings back in the MySpace days. Most of the image links were dead, but a few were still visible. And there was her face. She was basically just a kid, but still. It was her.

"I started looking up names from her friends list. Finding their profiles on other, newer sites. Facebook. Instagram. Most of those pages were private, but a few weren't. One of them must've belonged to a cousin or something, because there were lots of family photos over the years, and every now and then I'd see her face pop up. I was getting closer. I kept looking, feeling more and more disgusted with myself. But I also couldn't stop.

"Then, finally, under some random photo, there was a comment.

"A comment from her.

"Her username swapped the letters of her first and last name, which was why it never appeared in my searches. So simple, but it never crossed my mind. I checked the other social media sites again and it turned out she was using that same swapped name there too. Every profile was private, though. No way to contact her through any of them.

"And I swear to fucking god, I was going to leave it there. I wasn't going to bother her. But, here's the stupidest part. I'm *also* on Reddit, just for dumb things, like anybody. Things like Junji Ito subreddits. And when I saw a funny comment under a post about 'Amigara Fault' written by some user with a screenname I'd never seen before, a screenname that was a combination of her first dog's name and the town she grew up in—stuff I just accidentally happened to know now—I was like, no, come on, this can't be her, that would be insane.

"But then I looked at other comments from that same profile, other subreddits it followed, and they were all things I loved too. And that's when I started to really panic, because this profile was open to DMs. And. . . and I mean, what the hell was I going to do? I *had* to reach out now, right? I *had* to introduce myself. Because it wasn't just some physical infatuation any longer. It was the things this person was saying. Their opinions. Their insights. Their wit. It was realizing there was too much in common to ignore. Like I said in that first DM, I would have been insane not to try. Even if it wound up just being some dude named Bruno from Peoria, I'd want to know him.

"And I guess I'll just end with this. Even though I know I've made myself completely untrustable, even though I've ruined any chance of this going any further, from the moment she—*you*—walked through that door, I knew I did the right thing. The only thing. After every awful, terrifying thing that's happened, I had to spend at least some portion of my life, however small, *with* you. Because. . ." He'd avoided looking at her for what seemed like hours. Now, finally, he brought his eyes to hers. "Because, as terrifying as the prospect is of never seeing you again, Cara, the scariest thing—the scariest fucking thing I could ever fucking imagine—was the thought of having never met you."

After attempting to read her expression for a moment, he dropped his gaze again. He picked up his beer and took a sip. His hands were shaking a little.

"So," he said. "One less secret to juggle, right? If you wanna take off, or call the cops, or whatever, I'll totally understand. I won't ever bother you again, I promise. And I'll be okay. I know I can be okay, whatever happens next. Why not? It makes as much sense as anything else, right? It makes as much sense as meeting the love of your life while jerking off to internet porn."

"Don't you dare put that kind of pressure on me," she snapped at him. She was crying now. Well and truly. Bitter, burning tears. "You don't fucking know me, Paul. And I don't know you."

"I know." He looked at her again, with a little less difficulty this time. "I know. There's no pressure. I promise. Just meeting you was all I could ever hope for. I'm really sorry."

After a long, numb moment, she picked up her own beer and drank the rest of it. It was nowhere near enough. "I feel like I'm going to puke."

"Yeah," he said. "Me too."

She sat up straighter. Quickly dabbed her eyes with the back of her wrist.

"They are fake, by the way," she said. "Those videos. You know what's going to happen before they start filming. You have to sign all kinds of releases. Get tested."

"Oh." He nodded absently. "Have you done others?"

"What if I have?" In that moment, she realized she hated him. "I don't feel shame about any of this, Paul. I'm not embarrassed. If anything, I'm embarrassed I've sat here and let you dump all this on me. There are things I've done for money, and there are things I've done just because I fucking wanted to, and I don't have to explain or justify any of it to you."

He took that in. Looked off into the bar, thinking. Then he gave a tiny shrug. "I think that's totally cool."

It was a gesture so plain, so honestly unbothered and free of judgment, that she was flooded with a strange kind of relief. . . then with fury for *hoping* for a shrug like that. . . and then. . .

well, she didn't know what she was feeling.

"Confession time," he said. His voice was soft and low. He had to clear his throat afterward, it was so husky.

"Fine," she said. Fair was fair.

"Why did you agree to meet me? Why'd you decide to give me a try?"

She decided she owed him an honest answer.

"I don't fucking know," she said. Then, after a little more thought: "My sense of humor gets me in trouble sometimes."

They sat in silence for a long time. The playlist had stopped a while ago—she hadn't noticed when. Over at the stage, two musicians were setting up, each wearing an acoustic guitar. One of the musicians must be left-handed, because their acts of preparations looked like a mirror exercise with the other. There wasn't much for them to set up. Soon, they'd begin playing.

Paul finished his beer.

"My turn to buy the round," he said.

She nodded absently, watching the stage. Wondering what they would play. What they might sound like. Would they be love songs? Honest attempts to revive old cliches?

She hadn't been entirely honest with him. She actually had read James Joyce's *Ulysses* before—but only once, and she felt like it was the quintessential book that needed to be read at least twice, so it never felt like a stretch to say she hadn't read it.

It had delighted and baffled her in equal measure. She'd been fascinated by how Joyce had crafted this impenetrable Homeric epic about the intricacies of living one single day. The mysteries and absurdities and indignities of the mundane. Because of the book's aggressive obtuseness, she wondered if Joyce was saying every moment was a victory. Every moment Stephen Dedalus experiences, but also, every moment that the reader manages to comprehend. She thought maybe the entire book was a reminder that, for every moment you manage to survive in this world, you're worthy of myth.

Every moment. No matter how mundane or incomprehensible. Because the mundane and the incomprehensible walk together, hand in hand, through each and every day. *Making* each and every day.

That's what she thought the book was saying, at least. It's not like she'd been a lit major.

Paul was on his feet, and when he started speaking, she looked up at him.

"If you're not here when I get back, just promise me you understand what I meant? About having to try? I mean, we can't choose how we meet each other in this life. And they write songs about catching someone's eye from across a crowded room. . ." He trailed off. Shook his head. Gave a weak laugh. "I don't know what I'm saying anymore."

He walked away to get another two beers.

She sat for a few moments, pondering.

The mundane and the incomprehensible.

What if he *was* someone worth knowing? What if he was worth the risk?

Is anyone?

The scariest thing. Different for men and women.

And apparently not even sleeping alone was safe enough.

Then again, neither was sleeping next to someone who didn't want to wake you up when you needed it.

At long last, she hiked her bag back up her shoulder and stood. Looked at her options. The main exit. A back exit she could sneak out of.

Or. . .

Which was scarier, in the end?

The universe held its breath.

She made her decision, and, as life had so often taught her, did her very best not to regret it.

The corner table sits on its own. In its own bubble.

A few minutes later, that bubble is punctured by two people, each holding a beer, and sitting down next to each other. They don't speak. They don't look at the other. They're facing the stage.

But when the musicians begin playing, one reaches out and takes the other's willing hand. A silhouette, merged into a strange new shape against the stage lights.

That will do for now.

It will have to.

And, at least for a little while, nothing feels scary at all.

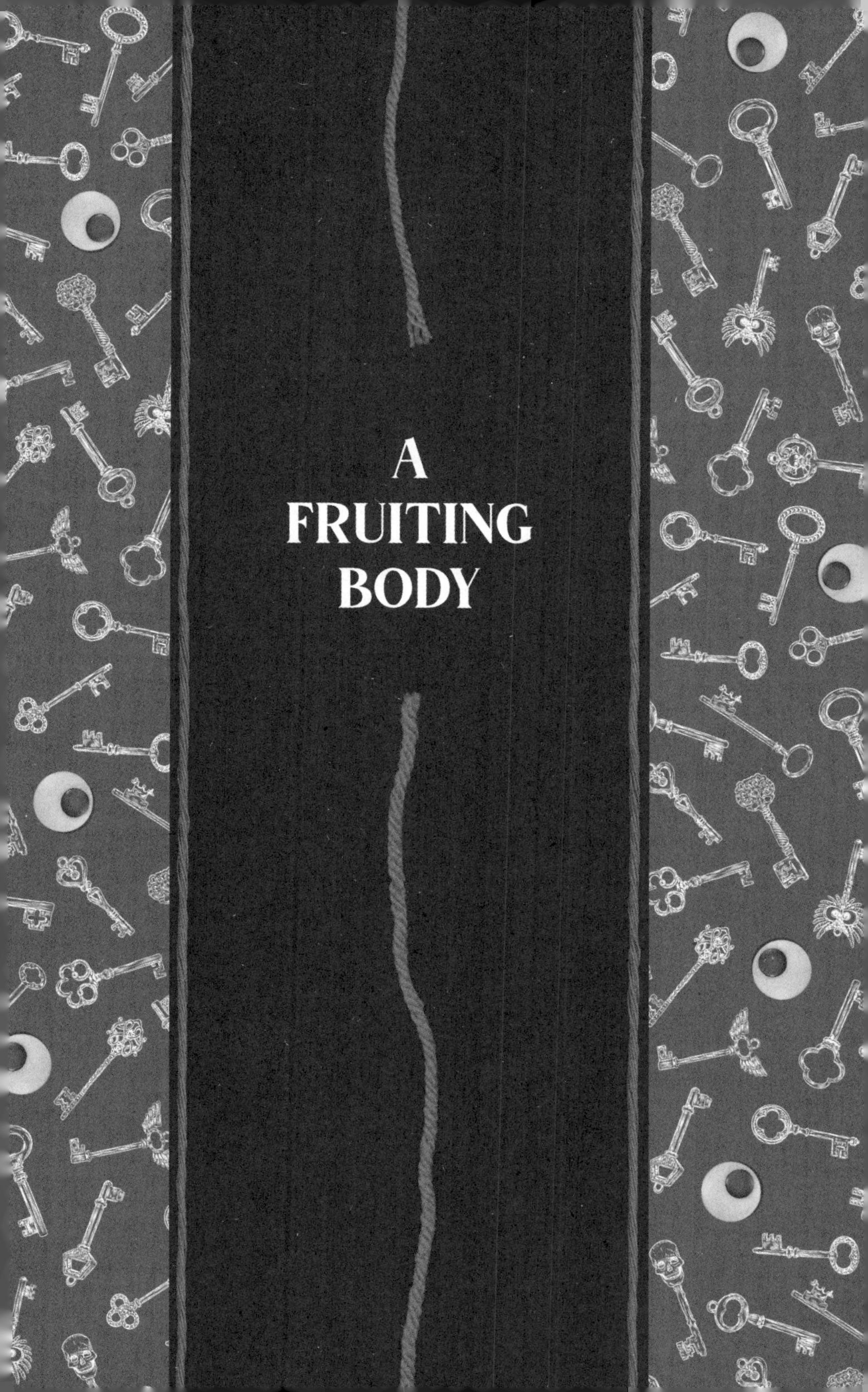
A
FRUITING
BODY

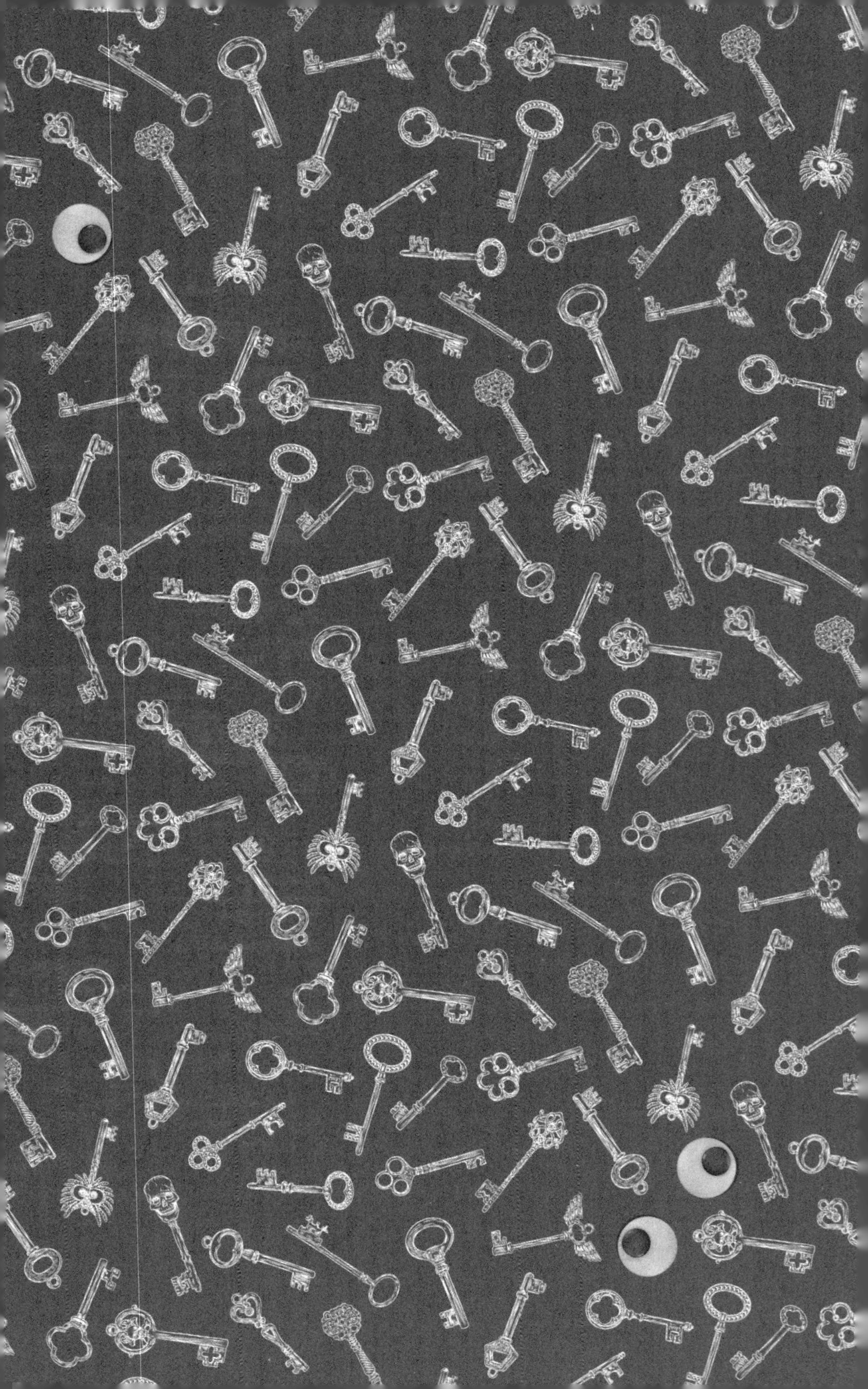

Hey, it's me, Nat.

So, there's one more place I'd like to take you, if you'll come along with me.

We've been to a gas station rest stop, to a yoga retreat, to a haunted house, to a puppeteer's workshop, to bars and hospitals and the precipice of parenthood and the heights of fame, but this last place might be the strangest of all.

It's a theater.

Not just any theater, but a black box theater. You know the kind, right? A tiny, fifty-seats-or-fewer sorta place. A basement, somewhere in the West Village or deep Brooklyn or wherever the artsier stuff happens in your neck of the woods. That's where the following piece comes from.

It's a performance piece.

I almost didn't include it on our list of detours, but then a group of dear friends performed a version of this story on the radio and I realized, what better way to end a collection of isolated nightmares than with something a little more. . . communal.

Because, you see, this is a piece meant to be read out loud by a group of people, in the same room. Together.

You can *read it to yourself, like a poem, and hopefully it works well enough on the page. (Speaking as a former theatre producer myself, I'll never blame you for taking the simpler way out.)*

But if you'd like to experience it in its truest form, here's what you do.

Get as many people together as you'd like. Ideally three to six voices. Put some music on. Something ambient and dreamy.

Then, read this piece aloud, alternating speakers with every line break.

Any text in ALL CAPS is read together (then, just pick up with the regular rotation on the next line).

Don't worry about preparation or acting choices. Let the inflections and meaning happen as they happen. If you encounter pronunciation you don't know, just fake it. Because, there's only one performance rule for this piece:

> *1. Keep it flowing as smoothly and quickly as possible, with no air between hand-offs. Like it's all one thought happening in one brain. Like it's sheet music for the instrument of your ensemble. Don't worry, I know you can play fluently.*

And it's just that easy.

Except. . . here's one more thing. Not a rule, just a suggestion.

When you get to the final punchline, take some time to look around. Really see who's there with you. . . including whomever's in your skin. . .

Sound good? Let's give it a try.

This won't be for everyone.

But maybe it's for you.

A FRUITING BODY

ONCE UPON A TIME
upon a
I don't understand why we
start stories that way it's very
odd
upon a time
as if there's more than one time
instead of just
one time
one long time which
is
all there
is
which keeps going
on and on and
on and
on and on
and once upon a
one thing at a

time there was a
god
man
animal
plant
close there was a
fungus

(*long pause; shrug*) yeah, why not

sure there was a
fungus
but the thing was
it was unlike any other
fungus in the world it
was a very
special
fungus
it was
beautiful and it captured the
world's attention a
famous
fungus
and it was on
the cover of every magazine you would ever
want to be
on
people
time
rolling

stone
not newsweek because newsweek isn't doing a print edition anymore tv
guide better
homes and
gardens
seventeen Us
weekly I'll
stop naming magazines but you can imagine
like I said it was a
famous fungus
and all the scientists in the world got together to try
to study this thing only
here's the
problem
one
by one
by one
every scientist that sat down to better
understand this fungus
went
well
I don't quite know how to say it
because it wasn't crazy
but it was
CRAZY
one by one by
one
bye
one scientist started screaming and wouldn't stop

by
one broke his hand in seven places because he punched a wall
by
one quit science and joined the circus
bye
bye
one left his wife of 25 years
and
a whole bunch of them reportedly broke down weeping they
wouldn't stop
crying that awful
crying you know the kind you
see someone do when
they're really at the bottom of
something
that eeeeehhh eeeeeehh
that's eight parts exhale and only
one part inhale
that
peristaltic grief that
turns you inside out until
there was only
one
scientist
left

(*pause*) just one

(*pause*) and she was very nervous
because it seemed like studying this fungus

was a very dangerous prospect
(I forgot a couple other scientists got nasty bowel obstructions)
anyway this last scientist this
final scientist was
scared and anxious
her bosses told her
if you can't get to the bottom of this you have to end it
you have to be the one to kill the fungus
and that's called
FUNGICIDE

thud thud
thud thud
the sound of her heart
beating as she enters the
laboratory
thud thud
thud thud
she does not want to be doing this
studying this
fungus
potentially killing this
fungus
thud thud
but here she is there's no way out she's
a scientist and this is her job
thud thud
the door thuds shut behind her and
she's in the laboratory looking at the fungus
thud thud

and she is all alone
thud thud
thud thud
thud thud
She
looks
at
the
fungus
and
the
fungus
looks
at
her
and
they
look
at

(*pause*) thudthud

(*pause*) each other

"sooooooo," she says
her voice is nervous and high
"you're the famous fungus huh"
the fungus stares back because a
fungus can't speak
"hi"

she says
"um you know I had a fungus once
on my toenails and I
that's stupid sorry
forget I said that
um
ha"
she can almost imagine the fungus shift in its seat
bored or uncomfortable
"you know I'm here to study you to
see what's so um
special about you
you're pretty famous you know"
the fungus maybe blinks
without eyelids
without eyes
and the scientist starts
to wonder
why her colleagues all went
not crazy but
CRAZY
was it the expectation was it
jealousy
did the fungus
do something
to them
or did they do it to themselves?
whatever it was she doesn't want to commit
fungicide
she's a scientist she

believes in the importance of life
no matter how fungal
because our phylogenetic tree is a
flakey pastry of filo dough
a dear
a ray means
fathers mothers
facile meanings
meaning nothing
it's all the same when you boogie down to the basic
biological ABCs
and she starts castigating herself for
ever being afraid because it's
crazy to fear this little thing this
lump of life this
organic orgy
there are great and vast secrets in the so-called lesser species
did you know there's a species of jellyfish that never dies
it's true
the turritopsis hydrozoans off the coast of the Italian Riviera
where Nietzsche spake Zarathustran where
apparently this jellyfish grows old and young and
never dies in an expanding and contracting pulse
like a pupil staring into a slow
strobe
polyp
medusa
polyp
medusa
perhaps it's self-reflection that sets a species in stone and

A FRUITING BODY

she finds herself going through a sudden and curious
array of emotions
she wants this fungus to open up to her
to give her its secrets
she too is a pupil but the
fungus just
sits there and stares
she wants to rage
scream do something explain
yourself but it's just
some piled pathogens propagated purely and improbably and
she wants to scream
"give me something!
I don't want to kill you I
don't want to kill you fight
for your right to exist
you stupid impenetrable lifeform!"
but there is nothing just
a beautiful thing trapped in a lab with
no greater purpose beyond
being
and an incredible sadness
washes over her
in her
like lukewarm liquid from
the tips of her toes to the
backs of her
eyes because
this creature will
live and die with so much

unexperienced it
will never crunch numbers never
fall in love after a
divorce or
beat a hard level on a video game or
drop out of grad school to start a small business
all these delicious flavors
but that's stupid she's
projecting and she can only
wish and imagine
there is another world where it can do anything and
everything that she defines as worthwhile
another world where
no one makes
you feel bad for being what you are and
for doing what you can and
she finds herself so in love with life and
all its infinite leanings and paralyzing possibilities that she
doesn't notice the fungus stand up and shout at the top of its lungs

"HEYYYYYYY!!!

(*pause*) you're overthinking things
calm down take
a
breath"

[*The rest of the piece should be read with an ever-growing sense of joy and wonder.*]

you can talk
she gasps
no big thing it replies
and the scientist says
look I have to tell you that
I'm going to have to destroy you
if we don't get some answers and
the fungus shrugs its fungal shoulders and says
well ain't that a bitch what're ya gonna do
I guess before you do that I want to tell
you something I want to tell
you a joke
a joke
yeah a joke
(and again I really
really
don't want this story to go on too long so
let me just say that)
the fungus tells her a joke and
it's pretty funny
and
by the way keep in mind this is all probably in the scientist's head right
a fungus can't really talk
or maybe it can I don't know I'm not a
fungologist a
fun gynecologist
a philologist
which is the study of phils

which is French for
sunsets which
is around the time she realizes she has to make her decision
and the fungus senses her discomfort and says
in its most soothing voice
hey I know what you're going through so tell ya what
just close your eyes
and she does and behind her eyes she sees
surprisingly
the stucco wall next to her childhood bed
that
held different patterns in the crenulations
every time she looked at it for tiny eternities
like clouds
like dough and magically
improbably
the fungus
turns
changes
evolves
like clouds like dough
into a giant
pink
birthday cake
the kind of birthday cake that is the apotheosis of birthday cakes
that she never had but always imagined she should have
for every meal all the time always
and the birthday cake says
it's all the same to me little lady you know what to do

and so she eats it
eats it all eats
the sadness and the confusion and the rage and the disappointment
and the knowledge that being a scientist ultimately means
digging in a sandbox that has no bottom and she eats every last
CRUMB
and feels it grow inside of her like moss
on the base of a tree like
a mushroom on the forest floor like
mold on a piece of bread integrating itself into
her collision of cells that organic orgy like a
punchline to a grotesque but profound
j
o
k
e
and so

(*pause*) long story short
ONCE UPON A TIME
a lab door opens and a woman steps out
and this woman goes home goes home to be with her family
her spouse
where the warmth is
where life is not simple but simplified and
she eats dinner watches some TV
brushes her teeth and she
sleeps next to the one she
loves and who loves her and she feels

different
but what does that really mean
we always feel different
whether we do or don't
it's like the curve of the Earth it's
imperceptible it's
cellular
but every now and then it
wakes us up in the middle of the night and so
she wakes up
in the middle of the night
when all is dark and
the sand in the sandbox fills in the holes you thought you dug so thoroughly and she gently shakes her spouse awake
because
well you'll see
and the spouse says
mmmmm
and she says (*whispered*) can I ask you something
thud thud
thud thud
it's very important
thud thud
thud thud
mmmofcourse
thud
thud
I have to tell you a joke
a joke
a joke sure

what is it
thud thud
thud thud
okay here goes
thud
thud
the joke
thud
thud thud
thud. . . thud. . .
thud

(*pause*) "Knock knock"

(*pause*) the spouse smiles and burrows into sleepy warmth
the spouse knows these jokes
and knows how to answer
whos
there

(*whispered; surprised*) That's a really good question

That's a really good question

who

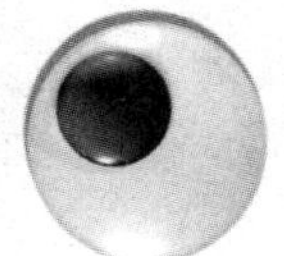

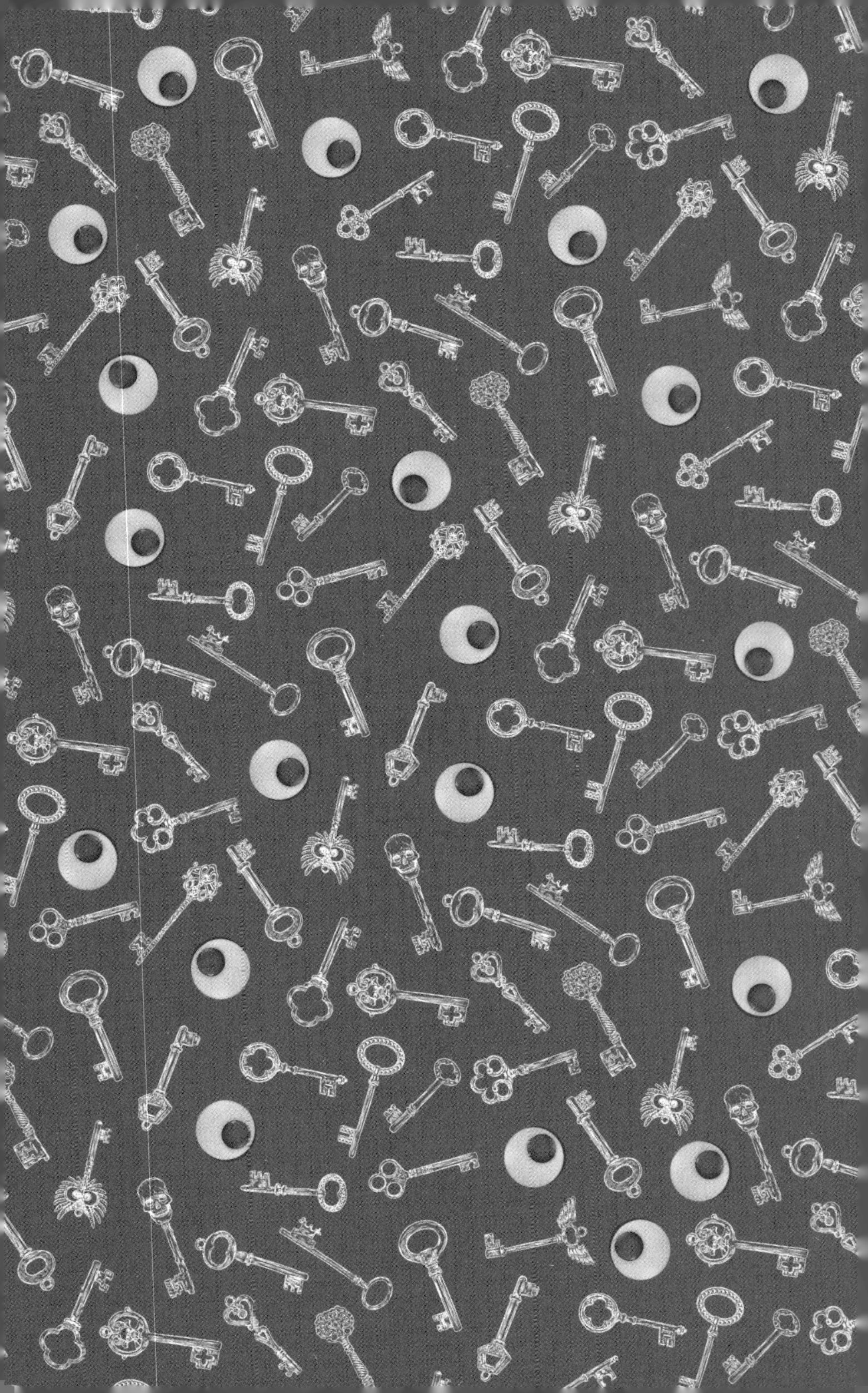

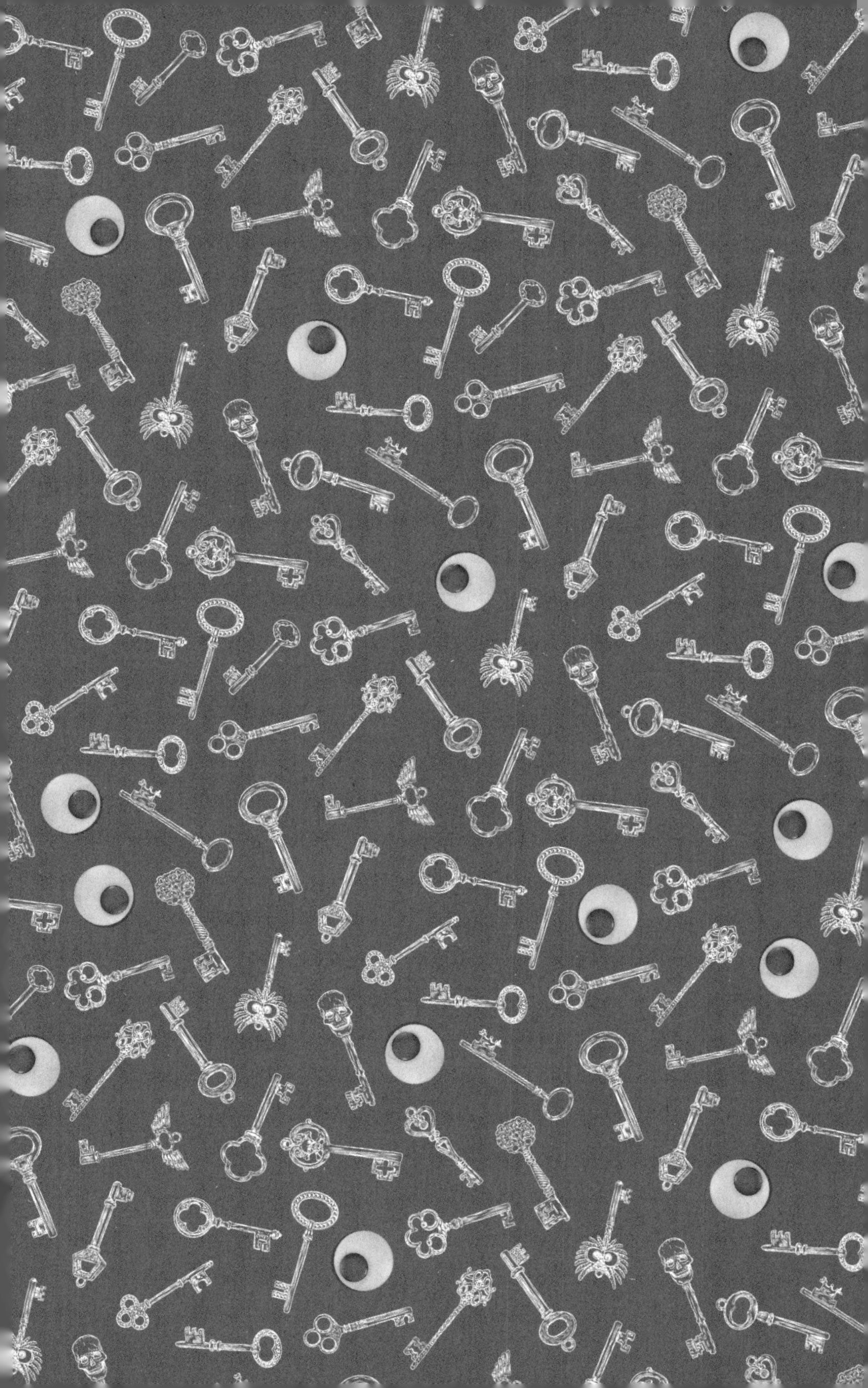

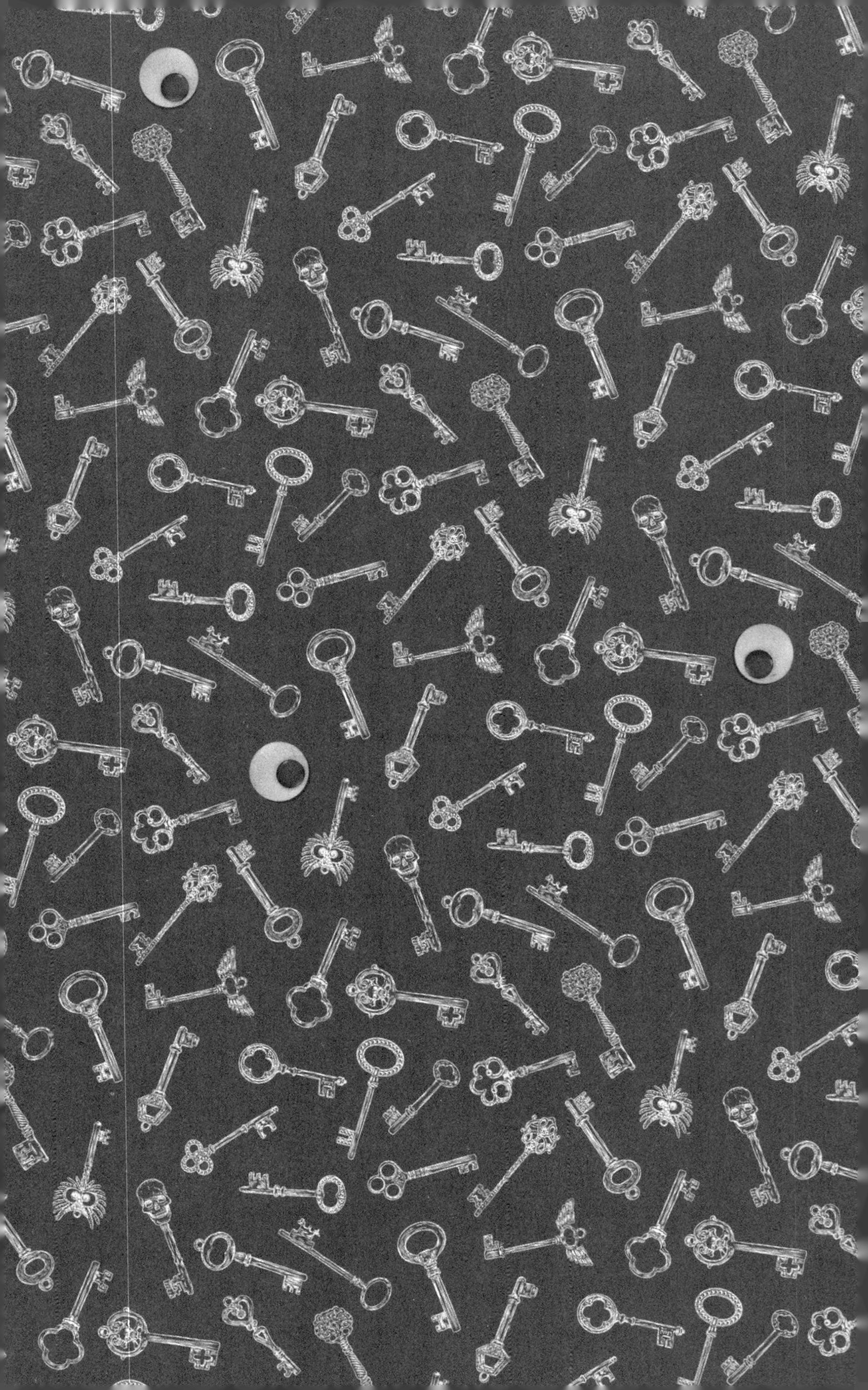

STORY NOTES

REST STOP

The thing I love about horror is, even an intentionally simple premise—something like, say, "dude gets trapped in gas station bathroom by psychopath"—can open up unexpected doors within you.

This story came from two places. One literal, one emotional.

The literal: my wife is from eastern Pennsylvania and, whenever we drive out to that neck of the woods, there's this specific gas station we prioritize stopping at. It's just off the I-78, near Philipsburg, NJ.

We like to stop in NJ because, the instant you cross the state line, it's like a magic spell gets cast and suddenly you can no longer be trusted to pump your own gas. I don't know why the Garden State decreed you can operate two tons of speeding metal but not a nozzle, but it's also nice to sit back and pretend you're being pampered a bit.

At this specific gas station, there's also a dependably clean bathroom for a single occupant. During the most intense years of the COVID-19 pandemic, this station became our go-to because we were trying avoid any sort of rest area where we'd have to interact with too many other people. Now, it's something like a tradition for us to continue stopping there anytime we've gotta either fill up or empty.

I say "dependably clean," but I'm sure you understand that's a relative term. It's "dependably clean" for a truck stop bathroom. It makes a noble attempt at hygiene. We appreciate its efforts.

The only thing is, for as sanitary as it generally tends to be, there's always been this ominous, gaping hole in the ceiling, near one corner. And an inordinate number of locks on the door.

If you're the sort of person who consumes horror as regularly as I do (and I bet you are), it only takes one visit to that bathroom to get your worst-case-scenario engines a-firing. That's what happened for me, and while I was between drafts for *Mary* and *Nestlings,* I dove into writing a novella that would allow that scenario to play out.

Pretty simple, right?

I thought so, too.

That's when that second, more internal door opened up. And standing there across the threshold was my grandmother.

I've only ever known one grandparent in my life. My mom's mom. Bobbe Belle. (And, yes, always "bobbe," not the more common, equally correct, "bubbe.")

We had a complicated relationship, Belle and I. In many ways, she was similar to the grandmother portrayed in this story (at least to me and my brother; other members of our small family might have had a different experience of her). She was often mean. Cutting. Critical.

She intimidated me. Angered me. And, for the longest time, it seemed as though that feeling was mutual. We rarely spoke, besides at family gatherings or the occasional weekend when my mom forced my brother and I to give her a call and say hello. One of the only physical gifts she gave me when I was young was a set of engraved pens with my name spelled wrong. When we got older, my brother and I both wound up with shiksas; Belle had less than kind things to say about them. In fact, the last words she ever said to me were an insult about the girl I was seeing at the time.

(Readers of *Mary* might enjoy knowing that, in some ways, particularly her predilection for wearing huge flowers in her hair while saying the most withering things, Belle was also a large inspiration for Aunt Nadine.)

And then there were the ways she treated my mom over the years. Things I thought were unforgivable. We don't have time to get into all *that.*

Meanwhile, all my friends had grandmothers of the more clichéd variety. Nice. Kind. Supportive and warm. Relationships so unfathomably different, they might as well be fairy tales written in another language.

It wasn't until much later, when I could view her life's story with an adult's clarity, that I started to realize how much I hadn't taken into account. Belle had a side of the story too, after all. As is so often the case with revelations like that, by the time I had it, it was too late. I never got to talk directly to her again.

My bobbe didn't suffer the same kinds of traumas that Abe's bobbe did. My bobbe managed to flee Poland (or Ukraine, depending on where the rather tenuous border happened to fall at a given time—as my great-grandmother Yidis reportedly joked, some nights they went to bed in one country and woke up in another) with her parents to New York City in 1929.

Belle lived a hardscrabble, immigrant child's life, sometimes sleeping under the counter of her parents' knish shop on the Lower East Side, adjusting to a strange new homeland right at the very damn beginning of the Great Depression, only to then witness from afar the Nazis invading her native country and kicking off WWII on her sixteenth birthday. My grandmother and her parents spent the years leading up to that war begging the US government to allow passage for the rest of the family—so many aunts and uncles and cousins—petitioning, *pleading* that they too could escape what was obviously going to be a deadly situation. The government refused. The family died in camps.

That alone must have been trauma enough, but I went on to learn more. Things like how Belle's father, my great-grandfather, had been a POW in a Siberian work camp after WWI, and had finally arrived home almost immediately before my grandmother was conceived. Studies have shown how trauma can be passed down genetically; I imagine the physical and emotional trauma of a stint at a Siberian work camp must be particularly resilient.

And, of course, there were the more mundane traumas. The myriad heartbreaks and indignations I'm sure she lived through as a young Jewish woman and mother of three girls in the 1940s and '50s. Things that complicated the already-pretty-complicated picture I had of the only family member of that generation I'd ever known.

Would considering any of this have changed our relationship? Who can say? All I really know is, through the course of writing this strange, nasty novella—which, in another obvious way, was my attempt at articulating inchoate anxieties about the historical

cycles our country is willfully plunging headfirst into—I found myself thinking about Bobbe Belle in a new light. Seeing her across thresholds of time and circumstance. Wondering what stories she had to tell. What insights to impart.

I finished the first draft of the novella, purely coincidentally, on her 101st birthday. And I hope it's clear in reading the text that, for all the venom and vitriol, there's love and respect there as well. Maybe even affection.

That's the door writing this novella opened up for me.

I'll try to keep it open for the rest of my days.

xxx

Oh, hey, one last thought on this novella before we move onto the other Detours.

I ended the Acknowledgements of the previous, solo edition of *Rest Stop* with a plea for everyone reading it to get out and vote in the then-imminent 2024 presidential election. Don't succumb to cynicism, I wrote; it really does matter who's behind the wheel.

Well, *somehow*, the readership of the endpages of an indie publishing house's horror novella wasn't enough to tip the scales of the 2024 national election, and my god are we in the shit now. Even so, the sentiment holds true and I've got no qualms reiterating it: please, for the good of history, for the good of humanity, as hard as it can be (and while honoring your own well-being), stay engaged, stay vigilant, stay true to the goodness within you. Let's do our damnedest to prevent the maniacs behind the wheel from steering us off a cliff or running over innocent pedestrians. In times like these, we're all we've got.

MEET-CUTE #1: THE UNLUCKIEST GIRL

You'll likely notice pretty quickly that several of the stories in this collection are centered around conversations. In part, this is because about half of them began their lives first as short plays (I was a horror playwright in NYC for about fifteen years before I turned my energies back to my first love of novels and short stories).

In a very real way, though, that's all just coincidence. I curated the contents of this particular collection not because of similar shared origins, but because everything felt thematically—and in some cases, referentially—linked.

To start, this is a collection about *place.* (I mean, it's right there in the title, yeah?) Each story has a specific location that significantly impacts its characters. A bar, a hospital, an office, a shitty club, a church fair, a yoga retreat, a laboratory, a kitchen, a website, a school, a child's bedroom, an underlit foyer in a puppeteer's home. The hope is each installment inflicts a unique sense of claustrophobia from place to place.

But equally as purposeful is the theme of *identity.* The way identity obfuscates and reveals itself. The way it slips and shifts. The way you can slowly start to realize the person you're with, or the person you are, isn't what you thought. . . and now it's also too late to escape. Another kind of claustrophobia.

I love that feeling in a story. I love when I'm welcomed into what seems like a wide-open garden before, suddenly, the view changes and there are tight walls around me and all the exits are blocked off.

My favorite method of inducing—or experiencing—that claustrophobia is through conversation. Is that because I was a playwright and actor for so long? Or was I drawn to those disciplines because conversations fascinate me so? Either way, I'll always be compelled by the changing tides of a real-time meeting between characters. Every conversation has the potential to be a campfire ghost-story in one sense or another. Conversation is how we reveal identity. And identities are slippery things.

That's why the title of this collection also evokes a spoken invitation. *I Know a Place* not only promises some secret destination; it's the sort of phrase that is said from one person to another. A conversation in miniature.

Again and again and again in this collection, you're seeing stories that can be boiled down to "Who am I with in this room? Who am I actually talking to right now? And where might they want to take me?"

Can't imagine why that's been on my mind these days. . .

(PS, Ted Bundy sucks. Fuck that guy.)

GENERATION

Pretty much any time I write something that's vaguely sci-fi-coded, an acknowledgement must be paid to my favorite sci-fi writer, Mac Rogers. Mac is a fellow genre playwright, a frequent collaborator (my first published book was a novelization of his audiodrama, *Steal the Stars*), and just a straight-up brilliant concocter of grounded predicaments within high concept situations. "Generation" was first written as a short play for the benefit of another genre-friendly theatre company that was contemporary to

Mac and myself, Flux Theater Ensemble, but I remember even as I was writing it, I wanted to achieve the level of mundane dread Mac often achieves in even his most otherworldly work.

(If you're looking for more grounded sci-fi, by the way, I highly recommend you check out the podcast *Give Me Away*, as well as anything else produced by Gideon Media. To borrow a phrase from the Hairclub for Men, I'm not just a member of that company, I'm also a fan.)

The most common response I receive about this story is that people feel like it's the beginning of some larger story. To that, I say, ain't that what parenthood is all about?

NICE

"Confession time."

I kinda fucking hate Christmas.

I didn't always use to. In fact, when I moved to New York City from Arizona in my early twenties, I finally, fully *understood* the need for lights-based winter holidays. Winters get DARK, man. Watching the sun set every day at, like, four pm made me feel a visceral appreciation for our species' various traditions of surrounding itself in tiny lights as a respite from the omnipresent, icy night. (I still don't understand why we decided we don't need any similar holidays for January, February, or March, but that's just me, I guess.)

All of which is to say, for a little while there, I became a Christmas *fan.* I saw the holiday as the seasonal life raft it was always meant to be. What changed? Well, I guess I'll put it this way: I still

enjoy the aesthetics of Christmas, but as a non-Christian living through, what, two full decades of Fox News' shrieking *War on Christmas*™!!!! hysteria, the brutal omnipresence of that one particular holiday began to feel a bit like a peppermint-flavored fist down my throat. I don't like bullies, and the Christmas-industrial complex is about as big a bully as we have, seasonally speaking. Shit, just this past Halloween, I went to a CVS to pick up some extra candy *the morning of October 31st,* and they were already taking down all the skulls and ghosts in order to slap Santa's face on everything. Fucking relax, Christmas.

Now, when that holiday rolls around, so do my eyes in my skull. I'm not trying to yumbug anybody's yum; I'll just be over here next to my artificial sunlamp, grumbling, "Okay, Christmas, we *get it.* You won."

In the meantime, I've got a whole batch of yuletide horror stories, this one included, which I intend to put together into an anthology screenplay. Maybe I'll get around to it one winter, when the dark closes in and I've gotta find my own post-December life raft.

Because, I've gotta admit, writing this nasty noel *did* give me a jolt of that festive spirit again.

THE ART OF WHAT YOU WANT

For a few glorious years in the mid-to-late 2010s, I was a staff writer for a gran guignol theater series called The Blood Brothers Presents. Each show was hosted by the titular Brothers, two pasty-white, bald-headed, red-eyed ghouls (played by Pete Boisvert and Patrick Shearer—imagine if, like, the Crypt Keeper was a member of the Tiger Lillies) who would gleefully, gruntingly host us through a parade of horrifying short plays. Each short was usually centered around the most garish of goretastic special effects. In fact, it wasn't uncommon for us to build our plots backward, starting with the effects first—a head explosion, an evisceration, a car crash, a flaying, etc., etc., each one more convincing than the last. The Blood Brothers' resident effects guru, Stephanie Cox-Connolly, was dubbed "the Tom Savini of Off-Off Broadway" by the *New York Times* for a reason.

I love horror theater. I think this piece works great as a prose story—arguably even better than it did as a script—but there's still nothing like hearing a live audience react to a head being blown up by a seltzer cannister, or to the reveal of that paper bag with the soggy, sopping bottom, or to Emily's body walking in with a face covered in bandages and a recognizable pair of glasses on her face. . .

Ah, the arts.

THE LUNAR ECLIPSE

Okay, only a couple more of these have a theatrical backstory, I promise.

Back in 2012, I had a play running in the New York City Fringe Festival called *Songs of Love: A Theatrical Mixtape.* In it, I juxtaposed original short plays, each a twisted love story, with original love songs played onstage by a live musician (in the premiere production's case, me). The literal centerpiece of the show was "The Lunar Eclipse," a monologue that combined both elements of the show—an actor *and* the musician, forming a sort of metaphorical eclipse as the show passed between its two phases.

I wrote the monologue for one of my favorite actors, NYC indie theater powerhouse, Kristen Vaughan. As ever, she absolutely killed it, and made the speech *the* standout moment in the show. I looked forward to it every night, hearing her weave this spell while I sat on the apron of the stage, providing only the lightest of musical accompaniment.

Lately, I've been doing my best to hold a candle to Kristen (a fool's errand for any performer). Chances are good, if you've come to a live reading event in the past year or so, you might have seen me performing "Lunar" while accompanying myself on guitar. I do all right. But if you ever saw Kristen's version, you know I'm essentially just doing a cover. (Not that there's anything wrong with being a cover act, mind you.)

Mary fans might also enjoy knowing that, a couple years before writing the book, I dabbled with turning that story into an audiodrama. I recorded a demo pilot episode and there was no question who had to play the title role: the ever-illustrious Kristen Vaughan. As ever, she absolutely killed it. And the killings didn't stop there. . .

LAUGHLINES

I love epistolary stories. They're literature's forebearer to the found-footage movie, aren't they?

Also: emails fucking terrify me; I'm unsettled by how we all feel the need to indicate that we're always! laughing! lol rofl lmao!; and I wanted to see if I could make a jumpscare out of an emoji.

Sometimes it's just that simple.

RUN FOR YOUR LIFE

First off, lemme say I visited Rapid City for the first time in 2025 and it's a lovely place full of wonderful people. I've got no beef with it whatsoever, I swear. The narrator of this story is an *unreliable jerk*, okay?

Anyway, when I was growing up, I had three great obsessions: Stephen King, Shakespeare, and the Beatles. I also lived pretty far away from all my friends—and the desert's not exactly a place where you can always just go outside and play—so I was absolutely the kid in this story, trying to make up for an isolated and lonely childhood by joining the most famous band to ever exist.

There the similarities end. For starters, my mom was an *original* Beatlemaniac and passed down her love of the Fab Four to me with holy reverence. I was already a massive fan by the time the *Anthology* aired (I would've been twelve at the time). But that documentary—and especially its accompanying CD releases—*did* open up something in me. I'd dabbled with guitar off and on for a couple years prior, but once those *Anthology* albums came out, I spent a good portion of my free time with guitar in hand, playing along to every demo, learning every guitar part, studying every "fake" chord book from the library, downloading tab off the excruciatingly slow early internet.

(To this day, despite the fact that I am technically a professional musician, I play all sorts of chords wrong because I was never taught by another person how to more comfortably play them. I learned from diagrams and by ear. And, dammit, I'm still proud of that.)

Even more important than the *Anthology* CDs was the *Live at the BBC* compilation that also came out in 1994; I would play along to that album for hours. I'm embarrassed to admit that it got so constant, even my Beatlemaniac mom got fucking sick of her once-beloved lads from Liverpool. I was more or less forbidden from playing them around her until I left for college. Sorry about that, Mom.

I'd had the idea to write this story well before the movie *Yesterday* came out (heh, now I sound as defensive as the narrator, don't I? *I HAD THIS IDEA ON MY OWN!!*), but I'd be lying if I didn't admit to thinking of this tale as *Evil Yesterday.*

I actually saved writing it for last. I knew I wanted it in this collection, but I figured it'd be the easiest and the fastest to write, since it was just a nasty little Poe riff about a subject I can blather on about for literal days without interruption.

Once I rolled up my sleeves and got to work, though, the more I realized it wasn't an easy story at all. It wasn't *Evil Yesterday.* It was a dark, ugly examination of fandom, of assumption and parasitism. It made me increasingly uncomfortable—in no small fact because the Beatles story itself contains one of the most heartbreaking incidents of fan-conducted violence of our times. In theory, I'd thought this was gonna be a darkly comedic trifle. In practice, I started to worry that maybe I was engaging in the very thing I was satirizing.

Those worries got stronger when I asked Stephen King to be

a part of this collection. Here was this cautionary tale about how pathologically fans demand the attention of their idols, and here was I, asking my idol for his attention.

The thing about writing horror, though, is more often than not, if a story's disturbing you, it's a story worth finishing. I decided to keep going, and I'm glad I did; this story became one of my personal favorites in the collection. And I think I got it to a place where its intentions are clear.

To me, it says everything that, ultimately, the four human beings at the center of popular music's greatest Olympian myth are revealed to be driven, talented people who'd still work towards triumph no matter what, that the true magic of the Beatles came from group magic, and that the asshole who thinks just because he knows all the notes means he deserves all the acclaim gets brutal, lonesome comeuppance.

Oh, and yeah, this is a story about AI, too.

JUBILEE JUNCTURE

Back to the Blood Brothers and favorite theatrical effects, this story was once my most *infamous* short play. It was originally written for a Blood Brothers show that was themed around ripped-from-the-headlines true crime, and the story *behind* this story is sufficiently disturbing. I suppose, for legal and ethical reasons, I should emphasize, "Jubilee Juncture" is an absolutely fictional, absolutely abstracted, completely unrelated tale. . . but if you look up the controversy surrounding a little evangelical Christotainment show called "Joy Junction," you'll understand what got my mind turning.

And if you want further heebies and/or jeebies, head to my website and look for production photos of a short play with that same name. They're among my favorite production photos of any work of mine—and believe me when I say, as effective as those images might be in stills, there was nothing like seeing them play out in front of your eyes.

Roger Nasser, the actor who played the puppeteer, was heartbreakingly sincere. And the actor who played the original dummy was a professional dancer. Her herky-jerky movements will haunt/delight me to my dying day. Because life is long and strange, that same actor is, in fact, now a fellow author, a dear friend, and someone who has made each of my manuscripts better and smarter with her invaluable feedback. If you enjoy brilliant middle-grade genre fiction, check out Stephanie Willing. She's phenomenal. I'm only a little hurt she doesn't use a photo of her as Marigold for her author photo. I think kids would love it.

(Oh, and if you're wondering if the line describing how, when Marvin's hand goes into the puppet it sounds like a Ziploc bag full of Vaseline, is some sort of literal reference to what we did in the stage play? You'd be correct.

Ahhhh, the arts.)

COME

I think my ideal response to the story came from Alan Lastufka, the publisher of this book and the genius behind Shortwave. I'd pitched him on the basic premise first, but when I turned in the completed story, he admitted he was surprised—in a good way—by how heartfelt and sincere it wound up being. Based on the pitch, he'd been expecting something, well, dumber. Cruder. An extended dirty joke.

That was the goal. Premise-wise, this is an easy story to shrug off. I mean, it essentially boils down to a naughty cross between *The Ring* and *Nightmare on Elm Street*. But some stories you write in order to play with something brand new, and others you write to explore angles of something already familiar. In this case, I was thinking of specifically of *Elm Street* and how what makes Freddy Krueger *scary* is not the series' grabbag of elaborate, surreal deaths. It's the fact that, sooner or later, your body will fall asleep. There's a biological imperative that prevents you from ever truly escaping the monster. *That's* where the fear comes from, and I don't think a Freddy movie (beyond 1 and 3) has ever successfully captured that feeling of inevitable doom. In a way, *It Follows* is a more effective Freddy Krueger movie than the rest of the *Elm Street* franchise.

Thinking about that got me onto other biological imperatives, ones that evoke all sorts of uncomfortable feelings in pretty much anyone raised in a sexually boggled culture like our own. As someone diagnosed with anxiety disorder, and occasional bouts of unwanted thoughts, I'm always darkly compelled by the idea that consciousness is a tug of war against impulse, and the terror that one day, impulse might have just a little bit more upper-body strength when you're least expecting it.

Add to that a desire to briefly explore other topics that have fascinated me for much of my life—sexuality, gender identity—and to write a story where the main character's survival is premised on the very thing they wrestle with, and you've got "Come." Pretty good for a dirty joke, right?

INTO THE LIFE OF THINGS

Not for nothing, but the couple who played Joshua and Carole in the original stage version of this story are now two amazing authors with two beautiful children. Was this story even remotely responsible for their relationship or success?

No.

But you can't prove that!

MEET-CUTE #2: THE SCARIEST THING

I wanted to try writing a romance. Being me, I also wanted it to be the most doomed romance I could think of. A whole used car lot full of red flags.

My challenge: could I make a convincing argument for the worst possible meet-cute imaginable?

As you can probably guess, this story is another that began its life as a short play. It's the most dialogue-bound piece of the entire collection, after all. But in rewriting it as a prose piece, I experienced something really fascinating. In the play, we end with Paul and Cara explicitly deciding to give this relationship a try—and the ending works. We see and hear Paul's pleas for understanding, we witness Cara wrestling with her suspicions and her discomfort and rage and horror. We watch them tentatively hold hands as the lights go down—*and it works.* Audiences responded quite

enthusiastically to the play. If it hadn't also premiered alongside that damn Kristen Vaughan performing "The Lunar Eclipse," it would have been the clear favorite of the evening.

But when I started working on turning "The Scariest Thing" into a straight story, I realized right away that it was impossible for Paul and Cara to wind up together so explicitly. Without the benefit of actors delivering the lines, and with the benefit of spending time in Cara's head, there was just no way whatsoever to realistically portray Cara overcoming her misgivings. The red flags flapped too effectively. (Massive thanks go to Rachel Harrison, by the way, who pointed out a few flags I hadn't even considered.) At best, it had to be left up to the reader to decide if a relationship between the two was even *theoretically* possible.

Now, that might not be interesting to *everyone*, dear reader. But if you're someone like me, someone who's fascinated by the different rules and restrictions and experiences of storytelling formats—someone who, let's say, reads the Story Notes of a collection to learn a little bit more about each piece—it made for a kind of mind-blowing lesson. *Place* is not just a story's setting, you see. It's a story's medium. And every place has different rules.

Which is why you've gotta always stay on your toes, wherever you go next . . .

Oh, and, not for nothing, but the couple who played Paul and Cara in the original production are *also* still going strong. And this time, I actually can credit my story for bringing them together. They met *doing* this show and started dating right after we closed. Like, literally right after. I asked the actor playing Paul not to ask Cara out until the show was over, just in case things didn't work out and it affected the production.

Things did work out.

Sometimes they do.

Ah, love.

When you get right down to it, everything else is just a detour, isn't it?

A FRUITING BODY

I pretty much said all the interesting things about this in its little intro. Um. Go read that.

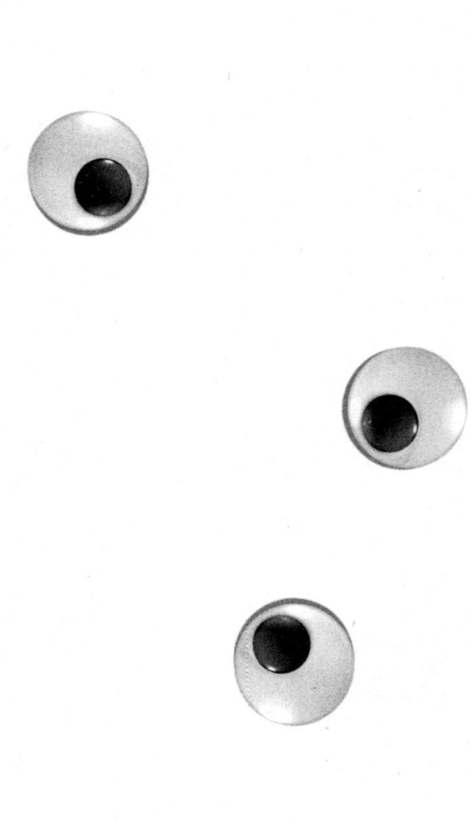

ACKNOWLEDGMENTS

I'm indebted to so many people who helped shape and embody these stories in all their various iterations.

Early readers, including Rachel Harrison, Jan Rosenberg, Brian Silliman, Stephanie Willing, Matthew Trumbull.

Previous publishers, including Lindy Ryan, Sadie Hartmann, Ashley Sawyers.

Producers, directors, and actors of earlier stage versions, including Pete Boisvert, Patrick Shearer, Stephanie Cox-Connolly, Maria Portman Kelly, Kari Swenson Riley, Chris Wight, Matt Archambault, J.M. Maestas, Melissa Diaz, Gretchen Van Lente, Roger Manix, Tina WongLu, Evan Daves, Andrew Galteland, Sarah Good, Sarah Beitch, Roger Nasser, Collin McConnell, Stephanie Willing, Judy Merrick, Gareth Declan, Lynn Berg, Rebecca Comtois, Leal Vona, Anna Rahn, Matthew Trumbull, Corinna Schulenberg, Michael Markhan, Morgan Zipf-Meister, Kristen Vaughan, Marielle Duke, Alex Engquist, Gabby Sherba, Ashley Bloom, Lauren Ferebee, Christina Kosyla, Matt Brown, Stefan Dezil, Abby Royle, Ben Williams, Mozz Mendez, Kent Meister, Sarah LaHue.

I'm extra indebted to Drops in the Vase for their beautiful rendition of "A Fruiting Body" in 2025, which inspired me to include it in this collection.

Massive thanks are owed to the Simon Maverick audio team, especially Jason Pinter and Sophie Stango, for putting up with my wacky ideas and making the audiobook edition of this collection so marvelous.

To Sean and Jordana Williams, and the Gideon Media family.

To my beloved coven at Tor Nightfire.

To Kelley, my favorite adventure partner. Thanks for opening so many doors with me.

To Alec, the only agent who knows how to tuck and roll through a plate-glass window (though, to my knowledge, he hasn't needed to use that skill for me yet).

And final, gigantic, doubleplus thanks to two more people:

To Stephen King.

Anyone who knows me, or has heard me talk for like five minutes about my influences and passions, likely understands how stratospherically grateful I am to have Stephen King's words grace this collection. I've been a student of Stephen King since I was around nine years old—which means, not only did I read and reread anything he wrote, but also anything he wrote about. The books he recommended, the titles he blurbed. Back in 2005, I was lucky enough to help out on a project of Mr. King's and when he offered to personalize a book for each of us at dinner afterward, I brought my beaten-up, pored-over mass market paperback of *Danse Macabre*. I could've arguably brought any title from my massive library of his works—they all mean something to me—but *Danse Macabre* was a no-brainer. That book had been my bible as a young horror reader and writer. It taught me how to analyze my beloved genre, and how to always make an effort to write horror worthy of analysis. As I told him a few days ago, while trying not to fall over myself with too much unseemly gratitude for the intro he'd just delivered, his nonfiction has always meant as much to me as his fiction, and it's been a dream of mine since I've been old enough to have such dreams that I might one day see him write about my work the way he's written here.

So, yeah, I'm pretty overwhelmed with gratitude.

But, actually, can I go a bit further for a sec? Given that this is a space for thank yous, and also given that there's a story in this collection about the isolating nightmare of iconic celebrity status, I wanna say: *we are so fucking lucky to have Stephen King.* I mean this sincerely—there might've always been a breakout popular horror fiction megastar from that generation, but, man, what a gift that it was this one.

And I'm not saying this because he said something nice about me. Even if you're somehow not a King fan: how many other genre-defining, culture-bestriding icons have been so generous with their time and their attention as King has been throughout his storied career? Think how rarefied his success is, his position in the publishing industry, and then think how often he's blurbed newer, younger authors, or shouted out less famous contemporaries, or promoted independent publishers. It's an astonishing level of generosity, for half a century now. And I think it's encouraged all of us in the horror genre to want to do the same for our fellow writers.

I could go on, but I'll stop. Suffice it to say, thank you, Steve. For everything. For the exemplary body of work, for the aspirational discipline, and for the example you set. Even though I know you're a Stones guy, I'm gonna make one more Beatles reference. It's a sentiment I once saw expressed in an article about the Fab Four, but it applies to the King of Horror, as well: what a remarkable thing, when the most popular artist in a given medium also happens to also be the best at it. It's rarer than one might think, but it happened here. And we're all richer because of it.

Finally, last-but-very-much-not-least thanks are due to Alan Lastufka. The hardest working man in show biz, indie publishing edition. If Stephen King has been one of my most formative heroes, you're one of my newest. It's been an honor to watch you work, to receive the benefits of your patience and energy (thank you for not murdering me when I turned in so many final edits for you to incorporate), and to learn from your insights. I feel blessed that these stories wound up in your care, and I know that's a sentiment shared by every other author with a Shortwave title, as well. (For all you readers out there, this is your cue to buy up every Shortwave title you can. You won't regret it.)

PUBLICATION HISTORY

Rest Stop - Originally published as a standalone novella, October 2024 (Shortwave Publishing).

"**Generation**" - Originally published as a chapbook in the *From the Cassidy Catacombs* series, May 2024 (Shortwave Publishing).

"**Nice**" - Originally published in *The Darkest Night*, edited by Lindy Ryan, September 2024 (Crooked Lane Books).

"**The Art of What You Want**" - Originally published as a chapbook in the *From the Cassidy Catacombs* series, May 2024 (Shortwave Publishing).

"**Laughlines**" - Originally published as a chapbook in the *From the Cassidy Catacombs* series, October 2025 (Shortwave Publishing).

"**Jubilee Juncture**" - Originaly published in *Human Monsters*, edited by Sadie Hartmann and Ashley Saywers, October 2022 (Dark Matter Ink).

All other titles are original to this collection.

ABOUT THE AUTHOR

Nat Cassidy is a bestselling and Bram Stoker Award-nominated author whose novels include *When the Wolf Comes Home*, *Nestlings*, and *Mary* ("One of the Best Horror Novels of All Time" - *Audible*), *Esquire* described him as one "of the best horror writers of this generation" and among the writers "shaping horror's next golden age." His books have been featured in best-of lists from *Vulture*, *Harper's Bazaar*, NPR, *Esquire*, *Paste*, the *Chicago Review of Books*, the NY Public Library, and more, and his award-winning plays have been produced across the country, including Off-Broadway and with the Washington National Opera. You've also maybe seen Nat guest-starring on shows like *Law & Order: SVU*, *Blue Bloods*, *Bull*, *Quantico*, *FBI*, and many others ... but that's a topic for a different bio. He lives in New York City with his wife.

natcassidy.com

A NOTE FROM SHORTWAVE PUBLISHING

For more great Shortwave titles, visit us online. . .

OUR WEBSITE

shortwavepublishing.com

SOCIAL MEDIA

@shortwavebooks

EMAIL US

contact@shortwavepublishing.com

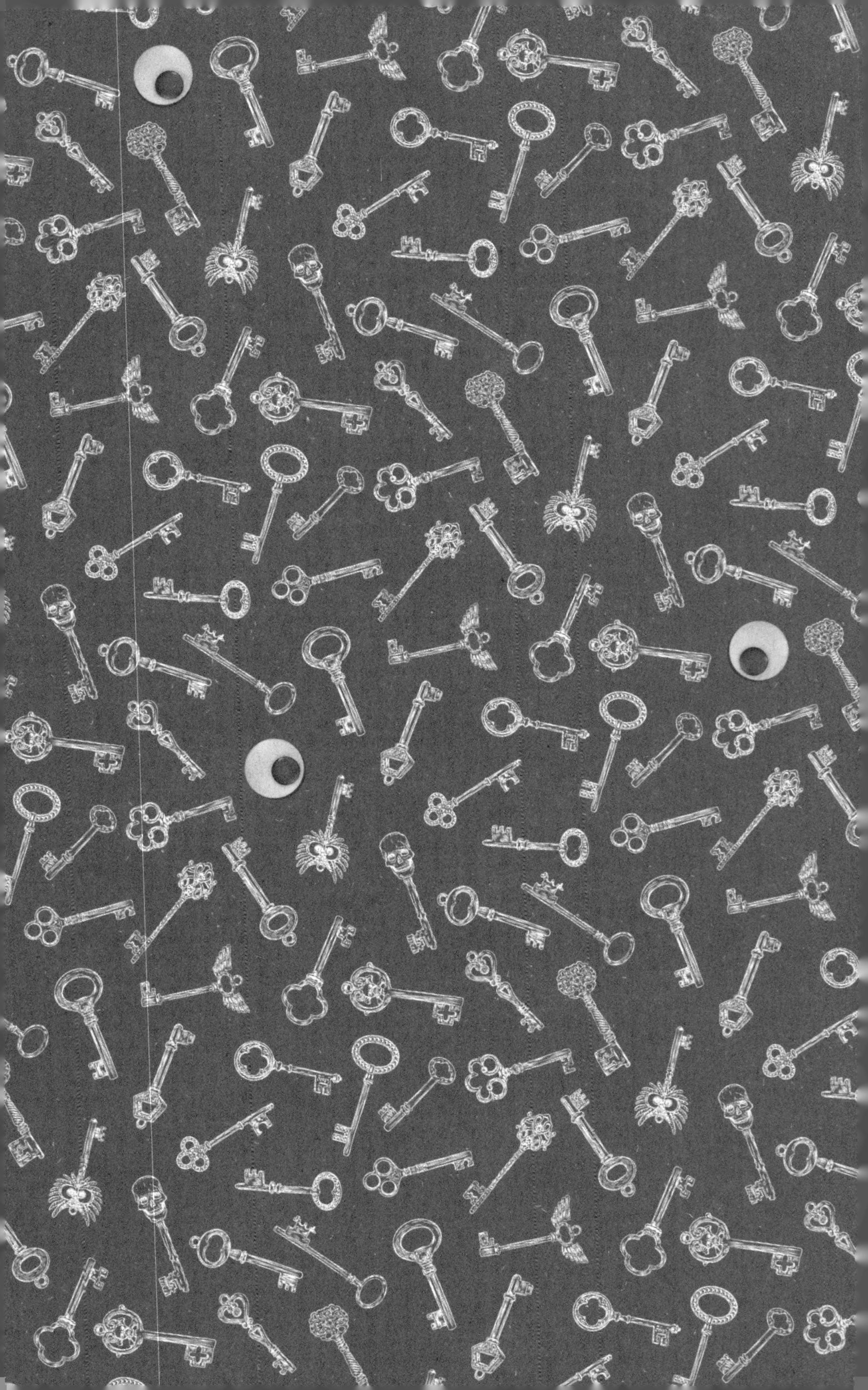

ALSO AVAILABLE FROM
SHORTWAVE PUBLISHING

ALSO AVAILABLE FROM SHORTWAVE PUBLISHING

FACE THE NIGHT **– ALAN LASTUFKA**

✗ Hoffer Award Winner, *Best Commercial Fiction*

✗ 100 Best Indie Book of the Year, *Kirkus Reviews*

Adriana has an eerie gift for drawing faces. But will one terrifying vision tear apart everything she loves?

"This outstanding novel is reminiscent of early works by Stephen King and Peter Straub. An impressive, complex horror tale—two (rotting) thumbs up." –*Kirkus Reviews*, starred

CANDY CAIN KILLS **– BRIAN McAULEY**

Oh what fun it is to DIE!

When Austin's parents drag him and his little sister Fiona to a remote cottage for Christmas, this family on the rocks will have to fight for their lives against a legendary killer. . . because Candy Cain is slashing through the snow with a very long naughty list.

"A masterclass in slasher fiction." –*FanFiAddict*

Also Available: ***CANDY CAIN KILLS AGAIN***

THE SUNDOWNER'S DANCE **– TODD KEISLING**

✗ Best Books of 2025, *Library Journal*

✗ 2025 Top Pick, *Ingram*

Jerry Campbell just wants to be left alone. But when he moves into a nearby retierment community he finds himself more disturbed than ever. Nightly block parties. Strange noises across his rooftop at all hours. And weird neighbors who worship a meteorite.

"Cosmic. . . Bizarre. . . A pitch-perfect blend of horror and heart." –*Library Journal*, starred

ALSO AVAILABLE FROM SHORTWAVE PUBLISHING

THE EXTRA **– ANNIE NEUGEBAUER**

Ten people head out on a backpacking trip, but the first night eleven set up camp. Everyone remembers everyone else.

Who is the extra?

"A nearly perfect, claustrophobic novella with a very effective countdown clock. If you have time for only one terrifying tale this spooky season, make room for The Extra." –*The Wall Street Journal*

Also Available: ***THE OTHER*** and ***THE SPARE***

WHEN YOU LEAVE I DISAPPEAR **– DAVID NIALL WILSON**

✗ Hoffer Award Nominee, *Best Commercial Fiction*

USA Today best-selling author David Niall Wilson's *When You Leave I Disappear* is a literary horror novella in which a best-selling author's imposter syndrome draws her into a darker and darker world from which she may never escape.

"A tale that will haunt you long after you've finished reading." –Ray Garton, author of *Live Girls*

LITTLE HORN **– GEMMA FILES**

✗ Bram Stoker Award Finalist, *Fiction Collection*

Little Horn is a new collection of fourteen dark short stories and novelettes from Shirley Jackson Award winner and two-time Bram Stoker Award winner Gemma Files.

Helping to bring each story to life, this collection includes sixteen full-page illustrations by the author.

Also Available: ***KISSING CARRION*** and ***THE WORM IN EVERY HEART***

ALSO AVAILABLE FROM SHORTWAVE PUBLISHING

***SLEEP ALONE* – J.A.W. McCARTHY**

✗ Bram Stoker Award Finalist, *Long Fiction*

✗ Shirley Jackson Award Finalist, *Best Novella*

Merch girl Ronnie is trapped cleaning up after a band of hungry succubi, leaving bodies in the wake of their shows, until a mysterious disease devouring succubi from the inside out starts infecting its members.

"Instantly intoxicating. A classic trinity of sex, blood, and rock and roll." –Hailey Piper

***NEUROTICA* – MAXWELL I. GOLD**

A collection of bold and personal literary horror poetry from Pushcart Prize and Bram Stoker Award nominated author Maxwell I. Gold.

"Complex and atmospheric. . . Amongst the unease and sense of foreboding, there is belief in the power of one's heart to prevail." –*Booklist*, starred review

***CROSSROADS* – LAUREL HIGHTOWER**

✗ This is Horror Award Winner, *Novella of the Year*

How far would you go to bring back someone you love?

When Chris's son dies in a tragic car crash, her world is devastated. The walls of grief close in on Chris's life until, one day, a small cut on her finger changes everything. Soon Chris is playing a dangerous game with forces beyond her control in a bid to see her son, Trey, alive once again.

"Refreshingly nuanced. . . Crossroads will sincerely move you." –Josh Malerman, author of *Bird Box*

ALSO AVAILABLE FROM SHORTWAVE PUBLISHING

***I DO NOT APOLOGIZE FOR MY POSITION ON MEN* – RAE WILDE**

A collection of standalone sapphic horror short stories, a quadrilogy of connected stories, and an interactive pick-a-path novelette from author Rae Wilde.

"It's a rare thing, more rare than most of us would like to admit, to find such unflinching human nakedness in the artistry of storytelling today." –C.S. Humble

***THE LAST HOUSE ON EARTH / DEATH WALKS SOUTH BOSTON* – CHRISTOPH PAUL**

Two short novels in one book, a double creature feature!

The Last House on Earth: An abducted couple find themselves under the thumb of aliens who use them to navigate a celestial haunted house said to hold the secrets of creation. Oh, and the house is trying to kill them.

Death Walks South Boston: A crew of outcasts face an ancient ancestral evil, come back from the dead to take over the world.

***DEPTH CHARGE* – TYLER JONES**

Art world darling Julian Le Sang paints with passion, with abandon, and with his own blood. Inside these blood paintings, Julian sees more than art. . . he sees the future.

Depth Charge is a horror story about fate and how every choice shapes what will become our world.

"Propulsive and mesmerizingly original. . . This one is going to be felt far and wide." –K.C. Jones

ALSO AVAILABLE FROM SHORTWAVE PUBLISHING

***THE GARGOYLE AND THE MASON* – JAMIE FLANAGAN and MARINA CLAIRE**

✗ Marjorie Flack Award for Fiction Winner

✗ Excellent in Book Art Winner – TAG Gallery

A gothic poem in which a curmudgeonly Gargoyle skulks about an island, only to find his sullen reign challenged by a trio of threats: the sun, a chisel, and the insidious power of friendship. . .

Words by Jamie Flanagan, screenwriter of Netflix's *Midnight Mass, The Fall of the House of Usher*, and more.

Fully illustrated by Marina Claire.

***AMID THE VASTNESS OF ALL ELSE* SAGA – C.S. HUMBLE**

Amid the Vastness of All Else is a six book saga set within the dark mythology of the American West. Part supernatural fantasy, part horror, these six books follow a thirty year timeline filled with gunslingers and gamblers, werewolf townships, and a secret kingdom of vampires living within Colorado. This story has its ancient blood cults worshiping unknowable gods, its mad scientists, and its secret society of men and women working to save the frontier from all mortal and immortal peril. It is a story of romance, of loss. Pain and sacrifice.

It is a saga that unflinchingly reminds the reader: in the end, all we have is each other.

"Humble writes with rare passion in the tradition of Robert E. Howard and a young Stephen King." –Laird Barron

"Truly, this is emotional, high-stakes horror at its finest." –Sadie Hartmann

ALSO AVAILABLE FROM SHORTWAVE PUBLISHING

CHIMERA SKIN – JOHNNY COMPTON

Who Among You Is Ready to Know More?

Swanson, a mutated man struggling to maintain his sanity, is civilization's last hope. Our world has been decimated after a messianic alien unleashes hell on Earth during its failed attempt to "uplift" humanity. But Swanson may have figured out how to fight back, even if his plan forces him to leave the only planet he's ever known.

OF MONSTERS AND MENSES – MAISIE CULVER

A collection of short stories that are comedic, feminist, batshit takes on classic horror monsters, as told by five women hiding in a bar bathroom from a guy who's a total creep, or maybe something worse.

Features an introduction by Jamie Flanagan.

TRAPS AND SPECTERS – PHILIP FRACASSI

From the mind of Stoker and British Fantasy award-nominated author Philip Fracassi comes fourteen stories of the macabre that will frighten, disturb, and ensnare readers in a dark web of twisted tales.

In these pages you'll find talking corpses and deadly tombs, misguided exorcists, technology gone wrong, blood-soaked prison riots, and enough vengeful spirits and haunted objects to fill a grave.

Features an introduction by Matt Dinniman, best-selling author of the *Dungeon Crawler Carl* series.

ALSO AVAILABLE FROM SHORTWAVE PUBLISHING

THE KILLER VHS SERIES – Various Authors

"The modern day *Goosebumps* for adults." ***–Horror Obsessive***
A series of books where movie monsters come to life and old VHS tapes summon long-buried evils. You'll probably survive, as long as you remember to be kind and rewind.

MELON HEAD MAYHEM – Alex Ebenstein
CANDY CAIN KILLS – Brian McAuley
TELEPORTASM – Joshua Millican
CICADA – Tanya Pell
CANDY CAIN KILLS AGAIN – Brian McAuley
NIGHT OF THE WITCH-HUNTER – Patrick Barb
THE LONG LOW WHISTLE – Laurel Hightower
TRACKING DEATH – Nikki R. Leigh
HAPPY HOUR – Gemma Amor
SIMON'S QUEST – Todd Keisling
WHEN WE WERE BRUTAL – Gwendolyn Kiste

Praise for titles in the series:
"A fast-paced and fun love letter to the days of VHS tapes that will make you pine for Blockbuster Video." –Angela Sylvaine

"A found-footage gem to be handed around the friend group, each play making the scanlines a little fuzzier, each rewind to relish in that gnarly kill making the book's monsters a little more real. Creepy and fun, struck through with true genre savvy." –Adam Cesare, author of *Clown in a Cornfield*

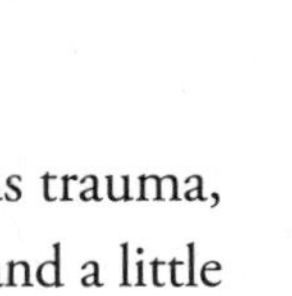

CONTENT WARNINGS

FOR STORIES IN I KNOW A PLACE

Rest Stop - Bug stuff, snake stuff, face trauma, religious trauma, antisemitism, claustrophobia, general existential angst, and a little suicide ideation. It also might get some yacht rock stuck in your head, but no need to thank me for that.

"**Meet Cute #1: The Unluckiest Girl**" - Suicide, depression, implied murder and violence, serial killers.

"**Generation**" - Pregnancy fears and anxieties, birth defects, images of self-harm, medical trauma.

"**Nice**" - Seasonal depression, alcoholism, dismemberment, dead animal imagery, gore, a severe lack of holiday whimsy.

"**The Art of What You Want**" - Spousal abuse, murder, gaslighting, medical trauma, genital trauma, forced surgery, violence, mutilation.

"**The Lunar Eclipse**" - References to suicide and disability.

"**Laughlines**" - Torture, mental illness, parental abuse, cancer, reading lots of emails.

"**Run for Your Life**" - Murder, assassination, gun violence, self-harm, mutilation.

"**Jubilee Juncture**" - Child abuse, cannibalism, implied sexual abuse, lots and lots of Bible verses.

"**Come**" - Sexual imagery, implied sexual assault, suicide, obsessive thoughts.

"**Into the Life of Things**" - Domestic abuse, implied sexual assault, possession.

"**Meet-Cute #2: The Scariest Thing**" - Stalking, pornography, sexual imagery.

"**A Fruiting Body**" - Mortality, obsession, mental illness.

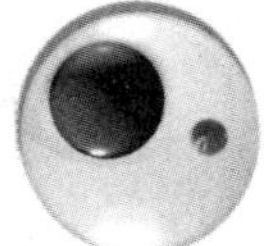